a&b

Ghost Town

The Morganville Vampires

BOOK NINE

RACHEL CAINE

First published in Great Britain in 2010 by
Allison & Busby Limited
13 Charlotte Mews
London, W1T 4EJ
www.allisonandbusby.com

A CIP catalogue record for this book is available from
the British Library.

10 9 8 7 6 5 4 3 2 1

ISBN 978-0-7490-0804-8

Typeset in 11/17pt Century Schoolbook by
Allison & Busby Ltd.

The paper used for this Allison & Busby publication
has been produced from trees that have been legally sourced
from well-managed and credibly certified forests.

Printed and bound in Great Britain by
CPI Bookmarque Ltd, Croydon, Surrey

RACHEL CAINE is the bestselling author of over thirty novels, including the *New York Times* bestselling Morganville Vampires series. She was born at White Sands Missile Range, which people who know her say explains a lot. She has been an accountant, an insurance investigator and a professional musician, and has played with such musical legends as Henry Mancini, Peter Nero and John Williams. She and her husband, fantasy artist R. Cat Conrad, live in Texas with their iguanas, Pop-eye and Darwin, a *mali uromastyx* named (appropriately) O'Malley, and a leopard tortoise named Shelley (for the poet, of course).

www.rachelcaine.com
www.myspace.com/rachelcaine

Available from
ALLISON & BUSBY

The Morganville Vampires series

The Weather Warden series

To a great many wonderful people in my life who've been so helpful and supportive this time around... Heidi, J.T., Wendy, A.J., Pat, Jackie, Bill, Jo, Jean, and Sondra especially.

I hope one day to deserve all your faith and kindness.

And you, Cat. Bless you.

INTRODUCTION

WELCOME TO MORGANVILLE. YOU'LL NEVER WANT TO LEAVE.

So, you're new to Morganville. Welcome, new resident! There are only a few important rules you need to know to feel comfortable in our quiet little town:

- obey the speed limits,
- don't litter,
- whatever you do, don't get on the bad side of the vampires.

Yeah, we said vampires. Deal with it.

As a human newcomer, you'll need to find yourself a vampire Protector – someone willing to sign a contract to keep you and yours from harm (especially from the other vampires). In return, you'll pay taxes...just like in any other town. Of course, in most other towns, those taxes don't get collected by the Bloodmobile.

Oh, and if you decide *not* to get a Protector, you can do that, too...but you'd better learn how to run fast, stay out of the shadows, and build a network of friends who can help you. Try contacting the residents of the Glass House – Michael, Eve, Shane, and Claire. They know their way around, even if they always end up in the middle of the trouble somehow.

Welcome to Morganville. You'll never want to leave.

And even if you do...well, you can't.

Sorry about that.

CHAPTER ONE

'Oh, *this* doesn't sound like a good idea,' Claire said, looking down at the paper that had been shoved into her hand by a passing student. She paused in the shade of the Science Building porch to read it. Only idiots stood around in full sun at Texas Prairie University in the middle of the afternoon – well, idiots and football players – so Claire angled herself into a corner where she wouldn't get buffeted by the streams of people pouring out after the end of class. There were a few hardy salmon trying to swim upstream, but she didn't think they'd make it.

People all around her were carrying the same goldenrod sheet of paper she had – stuffed into pockets, crammed into books, held in hands.

She was one of the last ones to get pamphleted, she guessed. She was just a little surprised anybody had bothered at all, given the fact that she, Claire Danvers, was small for her age, looked younger than her mid-seventeen-going-hard-on-eighteen years, and tended to blend into the crowd at the best of times. This even though her ultra-fashion-conscious housemate Eve – with all the best possible intentions – had made her sit down in the bathroom and get her brown hair all highlighted so it glowed red in the sun. Still. She just wasn't...noticeable.

She'd learnt it the hard way: early admission to college *sucked*.

Someone stopped next to her in the relative quiet of the shade. It was a tall, good-looking boy, and he dropped his backpack on the tiled floor with a thump as he looked over the same flyer she held. 'Huh,' he said, and glanced over at her. 'You going?'

Once she got over the dazzle of his good looks (truthfully, it didn't take that long; her boyfriend was just as cute), she checked his wrist. He was a Morganville native; he was wearing a bracelet around one wrist made out of copper and leather, with an ornate-looking symbol engraved on the central plate. It meant he was vampire property – property of Ming Cho, who was one of those vampires that Claire had never directly run into. She liked it that way. Really, her circle of vampire acquaintances was way, way too large as it was.

'Hey,' he said again, and rattled the paper in front of her face. 'Anybody in there? You going?'

Claire looked down at the paper again. It had a bunch of pictures and symbols on it, no words. A musical note, which meant a rave was on the menu. Some pictures of party favours, which meant that mostly illegal stuff was going to be floating around. The address was coded in the form of a riddle, which she solved easily enough; it was an address on South Rackham, among all those decaying warehouses that used to be thriving businesses. The time was pretty obvious: midnight. That was what the graphic of the witch was for – the witching hour. The date was several days out.

'Not interested,' she said, and handed him her copy. 'Not my thing.'

'Too bad. It's going to be out there.'

'That's why.'

He laughed. 'You a training-wheels partyer?'

'I'm not much of a partyer at all,' Claire said, and couldn't help but smile; he had a really nice laugh, one that made you want to laugh with it. He wasn't laughing *at* her, at least. That was different. 'Hi, by the way. I'm Claire.'

'Alex,' he said. 'You coming from Chem?'

'No, Computational Physics.'

'Oh,' he said, and blinked. 'And I have no idea what

that is. Right, carry on, Einstein. Nice to meet you.'

He picked up his backpack and moved off before she could even explain about many-body and nonlinear physical systems. *Yeah, that would have really impressed him. Instead of walking away, he'd have been running.*

She felt a little hurt, but only a little. At least he'd talked to her. That was ninety-nine per cent better than her usual score with college guys, except the ones who wanted to do something terrible to her. *Those* guys were very chatty.

Claire squinted against the bright sunshine and looked out onto the courtyard. The big open brick space was clearing, although there were, as always, a knot of people around the central column where flyers were posted for rides, rooms, parties, and various services and causes. She had time before her next class – about an hour – but hiking all the way in the unseasonably late heat to the University Centre coffee bar didn't sound attractive. She'd get there, have maybe half an hour, and then she'd have to walk another long way to get to her next class.

TPU really needed to look into mass transit.

The Science Building was closer to the edge of campus than most others, so it was actually a shorter walk to one of the four exit gates, across the street, and then to Common Grounds, the off-campus coffee house. Of course, it was owned by a vampire, and not a nice one, either, but in Morganville, you couldn't be too choosy about those kinds of things if you valued your caffeine. Or your blood.

Besides, Oliver could mostly be trusted. Mostly.

Decision made, Claire grabbed her heavily laden book bag and set off in the withering sunshine for Vampire Central.

It was always funny to her now – walking through town she could tell which people were 'in the know' about Morganville, and which weren't. The ones who weren't mostly looked bored and unhappy, stuck in a nothing-doing small town that rolled up the sidewalks at dusk.

The ones who did know still looked unhappy, but in that hunted, haunted way. She didn't blame them, not at all; she'd been through the entire adjustment cycle, from shock to disbelief to acceptance to misery. Now she was just...comfortable. Surprising, but true. It was a dangerous place, but she knew the rules.

Even if she didn't always *obey* the rules.

Her cell phone rang as she was crossing the street – the *Twilight Zone* theme. That meant it was her boss. She looked down at the screen, frowned, and shut it off without answering. She was pissed at Myrnin, again, and she didn't want to hear him go on, again, about why she was wrong about the machine they were building.

He wanted to put a human brain in it. *So* not happening. Myrnin was crazy, but normally it was a good crazy, not a creepy crazy. Lately, he seemed to be pushing the far end of the creep-o-meter, though. She wondered if she seriously ought to get some vampire psychologist to look at him or something. They probably had someone who'd been around when Dr Freud was just finishing medical school.

Common Grounds was blessedly dim and cool, but mercilessly busy. There wasn't a free table to be had, which was depressing; Claire's feet hurt, and her shoulder was about to dislocate from the constant pull of her book bag. She found a corner and dumped the weight of knowledge (potential, anyway) with a sigh of relief and joined the line at the order window. There was a new guy working the counter, again, which didn't surprise Claire much; Oliver seemed to go through employees pretty quickly. She wasn't sure if that was just his strict nature, or whether he was eating them. Either one was possible, but the latter wasn't likely, at least. Oliver was more careful than that, even if he didn't really want to be.

It took about five minutes to reach the head of the line, but Claire put in her order for a café mocha without much trouble, except that the new guy spelt her name wrong on the cup. She moved on down the counter, and when she looked up, Oliver was staring at her from behind the espresso machine as he pulled shots. He looked the same as always – aging hippie, greying hair pulled back in a classy-looking ponytail, one gold stud in his right ear, a coffee-splattered tie-dyed apron, and eyes like ice. With all the hippie-flavoured details, you didn't tend to notice the pallor of his face, or the coldness of his stare, right away unless you already knew him.

In the next second, he smiled, and his eyes changed completely, like another person had just stepped into his body – the friendly coffee-shop guy he liked to pretend to be. 'Claire,' he said, and finished dumping shots into her mocha cup. 'What a nice surprise. Sorry about the lack of seating.'

'I guess business is good.'

'Always.' He knew how she liked the drink, and added whipped cream and sprinkles without asking before handing it over. 'I believe the frat boys by the window are about to leave. You can get a seat if you hurry.'

He was right; she could see the pre-leaving preparations going on. Claire nodded her thanks and grabbed her bag, pushing between chairs and apologising her way to the table so that she arrived just as the last frat boy grabbed his stuff and headed out the door. She was one of four aimed for the vacancy, and missed it by the length of one outstretched, well-manicured hand.

'Excuse me, *our* table,' Monica Morrell said, looking down at her with unconcealed delight. 'The junior skank section is over there, by the trash. Beat it.'

The mayor of Morganville's sister sank down on one of the four chairs, flipping her shiny dark hair back over her shoulders; she'd added some blond highlights to it again, but Claire didn't think they did her any favours. She'd accessorised with arm candy, though, in the form of a big linebacker-style guy with one of those faces that was beefy but still handsome. He was blond, which seemed to be Monica's new type, and (Claire knew from the one class she'd shared with him) dumb, which was *always* Monica's type. He was carrying Monica's coffee, which he put down in front of her before taking a seat next to her, close enough to drape his big arm around her shoulders and stare down her cleavage.

It would have been the safe thing to just back off and let Monica claim her petty victory, but Claire was really not in the mood. She wasn't afraid of Monica anymore – well, not normally – and the last thing she wanted to do was let Monica spoil the one thing she'd been looking forward to during the entire walk over: a decent seat in which to enjoy her drink.

So Claire put her café mocha down at the third place and sat down, just ahead of Jennifer, who was making for the space. Gina, Monica's other ever-present girlfriend/minion, had already taken the last seat.

Monica, oddly, didn't say anything. She stared at Claire as if she couldn't quite figure out what the hell *that* was doing sitting down at her table, and then, once she got over the shock, she smiled, as if it occurred to her that maybe this could be fun. In a nasty sort of way. Her new temporary boyfriend didn't seem to be noticing any of it as he smirked and did a virtual high-five with some friends across the room.

Jennifer stood there glaring down at Claire, clearly not sure what to do, and Claire was acutely aware that she had her back to the girl. Never a good plan. She didn't trust *any* of them, but she trusted Jennifer these days least of all. Gina had kind of discovered humanity, in a vague sort of way, and Monica...well, Monica could usually be counted on to do what was good for Monica.

Jennifer was unpredictable, and six of the worst kinds of crazy. Gina was mean, and Monica could be vicious, but Jennifer didn't seem to have any sense of boundaries at all. Plus, Jennifer had been the first one of the three to push her. Claire hadn't forgotten that.

Claire sensed a movement at her back, and almost ducked, but she forced herself not to flinch. *Nothing will happen, not here. Not in front of Oliver.* It wasn't that Oliver was fond of her, exactly, only that he didn't like conflict inside of his business that he, himself, hadn't started.

Monica's eyes went to Jennifer – wide and a little odd, as if Jennifer spooked her, too. 'Jesus, Jen, get a grip,' she said, which made Claire want to turn around and see if the other girl was getting out a knife, but she managed to resist. 'Just get another chair. It's not rocket science.'

Jennifer's tone of voice made it clear she was still glaring at the back of Claire's head. 'There aren't any.'

'Well? Go scare somebody out of one. It's what you do.'

That was cold, even for Monica, and Claire suddenly felt uneasy about this. Maybe she should just...move on. She didn't want to be in the middle, because if Monica and Jennifer really went at it, the one in the middle was going to get killed.

But before she could decide what to do, she heard Jennifer walking away, towards a team of people studying in the corner with books and calculators and notes spread on every available table inch. She zeroed in on the biggest guy, tapped him on the shoulder, and whispered in his ear. He stood up. She grabbed his chair and carried it back with her, as he stood there in complete bafflement.

It was, Claire realised, a really good strategy. The

guy didn't seem like the type to come and pick a fight over something that small, especially with a girl of Jennifer's size (and reputation). So he finally shrugged and stood there awkwardly, resigned to his fate.

Jennifer jammed the chair in between Monica and Claire and sat down. Monica and Gina clapped, and Jennifer, finally, stopped glaring and grinned, proud to have earned their approval.

It was just...sad.

Claire shook her head. She still wanted to sit down and rest, but it really wasn't worth the small victory to be part of this. She stood up, grabbed her chair, and towed it across the crowded room to slide it next to the guy Gina had stolen the chair from, who was still standing. 'Here,' she said. 'I'm leaving anyway.'

Now he *really* looked confused. So did Monica and her Monickettes, as if the concept of givebacks had never crossed their path before. Claire sighed, shifted the weight of her backpack, and prepared to leave, mocha in hand.

'Hey!' Monica's grip on her elbow dragged her to a stop. 'What the hell? I want you to stay!'

'Why?' Claire asked, and jerked her arm free. 'So you can needle me for an hour? Are you really that bored?'

Monica looked even *more* confused. Nobody ever turned down being part of the queen bee's inner circle.

After that second of vulnerability, though, her face hardened. 'Don't diss me, Danvers. I'm warning you.'

'I'm not dissing you,' Claire sighed. 'I'm ignoring you. There's a difference. Dissing you implies I think you're actually important.'

As she walked out, she heard someone behind her laugh and clap. They were quickly hushed, but it still warmed her just a little. She didn't often get up in Monica's grille that directly, but she was sick of the games. Monica just needed to move on and find somebody else to poke her pins into.

The mocha was still delicious. Maybe even just a little bit *more* delicious for being outside in the open air, come to think of it. Claire nodded to a few people she knew on the street, all of them permanent residents, and strolled down the block. She wasn't in the mood to shop for clothes, but the little, faded bookstore farther down beckoned her.

Book Mad was a dusty hole-in-the-wall, crammed floor to ceiling with stacks of volumes in – as far as Claire had ever been able to tell – only a vague sense of order. Generally, non-fiction was at the front and fiction at the back, but you really could never tell. The stacks never seemed to get any smaller, nor was the dust ever disturbed, but she was always finding new stuff she hadn't seen before.

That was weirdly entertaining.

'Hi, Claire,' said the proprietor, Dan, a tall guy about her father's age. He was thin and a little nerdy, but that might just have been the glasses, which were either wickedly retro or seriously lame; Claire could never decide. He had on a funny T-shirt, as usual. Today's featured a cartoon figure running from a giant T-rex that said underneath, Exercise: some motivation required. She tried not to smile, but lost the battle. It really *was* funny. 'Got some physics stuff that just came in. It's over there.' He gestured vaguely off into the distance. Claire nodded.

'Hey,' she said. 'Where do you get the books? I mean, they're old. Some of them are really kind of ancient.'

He shrugged and looked down at the antique register on the counter, and brushed some dust off the keys. 'Oh, you know. Around.'

'From a storage room in the library? Maybe on the fourth floor?' She had him. He looked up at her, eyes narrowing. 'I've been in there. I was wondering what they were going to do with all that stuff once they were done with it. So, who gives you the books?'

'I don't know what you're talking about,' Dan said, and all the warmth was gone suddenly. He looked uncomfortable and suspicious, and the funny T-shirt didn't fit his mood at all. 'Let me know if you find anything you want.'

The fourth floor of the school's library had been

a locked maze of boxes of old books, gathered from who-knew-where by the vampires. At the time Claire had visited – well, broken in – vampires (no doubt reporting to Amelie, the town's Founder) had been combing through looking for one *particular* book. She'd wondered what they'd planned to do with all the rest once their quest was finished.

Naturally, it turned out Amelie was making money off of the extra books. Vampires were nothing if not practical.

As Claire was thumbing through the dusty stacks, squinting to read faded titles, occasionally sneezing from the smell of old paper, she found a slim, leather-bound volume that was still in pretty good condition. No title on the spine, so she pulled it out and looked at the front. Nothing on the front, either.

Inside, on the first page under a sheet of old onionskin, was a black-and-white photograph of Amelie. Claire blinked and took her time looking; yes, it really was her. The Founder of Morganville looked young and fragile, with her white-gold hair piled up in a complicated style on top of her head that showed off her very long, elegant neck. She wore a black dress, something from the 1800s, Claire guessed, with lots of sleeve and tons of skirts and petticoats. There was something about her eyes – the photograph had made them even lighter than the icy grey they usually were.

It was deeply spooky.

Claire flipped a page and read the title:

A HISTORY OF MORGANVILLE

ITS IMPORTANT CITIZENS AND EVENTS

A CHRONICLE OF OUR TIMES

She blinked. Surely they hadn't meant for *this* to end up in the used bookstore, where anybody could pick it up and find it. She'd never seen anything like it before.

And, of course, she *had* to have it. She'd been burning up with curiosity about Amelie ever since she'd met her; the Founder seemed to have so many secrets that it was hard to know where they started and stopped. Even though Amelie had, from time to time, helped her out, and had given her Protection that had saved her life at one time, Claire really didn't know that much about her, except that she was old, regal, and scary.

The pencilled price on the inside of the cover was only five dollars. She quickly found a few more obscure science titles, buried the history in the stack, and hauled it up to the front.

Dan snorted. 'You're never going to cram all that in your backpack.'

'Yeah, probably not,' she agreed. 'Could I have a sack?'

'What do I look like, Piggly Wiggly? Hang on.' He

rooted around behind the counter, sending up choking clouds of dust that made even *him* cough, and finally handed over a battered old canvas bag. She started counting out money, and he quickly flipped open the books and added up the totals. He wasn't paying attention, which was good; he just added it up and said, 'Twenty-seven fifty.'

That was an awful lot, pretty much all she had at the moment, but she kept smiling and handed it over. As soon as the cash had left her palm, she grabbed the bag and started stuffing things inside.

'What's your hurry?' he asked, counting out the fives and ones. 'It's not close to sundown.'

'Class,' she said. 'Thanks.'

He nodded, opened the register, and put the cash inside. She felt him watching her all the way to the door. It occurred to her that she didn't know which vampire owned this business, or how he (or she) might feel about the sale of the book…but she couldn't worry about that now.

She really *did* have class.

CHAPTER TWO

It didn't take long at all to read the book. She stopped in a park on the way home, sitting in a sun-faded rubber swing seat, rocking slowly back and forth as she flipped pages.

It was about people she'd never heard of...and people she knew. Amelie, for one. Amelie's disputes with various vampires. Amelie's decisions to sentence this person for his crimes, spare that one. There were other vampires profiled, too. Some she'd never heard of; she supposed that they'd died, or left, or maybe they were just reclusive. Oliver wasn't in the book, because he was a latecomer to town. Neither, curiously, was Myrnin. She supposed Myrnin had been a closely guarded town secret from the very beginning.

It was weirdly interesting, but overall, she didn't know what good it was going to do her to know that

Amelie had once filed a complaint against a man who owned a dry-goods store (what *was* a dry-goods store?) for cheating the human customers. And that the complaint had got his store taken away from him, and he'd opened the town's first movie theatre.

Boring.

In the end, Claire dropped the book into her backpack and thought about mailing it anonymously to the library. Maybe that was where it really belonged, anyway. She thought about it on the way home, but she ended up worrying about whether or not vampires could somehow sense she'd handled it. *CSI: Vampire.* Not a comforting thought.

'You're late,' Michael remarked, as she walked into the Glass House through the kitchen door. He was standing at the sink washing dishes; there was nothing odder to her than seeing her housemate, who was all kinds of smoking hot, not to mention all kinds of vampire, up to his elbows in suds at the sink. Did rock stars really do their own housework? 'Also, it's not my day to do the kitchen. It's yours.'

'Is that your passive-aggressive way of trying to get me to pick up your laundry duty?'

'I don't know. Is it working?'

'Maybe.' She put her bags down on the table and went to join him at the sink. He washed plates and handed them over, and she rinsed and dried. Very domestic. 'I was reading. I forgot what time it was.'

'Bookworm.' He flicked suds at her. Michael was in a really good mood, no question about that; he had been for the last couple of months. Getting out of Morganville and recording his music with a real, genuine recording company had been good for him. Coming back had been hard, but he'd finally settled into the routine. They all had. It had been a crazy, weird vacation, almost like something they'd dreamt, Claire decided.

But damn, it had felt good to be out there with her friends, on the road, without the shadow of Morganville hanging over them.

Michael abruptly stopped laughing, and just looked at her with those big blue eyes. That made her go momentarily dizzy, and she felt a blush coming on. Not that he was flirting with her – not more than normal – but he was looking at her a lot more deeply than usual, and he didn't blink.

Finally he did, turning his attention back to the sink, and washed another plate before he said, 'You're nervous about something. Your heartbeat's faster than normal.'

'You can hear – Oh. Of course you can.' He hadn't been staring at *her* so much as the blood moving through her veins, she thought. And that was kind of creepy, except it was *Michael*. He made creepy adorable, most of the time. 'I ran part of the way home; that's probably it.'

'Hey, if you don't want to tell me, don't. But I can tell when you lie.'

OK, that was *super* creepy. 'You can?'

He smiled grimly down at the dirty dishwater. 'Nope. But see? You fell for it anyway. Careful, or I'll read your mind with my incredible vampire superpowers.'

She sighed and wiped her hands as he pulled the plug on the dishwater and let it swirl away into the dark. The kitchen looked like someone actually cared. She really did owe him laundry, probably.

Claire tossed him the dish towel. 'That was a mean trick.'

'Yeah, still a vampire. Spill it.'

As he wiped his hands and arms free of suds, she opened up the bag on the table, rooted around to find the slim volume, and handed it over. He sank into a chair. As he looked it over, his eyebrows went up and up. 'Where'd you get this?'

'The used bookstore,' she said. 'I don't think Dan – you know, the guy who runs it? – knew it was there. Or if he did, maybe it's...I don't know...full of lies? But that's a picture of Amelie, right?'

'I didn't know there were any, but that's definitely one.' Michael closed the book and handed it back. 'Maybe it's Morganville propaganda. Seems like

Amelie's done that from time to time, in which case, no big deal. But if it's not—'

'If it's the real history of Morganville, then I should take it to Amelie before I get in trouble, yeah, thanks, *Dad*. Already figured that one out.'

He leant forward on his elbows and grinned. 'You are a difficult kid. But a smart one.'

'Not a kid,' she said, and shot him the finger, just like Eve or Shane would have done. 'Hey, who's on dinner patro—'

Before she could finish the last word, the front door banged open, and Eve's cheery voice echoed down the hall. 'Hellooooo, creatures of the night! Put your pants back on! Food's here, and I don't mean me!'

Michael pointed mutely in that direction.

'Tell me she's not bringing leftover sandwiches from the University Centre,' Claire moaned, as Eve burst into the kitchen door with a white paper bag in hand.

'I heard that,' Eve said, and opened the refrigerator to dump the bag inside. 'I got you the bacteria special; I know how much you like that. The UC kitchen staff send their love. Whassup, dead guy?'

'Not dead yet,' Michael said, and rose to kiss her. Except for the cool bluish tone to his skin, he looked like any other boy of nineteen; the sharp, pointy teeth were folded up, like a snake's, and when he was like this Claire actually kind of forgot he was a vamp at all. Although he was wearing a faded T-shirt that had a happy face on it, with vampire fangs. Eve had probably bought it for him.

Eve herself had to stand just a bit on tiptoe for the kiss, which went on about five seconds too long for it to be just hi-honey-welcome-home, and when they parted, Eve's cheeks were flushed even under the white Goth make-up. After a hard day of pulling shots at the TPU coffee shop – she alternated now between there and Common Grounds – she still looked cheerful and alert. Maybe it was all that caffeine. It just soaked right into her body without her even having to drink it. She was wearing black tights with orange pumpkins on them – left over from Halloween, Claire assumed, but Halloween was a year-round holiday for Eve – a tight black skirt, and three layers of thin shirts, each a different colour. The one on top was sheer black, with a sad-eyed pirate skull printed on it.

'I like the new earrings,' Claire said. They were silver skulls, and the little eye sockets lit up red whenever Eve turned her head. 'They're you.'

'I know, right? Couldn't be cooler.' Eve beamed. 'Oh, and actually, they were out of the bacteria special, so I got you the ham and cheese. That's usually the safest one.'

Safe being a relative term, when it came to UC food.

'Thanks,' Claire said. 'Tomorrow I'm making spaghetti. Yes, before you ask, with meat sauce. Carnivores.'

Eve made a chomping sound with her teeth. Michael just smiled. The smile faded as he asked, 'You don't have to go see Amelie tonight, do you?'

'No, probably not. The book's been sitting in that shop for who knows how long. It can wait until tomorrow. I have to go to the lab anyway. Amelie will be a nice break, after my mandatory crazy-boss time.'

Eve got herself a cold Coke from the fridge and popped the top as she dragged Claire's bag off of a chair and dumped it in the corner. 'How is crazy boss man, anyway?'

'Myrnin's...well, Myrnin, I guess. He's been getting a little weird.'

'Sweetie, coming from you, that's alarming. You have an awfully large scale of weird.'

'I know.' Claire sighed and sat down, propping her chin on both fists. She debated how much to say, even to her friends, but honestly, there weren't any secrets. Not in the Glass House. 'I think he's under a lot of pressure to get the machine fixed; you know the one—'

'Ada?' Eve asked. 'Ugh, seriously, he's not bringing *that* back to life, is he?'

'Not...exactly, no. But Ada wasn't all bad, you know. Well, *Ada* was, the personality, but the machine did all kinds of things that the vamps need, like maintain the borders of the town, give alerts when residents leave, wipe memories when they want it done…and run the portals.' The portals were the dimensional doorways that ran through town. Myrnin had discovered some freaky way of accelerating particles and constructing stable tunnels through space-time, something that Claire was still struggling to understand, let alone master. It wasn't *quite* magic, but sometimes, there didn't seem much of a boundary between magic and Myrnin's science. 'It's important. We're just trying to, you know, take the Ada factor out of the equation and get the mechanical piece working without the mind-of-its-own part.'

'Killer computers.' Eve sighed. 'Like we didn't have enough trouble in Morganville already. I'm not so sure any of those things you're talking about are good for us, Claire Bear. You feel me?'

'If by *us* you mean the regular humans, yeah, I know. But…' Claire shrugged. 'Fact is, having those safeguards lets them trust us, at least a little, and trust is all that keeps this town going.'

Eve didn't have a comeback to that. She knew Claire was right. Morganville existed on a teetering, dangerous balance between the paranoia and violence of the vampires, and the paranoia and violence of the humans who outnumbered them. Right there, at the balance point, they could all coexist. But it didn't take much to tilt things to one side or the other, and if that happened, Morganville would burn.

Claire chewed her lip and continued, 'We're getting it done; really, we are, but he's got some kind of deadline he's not telling me about, and I'm worried he's going to...do something crazy.'

'He lives in a hole in the ground, dresses funny, and occasionally eats his assistants,' Eve said. 'Define *crazy.*'

Claire closed her eyes. 'OK. I think he wants to put my brain in a jar and wire it into the machine.'

Dead silence. She opened her eyes. Michael was staring at her, frozen in the act of opening the refrigerator door; Eve had put her Coke down, her eyes as wide as anything ever drawn in animation. Michael finally remembered what he was doing, reached in, and grabbed a green sports bottle, which he carried to the table and sat down. 'That's not going to happen,' he said. 'I'm not going to let it happen. Neither will Amelie.'

Claire wasn't so sure about that last part, but she was sure Michael meant what he said, and that made her feel a little better. 'I don't think he's serious about it,' Claire said weakly. 'Well, not most of the time. But he keeps going on about how the brain is a much better CPU—'

'Not going to happen,' Michael repeated flatly. 'I'll kill him first, Claire. I mean it.'

She didn't want Myrnin dead, but it did make her feel better to have her friend say it. Michael was a sweetheart most of the time, but the truth was, there was something cold inside him – and it wasn't just that his heart didn't beat. It was...something else. Something darker. Mostly, it didn't show.

Sometimes, she was grateful it did.

'Shane's late,' Eve said, changing the subject. 'Where's Mr Barbecue McStabby?'

'Working late,' Claire replied. 'Somebody cancelled on the night shift, so he had to work dinner service. He said it was OK; he could use the overtime. And he doesn't like you to call him Mr McStabby, you know.'

'Have you ever *seen* him cutting up that meat? He is like an artist with slicing. And that knife is as long as my arm. Mr McStabby it is.'

They debated it for a while, with Michael staying out of it and sipping his sports bottle of – probably – blood, until Eve got the sandwiches out and they ate a cold, and somewhat mushy, dinner. After that, Claire fidgeted around, too restless to study, missing Shane, until Eve finally snapped at her about pacing and moving stuff, and she went up towards her room.

On an impulse, she didn't go there; she stopped in the hallway, reached out, and found the hidden catch to the secret room. The panelling clicked open, and she went in and shut the door behind her. No knob on this side, but that was OK; she knew where the release was. She ran up the narrow flight of stairs and came out in the windowless, dusty room that they'd always figured had been Amelie's retreat, when she'd once lived in this house. It *looked* like her, somehow – old Victorian furniture, tapestry hangings, multicoloured Tiffany lamps that were probably worth a fortune. It was always a little cold in here, for some reason. Claire stretched out on the old velvet sofa, staring up at the ceiling, and thought about how many times she'd come here with Shane. It was their private place, where they could just get away from everything, and the blanket draped over the back smelt like him. She pulled it over her and smiled, feeling like the ghost of Shane was here with her, snuggling up close.

She had no idea she'd fallen asleep at first, and then she thought she was dreaming, because someone was touching her. Not molesting her or anything, just a fingertip being drawn down her cheek, across her lips...a slow, gentle sort of caress.

She opened her eyes to see Shane crouched down next to her. His hair was – as usual – mussed, hanging long around her face, and he smelt like barbecue and wood smoke, and his smile was the most beautiful thing she'd ever seen.

'Hey, sleepyhead,' he said. 'It's three in the morning. Eve thought vampires stole you, but that's only because you didn't make your bed this morning. I think I'm a bad influence.'

Her lips parted, and his finger paused there, tracing her mouth slowly. She didn't speak. His smile got wider.

'Miss me?'

'No,' she said. 'I wanted some peace and quiet. I didn't even know you were gone.'

He clapped his hands over his chest like she'd shot him, and fell on the floor. Claire rolled off the couch on top of him, but he refused to open his eyes until she kissed him, long and thoroughly. She licked her lips as she pulled away. 'Mmmm, barbecue.'

'Hungry?'

'Eve brought UC sandwiches.'

Shane made a face. 'Yeah, glad I missed that. But I wasn't exactly talking about midnight snacks.'

'Boys. Is that all you think about?'

'Midnight snacks?'

'Is that what the cool kids are calling it these days?'

He laughed, and she felt the rumble of it through her skin. Shane didn't laugh often, except when they were together; she loved the light in his brown eyes, and the wicked way his smile curled up on the ends.

'Like I would know,' he said. 'I never was one of the cool kids.'

'Bullshit.'

'Such language, Miss Danvers. Oh, wait, shit, I'm a bad influence.'

She settled her head down again, ear against his chest, listening to the rush of his breathing. 'Tell me what you were like in school.'

'Why?'

'Because I missed it.'

'You didn't miss much,' he said. 'Me and Mikey hung out a lot. He was Mr Popular, you know, but really shy. Girls, girls, girls, but he was pretty choosy. At least, up until our junior year.'

'What happened in your junior year?' she asked before she thought.

Shane's fingers kept stroking through her hair as he said, 'House burnt, my sister Alyssa died, my family went on the run. So I don't know how Mikey was the last two years of school. We caught up some when I came back, but it wasn't the same. Something happened to him. Sure as hell something happened to me. You know.' He shrugged, even with her weight on him, but then, she wasn't much of a burden, and he was a strong guy. 'There's not a lot to say about me. I was a pretty boring dumb-ass.'

'Were you in sports?'

He laughed. 'Football, for a while. I liked hockey better. More chances to hit people. But I'm not really a team player, so I ended up in the penalty box about twice as much as everybody else. Not as much fun.' He was quiet for a few seconds, then said, 'I guess you know Monica was after me for a while.'

That surprised her. 'Monica *Morrell*? You mean, after you, in the sense of—'

'I mean she slipped me really dirty notes and tried to rip my clothes off in a broom closet once. Which I guess to her was love. Not so much for me.' His face got hard for a moment, and then relaxed. 'I blew her off, and she got pissed. You know the rest.'

Shane believed – and Claire had no reason to doubt it – that Monica had set the fire that had burnt his home and killed his sister and destroyed his family's life. That wound was never going to heal; he was always going to hate Monica with a burning passion that was two seconds from violence. Not that Monica didn't egg him on, most of the time; she seemed to enjoy Shane's rage.

Claire couldn't think of much to say, so she kissed him again, and it felt sweet, warm, a little distracted on his part. She shouldn't have brought it up, she thought. He didn't like to think about those days at all. 'Hey,' she said. 'I didn't mean—'

'I know.' His smile came back again, and she thought

he was back in the here and now, with her, instead of in the bad old days. 'Glad you weren't here for all that, actually. I wasn't really all that good to know then. Plus, if you want to know the truth, I was kind of a jerk in junior high.'

'All boys are jerks in junior high. And mostly in high school. And then they grow up to be jerks.' She kissed him again. 'But not you, Mr McStabby.'

'Oh, man, Eve's not letting that go, is she?'

'Not remotely.' She felt herself smiling, too. Shane always brought out some crazy streak in her she didn't think she had – that was probably what worried her parents so much about the two of them. But Claire liked it. When she was with Shane, she could *feel* – feel the blood pounding in her veins, feel every nerve awake and alive and hungry to be touched. Everything was brighter, clearer, cleaner. A little crazy was a good thing. 'Want to make out?'

'Maybe I should take a shower. I smell like sweat and barbecue.'

'You smell great,' she said. 'I love the way you smell.'

'You're getting sappy, you know that? And maybe a little creepy.'

'Oh, shut up, you like it.'

He did, she could tell, especially when they were under the blanket, curled together on the couch, and

Amelie's refuge was their own, their private, sweet, warm heaven where nothing could intrude.

Well, except for Claire's cell phone alarm, which was set for seven a.m.

That sucked.

Morning was hard, partly because neither one of them had slept much, and partly because Claire just didn't want to *ever* leave the room, but she finally managed to kiss her way free and get down the stairs to the closed door.

It didn't open. 'Shane!' she yelled. 'I have to *go!*'

His evil laugh drifted down to her, movie-campy, but he pushed the button and let her out. She beat Eve to the shower, of course; Eve was not voluntarily an early riser, and it was her day off, so Claire could take her time in the hot water, and get herself pulled together without knocks rushing her along. When she opened the bathroom and stepped out, she found Shane sitting on the floor next to it, blocking the hallway with his legs. He had on his rumpled jeans, but he'd left off the shirt.

So not fair. She loved looking at his chest, and he knew it.

'We have got to get a second bathroom in this monster,' he said, and kissed her on his way through the doorway. 'You take way too long.'

'Do not!' she said, outraged, but the wood had

already closed between them. 'I take *half* the time Eve does!'

'Still too long!' he called from inside. 'Girls.'

She banged on the door, then winced and hoped it wasn't loud enough to wake Eve or Michael, and went down the hall to her room. Shane had been right: she had never made the bed yesterday, but she did it today, putting the pillows right and everything. Then she pulled out old, ratty clothes and her worst high-tops.

There was no sense in wearing good clothes to Myrnin's lab. They were just going to get splashed with icky stuff, or stuff that burnt holes, or stuff that never came out, no matter how creative you got with laundry add-ins. Claire gulped a bowl of cereal in the kitchen, standing over the sink, and started to wash the bowl – but it was Shane's kitchen day, and with a grin, she put the dirties down unscrubbed.

Served him right for trying to make her late.

She dumped most of the contents of her backpack, except for the things that were relevant to her project with Myrnin, then added in the slim history book and took off.

It was a beautiful morning. She'd missed sunrise, but it was still a little cool, and the sky was a beautiful clear blue with only a few scrubby clouds on the horizon. At this hour, the sun seemed friendly, not like the scorching monster it would become by noon. Claire skipped down the steps and out the gate, and set off for Common Grounds first. No Oliver, and this time both the baristas were new employees. Her name was spelt wrong, again.

Coffees in hand, she headed for Myrnin's lab.

Morganville was busy at this hour, with practically everybody who wasn't a vampire taking advantage of the sunshine and the safety it afforded. Kids walked in groups, even so; most adults didn't go alone, either, but go they did. Claire met several people she knew as she walked along.

It felt like home. That was actually a little sad.

A police car pulled up next to her on the street, idling and crawling along, and Claire saw Hannah Moses wave at her. The police chief of Morganville rolled down her window. 'You need a ride, Claire?'

Hannah was...impressive. She just had this completely competent air about her, and there was a scar on her face that should have looked disfiguring, but on her, it made her seem even more intimidating – until she smiled. Then she looked beautiful. Today, she was wearing her cornrowed hair back in a loose knot, elegant and kind of formal. For Hannah, anyway.

'No, thanks,' Claire called back. 'I appreciate it, but it's a really nice day. I should walk. And you're probably busy.'

'Busy is vampires fighting over the snack supply,'

Hannah said. 'This isn't it, trust me. OK, then, have a nice day. If you see Myrnin, tell him I said I want my slow cooker back.'

'Your – You let him borrow something you put food in?'

Hannah's smile disappeared. 'Why?'

'Um, never mind. I'll make sure it gets disinfected before you get it back. But don't lend anything to him again unless you can put it in some kind of steriliser.'

That made even *Hannah* look nervous. 'Thanks. Tell crazy boy I said hey.'

'I will,' Claire promised. 'Hey, if you don't mind me asking – when did he borrow it from you?'

'He just showed up at my door one night about a week ago, said "Hi, nice to meet you, can I borrow your Crock-Pot?" Which I understand is pretty typical Myrnin.'

'Very,' Claire agreed. 'Well, I should go; the coffee's getting cold—'

'Be safe,' Hannah said, and accelerated away. Claire increased her pace, too, walking faster as she passed through a couple of neighbourhoods and arrived in the street with the Day House – a mirror of Michael Glass's, because they were both Founder houses, the original houses built by Amelie and Myrnin. The Founder Houses not only looked the same; they had

the same kind of energy to them, Claire had found;
in some it was stronger than others, but they all had
that slightly unsettling sensation of...*intelligence*. It
was strongest in the Glass House, almost a personality
of its own.

The Day House was at the end of the cul-de-sac.
Hannah's relatives lived there, or at least Gramma Day
still did; Claire didn't know where Lisa Day had gone,
except that she'd chosen wrong during Morganville's
civil uprisings of a few months back, got jailed, and
been released after a couple of weeks. She'd never
come back to the Day House; that was certain. Claire
knew Hannah was still looking for her cousin. There
were only a few possibilities – Lisa had managed to
escape Morganville, or she'd gone into hiding, or she'd
never made it out of jail alive. For Gramma Day's
sake, Claire hoped Lisa had escaped. She wasn't the
friendliest person, but the old lady loved her.

Claire wasn't planning to stop at the Day House,
although Gramma Day, an ancient little old woman
sitting outside in a big rocking chair, called to her and
asked if she wanted any breakfast rolls. Claire smiled
at her and shook her head – Gramma didn't always
hear too well – and got a friendly wave in return as she
turned right, down the narrow fenced alley between
the Day House and the anonymous tract home on its
other side. It was too small for a car, this alley, and it

got narrower as it went, like a funnel. Or a throat. It was suspiciously clean, too — not a lot of trash blown in, and even the tumbleweeds had stayed away.

And here she was, walking right into the trap-door spider's lair.

The door to the rickety shack at the end of the alley banged open before she could reach it, and the spider himself charged out, grabbed his coffee out of her hand, and dashed back inside at vampire speed before she could say a word. From the glimpse she had of him, he'd been wearing black cargo-style pants that were too big for him, flip-flops with daisies on top, and some kind of satin vest with no shirt, probably because he just forgot to put one on. Myrnin didn't dress for vanity. More completely at random, really, like he just reached into the closet blindfolded and put on whatever pieces he touched first.

Claire went at human speed into the shack and down the steps, and emerged into the big room that was Myrnin's lab and sometimes his home. (She thought he had a separate one, but she rarely caught him absent from this one, and there was a room in the back with castoff clothes he rummaged through when the mood took him.) Myrnin was bent over a microscope, studying who-knew-what. He had all the lights on, which was nice, and the lab looked clean and cool today, all its steampunky elements gleaming. She wondered if he had a mad-scientist cleaning service.

'Thank you for the coffee,' he said. 'Good morning.'

'Morning,' Claire said, and dumped her backpack on a chair. 'How did you know which coffee was yours?'

'I didn't.' He shrugged. 'You haven't been returning my phone calls. And you know how much I dislike making them in the first place. Telephones are so cold and impersonal.'

'I didn't answer because I didn't feel like rerunning the argument again. We're not getting anywhere with it, are we?'

He looked up from the microscope, shoved old-fashioned square spectacles up on top of his long, curling black hair, and looked at her with a devastating smile. Myrnin was – for a vampire who *looked* about twice her age, but was thousands of years older than that – pretty hot. He could be sweet and affectionate one minute, cold and predatory the next, and that kept her from having any kind of crush on him, mostly. Truth was that he'd make a terrible, possibly fatal boyfriend.

She also really had no idea how he felt about her, deep down. He treated her like a particularly clever pet, most of the time.

'I love arguing with you, Claire. You always surprise me. And occasionally, you even make sense.'

She could have said the same about him, but not in

a flattering kind of way. Instead of trying to put that into words, she took her coffee over to the granite-topped lab table. He was using a modern microscope, digital, that she'd ordered for him special. He seemed happy with it, for now, though he'd probably go back to his old brass-and-glass monstrosity soon. Myrnin was just more comfortable with Victorian technology. 'What are you doing?'

'Checking my blood,' he said. 'I do it every week. You'll be happy to know that there's still no trace of the Bishop virus.'

The Bishop virus was what they'd named the cruel sickness that had attacked the vampires long before she'd arrived – a manufactured virus that Amelie's father, Bishop, had released, because only he had the cure. Unfortunately for him, since he'd first used the cure on himself, his blood had been the cure for everybody else, and now the evil old vampire was locked down, under maximum security, somewhere in Morganville. Nobody knew where, except Amelie and the people guarding him.

Claire liked it that way. The last thing she wanted to think about was Bishop getting away and coming after all of them for revenge. She'd met some nasty vampires, but Bishop was, as far as she was concerned, the worst.

'I'm glad you're OK,' she said. The Bishop virus had

caused vampires to lose themselves, their memories, their self-control. It had happened slowly for most, which made it worse – like human Alzheimer's, only a vampire stripped of all of those things was an unpredictable, dangerous beast. Unlike the others, Myrnin hadn't recovered completely – or, more likely, he'd always been a little off the bubble from normal. 'Can I see?'

'Oh, certainly,' Myrnin said, and stepped back to let her squint into the eyepiece of the microscope. There, in vivid colour, was the busy life of Myrnin's drop of blood – which wasn't his own blood, really, so much as that of others. There was a lot of difference between vampire blood and human, and Claire was still fascinated by how it worked. 'See? I'm in fine shape.'

'Congratulations.' She shut down the microscope – no sense in running up the lab's probably horrible electric bill – and sipped her coffee while he drank his. 'What are we doing today?'

'Oh, I thought we'd take a day off. Go to the park, stroll, watch a film...'

'Really.'

'You know me too well. Since you weren't talking to me this week, I designed some new circuitry. I'd like to see what you think of it.' He darted over to another table, this one covered by a white sheet. For a horrible few seconds she thought there was a *person* under there...but then he whipped it off, and it was just piles of metal, glass, and plastic. It didn't look like circuitry. Most things Myrnin built didn't look right. They just worked.

Claire came over and tried to figure out where to start – probably there, at the open pipe, that wound around and led to some kind of vacuum-tube arrangement, then into what looked like a circuit board scrounged from something more rational, then into bunches of wire, all the same colour, that snaked out like spaghetti to other things buried under more coils of tubing.

She gave up. 'What is it?'

'What do you think it is?'

'It could be anything from a lawn trimmer to a bomb, for all I know.'

'I would never build a lawn trimmer,' Myrnin said. 'What did the lawn ever do to me? No, it's an interface. For the computer.'

'An interface,' Claire repeated slowly. 'Between what and what?'

He gave her a long look, one of those 'don't ask me questions you already know the answer to' looks, and she felt her stomach clench.

'I'm not going to let you do that,' she said. 'No building brains into your machines. No. You can't kill someone just to power your stupid computer, Myrnin; it's *wrong*!'

'Well, I kill people for blood, you know. I thought this would be more like conservation – waste not, want not, and all that. If I'm killing them already.'

Claire rolled her eyes. 'You *don't* kill people for blood, not in Morganville. I know for a fact that since you got better, you haven't—' Well, *did* she know that, actually? Was she sure? 'I'm pretty sure you haven't.'

He smiled, and it was a sad, sweet smile, the sort that broke her heart from him. 'Oh, Claire,' he said. 'You think me a far better man than I am. That's kind, and flattering.'

'Are you saying that you—'

'Doughnuts!' Myrnin interrupted her, and darted away, to zip back in seconds with an open box. 'Chocolate glazed. Your favourite.'

She stared at him, helpless, and finally took one. They were fresh, so he'd actually gone out and got them. She could imagine how *that* had gone over at the local doughnut shop, especially given what he was wearing today. 'Myrnin, have you been hunting?'

He raised his eyebrows and bit into a jelly-filled doughnut. Raspberry jam oozed out, and Claire swallowed hard.

After he licked his lips clean, he said, 'Let's look at *your* latest breakthrough, shall we?'

She followed him across to the back of the lab, where her own much saner-looking circuitry was sitting on another table, under another sheet. He'd made some...additions, she saw, in his usual non-traditional style. She couldn't imagine how copper pipes and old-fashioned springs and levers were supposed to improve her work, and for a second she felt righteously angry. She'd worked *hard* on that, and like a bratty little kid, Myrnin had *ruined* it.

'What did you do?' she asked, a little too sharply, and Myrnin turned around slowly to stare at her.

'Improved the design,' he said, and this time his voice was cool, and not at all amused. 'Science is collaboration, little girl. You are no scientist at all if you can't accept improvements on your theory.'

'But—' Frustrated, she bit into her doughnut. She'd spent *weeks* working on this, and he'd promised he wouldn't touch it while she was gone. She'd been so *close* to making it work! 'How exactly did you *improve* it?'

For an answer, he reached over to the power cord – still modern, thank God – and plugged it into the outlet at the side of the table.

The computer monitor – LCD, perfectly good – had been given the Jules Verne treatment, too. It was almost invisible in a nest of pipes and springs and gears...but it came on, and Claire recognised the graphic interface she'd designed for him. She'd made it steampunky, of course, because she knew that made him happy, but with the ornaments on the *outside* it looked half-crazy.

Perfect for Myrnin, then.

She went through the touch-screen menus rapidly. *Town security, town memory control, town transportation...*Transportation and memory control had been the two things that hadn't worked, but now, at least according to the interface, they did. She pressed the on-screen button for town transportation, and a map popped up, with glowing green spots for each of the stable doorways – like wormholes – that ran between Founder houses in town, and throughout most of the public buildings. There were two at TPU, and two at the courthouse, one in the hospital, some in places that she didn't recognise.

But just because they were green on the screen didn't mean they actually worked, of course.

'Have you tested it?' she asked.

Myrnin was finishing his doughnut. He wiped red from his lips and said, 'Of course not. I'm far too valuable to waste on experiments. That's your job, assistant.'

'But it works?'

'Theoretically,' he said, and shrugged. 'Of course, I wouldn't recommend a first-person test just yet. Try something inorganic first.'

Despite herself, Claire felt a little thrill of

excitement. *It's working. Maybe.* Transportation and
memory control had been two impossible problems,
and maybe, just maybe, they'd actually solved one of
them. That meant the second wasn't insurmountable,
either.

She tried to keep that out of her expression, nodded,
and walked to the wooden cabinet that covered
the doorway that led to the lab. She tried to slide
it. It wouldn't budge. 'Did you lock this in place or
something?'

'Oh, no, I just stored some lead inside,' Myrnin said
cheerfully, and with one hand he slid the heavy beast
out of the way. 'There you go. I forget you can't actually
move mountains; you do such a good imitation of it. I'll
move the lead to another location.'

She wasn't sure if that was meant to be a
compliment, so she said nothing, just focused on the
portal in front of her. He'd put in a new locked door
to cover it, and she had to go in search of the key to
the padlock, because of course it wasn't hanging on
the hook where it was supposed to be. It took twenty
minutes to locate it in the pocket of Myrnin's ratty old
bathrobe, which was hanging on an articulated human
skeleton wired together in the corner of the lab – one of
those old teaching tools, she hoped, and not a previous
occupant of her own job.

Once she'd opened the door, what was beyond was

an empty, dark space, leading...well, potentially to a horrible death.

Claire reached over and grabbed a book from a nearby stack, checked the title, and decided they could do without it. Then she concentrated, imagining the living room at the Glass House. It was harder to project that image into the portal than before, almost as if there were some kind of force fighting *not* to open the connection, but then the image resolved through with an almost audible *pop* and colour spread out in front of her. Blurry at first, then slowly coming into focus.

'My God,' she breathed. 'He actually made it work.'

Facing her was the back of the battered couch at home. She could see Michael's acoustic guitar still propped up in his chair off to the side. The TV was off, so obviously Shane wasn't up yet.

She flinched as a shadow walked in front of her, but it was only Eve, who crossed between the TV and the couch, still fastening her pigtails as she headed towards the kitchen.

'Hey!' Claire called. 'Hey, Eve!'

Eve, puzzled, stopped and turned around, staring up towards the second floor, then looking at the TV.

'Over here!' Claire said. 'Eve!'

Eve turned, and her eyes widened. 'Claire? Oh, are the portals working?'

'No, stay there. I'm testing it.' Claire held up the book. 'Here. Catch.'

She tossed the book through the open connection, and on the other side she saw Eve raise her hands.

The book hit Eve's palms and crumbled into dust. Eve, surprised, let out a little squawk and jumped back, shaking the dust from her hands.

'Are you OK?' Claire asked anxiously.

'Yeah, just surprised. And filthy.' Eve held up her smudged palms. 'Not quite there yet, right? Unless you *wanted* to pulverise people.'

'Not exactly.' Claire sighed. 'Thanks. I'll keep working on it. Sorry about the dirt.'

'Well, it's not like we don't have *that* on the floor. Michael was supposed to sweep; do you really think he's done it?' Eve grinned. 'Nice try with the weird science, but for now, I think I'll stick with walking.'

She blew Claire a kiss, and Claire waved and stepped back. The colour faded out again, turning Eve and the room to black-and-white, and then to just a sea of liquid darkness.

Myrnin was standing by her elbow when she looked over. He was tapping a finger on his lips. 'That,' he said, 'was very interesting. Also, you owe me a third-edition Johannes Magnus.'

'You have six of them already. But the important thing is, it's almost working,' Claire said. 'The stabilisation's off. But the connection's working. That's a huge step forward.'

'Not much of one if it turns us to ashes upon arrival. I can do that all on my own by strolling long enough in the sunlight. Well, it's your problem now, Claire. I'm working on the other part.'

'What other – Oh. Wiping people's memories when they leave Morganville.'

'Exactly. I'm actually getting quite close, I believe.'

'But you're not going to use a brain. Other than your own, I mean.'

'Since you insist, I am trying it the hard way. I am not optimistic at all that this will ever work,' he said, and produced the box of doughnuts again, with a magician's flourish. 'One more?'

She really couldn't resist, when he gave her that smile.

CHAPTER THREE

Over the next three days, Claire didn't go home for long. She was obsessive when she got into a problem, and she knew it, but this was so *cool*. She went to the store and bought cartloads of cheap plastic toys, which she spent hours tossing through the portal to an increasingly bored Eve, then Michael, then Shane. They had their own supply of toys, too, and pitched them through in the opposite direction.

All she got out of it, for two and a half days, was dust – so much of it that Shane told her she was on permanent vacuum duty at home, if she ever came home again. She knew that he was grumpy, both because it was boring pitching toys back and forth, but also because she'd barely seen him for days, except to come home, shovel in food, and fall into bed. She was grumpy about it, too, but there was something inside of her that was locked on target about this stupid problem, and she couldn't walk away from it. Not until something worked, or she broke.

She didn't break.

On the third day, Shane was still on catching duty. He was sitting cross-legged on the floor, leaning against the back of the sofa and wearing one of those white cotton breathing masks. He'd bought it in self-defence, he'd told her; he didn't want to be breathing in plastic toy dust and coughing up a lung.

She didn't blame him, but it did make a funny picture, at least until she'd realised the same thing on her end and got a mask out of Myrnin's jumbled stash of supplies. And goggles. Shane now envied her the goggles.

'Hang on,' she said, after her last attempt at pitching a neon plastic ball through had turned it to dust on the other end. 'I have an idea.'

'So do I,' Shane said. 'Movies, hot dogs, and not doing this anymore. Like it?'

'Love it,' she said, and meant it. 'But let me do this one thing, OK?'

He sighed and let his head fall back against the sofa. 'Sure, whatever.'

She really was a terrible girlfriend, Claire thought, and raced across the lab, careful of all of Myrnin's various scattered trip hazards that she couldn't seem to convince him were dangerous. She arrived at the worktable, where her circuitry (with Myrnin's incomprehensible additions) quietly hummed away.

She shut the power off and checked the connections again. All of the voltage was steady; there was no reason why the other end would be unstable, unless...

Unless it was something Myrnin had done.

Claire began tracing the piping, which led to a spring, which led to a complicated series of gears and levers, which led to a bubbling ice-green liquid in a sealed chamber...

Only it wasn't bubbling. It wasn't doing anything, even when she turned the power on. She distinctly remembered him explaining that it was supposed to bubble. She had no idea why that was important, but she supposed that maybe the bubbling created some kind of pressure, which...did what?

Exasperated, she thumped the thing with her finger.

It started to bubble.

She blinked, watched the whole thing for a while, decided that it wasn't going to blow up or boil over, and went back to where Shane was pretending to snore on the other side of the portal.

'Heads up, slacker!' she said, and pitched another neon ball at him, hard.

Shane's reactions were really, really good, and he

got his eyes open and hands up at the same time...

...and the ball smacked firmly into his grip.

Shane stared down at it for a second, then stripped off his mask as he turned it over in his fingers.

'Is it OK?' Claire asked breathlessly. 'Is it—'

'Feels fine,' he said. 'Damn. Unbelievable.' He pitched it back to her, and she caught it. It felt exactly the same – not even a little warm or a little cool. She threw it back, and he responded, and before long they were laughing and whooping and feeling incredibly giddy. She raised the ball over her head and jumped around in a circle, just like Eve would have, and made herself dizzy.

She whirled around to an unsteady stop, and Shane caught her.

Because he was *here*, in the lab with her, instead of on the other side of the portal. Her brain sent a message of, *Oh, he feels so good*, just about a half second before the logical part kicked in.

Claire shoved him backward, appalled and scared. 'What the hell are you doing?'

'What?' Shane asked. 'What did I do?'

'You...you came through?'

'The ball was fine.'

'The *ball* doesn't have internal organs! Squishy parts! How could you be so crazy?' She was literally shaking now, deeply terrified that he was about to burst into a dust cloud, melt, die in her arms. How could he be so *insane*?

Shane looked a little off balance, as if he hadn't really expected this kind of reception, but he looked back at the portal, the piles of dust, and said, 'Oh. Yeah, I see your point. But I'm fine, Claire. It worked.'

'How do you know you're fine? Shane, you could *die!*' She rushed at him, threw her arms around him, and now she could feel his heart beating fast. He hugged her, held her while she tried to get her panic under control, and gently kissed the top of her head.

'You're right; it was dumb,' he said. 'Stop. Relax. You did it, OK? You made it work. Just...breathe.'

'Not until you go see the doctor,' she said. 'Dumbass.' She was still scared, still shaking, but she tried to get the old Claire back, the one who could face down snarling vampires. But this was *different*.

What if she'd just killed him? Broken something inside him that couldn't grow back?

Myrnin came in from the back room, carrying a load of books, which he dropped with a loud bang on the floor to glare at the two of them. 'Excuse me,' he said, 'but when did my lab become appropriate for snogging?'

'What's snogging?' Shane asked.

'Ridiculous displays of inappropriate affection in front of me. Roughly translated. And what are *you* doing here?' Myrnin was genuinely offended, Claire realised. Not good.

'It's my fault,' Claire said in a rush, and stepped away from Shane, although she kept holding his hand. 'I...He was helping me with the experiments.'

'In what, biology?' Myrnin crossed his arms. 'Are we running a secret laboratory or not? Because if you're going to have your friends drop in anytime they please—'

'Back off, man; she said she was sorry,' Shane said. He was watching Myrnin with that cold look in his eyes, the one that was a real danger sign. 'It wasn't her fault, anyway. It was mine.'

'Was it,' Myrnin said softly. 'And how is it that you do not understand that *here*, in *this* place, this girl belongs to me, not to you?'

Claire turned cold all over, then hot. She felt her cheeks flare red, and she hardly recognised her voice as she yelled, 'I don't *belong* to you, Myrnin! I *work* for you! I'm not your...your slave!' She was so furious that she wasn't even shaking anymore. 'I fixed your portals. And we're leaving.'

'You'll leave when I – Wait, what did you say?'

Claire ignored him and picked up her backpack. She led the way up the stairs. Three steps up, she glanced back. Shane still hadn't moved. He was still watching Myrnin. Still *between* her and Myrnin.

'Wait,' Myrnin said, in an entirely different tone now. 'Claire, wait. Are you saying you successfully transported an object?'

'No, she's saying she successfully transported *me*,' Shane snapped. 'And we're leaving now.'

'No, no, no, wait, you can't. I must run tests; I need to have a blood sample.' Myrnin rooted frantically in a drawer, came up with an ancient blood-drawing kit, and came towards Shane.

Shane looked over his shoulder at Claire. 'I'm seriously going to kill this guy if he tries to stick me with that thing.'

'Myrnin!' Claire snapped. 'No. Not now. I'm taking him to the hospital to get him checked out. I'll make sure you get your sample. Now *leave us alone*.'

Myrnin stopped, and he actually looked wounded. *Oh stop it*, Claire thought, still furious. *I didn't kick your puppy.*

She was almost at the top of the steps, and Shane was right behind her, when she heard Myrnin say, in a quiet voice that was like the old Myrnin, the one she actually liked, 'I'm sorry, Claire. I never meant – I'm sorry. Sometimes I don't know...I don't know what I am thinking. I wish...I wish things could be like they were before.'

'Me too,' Claire muttered.

She knew they wouldn't be, though.

Getting Shane seen by a doctor was trickier than she'd thought. Claire couldn't exactly explain to the emergency room what *might* be wrong with him, so after a complete fail at the ER, she went in search of the only doctor she knew personally – Dr Mills – who'd treated her before, and knew about Myrnin. He'd actually helped create the antidote to the vampires' illness, so he was pretty trustworthy.

She still didn't explain about the portals, but he didn't push. He was a nice guy, middle-aged, a little tired, like most doctors usually seemed to be, but he just nodded and said, 'Let me take a look at him. Shane?'

'I'm not dropping my pants,' Shane said. 'I just thought I'd say that up front.'

Dr Mills laughed. 'Just the basics, all right? But if Claire's concerned, I'm concerned. Let's make sure you're healthy.'

They walked off towards his office, leaving Claire in the waiting area with piles of ancient magazines that still wondered whether Brad Pitt and Jennifer Aniston would stay together. Not that she read that stuff anyway. Much.

She was still mad at Myrnin, but now she realised that it was mostly because she'd been so tired and stressed out. He hadn't been any worse than normal, really. And how much did *that* suck?

It doesn't matter, she told herself. *I did something*

amazing, and nobody got hurt. She knew they'd both been lucky, though. It still turned her cold to think what could have happened, all because she hadn't thought to tell Shane not to come through the portal, no matter how safe it seemed.

Doctors always seemed to take for ever, and while Shane was getting checked out, Claire fidgeted and thought about the progress she'd made, and – what worried her more – the progress that *Myrnin* had made. Apparently. What was he thinking? It was impossible to know, but she was pretty sure he hadn't given up the idea of putting a brain – namely *her* brain – in a jar and hooking it up to a computer. It was the kind of totally cracked thing Myrnin would think was not only logical, but somehow *helpful.*

She really didn't want to end up in a jar, like Ada had before her. A ghost, slowly going mad because she couldn't touch, be touched, be *human.* Although in Ada's case, she'd been a vampire. But still, Ada hadn't exactly come through it with all her marbles. Oh, she'd seemed to do her job, running the systems; she'd kept the portals open and the boundaries closed, issued alerts when residents tried to flee, probably even done a lot more that Claire had never seen. But in the end, Ada had got less and less sane, and more and more determined to keep Myrnin all to herself, and never mind the rest of Morganville.

And Myrnin hadn't been able to admit that there was a problem.

That brought a bad flashback of Ada's proper Victorian schoolmistress image standing in front of her, hands folded, smiling. Waiting for Claire to die.

Well, I didn't die, Claire thought, and controlled a shudder. *Ada died. And I'm not ending up like Ada, some insane thing trying to stay alive at any cost...*

She flinched as someone touched her shoulder, but it was Shane. He grinned down at her. 'Hospitals freak you out?'

'They ought to,' she shot back. 'You're always ending up in here.'

'Not fair. You've had your turns, too.'

She had, more than she liked. Claire scrambled to her feet, grabbed her stuff, and saw Dr Mills standing a few feet away. He was smiling. That was a good sign, right?

'He's fine,' the doctor said, in such a soothing voice Claire knew she was looking anxious. Or panicked. 'Whatever he was accidentally exposed to, I can't find anything that's off. But if you start feeling odd, dizzy, experiencing any pain or discomfort, be sure to call me, Shane.'

Shane, his back to the doctor, rolled his eyes, then turned and said a polite thank-you. 'How much do I owe you, Doc?'

Dr Mills raised his eyebrows. 'I see you're wearing Amelie's pin.'

Shane was, haphazardly stuck in the collar of his shirt; he'd bitched about it at first, but Claire had insisted they all wear the pins, all the time. Amelie had promised that they would identify them as a special kind of neutral, free from attack by any vampires – though she'd yet to test out the theory.

Apparently, they were also gold cards, because Dr Mills continued, 'There's no charge for services for friends of Morganville.'

Shane frowned, and it looked like he might argue, but Claire pulled on his arm, and he let himself be led away to the elevators. 'Never turn down free,' she said.

'I don't like it,' Shane said, before the doors even closed. 'I don't like being some charity case.'

'Yeah, well, trust me: you couldn't afford his bill anyway.' She turned towards him as the elevator beeped its descent to the ground floor, and stepped closer. 'You're OK. You're really OK.'

'Told you I was.' He bent down, and she turned her face up, but they had time for only a quick, sweet kiss before the doors opened and they had to dodge out of the way of a gurney with a patient on it. Shane took her hand, and they walked out of the hospital lobby and into the late-afternoon sun.

On the way out, she caught a glimpse of a face in shadows, pale and sharp and hard. An older man, with a vivid scar marring his face.

Claire stopped walking, and Shane continued on for a step before looking back at her. 'What?' he asked, and turned to see where she was staring.

Nothing there now, but Claire was sure of what she'd seen, even in that brief flash.

Shane's father, Frank Collins, had been watching them. That was unsettling, and creepy. She hadn't seen Frank in a while – not since he'd saved her life. She'd heard that he'd been around, but seeing him was an entirely different thing.

Frank Collins was the world's most reluctant vampire, and besides that, she was sure that he was the person Shane least wanted to see.

'Nothing,' she said, and focused her attention back on Shane with a smile that she hoped was happy. 'I'm so glad you're OK.'

'So how do we celebrate my okayness? It's my day off. Let's go crazy. Glow-in-the-dark bowling?'

'No.'

'I'll let you use the kiddie ball.'

'Shut up. I do *not* need the kiddie ball.'

'The way you bowl, I think you might.' He grabbed her in an exaggerated formal dance pose and whirled her around, backpack and all, which didn't make her any more graceful. 'Ballroom dancing?'

'Are you *insane?*'

'Hey, girls who tango are hot.'

'You think I'm not hot because I don't tango?'

He dropped the act. Shane was a smart boy. 'I think you are too hot for ballroom *or* bowling. So you tell me. What do you want to do? And don't say study.'

Well, she hadn't been going to. Although she'd considered it. 'How about the movies?'

'How about borrowing Eve's car and going to the drive-in movie?'

'Morganville still has a *drive-in theatre?* What is this, 1960?'

'I know, goofy, but it's kind of cool. Somebody bought it a few years ago and fixed it up. It's the hot place to take a hot date. Well, hotter than the bowling alley, because...privacy.'

It sounded weird, but Claire thought that in fairness, it *did* seem more romantic than the bowling alley, and less old-folks than ballroom dancing. 'What's showing?'

Shane gave her a sidelong look. 'Why? You planning on watching the movie?'

She laughed. He tickled her. She shrieked and ran on ahead, but he caught her and tackled her down to the grass of the park on the corner, and for a couple of seconds she kept laughing and struggling, but then he kissed her, and the sensation of his warm, soft lips moving on hers took all the fight right out of her. It felt *wonderful*, lying here on the grass, with the sun shining on them, and for a few minutes she was floating in a soft, warm cloud of delight, as if nothing in the world could ever ruin this feeling.

Until a police siren let out a sharp burst of noise, and Shane yelped and rolled off of her and up to his feet, ready for...what? Fighting? He knew better. Besides, as Claire struggled up to her elbows, she saw that the police car that had pulled up to the curb was – once again – Chief Hannah Moses. She was laughing, her teeth very white against her dark skin.

'Relax, Shane; I just didn't want you scaring the little old ladies,' Hannah said. 'I'm not hauling you in. Unless you've got something to confess.'

'Hey, Chief. Didn't know kissing was against the code.'

'There's probably something about public displays of affection, but I'm not so much bothered by that.' She pointed at the western horizon, where the sun was brushing the edge. 'Time to be getting home.'

Shane looked where she pointed, and nodded, suddenly sobered. 'Thanks. Lost track of time.'

'Well, I can see how.' She waved and pulled away, off to deliver helpful encouragement to other wandering potential victims. It was different from the way Monica's brother, Richard Morrell, used to do things, and before him the old police chief, but Claire kind of liked it. It seemed...more caring.

Shane held out his hand and pulled her to her feet, and helped her dust the grass off, which was mainly just an excuse to be handsy. Which she didn't mind at all. 'Did you see my ninja move? That was fast, right?'

'You are not a ninja, Shane.'

'I've watched all the movies. I just haven't got the certificate from the correspondence course yet.'

She smiled; she couldn't help it. Her lips were still tingling, and she wanted him to kiss her again, but Hannah was right – sundown was a bad time to make out in public. 'I've thought about the drive-in.'

'And?'

She fell in beside him as they walked towards home. 'I don't care what's playing after all.'

His eyebrows rose. 'Sweet.'

Michael wasn't home when they got there, but Eve was, buzzing around upstairs. Claire could immediately tell, because either it was Eve in those shoes, or the hoof beats of a small pony. Not that Eve was large; she just...clomped. It was the big, heavy boots.

'It's chilli-dog night,' Shane said. 'How many?'

'Two,' Claire said.

'Really? That's a lot for you.'

'I'm celebrating the fact that you didn't fry out your brain being stupid.'

He crossed his eyes and let his tongue loll, which was disgusting and funny, and smacked the side of his head to put everything back right again. 'Jury's still out on that one. Two chilli dogs, coming up.'

'Hey!' Claire called after him, as she leant her backpack against the wall. 'No onions!'

'Your loss!'

'I meant for *you*! Not if you want to get kissed tonight!'

'Damn, girl. Harsh.'

She grinned and ran up the stairs, intending to use the bathroom – but Eve was breathlessly rushing towards it. 'Wait, wait, wait!' she squeaked. 'I have to finish my make-up! Please?'

Claire blinked. The outfit, even for Eve, was a little much…a skin-tight black minidress with all kinds of lacing and buckles, fishnet hose, and big plaid boots with two-inch-thick soles that came up to her knee. 'Sure,' she said. 'Uh – where are you going?'

'Cory – you know, the girl from the UC coffee bar, the one who isn't a butthead? – she's going to this rave thing, and I promised her I'd go with, just so she doesn't feel so weird. She's not much of a partyer. It'll be an early night, but I promised her I'd be ready by seven—'

'She's picking you up?'

'Yeah, why, you need the car?'

'If you're not using it.'

'Knock yourself out, just *please* let me have the bathroom!'

Claire sighed. 'Go ahead. And thanks. Oh, and be careful?'

'Please. I am the queen of careful. Also, princess of punk fabulousness.'

She was probably right about that last part, anyway. Claire continued on down the hall to her room, closed and locked the door, and opened up her dresser to go through her choices for underwear. She wanted something pretty. Something...special.

In the back of the drawer, neatly folded, was a bra-and-panties set that Eve had bought her for her birthday – way too revealing, Claire had thought, since it was mostly net and little pink roses. But... cute. Very cute. Eve had handed it to her and whispered, 'Don't open it in front of the guys. Trust me. You'll blush.' And she had saved it to open in private, and stuck it in the back of a drawer, although she'd been delighted. It was like a sexy little secret she hadn't known if she'd ever actually be brave enough to share.

Now she took a deep breath, stripped off her jeans and top and plain underwear, and put on the new bra and panties. They fitted perfectly – not that she expected anything else from Eve, who had an eye for that kind of thing. She was afraid to look, but Claire made herself walk over to the mirror on the back of the door.

After the blinding shock of *OMG*, she tried to be objective and not cover herself up with a blanket. She looked...naked. Well, almost. But...the longer she looked at it, the better she liked it. It made her tingle, just a little. What *really* made her tingle was the idea of what Shane would say when he saw her like this.

Because she intended him to see it.

The jeans and T-shirt didn't seem good enough anymore. Claire went to her closet, pulling out and rejecting things that just weren't right, until she found a top she'd almost forgotten about – an impulse buy in Dallas, like the pink wig up on the shelf that she wore when she was in a silly kind of mood. This was a soft, silky shirt, buttons down the front, in dark red, and it fitted really well – too well for her to feel comfortable wearing it to school, or to the lab, or anywhere else, for that matter.

But for this, it was perfect.

She dressed, added a touch of lipstick, and headed back. Eve was still in the bathroom, of course. Claire banged on it on the way by and yelled, 'Vampire attack!'

'Tell them to bite me later!' Eve yelled back. Claire

grinned and skipped down the steps, and arrived just as Shane came out of the kitchen, carrying two plates loaded with chilli dogs.

He didn't *quite* drop them. He put them on the table and said, staring at her, 'New shirt?'

She smiled. 'Bought it in Dallas. Do you like it?'

'Oh, come on. What's not to like? Especially with the easy-open buttons.'

'You did *not* say that out loud.'

'Huh. I thought I did, actually.'

Claire slipped into her chair. He'd got her a cold Coke, too, which was perfect. So were the chilli dogs. He'd even left off the onions. 'Delicious,' she mumbled around a mouthful, and then thought that probably spoilt her fancy new look.

Her fancy new look, though, was nothing compared to Eve's outfit, and just as the doorbell rang, Eve came clattering down the stairs in her buckles and laces and fishnets and boots, and Shane's eyebrows climbed high. He chewed chilli dog, swallowed, and said, 'Is there some holiday I'm missing? Girls' Dress-up Day?'

'Yes, Shane, and it's a secret you will never share,' Eve said. 'You just benefit. So shut up.'

'You look like a Goth factory exploded all over you!' he called as she ran down the hall.

'Love you too, jackass!'

The door slammed. Shane grinned and took a

huge bite of his second hot dog. 'She's so sensitive,' he mumbled.

'That's because you're not.'

'What?'

Claire sighed. 'Never mind. I should know better than to think guys would ever figure that out.'

'OK, this is not a conversation I ever intend to have. Did you get the car?'

'Eve said it's fine.'

Shane wolfed down the rest of his food in record time, before she'd even tried to start her second hot dog. She shook her head, took her plate into the kitchen, and put it in the refrigerator for later...although she was pretty sure Shane would sneak back and eat it, too, if she didn't get to it first.

He was practically bouncing up and down to leave when she came back with the car keys, which she pitched to him underhanded; he fielded them without a pause as he headed for the door.

'Shotgun!' Claire yelled.

He laughed and opened the door, and took a giant step back, because of all people, *Amelie* was standing there. She didn't come inside, although she could have; as Claire joined Shane, she looked at each of them in turn with her cool grey eyes reflecting the hallway light in a strange kind of way. Amelie was wearing her hair down these days, which was still odd to Claire, who'd become so accustomed to that white-gold hair being fastened up in a crown. The long hair made her look much younger. She'd changed how she dressed, too – instead of the formal, stiff suit jackets and skirts, she'd put on dark pants and a black, silky shirt. She was wearing a gold pendant in the shape of a lily, with a red stone in the centre. It looked beautiful, and expensive, and old.

'Uh...hi, Amelie. Come in?' Claire moved back to give her room. Amelie smiled slightly and nodded as she walked past them. She smelt like refrigerated roses. She walked ahead of them down the hall, paused in the living room, and turned back to face Claire.

Shane was still at the door. 'Where are the spear carriers?'

'Pardon?' Amelie raised pale eyebrows.

'You know, your guys. The guards.'

'They're outside. They shall stay there, unless they're needed. I trust they won't be, Mr Collins.'

Shane locked the door and came back to stand beside Claire. He folded his arms and waited.

Amelie seated herself on the couch and crossed her legs, still staring at the two of them. Suddenly, Claire felt like she'd been called to the principal's office. What had she done wrong?

Amelie said, 'Forgive the intrusion. I would have called, but I was in the area, and I had a moment to stop by.' Claire noticed she didn't ask *them* if they had a moment...but then, she wouldn't. 'Please sit.'

'No, thanks,' Shane said. 'We were on our way out.'

'Ah. Well, I will be brief.' She focused on him. 'Your father has come to me and asked to be included in the register of vampires in Morganville. I have allowed it. I feel that I owe it to him, despite the crimes he has committed against us; after all, it was my own father who sentenced him to this life, and I know he did not want it.' She was focused entirely on Shane, who had gone stiff and very still.

His eyes went flat and blank for a second, and then he straightened and took a deep breath. 'I don't care what he does,' he said. 'Include him all you want. But he's not my father. My father died.'

Claire and Shane had watched it happen. Frank Collins, fearless vampire killer, had been dragged in and attacked by Amelie's evil old vamp daddy, Bishop. He'd been drained. And he'd been brought back.

It had been beyond horrible having to see it, especially for Shane. But worse than that was knowing his dad was a vampire. And knowing that he was still walking around.

Which was why Claire hadn't mentioned her sighting of him earlier.

'I thought you might feel so,' Amelie said. Her tone

was cool, very neutral, and Claire shivered a little,
as if she'd caught a chill. 'I felt it worth the attempt
to give you a chance to reconnect. Frank Collins has
entered a training program we have established for
new vampires to break them of bad habits and reinforce
the rules of Morganville that they must live by; he will
finish this program within the week. Once he does,
he will have the same status as any other vampire
who has signed the Morganville accords. He may not
be harmed without my permission. Should anyone
attempt it, I will take it personally.' She continued to
stare at Shane. 'Anyone. I trust you do understand
what I'm saying to you.'

Shane just shook his head, face closed and hard.
Claire wanted to take his hand, but his arms were still
folded defensively across his chest. He wasn't meeting
Amelie's eyes.

'Shane,' the Founder of Morganville said, using his
name for the first time. 'I am sorry. I know this will
be...difficult for you, considering the history between
you and your father, and what has happened to him.
But according to the laws of Morganville, he will also
be allowed to become a Protector, if he wishes to do so.
He has said that he will gladly accept the responsibility
of acting as *your* Protector, should you choose—'

'No way in hell. Get out,' Shane interrupted her.
He didn't say it loudly, but there was a frightening,

out-of-control look in his eyes. 'Just get out. I'm not talking about this.'

Amelie didn't move. She stared at him. He'd met her eyes now, and after a long, tense moment, she spread her hands in a graceful gesture, unfolded her long legs, and stood. 'I have taken enough of your time,' she said. 'I am sorry to have upset you. Your father may well come to see you, so please remember what I've said: no matter how you feel, you cannot strike at him without consequences. Even a friend of Morganville has limits.' Her icy grey eyes shifted, and Claire froze in place. 'Claire, I rely on you to remind him if he should forget this.'

Claire nodded, suddenly unable to speak at all. She glanced at Shane, who wasn't moving, and hurried down the hall to the door to open it for Amelie. When she did, she found Amelie's two big vampire guards, in their black suits and ties, standing on the porch, facing out towards the road.

Amelie walked past her and down the steps without another word. The guards fell in behind her, helped her into the big black limousine that idled at the curb, and as it glided off into the dark, Claire stood there watching it go.

What just happened? Things had changed so fast, and so violently, that she felt shaky.

It occurred to her that standing here with the door

wide open was a victim-type thing to do in Morganville, so she quickly closed and locked it, took a deep breath, and went back to Shane.

He was sitting down on the couch at one end, staring straight at the not-currently-on TV. He was playing with the remote control, but he didn't press the power button.

'Shane...'

'I don't care,' he said. 'I don't care that Frank's still alive, because he's not my dad. He hasn't been my dad for years, not since Alyssa – not since she died. He's even less my dad now than he ever was, and he never was up for Father of the Year anyway. I don't want to know him. I don't want to have anything to do with him.'

'I know,' Claire said, and sat down next to him. 'I'm sorry. But he did save my life once, and I have to think maybe he can...change.'

Shane snorted. 'He already changed, into a bloodsucking freak. What bugs me is that he has one minute of regret, and he gets to wipe out years of being a drunken asshole, beating the crap out of me, nearly getting us all killed more than once – no. I'm glad he saved you. But that doesn't even *start* to make us even. I don't want anything to do with him.'

There didn't seem to be anything she could possibly say. He was really upset – she could see it; she could *feel* it. 'Are you OK?' What a stupid question, she thought, as soon as she said it. Of course he wasn't OK. He wouldn't be slouched like a boneless sack on the couch, staring at a dead TV with even deader eyes, if he was *OK*.

'If he comes here...' Shane swallowed. 'If he comes here, you have to promise me you'll stop me from doing something stupid. Because I will, Claire.'

'No, you won't,' Claire said, and finally took his hand. 'Shane, you *won't*. You're not like that. I know it's all complicated and crazy and it hurts, but you can't let him do that to you. I'll make sure Michael and Eve know that if he shows up, we just tell him to leave. He'll never get in the door.'

She felt cold again — icy, in fact — and felt a hum all along her nerves. What *was* that? Not a draft. Definitely not a draft. It felt like...anger. Cold, hard anger, like the kind that was inside Shane right now — but she was feeling it from the outside.

The house.

She'd got used to its not doing this kind of thing anymore; the Glass House had always seemed to have a kind of presence to them, something that reflected their feelings, their fears...but it had died with the portal system. So she thought.

You fixed the portal system, remember? Apparently, that put the house itself back on the grid, too, which was why it was reacting to Shane's mood. She was never sure what the house understood, but she was absolutely sure it was on their side. Maybe that even meant it would make sure Frank Collins never came here again.

She reached for a blanket and pulled it over her shoulders, still shivering. If the house was showing her any reflection of Shane's anger, he was deeply upset, even though he was struggling not to show it.

Shane finally pressed the power button on the TV and dropped his left arm over her shoulders. She felt the chill ease a little. 'Thanks,' he said. 'If you hadn't been here when she said all that, I probably would have done something pretty dumb. Or said something even dumber.'

'No, you wouldn't. You're a survivor.'

He kissed her on the forehead. 'Takes one to know one.'

'So, no drive-in?'

'It's a zombie movie.'

'Well, there are good points about zombie movies. There're usually smart girls in them, for some reason. And the smart girls hardly ever get killed.' Claire kissed him back, on the cheek. 'Besides, I know how much you like zombie movies. Especially with chain saws and everything.'

Shane flipped channels for a few seconds, then

shut the TV off, got up, and held out his hand. 'Chain saws,' he repeated. 'You're right. It's probably just what I need.' He didn't let go of her hand after he'd helped her to her feet; instead, he put it on his chest, over his heart. She felt the strong, steady beat beneath. 'You look great. You probably already know that.'

She kissed him, and they stood together, rocking slightly from side to side, until Shane broke the kiss and smiled down at her. 'Save it for the drive-in,' he said, and touched her lips with one finger. 'I'll drive fast.'

'You'd better.'

CHAPTER FOUR

Shane drove the hearse – Eve's, a huge, black, vaguely old-fashioned monster, with the fringed funeral curtains still in the back – down Morganville's poorly lit streets, winding through backstreets Claire had never visited even in daylight. She saw glints of eyes in the darkness, and if there were any streetlights in this part of town, they were broken or turned off. She felt relieved when he made a turn that took them onto a broader avenue...until she took a good look. Lots of people walking around in the shadows.

Not normal for Morganville. But normal for *vampires* in Morganville.

'Yeah, it's Vamp Central Station,' Shane said. 'Not like Founder's Square – that's where the upper-class bloodsuckers hang out. This is where the rest of them come. There's another blood bank down here, and nothing around gets much human business after dark. Don't worry; we're not stopping.'

And they didn't, not even for a light that was shifting from yellow to red; Shane just gunned right through it.

Claire was glad he did. Heads were turning to watch the car go by. Maybe Amelie's Protection extended out here. But she didn't want to risk her neck – literally – on that.

Two more turns and all of a sudden there was a giant white screen looming up out of the darkness ahead, surrounded by a fence. It looked like a parking lot inside, with some kind of vending stand at the back.

Just like in the old movies.

'Amazing,' Claire said. Shane pulled up to the ticket stand at the entrance and handed over a couple of dollars – it didn't cost much, apparently. Then he drove on in. The lot was about half-full, mostly with battered old cars and trucks that matched up with what the humans of Morganville drove. There were also a few heavily tinted late-model sedans – vampmobiles. Well, she supposed even vampires loved the movies. Who didn't?

'So how does this work?' Claire asked. 'How do we hear the sound?'

For an answer, Shane flipped on the radio and tuned

it to an AM channel. Immediately, she was treated to a burst of static, followed by extremely cheesy music that had probably annoyed people even back when her grandmother was young.

'Fantastic,' Claire said, in a way that meant it wasn't. 'You know, Eve went to a rave.'

'By herself?'

'With a friend. She's sort of doing the mother-hen thing.'

'Are you wishing we'd gone, too?'

'No,' Claire said, although secretly she thought it might not have been terrible. 'This is great.'

Shane looked over at her. 'Bullshit. You think it sucks.'

'I don't!'

'Just wait,' he said, and smiled. 'You'll see. You want a Coke? Popcorn?'

'Sure.' She sighed. Shane bailed out and set off for the refreshment stand at the back. Claire got out her cell and texted Eve. *R u OK?* She got a reply back in seconds. *Death by boring. College posers. Yak.*

Eve always made her laugh. *B safe*, Claire texted back. Eve sent a picture of herself with her friend, who looked intimidated and scared and very much as if she was wishing herself gone. Eve was winking. The message with it said, *Half an hour more tops. C u home.*

The car door opened, and Shane climbed in, handing her a cup of Coke and a giant bag of popcorn, which she tried to figure out how to balance in her lap. The Cokes went into cup holders, at least, and before she could take a handful of the steaming popcorn, there was a sudden flicker of colour out the front window, and the coming attractions started up.

Shane took the bag of popcorn from her, set it carefully in the backseat, and turned the radio down. 'Hey,' Claire protested. 'How can we hear if—'

He leant over and kissed her, and *kept* kissing her, and his lips were so hot and sweet and strong that she just felt herself melting against him. He eased her jacket off, and she didn't even think about objecting, because even though it was cold she felt warm, so warm, and then his hands were...Oh, that was good. Very good.

She wasn't thinking, not at *all*, not about anything except how incredible it felt to be with him, here, in the dark. When she finally came up for a gasping breath, most of her buttons were undone. *All* of his were undone. *Did I do that?* she wondered with a shock, because it really wasn't like her to be doing this out in public, where people could see.

But it felt like being alone. Deliciously, magically alone. Because they were in a crowd of people, but nobody was paying them the slightest bit of attention.

The movie had started, but she had zero idea what it was about, other than some crazy zombie guy stalking people. Oh, and there was a smart girl with glasses, and a hot guy who would probably survive, too. With the sound turned down to a whisper, she saw only flashes, and when she closed her eyes, she didn't see anything but sunbursts of light against the darkness.

'What's this?' Shane asked, and traced the line of her new bra with his fingertip. 'Sexy. What else you got?'

'I'll give you a hint. It matches.'

'Let's take a look...'

Things were about to get *very* interesting – and she wasn't thinking about the movie at all – when her cell phone rang. Claire yelped and flailed around for it, mostly to shut it off, but Shane sat up, and she squirmed around to get to a sitting position, holding her shirt closed as she squinted at the display.

'It's Eve,' she said. Shane smacked his forehead right into the steering wheel and made a sound of utter frustration. 'Should I get it?'

'Yeah,' he said, not too happily. 'I guess so. But tell her I hate her a whole lot right now.'

'You don't.'

'Oh, trust me. I could not hate her more.'

Claire pressed the button and said, 'Eve? Shane

says—' She was interrupted by the sound of screaming. It was so loud and shocking that she almost dropped the phone. 'Eve? Eve!'

Shane caught the alarm in her tone, and reached out for the phone. 'Give,' he said. She handed it over, shaking, and he put it to his ear. 'Eve? Eve, can you hear me? What's going on?' He stopped to listen, and gave Claire a look that made her shiver again. 'Yeah, I hear it. Are you safe?'

'Speaker!' Claire said. 'Put it on speaker!'

He did. Screaming blasted out of the phone, but it wasn't Eve's; she was trying to talk. Only part of it came through. '...define safe...trying to get...crazy... need help—'

'Hang on, Eve, we're coming,' Shane said, and tossed the phone to Claire as he fired up the hearse's engine, slammed it into reverse, and backed up with a squeal of tyres. 'Try to get an address!'

'I know where it is,' Claire said. She gave him the address, clear and sharp in her memory from the flyer she'd been handed days ago on the steps of the Science Building. 'That's not far, right?'

'Not far,' he agreed, and hit the gas, speeding towards the exit past rows of parked cars with fogged-over windows. 'Keep her talking.'

'Eve? Can you hear me?'

'Yes!' Eve's voice suddenly came through the

background noise loud and clear. 'We're OK for now, but we need back-up, big-time.'

'What's going on? Vampires?'

'Oh, you'd think, but no. Some jackass jocks started tearing up the place. They've been rampaging around through half the town... *Oh, shit!*' There was a rise in screaming and confused sounds. When Eve came back, she was out of breath. '*Now* there're vamps. And they are *pissed.*'

'Is Oliver there?'

'Didn't stop to read name tags. Oh, man – seriously not good here. People are dying – Cory! Cory, no, don't – *Cory!*' Eve's last word was a scream of utter horror, and then the phone just...died. Claire hung up and tried calling back. Eve's cheery voice mail took the call. She looked over at Shane, who was staring straight ahead with an expression as hard as stone. He shook his head.

'Hurry,' Claire whispered. She realised her shirt was still open, and quickly buttoned it up with trembling hands. 'Does Eve keep any weapons in here?'

'Probably in the back. Wait, check the glove box.'

Claire opened it and found two silver-coated, sharp-tipped stakes. They weren't her favourite vampire-fighting accessory, only because they weren't something she could use at a distance, but the heavy, cool feel of them eased a tight, anxious knot in her stomach. But

there was something odd about the way they felt...
Claire turned the stakes over in her fingers until
she saw what that roughness in the surface was, and
almost laughed.

'What?' Shane asked. Claire showed him the stake.
The dashboard lights caught the silver surface and
shone red from a skull design blinged out in fake
rubies.

'She BeDazzled her stakes,' Claire said.

'Yeah, she would.' He almost smiled, but his eyes
were wild, and he couldn't seem to get his face to relax.
'Get Chief Moses on the phone; get her to send the
marines.'

Claire nodded and speed-dialled Hannah's number.
Hannah sounded cheerful and alert, but on guard
when she answered. 'Moses.'

'Hannah, it's Claire. Eve's in trouble – well, a lot of
people sound like they're in trouble. You know about
the rave tonight?'

'I had some plainclothes officers there making
sure the kids didn't get into trouble. Except they did,
right?'

'Eve called me, and there was screaming. I think
you'd better send everybody. Just in case.'

'Done. And, Claire, don't you go running in there.'

'But *Eve's* in there!'

'And we'll get everybody out.'

Hannah hung up on her. 'Hannah says not to go there,' Claire said.

'Well, I like the lady, but screw that,' Shane said. 'Call Michael. Eve probably did, but just in case; he'd rip my ears off if I didn't let him know what was up.'

Besides which, Michael's vampire strength wouldn't be at all a liability right now. Claire tried his phone, but it went to voice mail. She left a message with the address, and texted him, too. That was all she had time for, because Shane skidded the hearse around the last corner and onto a street that should have been deserted after dark – well, was deserted most of the time – but was parked up with cars on both sides.

There were people boiling out of the doorway of one of the big, rickety warehouses on the left, and Claire had a blurry impression of open mouths and panicked faces as the hearse hurtled towards them.

Shane blurted out a curse that normally would have made her blush and slammed on the brakes. Somehow, he managed not to hit any of the running, screaming crowd, which just parted and flowed around the car, scattering into the dark in all directions. Shane threw the hearse in park and took his hands off the wheel. They were shaking. He stared at them a second, then snapped out of it and grabbed one of the stakes from Claire. 'Stay with me,' he said. 'I mean it. *Right* with me.'

She nodded. Shane took a deep breath and got out of the car, and she slid out after him as he ran to the back and opened up the hatch to grab a black canvas bag. 'Hope this isn't her make-up,' he said as he shouldered the strap and slammed the door. 'Let's go.'

People were still coming out. Claire noticed that most of them seemed OK, just freaked out, but there were a few who seemed like they might be injured. Maybe that was just from the general crowd panic – hard to tell. She hoped so. She heard the wail of sirens approaching, and had time to think, *Hannah's going to be really angry at us*, but then it was too late to have second thoughts. Shane was moving against the flow of people, heading inside, and she'd promised to stay with him.

She kept her promises.

Someone smacked into Shane as he started through the doorway, and he staggered back a step, then grabbed whoever it was and yanked her out into the street.

Monica Morrell. She looked just as scared as everyone else running from the building, and then, as she realised who it was who had hold of her arm, she looked...relieved. *Relieved?* Claire thought. *Really?* Because Shane and Monica made cats and dogs look like besties. 'Collins,' Monica said, and looked back.

'Jennifer's still in there. I think...I think she's still in there.' She was trembling, and she looked cold in her red-and-white minidress.

No, it wasn't red and white. It was white. Claire parted her lips, realising what all the red was, and looked sharply at Shane. He was staring at Monica with a very odd expression – pity, mixed with distaste. But mostly pity. It was almost *concern*.

'What happened?' he asked. She didn't answer, so he shook her, not too gently. 'Monica, snap out of it. What *happened*?'

'It was all going OK, and then the Epsilon Epsilon Kappa guys showed up. They were all drunk and crazy, started yelling about being in a fight and how they kicked somebody's ass. They busted stuff up.'

Shane went from concerned to pissed. 'That's it?'

'No! No, they...they were followed.' Monica swallowed. She looked pale and shaky. 'The vamps came. I guess the ass they kicked belonged to one of them. It got ugly. It's getting worse.' She looked down at Shane's hand around her arm, and got a little of the old Monica 'tude back. 'Who said you could go all bad-cop on me, Collins? Back your wannabe ass off!'

He didn't let go. 'Did you see Eve?'

'Little Miss Goth Princess had some boring chick with her. She's—' Monica looked over her shoulder. 'I don't know. Everybody was running. I didn't see where she went.' Shane let go of her. Monica grabbed him instead. 'Hey,' she said. 'Look for Jennifer. I didn't see her come out. She was right behind me. I think.'

Shane said, 'Let go or lose the fingers,' and she did, instantly, stepping back and wrapping her arms around her torso – for warmth, not in defiance. Shane looked back and held out his hand. Claire took it. 'Ready?'

'I guess.'

'Watch your back.'

The oncoming wail of sirens meant help was coming, but Claire knew Shane wasn't going to wait. She didn't want to, either. That had been real fear in Eve's scream.

They plunged onward, into the warehouse.

The place smelt like smoke – not burning-insulation smoke, but the kind of bong smoke college students liked a lot better. It made Claire's eyes water. The rave lights were still on, cycling through all kinds of colours and patterns, strobing white every few seconds. The music was still thundering, too – the deejay had left tracks running and bugged out from behind the console in the corner. Claire could feel the vibrations in her bones, and her ears went instantly into shock. She could still hear, but it was like hearing through earmuffs.

A few people were too scared to make a break for the door; she could see them hiding behind the speakers, or pressed against the walls in a huddle, trying to pretend it all wasn't happening. The usual Morganville strategy. It was hard to make out details in the weird lights, but none of them had Eve's Goth style. Mostly college kids, Claire thought. Well, they'd got their tuition's worth tonight.

There were bodies on the warehouse floor. They weren't moving. Some of them had very, very pale faces, and wide eyes, and mouths still open in silent screams. Bite marks on their throats.

There were also a couple of vampires down – also pale, but with stakes in their chests; that didn't necessarily mean they were dead, just wounded. There was one who was definitely dead, because – and Claire had to control an urge to retch – his head was missing. There was still a stake in his heart, too.

She thought she saw the head a few feet away in the corner, but no way was she going to go take a closer look. She was thankful Shane turned away from all that, heading into a hallway that channelled the thundering music into waves. It was still too loud to talk. In strobe flashes, Claire saw blood on the walls in smears.

The hallway opened into another big room, and the music wasn't quite loud enough here to cover the screams. Or the sound of fighting.

Shane stopped, zipped open the bag, and pulled out

a crossbow. He stuck the silver stake he'd been gripping into a pocket of his jeans, loaded the crossbow, put another bolt between his teeth, and nodded to Claire to follow. She nodded back.

When they came around the corner, they saw where the noise was coming from. A group of people were hemmed tightly into a corner, mostly cowering, but some were big, drunk-looking frat dudes who were yelling challenges and smashing wooden crates over the heads of the vampires who were closing in on them. The lights in here were dim, dirty fluorescents, and flickering like mad, but somehow Claire saw what happened next with high-definition, slow-motion clarity.

A male vampire – young-looking, with long blond hair tied back in a ponytail, wearing a black leather jacket – grabbed hold of one of the frat boys (who was, she realised, wearing an EEK T-shirt) and dragged him away from the others. The boy was football-big, but the slender vamp lifted him right off the ground by the neck, glaring up at him as he struggled and tried to scream.

Then the vampire said, 'You think you can defy us and live? Who do you think you are, meat? This is *our* town. It's always been ours. You have to pay for your disrespect.'

And then he closed his fist and crushed the boy's big,

muscular throat like crunching up a sheet of paper.

Shane brought the crossbow up almost as fast and fired. The bolt hit the vamp in the back, on the left side, just about dead centre in the heart.

The two bodies hit the floor together.

And then all the vampires turned on Shane and Claire. Shane loaded the second bolt and dropped the bag between the two of them. Claire didn't need any instructions; she crouched down and groped around inside the bag. No extra crossbow, unfortunately, but plenty more bolts, which she took out, and two vials of silvery liquid – silver nitrate. Claire handed Shane another bolt to put between his teeth and popped the cap on one of the vials.

The vampires didn't look familiar to her, but then, she didn't keep up with every bloodsucker in Morganville; she thought these were probably some of the ones Amelie had been concerned about, who weren't taking the new human-rights decrees of the town quite so well. Well, vampires liked to be in charge, no doubt about that. And they didn't like being challenged.

I just saw that boy die, she thought, but then shut that thought off, walled it away, because it wouldn't help to think about it. Not at all. 'Eve!' she yelled. 'Eve Rosser!'

From somewhere near the far edge of the human crowd, she saw a very white face turn towards them under a sleek cap of black hair. Eve didn't say anything, but there wasn't any time, because the vampires were coming for them.

Shane fired once, taking down one of the five, and as he reloaded, Claire threw the contents of the vial in an arc across the other four. Where the silver nitrate hit vampire skin, it hissed and bubbled like acid. That stopped at least one, and slowed down the others long enough for Shane to get off another shot. It went wide as the vampire batted the bolt aside in midair and lunged for them. Claire dived one way, and Shane the other; he hit the floor and rolled, came up on his knees, and reloaded another bolt in time to get the vamp square in the chest as it rushed him. It still reached him, and Claire uncapped the other vial of silver nitrate, heart pounding, but Shane rolled again, out of reach, and the vamp collapsed on the floor before it could claw him.

The other two still in the fight were women – one about her mom's physical age, with grey streaks in her long hair, and a lean, mean face. The other looked barely older than Claire herself, with short red hair and a round face that might have been sweet-looking, if it weren't for the glowing eyes and pointy teeth. Both had got burnt by the silver nitrate, and they weren't in a hurry to get another dose, but Claire realised that Shane was out of crossbow bolts, and she'd dropped the rest by the bag, ten feet away.

She made a dash for them. The red-haired vamp cut her off, laughing, and kicked the bolts into the far corner, along with the black canvas bag.

Claire yanked her silver stake out of the waistband of her pants. She was terrified, but she was also angry – angry that Eve had been penned up in the corner with all those people, like so many cattle. Angry about all the dead people. Angry for the probably stupid boy who'd just got killed right in front of her. Angry that this was all happening because some vamp's *pride* had got hurt.

'Hey!' Shane yelled, and tossed his empty crossbow to the ground as he jumped to his feet. 'You going to let her have all the fun? Come on, Vampirella! Let's go!'

The older vamp turned on him with a snarl, and in one leap was all over him like some horrible jumping spider. Shane hit the ground hard, on his back, and tried to roll, but the vamp was too strong. She snarled again, jaws gaping wide, and Claire desperately threw the silver nitrate at her. It hit, but the vampire ignored the burns.

A blur flashed out of the hallway and hit the vamp in a full tackle, taking her completely off of Shane as she tried to bite him. Both Shane's attacker and the newcomer hit the far wall with a hollow boom, and then jumped apart. Both snarling.

Both vampires.

Michael. He looked tremendously scary when he was like this, all eyes and teeth, and he looked *strong.* Claire swallowed hard and focused on the vamp in front of her, the redhead, who had been as surprised as Claire at Michael's furious arrival...but was getting over it fast.

The vamp lunged for her, but came up short with a kind of funny squawking sound as her head was yanked backward, hard.

Behind her stood Eve, both hands in the vamp's hair. 'That's my *friend,* you bitch!' Eve said, and – when she was sure Claire was ready – shoved the vamp at her, off balance.

Onto the point of Claire's silver-coated, blinged-out stake.

The vamp cried out, and for a second her eyes met Claire's, and Claire felt something terrible: guilt. There was terror in those alien eyes, and hurt, and surprise...and then the vamp went down at her feet, taking the stake with her.

The vamp girl had been somebody's daughter once. Somebody's sister. Maybe even somebody's girlfriend. Maybe she hadn't asked to be what she was now.

Claire felt sick and she wanted to cry, but there wasn't time, because Shane was at her side now, pulling her into his arms.

'Eve?' he asked. 'You OK?'

Claire turned her head to look at her friend. Eve didn't look OK. Her Goth make-up was a mess, mascara smeared and running in thick, uneven streams down her face; her dress was torn at the shoulder, and she had long, red scratches down one arm that were still bleeding.

But it was her eyes that really told Claire how not-OK she was. They were wide and full of misery. Without even knowing why, Claire let go of Shane and hugged Eve, who hugged her back so hard it hurt. Eve was trying not to cry, from her hiccupping little gasps for breath.

'You're OK now,' Claire whispered in her ear. 'We came as fast as we could.'

Eve nodded and tried to smile. 'Guess I can't say "you losers" for at least a week, then.' Her voice sounded odd and muffled, but she blinked back the tears. 'Thank you.' She kissed Claire's cheek, then Shane's. Shane stepped away, clearing his throat. 'Oh, don't go all boy on me.'

'Mikey!' Shane yelled. 'You'd better finish it up! Your girlfriend's trying to kiss—'

He didn't finish, because all of a sudden the fight was over...

...and Michael *lost*.

It happened so fast Claire hardly had time to comprehend it, but one second, the two vamps were a blur of movement, and then next, Michael was down on the ground, crumpled like a broken toy.

The other vamp grinned with her sharp, sharp teeth gleaming in the light, and licked blood from her lips. Her eyes looked brilliant and insane, and redder than the blood. She kicked Michael's limp body out of the way and came for the three of them, doing that creepy jumping-spider thing again.

Suddenly, there was a cold, still presence standing in front of them, and a white hand reaching up, grabbing the vamp in mid-air and slamming her down to the floor.

Amelie.

The Founder of Morganville had arrived, and she'd done it in force; as Claire looked behind her, she saw at least a dozen vampires, all looking very seriously dangerous, including Oliver and a number of others she knew by sight. They were all dressed in long black leather coats, like a kind of uniform, with the symbol of the Founder stamped into the leather on every one of them.

Amelie was wearing white. Pure ice white, almost shimmering in the dim light. Her hair was up in a woven crown, nearly as pale as her elegant silk suit.

'Do be quiet,' she told the fallen vampire. 'You're a worthless idiot, but I don't want more blood tonight.

Don't make me kill you for what you've done.' Amelie's voice was so cold that it seemed to drop the temperature in the overheated, stifling room by at least fifty degrees. 'Get up.'

The other vamp did, moving slowly. Claire didn't see Oliver step forward, but suddenly he was right there, holding both the woman's arms in a bone-shattering grip behind her. 'No foolish moves, Patrice,' he said. 'I don't believe the Founder is joking.'

'Get her out of my sight,' Amelie said, and looked at the other fallen vampires. The one who'd been burnt badly by Claire's silver nitrate got up and limped over, looking thoroughly terrified. 'This one too. And release those others.' She waved a hand at the vampires Shane had nailed with the crossbow bolts. One of Oliver's black-coated troopers glided over and pulled the arrows out. The two downed bloodsuckers, released from their paralysis, coughed and sputtered blood.

They'd live.

'Michael,' Claire whispered. Eve broke free and ran to him, throwing herself down on the floor and taking his head into her lap. He looked – oh, God – he looked...dead. His eyes were open, and he looked so pale, so still; there was a hole in the side of his throat, but not much blood. Claire skidded to a stop and put her hands to her mouth, trying to hold in a scream. She felt Shane's hands close hard around her shoulders – that was probably his version of feeling the same rush of horror and denial.

Then Michael finally, slowly, blinked. Eve screamed. 'Michael? Michael! Talk to me!'

'He can't,' Amelie said. She had come up behind them, and was looking at Michael with a slight softening of her usual cool expression. Maybe, Claire thought, because Michael still reminded her of Sam, her lost love. Apart from the colour of their hair, they'd looked a lot alike. 'He'll be all right once we get some nourishment into him. I'll have my people take him directly to the blood bank.'

'I want to go with him!' Eve said.

'I'm not sure that's wise. Drained and hungry vampires, even ones you know well, can be very unpredictable. I would hate for anything to happen that Michael might regret later.'

'What about what *we* might regret later?' Shane asked under his breath. 'Oh, right. Humans don't count.'

Amelie heard him, and her head swivelled smoothly as she focused her cool grey eyes on his face. 'I only meant that you would likely not be around to regret anything, Mr Collins. Ms. Rosser. Explain what happened here. Now.'

Eve was combing her fingers through Michael's blond hair, but now she looked up, startled. That lasted only a second, though, and then her attitude snapped back in place. 'Gee, I don't know, maybe a *vampire attack?*' she snapped. 'It was a party; then the frat idiots crashed and started boasting about how tough they were; then these freaks showed up to teach us all a lesson. That's what they said. They wanted to put us in our place.'

'I see,' Amelie said. 'And you did nothing to provoke them.'

'My friend—' Eve's voice failed. Claire could see she was trying once again not to cry, and how much it hurt. 'My friend Cory was just trying to have fun. That one, the redhead, she grabbed her and just...tore her up. Cory's *dead.* I saw it happen.'

'Oh, man,' Shane whispered. Claire put her hand on top of his, where it lay on her shoulder. 'Eve...' It sounded like he wanted to say something, but he had no idea what. She loved him for that.

Amelie waited a moment, and then said in a very low voice, 'I am sorry for this experience, and for the loss of your friend. All who broke the law will be punished.'

Eve's eyes grew brighter, but not with tears. With fury. '*Punished?* What, like little kids going to bed without their blood supper? No TV for a week? *Time-out?*'

'I can assure you that the punishment will be severe.'

'Not enough!'

Now Amelie's voice turned cool again. 'It is enough for me, and that *will* be enough for you, Ms. Rosser.

Enough for all of you. Do I make myself clear?' She didn't wait for an answer; she turned to Oliver, who was standing nearby, hands folded behind him, watching as the vampire prisoners and humans were herded out. 'Vampires are dead here. I will expect a full investigation.'

'Of course,' Oliver said without turning. 'And I expect the appropriate punishments will be meted out, according to the law.'

'Sir,' called one of Oliver's men, who was kneeling over the red-haired girl with Claire's stake in her chest. 'You should see this.'

Oliver walked over, frowned, and crouched down to examine the girl more closely. 'Silver,' his man said, and Oliver nodded. Oliver tugged on a pair of leather gloves and grabbed the stake, which he pulled out and immediately dropped with a clatter to the floor.

The girl didn't breathe, move, or react.

Claire gripped Shane's arm tightly, and waited, but the vampire stayed still on the floor, unmoving. There was a burnt patch where the stake had gone in that continued to slowly burn outward.

'She's dead,' Oliver said. 'Silver poisoning. She must have been unusually allergic.'

Claire had killed her.

And the appropriate punishment for a human killing a vampire was death.

CHAPTER FIVE

'But it was self-defence!' the guy seated next to Claire said. He'd been saying it a lot, and at a loud volume, and she thought his anger probably wasn't helping any.

They were sitting in a quiet, wood-panelled room in the Elders' Council building, a big faux-Greek temple that always felt to Claire like a funeral home. A really nice one. This particular room featured a long, highly polished table of dark wood, fancy chairs, and – of course – no windows. There were two doors, one at either end, but they were both guarded by Amelie's personal security men. Claire knew them, slightly, but now they had their sunglasses hiding their eyes, and she knew they wouldn't give her any breaks. They had their serious faces on.

Amelie sat at one end of the long table. Oliver sat

at the other. Police Chief Hannah Moses was seated on one side, along with Mayor Richard Morrell, who'd taken his father's seat on the council along with the not-too-fun job of governing the human side of Morganville. Richard was a nice-looking man, Claire had always thought, but he usually also looked tired, and like he didn't smile nearly enough. But then, being Monica Morrell's brother would probably take most of the sparkle out of life in general.

On the other side of the table, shackled, were one of the big EEK frat boys with blood all over his shirt, and Claire. Shane, Michael, and Eve had been shut out of the room, and Claire hoped they'd taken Eve home; she'd been pretty shaky, once the emergency was over, and had badly needed to clean up and change clothes.

Though Shane had wanted to stay, of course. It had taken all of Claire's powers of persuasion to convince him not to start throwing punches when Amelie gave the order to leave. *I'll be OK*, she told him, with confidence she didn't completely feel. *Amelie won't let anything happen to me.*

Looking at Amelie right now, sitting so cold and emotionless at the end of the table, Claire felt she'd probably overstated that. Maybe a lot.

'According to the testimony of both humans and vampires on the scene, the two of you are guilty of the deaths of two of my people,' Amelie said into the silence. The frat boy beside Claire shifted, and his chains rattled, but he didn't say anything. He had a leather bracelet on his wrist, a Morganville band that identified him as belonging to some vampire in town. Claire wondered why the vampire wasn't here. He or she was supposed to be, at any legal thing that involved their people.

'We'll start with you, Mr...' Oliver consulted a file in front of him. 'Kyle Nemeck? Testimony of vampires and humans says that the trouble started with you and others from your fraternity group who arrived at the warehouse. Vampires tell us that you attacked a vampire, Ioan ap Emwnt, on the street, beat him severely, robbed him, and left him for dead. He is not dead, fortunately for you.' Oliver closed that file and opened another. 'This vampire, unfortunately, was not as lucky.' He slid a colour photograph out onto the table, and Claire had to look away. It was the decapitated body she'd seen in the club. Once had been enough. 'Here's his missing piece.' Another photo, this one probably the head; Claire *definitely* didn't look. 'While your friends held this unfortunate down, you severed his neck. Comments?'

The frat boy – Kyle – was sweating. He looked younger now, and very scared. 'I...sir...ma'am – it was self-defence. They came after us.'

'They thought you had killed one of our own,' Amelie said. 'Any vampire can, by law, pursue such an offender and claim him for trial. Your actions, defensive or not, sent this legally pursuing group into a blood rage. Everything that followed, including all the human deaths, can be laid directly at your door. Am I correct, Mayor Morrell?'

Richard was reading his file, frowning. Now, he looked up, directly at Kyle. His brown eyes were narrowed, and there wasn't any hint of sympathy. 'Correct,' he said. 'If it were only the human deaths, I could argue for a life sentence. With vampire deaths involved, it's out of my hands. You're a native, Kyle. You know better.'

Kyle looked as if he might start to cry. Oliver took the photos back, neatly stacked them, and closed that folder, too. 'Any defence?' he asked, not as if he really cared.

Kyle's mouth opened, closed, and opened again. 'I... Look, we didn't know that first dude was a vampire. I mean, we never would have...I swear.'

'So your defence is that you'd have done the same thing to a human. Which would almost certainly have killed him.'

'I—' Kyle clearly didn't know what to say to that. 'I just mean we didn't know he was one of you.'

'Weak,' Oliver said. 'And the vampire you did

manage to kill, do you claim to not know what *he* was? Because I think you recognise him very well, since his name appears on the bracelet you wear around your wrist.'

Claire took in a slow breath. Kyle had killed his own Protector. She didn't know if there was a law for that, but if there was, the punishment wasn't going to be anything less than gruesome.

Kyle shut up. He looked so pale he might have been a vamp himself.

'Well?' Oliver snapped. 'Yes or no, did you recognise your Protector before you *beheaded* him?'

'I...The lights...I don't...No, I didn't know who it was; I just knew it was a vamp coming after my friends.' He gulped. His voice sounded faint and rusty. 'I'm sorry.'

'Well,' Oliver whispered. 'I suppose that excuses everything, doesn't it? He was *seven hundred and sixty years old.* But you're *sorry.*' Oliver shoved his chair back from the table as he stood up, so hard it tipped over and crashed against the floor with a bang. 'This is what being soft with the humans gets us, Amelie. You already know my vote. Guilty. I'm done with this nonsense.'

'And what about Claire?' Amelie asked quietly. 'She's charged with a similar offence.'

Oliver was heading for the door, but he hesitated,

just a brief step. He didn't look back. 'Guilty,' he said. 'She should have left it to us to police our own. I'd be hypocritical if I said anything different, wouldn't I?'

The security guard let him out, closed the door behind him, and took up that waiting, alert pose again.

Claire was having trouble breathing. *Guilty.* She'd been defending herself. Defending her friends. And Oliver knew that, and he'd still voted against her.

'Mayor Morrell,' Amelie said. 'Your vote on Mr Nemeck.'

Richard rose slowly, put his hands flat on the table, and looked at Kyle as he said, 'Guilty. I'm sorry, Kyle, but you left me no choice.'

'Chief Moses?'

Hannah got up, too. She looked as focused and cold as Amelie. 'Kyle,' she said. 'One question first. Do you swear you really didn't know who you were killing?'

'Yeah, I swear!'

Even Claire could tell that he was lying. He'd known. He'd thought he could get away with it in all the confusion.

Hannah shook her head. 'Guilty as hell, I hate to say.'

Amelie hesitated, then rose smoothly to her feet. 'By unanimous verdict, Kyle Nemeck, you are found guilty of the highest crime of Morganville: the murder of your own Protector. I had sworn that the more barbaric punishments we once practiced would be outlawed, for the sake of harmony with humans, but I see no alternative than to punish you as harshly as you deserve. You will be placed in a cage in the middle of Founder's Square for two days and nights, so that all may come and read an account of your crime. After that, you will die in the traditional way. By fire.'

'No!' Kyle screamed, and threw himself out of his chair, stumbling around in his hobbling chains. 'No, you can't do this to me! You can't! No!'

Claire stood up. She wasn't shackled; maybe that was a sign they respected her more, or just weren't afraid of her at all. She didn't know. But she looked directly at Amelie and said, 'Don't do this. Please don't do this.'

'He's guilty of the worst crime that may be committed, short of attempting to kill me,' Amelie said, and Claire had the feeling she was no longer talking to the sometimes-almost-kind person Amelie could become. She was talking to the Founder, or to the long-ago royal princess Amelie had once been. 'There are times one cannot afford mercy without showing weakness. Weakness invites worse outrages.' She nodded to her guards. 'Remove him to the cage.'

Claire opened her mouth to protest again, but she saw both Richard and Hannah sending her warning looks. Hannah actually made a 'sit down' gesture and mouthed, *Don't be stupid*.

Claire slowly sank into her chair as Kyle was dragged out of the room. She felt sick and angry, but mostly, she was scared. While the guards were busy, she could have made a run for it, found Shane, done...what? Tried to get out of Morganville? She knew better than to even try it. Security was tight, and getting tighter.

Amelie was still watching her, and anyway, Amelie could catch her before she got within touching distance of the door.

'Now to you,' Amelie said, as Kyle and the security detail disappeared down the hall, and his screaming was muffled by distance. Another security guard, this one female but dressed in the same black suit and sunglasses, stepped into the room and shut the door behind her.

It seemed very, very quiet.

The Founder sighed and sat back in her chair, and it seemed to Claire as if she became a different person. One who was irritated and unhappy and sad. Hannah and Richard sat down, too. After a moment, Amelie continued, 'Claire, this is a very unfortunate situation. You know that, don't you?'

Claire nodded, thinking, *It's really damn unfortunate for me*. But she didn't say it.

'Having just harshly sentenced Kyle, I can now afford

to show leniency towards you. There are mitigating factors – you were definitely acting in defence of your own life, and all of the witness statements support it. The vampire you staked was known to be extraordinarily violent, and we have been considering for some time what to do to restrain her appetites; you have removed this problem for me, and although I can't be seen to celebrate this, I must acknowledge that you did me a service in this matter. Again.'

Amelie's long white fingers tapped the table in a little dry clicking rhythm, and her eyes went half-closed as she stared at Claire. Finally, she looked to Richard Morrell. 'What say you?'

'She acted in self-defence. It's unusual, but there are plenty of precedents – I did it myself once, and you found that what I did was justified. I don't support any kind of punishment for her.'

Amelie looked at him for several long beats after he'd finished, and neither of them blinked. She turned her attention to Hannah. 'And you?'

'Not guilty,' Hannah said. 'You changed the rules in Morganville. You gave humans rights to defend themselves, even if it cost vampire lives. Claire was within the law to do what she did, and she saved her own life and the lives of at least some of the people in that room.'

Amelie closed her eyes for a moment, and said, 'I'd

have preferred you to use nonlethal methods in your heroic defence, but I cannot deny that there is right on your side. On mine, there is only tradition, but tradition is a very powerful force to vampires. It will be quite difficult to convince them that you shouldn't join young Kyle in the cage. Oliver already cast his vote. I will be obliged to overrule him.'

Claire knew, without Amelie saying so, that overruling Oliver in his angry mood would be hard, if not impossible. Amelie and Oliver had struggled for control of Morganville in the past, and even though they had developed a kind of respect, that didn't mean they couldn't fight. Viciously, if necessary.

Amelie opened her eyes and said, 'As the Founder of Morganville, I rule that Claire Danvers is innocent of the crime of deliberate murder. However, she is *not* innocent of all charges. Claire, I give you two alternatives. First, you will be given into Myrnin's charge until you complete the repairs for which he requires your assistance. During this time, you cannot leave his lab, nor see your friends or family, nor rest until the repairs are completed to Myrnin's satisfaction. I will not deny you food and water, however.'

Claire swallowed. 'What's the second alternative?'

'You can choose someone to suffer punishment in Founder's Square in your place,' Amelie said. 'One of your friends, or your family. It will not be the punishment Kyle faces, but it will be severe, and it will be public.'

If a *vampire* said it was severe, then it was nothing Claire even wanted to think about. And choosing one of her *friends*? Her mom or her dad? She couldn't do that. She could never do that.

'Think carefully,' Amelie said softly. 'The first alternative may sound reasonable, but there will be no sleep, no rest, no contact until you have finished your work. It may well be a death sentence on its own, if the problem is as complex as Myrnin tells me. You'll find that such a sentence is brutal in itself.'

'At least it's my risk to take,' Claire said. 'I'll do it.'

Hannah sighed and looked grim, and Richard shook his head. 'For the record, I lodge an objection to this,' he said. 'She isn't guilty. You're bending the laws to benefit vampires.'

Amelie raised her pale eyebrows. 'Of course I am,' she said. 'Morganville is still my town, Richard. You'd do well to remember that.'

'Then why have us sitting here? Just to make it look legitimate?' Richard shoved his chair back. 'The kid's not guilty. And you're manipulating things to get what you want.'

Amelie didn't bother to reply this time. She looked at the security guard instead. 'I believe Mayor Morrell and Chief Moses are finished,' she said. 'Please see them out.'

The vampire woman nodded, opened the door, and gestured for the two humans to proceed. Hannah looked like she might protest, but it was Claire's turn to shake her head. *Don't*, she mouthed. *I'm OK.*

'No, you're not,' Hannah muttered, but Richard put a hand on her shoulder, and they left the room together.

That left Claire and Amelie. No guards. No witnesses.

'You knew I wouldn't let anybody else take my place,' Claire said. 'Why'd you even ask?'

'Because if I had not, Oliver would demand that I did so,' Amelie said. 'I asked, you chose; there is not much room for him to disagree with the outcome.'

'This is bad for you, isn't it?'

Amelie looked down at her clasped hands. 'It is not the best situation I can imagine. Oliver has been increasingly unhappy with the attitude of the younger humans, and the liberties they're taking. I can't blame him; I am less than happy myself. This incident...We cannot allow humans to roam in packs like animals, victimise our people, and commit cold-blooded murder. It would destroy us. Measures must be taken.'

'Why not? You allow *vampires* to do it!'

'It isn't the same.'

'But you promised that things would change! You promised at Sam's funeral!'

Amelie looked up sharply, and said, 'Mind your place, Claire. I know what I said. And I know what Sam would have said, were he here. He would agree with me, though it would pain him. You hardly knew him at all. Don't presume to lecture me on the rights of humans, or my responsibilities.'

There was a restless fire in her eyes, something that made Claire shiver, and she couldn't help but look away. 'You said I could stop to eat,' she said. 'Can I go home for that?'

'Myrnin will provide you with meals. I will guarantee it.'

'What...what do I tell everybody? Shane, Michael, Eve, my parents?'

'Nothing,' Amelie said. 'Because you will not speak to them at all. You leave this room and go directly to Myrnin's lab, and you begin your work. I will speak with those who need to know of your choice.'

'That's cruel.'

'It's merciful,' Amelie said. 'I am sparing you goodbyes to those whose tears will cause you pain.' She hesitated, then said, very quietly, 'And if you fail me in this, Claire...then you will never see them again. That is my wish.'

'But—' Claire couldn't seem to find the words, and then they came in a rush of clarity. 'You mean, if I don't fix the machine, you'll *kill* me?'

Amelie didn't answer. She looked into the distance, face a blank mask, and Claire felt sickeningly sure that she had it right: Amelie expected results, or else.

The female vamp guard came back, and Amelie pointed to Claire. 'Take her to Myrnin,' she said. 'No stops. She speaks to no one. I will tell Myrnin what must be done.'

The guard nodded and gestured to Claire, who suddenly didn't want to get out of the chair, uncomfortable though it was; she was scared, and cold, and she wanted to go home. She asked, 'Amelie? What if I can't? What if I can't fix it?' Because that was, after all, a very real possibility.

Amelie was silent for a moment, then rose from her chair and looked down at her from what seemed like a million miles away. 'You *must* fix it, the consequences of this town remaining unprotected are too severe. This is the only chance I can offer you, Claire. Prove yourself worthy, and live. Fail, and you will wish you'd taken the second option I offered, harsh and unforgiving as it was.'

Amelie swept out of the room, head high, not looking back. Claire slowly got up, tested her trembling legs, and walked over to the waiting guard.

'What's your name?' Claire asked.

'As far as you're concerned, I don't have one,' the vamp said. 'Move.'

She'd never thought of Myrnin's lab as a prison
before. The unnamed vampire guard – Claire
decided to call her Charlotte, at least in her own
mind – escorted Claire to the underground parking
lot beneath the council building, loaded her into
a standard blacked-out vampire sedan, and drove
her without making any further conversation. They
got out at the entrance of the alley next to the Day
House. It was dark, all the lights off. Overhead, the
moon was setting, abandoning everything to the
night.

The fence closed in on either side, narrowing and
narrowing, until it ended at the run-down wooden
shack that was the entrance to the lab.

Myrnin, wearing a gigantic red velvet hat with
feathers, and some kind of long cloak, was standing
outside the door, waiting. He nodded to Charlotte, took
Claire's arm, and, without a word exchanged, hustled
her inside. He padlocked the door from within, and
then escorted her – more like dragged her – down the
steps into the lab proper.

He stripped off the hat and cloak, dumped them on
a medieval-looking chair, and turned to look at her
with his hands in fists on his hips.

He was wearing a clean white shirt, a shiny blue
vest, and black pants. Even his shoes looked normal,
if a little pointy at the toes. His hair was clean and

curling around his shoulders, and his expression was very, very sober.

'Well, you really made a mess of things,' he said. 'And as a consequence, Amelie has been very clear about my responsibilities. No more Mr Nice Vampire, Claire. You must work, and work constantly, until we get the last security measure of Morganville running properly again. I can provide you with food and drink, but no rest periods. Personally, I think that's excessively cruel, but no one asked me for my opinion, only for my strict cooperation, which I will provide. How many hours have you been awake so far?'

'Um...' Claire's brain didn't seem to be working so well. 'About eighteen, I guess.'

'Unacceptable. You'll make no significant progress before you collapse or go insane. No one said I couldn't let you rest *before* you start work. I'll get your dinner, and then off to bed with you. I'll wake you at a reasonable hour.' Myrnin's expression softened, and he looked genuinely sad. 'I'm sorry for this, Claire. But she's trying to walk a razor's edge, do you see? Cruel enough to satisfy Oliver and his growing number of supporters, but providing you with an opportunity to redeem yourself and do good for our community. And should you fail, I think she is providing me an opportunity to—' He must have been about to say something that he shouldn't have, because he stopped, looked away, and shrugged. 'With an opportunity as well. In any case. Dinner. Do you prefer hamburgers or hot dogs?'

Hot dogs made her think of Shane, and that made her want to cry. She knew how he was taking the news; he'd be going crazy, and probably trying to do something stupid that Michael and Eve were trying to stop. 'Hamburger,' she said. 'I guess.'

'And french fries? And cola? Young people still like those things, I assume?'

She nodded, miserable already. Myrnin reached out and patted her awkwardly on the shoulder. 'Chin up, little one,' he said. 'I have faith in you. Well, in us, actually. I'll be back in five minutes.' His hand tightened on her, and she looked up into his face. 'I don't have to tell you what the consequences are if you try to flee while I'm gone, do I? I don't have to put you in a cage to be sure?'

'No,' she said. 'I'll stay.'

'Good. Because if you do manage to escape, Amelie has issued orders that your friends and your parents are to be immediately arrested, to join that unfortunate stupid boy in his doom. Do you understand?'

Claire's eyes flooded with hot, angry tears. 'I understand,' she said. 'I won't run.'

'I didn't expect you would. But I had to tell you.'

She hated him a little bit just then, but he patted her

on the shoulder, grabbed his flamboyant hat and cloak, and was up the steps and gone in a vampire flash.

Claire sank down on the dark medieval chair and put her head in her hands. She hadn't realised how tired she was, but her muscles ached, and she could feel a fuzziness in her thoughts that told her she was getting close to the end of her energy. Myrnin had been kind, as much as he could be. Rest would help her get through at least another day, maybe two.

Forty-eight hours, max, before she'd start losing focus, making mistakes, failing.

She couldn't fail. She *couldn't*.

The tears came then, even though she didn't really want them. She didn't know how long she cried, lost in a bleak fog of misery, until the smell of french fries made its way into her nose. She sat up, wiping her eyes, and saw Myrnin standing in front of her in that ridiculous pimp hat. He'd left the cloak somewhere.

He held out a paper bag stained with grease, and a gigantic paper cup with a lid and a straw. She took it and sipped the soda first. Pure, sweet, cold Coke. Somehow, it made her feel a little better.

'Follow me,' Myrnin said. 'Eat, then rest.'

She got up and followed him through the lab, through one of the doors at the back that was normally kept closed with a gigantic, ancient padlock dangling above the knob. He searched through his pockets and came up with a clumsy-looking iron key, which he used on the lock, and then swung the door open with a flourish. He swept off his hat and bowed, which was so ridiculous Claire almost laughed.

Inside was a little room with a little table, and a very plain cot with clean white sheets. There were lamps, and in the dim light Claire made out tapestries on the walls. He'd put some colourful rugs on the floor, too. It looked oddly...nice.

'Is this your bedroom?' she asked, and turned to look at him. Myrnin straightened and jammed the big red floppy hat back on his head. The feathers waved back and forth.

'Don't get any ideas,' he said. 'I'm far too young and innocent for that kind of thinking.'

He backed out, closed the door, and she heard the lock snap shut. Panic kicked in immediately; no matter how nice it was, this was a *prison*. Myrnin held the key, and she didn't trust Myrnin to remember tomorrow that she was still here. Claire dumped the food and drink on the table and rushed to the door, banging on the wood. 'Hey!' she yelled. 'I said I wouldn't run! I promised!'

She didn't think he'd answer, but he did. 'It's for your own good, Claire,' he said. 'Eat, rest, and I'll see you in the morning.'

No matter how much she shouted after that, he didn't answer.

Claire finally ran out of fury, although the fear seemed there to stay. She went back to the table, sat down, and took out the burger and fries. She didn't really feel hungry until the first bite, and then she was ravenous and ate everything, even the pickles. She was getting sleepy even before finishing the Coke, and had time to wonder what exactly Myrnin had done to her drink, then stumble to the bed, before she collapsed and fell into a deep, dark sleep.

CHAPTER SIX

The next day started with breakfast, provided by Myrnin again. He set it on the table while she was still lying on the bed, blinking at the lights. Claire said, 'You drugged me.'

'Well, only a little,' he said. He was wearing a violent-looking Hawaiian shirt, all pinks and yellows and neon greens, a pair of checked pants that had probably been ugly when checks were in style, and flip-flops. 'Did you sleep?'

'Don't drug me again.'

'It wouldn't be appropriate in any case. You won't be able to sleep, you know. Not until we're finished.'

'Don't remind me.' She got up, stretched, and wished she had fresh clothes. These were wrinkled, and starting to smell funky. Not that Myrnin would notice, probably. 'What's for breakfast?'

'Doughnuts,' he said cheerfully. 'I like doughnuts. And coffee.'

Claire was doubtful about the coffee, but he'd provided some cream and sugar, and the chocolate-covered doughnut helped wash the taste away anyway. She drank it all, with plenty of sugary bites to help; she was pretty sure she'd need all the caffeine she could get.

Breakfast didn't last nearly long enough.

She couldn't have said what made her aware that something had changed; she'd developed a kind of sixth sense for these things, being around Myrnin for a while. Maybe it was just that he'd fallen silent for what seemed like too long. She looked up and saw him standing in the doorway of the room, watching her with big, liquidly dark eyes that seemed…wistful? She wasn't quite sure. He could have moods about the oddest things.

He smiled, just a little, and it seemed very sad. 'You reminded me of someone, just then.'

'Who?'

'It wouldn't make you feel better to know that.'

She could guess, anyway. 'Ada,' she said. 'You had that thinking-about-Ada look.'

'I don't know what you mean.'

'You look like you miss her,' Claire said. 'You do, don't you?'

His smile faded, as if he didn't have the strength to hold it anymore. 'Ada was my friend and colleague for a very long time,' he said. 'And there was…a great deal of respect between us. Yes, I miss her. I've missed her every moment that she's been gone, strange as that may seem to you.'

He pushed away from the door frame, as if he was about to leave. She couldn't stand to see him walk off with that lost expression, so Claire asked, 'How did you meet her?'

That brought him, and the smile, back. It seemed less wistful this time. 'I heard of her first. She was brilliant, you know. Brilliant and charming and well before her time. She understood the concept of computing machines from the very beginning, but not only that; she was a student of a great many things, including people. That was how we met. She spotted me in a crowd one night, in London, and the next thing I knew she was demanding to know what I was. She could tell, you see. It fascinated her. No surprise, because her father and his friends were the original Gothic crowd, you know.' Claire must have looked blank, because he sighed. 'Really, child. Lord Byron? Percy Shelley? Mary Shelley? John Polidori?'

'Um…*Frankenstein*?'

'That would be Mary's work, yes. Doctor Polidori became famous for a similarly dark work of fiction…

about a vampire. So Ada was much more perceptive than one would have thought. And terribly persistent. Before long, we were...' He stopped himself, looked sharply at her, and said, 'Close friends.'

'I'm not *five*.'

'Very well, then, call it what you like. We became intimate, and we'll leave this discussion there, I think.' He cleared his throat, looked away, and said, 'Thank you.'

She was gathering up her oil-stained doughnut bag, and stopped to stare at him. 'What for?'

'For making me think of that,' he said softly. 'I do miss her. I really do.' He seemed a little surprised about it, then shook out of it with a visible effort. 'Enough. Let me show you what I've accomplished while you were out getting yourself in so much trouble.'

'I didn't—'

'Claire.' He gave her a long, reproachful look, and put his finger to his lips. 'Silence while I am speaking. We don't have time for you to quibble.'

He did have a point, sort of. She nodded, and he led her over to the nearest lab table, which held undefined lumps of things under a grey canvas. Myrnin whipped the canvas off like a magician unveiling a trick, complete with, 'Ta-da!'

It looked worse than it had when she'd last been here. It looked like a completely insane, random collection of parts, cobbled together without any sense of reason. Wires went everywhere, looping into snarls, and he'd used so many colours of wire that the whole thing had a strange rainbow look to it that made little sense.

There really wasn't much to say, except, 'What is it?'

'Oh, Claire, it's my latest attempt to bring up the barriers around the town; what do you think it is? Look, I added vacuum pumps here, and here, and a new gear assembly, and—'

'Myrnin, stop. Just...stop.' She closed her eyes for a second, thinking, *I'm going to die*, and finally forced herself to look at him again. 'Let's start from the beginning. Where's the input?'

'You mean the point at which energy enters the system?'

'Yes.'

'Here.' He touched something in the middle of the device, which made even less sense. It looked like a funnel made of bright, shiny brass. In fact, it looked almost like a horn.

'And then where does the...ah, energy go?'

'Isn't it obvious? No? I weep for the state of public schools.' He traced two wires, one that split off into a tangle of tubes, and one that went into what looked like a clock, only there were no numbers on the dial.

'It draws power during the daytime hours, but it's at its most powerful at night, under the influence of the moon, which is why I've made certain parts of it from elements that resonate with the lunar cycle. I tried to balance the effects of the different elements, day and night, to achieve a perfect oscillation. It's obvious.'

If you were *insane*.

Claire sighed. 'We need to start over,' she said. 'Just start from scratch and build it again. One thing at a time, and you explain to me what it does, OK?'

'There's no need to start over. I've been perfectly—'

'Myrnin,' Claire interrupted. 'No time to quibble, remember? It's going to take all day to tear this thing apart, but I need to understand what you're doing. Really.'

He considered it, looking at her for the longest time, and then grudgingly nodded. 'Very well,' he said. 'Let's begin.'

Autopsying Myrnin's mad-scientist machine was weirder than anything Claire had ever done in Morganville, and that was *definitely* a new record. Some of the parts were slippery, and felt almost... alive. Some were ice-cold. Some were hot – so hot she burnt her fingers on them. Asking why didn't seem to do any good; Myrnin didn't have explanations that she could follow, since they drifted out of science and off into alchemy. But she methodically broke down the machine, labelled each part with a number, and made a diagram as she did of where each thing fitted.

For a device that was supposed to establish a kind of detection field around the town limits, and then a second stage that would physically disable vehicles that weren't already cleared for exit, and then a *third* stage that selectively wiped memories, it was...

Incomprehensible, really. She could see pieces of what Myrnin was doing; the detection-field part was simple enough. She could even follow the purely mechanical part of how the machine broadcast a shut-off of a vehicle's electrical system – which led into the more complicated problem of how to rewire people's brains. But it was all just so...*weird*.

It took hours, but all of a sudden as she was drawing the plug-in for a vacuum pump that felt as if it was radiating cold, although she didn't know how, Claire saw...something. It was like a flash of intuition, one of those moments that came to her sometimes when she thought about higher-order physics problems. Not calculation, exactly, not logic. Instinct.

She saw what he was doing, and for that one second, it was *beautiful*.

Crazy, but in a beautiful kind of way. Like everything Myrnin did, it twisted the basic rules of physics, bent them and reshaped them until they became…something else. *He's a genius*, she thought. She'd always known that, but this…this was something else. Something beyond all his usual tinkering and weirdness.

'It's going to work,' she said. Her voice sounded odd. She carefully set the vacuum pump in its place on the meticulously labelled canvas sheet.

Myrnin, who was sitting in his armchair, with his feet comfortably on a hassock, looked up. He was reading a book through tiny little square spectacles that might have once belonged to Benjamin Franklin. 'Well, of course it's going to work,' he said. 'What did you expect? I do know what I'm doing.'

This from a man wearing clothing from the *OMG No* store, and his battered vampire-bunny slippers. He'd crossed his feet at the ankles on top of a footstool, and both the bunnies' red mouths were flapping open to reveal their sharp, pointy teeth.

Claire grinned, suddenly full of enthusiasm for what she was doing. 'I didn't expect anything else,' she said. 'When's lunch?'

'You humans, always eating. I'll make you soup. You can eat it while you keep working.' Myrnin set aside his book and walked into the back of the lab.

'Don't use the same beaker you used for poisons!' Claire yelled after him. He waved a pale hand. 'I mean it!'

She looked back down at the machine. The flash of intuition was gone, but the excitement remained, and she started in on the screws holding the next part.

She was exhausted, and she had no idea what time it was. Time didn't exist in Myrnin's lab; the lamps were always burning. There were no windows, no clocks, no sense of how long she'd been standing here over this table, tinkering. Days, it felt like. The only time she'd been able to sit down was when she had to go to the bathroom; even Myrnin admitted he didn't think Amelie had meant for her to be denied restroom privileges.

He kept bringing her cups of things. Soup, when she was hungry. Coffee. Sodas. Once, memorably, a glass of orange juice that tasted like sunshine – at least, as far as she was able to remember sunshine.

She was *so tired.* She could hardly hold on to her tools anymore, and her hands were clumsy and aching. Her back was on fire. Her legs trembled with the effort to stay standing. She couldn't work sitting down, as high as the table was, and when she tried to stop and sit for a moment, Myrnin was always there.

This time, as she inched towards the stool, he suddenly made a furious sound and knocked it away, and halfway across the lab, where it hit and rolled with a shocking clatter. 'No!' he barked. 'Stay awake. Do you think I *like* this?'

'I can't *do it!*' she cried, and felt tears stinging her eyes. 'Myrnin, I'm so tired! I need to sit down; *please* let me sit down! Amelie won't know!'

'She will,' came a voice from the shadows, by one of the storage room doors. Claire blinked and focused, and there was Oliver, leaning against the wall. 'You will always have observers, Claire. You chose this punishment, and now you have to survive it. Personally, I think that's unlikely; I believe you'll collapse long before you finish the work, and we both know that Amelie can't afford to be seen as merciful to you. If you fail, all the better. I never agreed with this compassion nonsense.' He sounded dismissive, and still angry that she wasn't in a cage in the middle of Founder's Square, waiting for a bonfire. She felt a surge of hate so hot it shocked her. If she'd had a stake, she'd have used it on him, and never mind the consequences.

She went back to work. She didn't know how, but she did, focusing so fiercely that every part was etched in her mind, every gleaming metal surface.

It could have been minutes later, or hours, but she became aware that Oliver was gone, and that Myrnin was, too. He'd moved all the chairs, and the distance of a few feet seemed so far away to try to walk. She wasn't sure she'd be able to make it, even if she dared.

Myrnin was pacing on the other side of the lab, head down, arms folded. He looked agitated. Her weariness painted strange lines around him, jagged patterns of colour that seemed to flow like oily rainbows.

He was muttering something. She had to concentrate to hear him.

'I never meant it,' he was saying. 'Never meant it to happen. Can't stand it, seeing her suffer. Must do something, do something, what do I do, what *can* I do...'

Claire thought he was talking about her, but just then, he stopped and pulled a small golden locket out of his pocket. He opened it and stared down at the picture. His face looked drawn and tortured, and she'd seen him like this before, her weary brain insisted. Back in the bad old days, before he'd got well, he'd had episodes like this.

It wasn't about her at all.

It was about Ada.

'So sorry,' Myrnin whispered to the picture in the locket. 'I never meant it to happen. I never meant to hurt you. But you were so *sick*. And it was so *easy*.'

Claire tried to move, and her legs threatened to collapse. She reached for the edge of the table for balance, and knocked over a glass beaker, which rolled off and smashed on the stone floor.

Myrnin whirled, and his fangs came out.

This is what happened to Ada, she thought, and felt a terrible sense of inevitability to it all. *She got sick and weak, and he couldn't help himself. Just like he can't help himself now.*

As Myrnin stepped towards her, though, she saw realisation come back into his eyes, driving out the alien energy she'd seen there. He looked appalled. And frightened. 'Claire?'

'I'm working,' she whispered. 'I'm just so...I don't think I can do this. I really don't.'

He hesitated, then came to stand beside her. Myrnin's cool hand closed around her wrist, drawing her attention back to him. 'Focus,' he told her quietly. 'You can do this. We're close. Very close.'

They weren't. They couldn't be. She'd thought she understood, but she was so *tired*, and everything was jumbled and confused and her eyes hurt and her back hurt and she couldn't feel her feet *at all...*

'Here,' Myrnin said, his voice still gentle and low. 'Amelie said you had to work. No one said you had to work alone.' He picked up the next part and slotted it in, took the screwdriver from Claire's numbed fingers, and fastened it with a couple of deft, fast movements. 'I'll be your hands.'

She wanted to cry, because it was sweet, but it wouldn't do any good. She couldn't *think* anymore. Even all her meticulous labelling and drawing just looked like so many puzzle pieces jumbled up in a box. She'd understood how it all fitted together, how amazing and beautiful it would be when it was finished, but...but now it was just noise in her head.

She felt her vision start to go grey, and her heart was pounding loud and fast.

Myrnin caught her around the waist. Claire hadn't even realised she was about to fall. 'Focus,' he told her. 'You can finish this. You're close.' He sounded a little desperate. 'Don't do this, Claire. Don't make me see you like this. It's too easy for me to...forget who I should be.'

She swallowed hard and tried, tried really hard, to stand on her own. 'How long has it been?'

'Forty-nine hours since you started,' Oliver said, from the shadows. 'Myrnin. I don't believe Amelie meant for you to actually hold her upright.'

Myrnin let go and stepped back, guilty relief flaring on his face. He nodded and moved away, out of reach.

Oliver watched him with a dispassionate kind of calm. 'I admit, you've done better than I would have expected. You can still choose to have one of your friends take your punishment for you. I won't protest the change.'

That steadied her; the thought of Eve or Shane or Michael having to suffer for her – or worse, her mom or dad – made her find the last little dregs of strength she still had. *Forty-nine hours?* The longest she'd ever stayed up before was thirty, and that had felt like dying.

She was still on her feet, still working, still thinking. That was some kind of victory, right?

Myrnin hovered near her, not trusting her balance, but she hardly noticed. Claire focused down on the machine, on the few parts remaining. She had to figure this out. She had to.

It was as she slotted one of the last pieces in place that she saw what was missing. 'Wiring,' she said slowly. Her voice sounded thick and strange. 'From here to here.' She pointed at the contact points. 'Should carry the current into the output.'

Myrnin bent over, frowning, and squinted at the place she'd pointed. He grabbed an enormous magnifying glass and looked closer. 'I think you're right,' he said. 'Hold on, Claire. We're almost there.'

She nodded and grabbed the edges of the table. Her body felt like it weighed five hundred pounds. Her legs were numb. She didn't dare try to shift at all, or she knew she'd fall.

Myrnin was back in seconds with a ball of black insulated wire and a soldering gun. He nearly burnt his hair with it, since he was bending so close, but he got it right.

Claire grabbed the last two parts – a clockwork mechanism that fastened on top, and a wiring assembly that connected it to the vacuum tubes – and slotted them into place. Myrnin finished fastening them.

And that was all of it. The machine stretched out in an endless, dizzying series of loops and whirls and weird mechanisms, sprouting wires like tree roots. It didn't look real to her. Neither did Myrnin, as he turned to her with a barely concealed red glow in his eyes.

'I think it's done,' she said. 'May I please sit down?'

'Yes,' Oliver said. 'I think you'd better.'

She fainted.

She awoke to the sound of a cell phone. She knew that song. It was the ring tone she'd assigned to Shane.

She tried to reach for her cell, but her hand felt like a balloon, and a million pounds heavier than it should. She was lying down in Myrnin's cot again, blankets pulled up neatly to her chin, and as she fumbled for the cell the door opened, and Myrnin zipped in and grabbed the phone. He put a cool hand on her forehead and said, 'Sleep. You're fevered.'

'Thank you,' she whispered. 'Thank you for taking care of me.'

He looked at her for a long, moment, and smiled. 'It's nice to not be on my own, at least for now,' he said. 'I'm sorry about earlier. I was...not myself. You understand.'

She did, she'd seen it often enough. She even understood what had pushed him close to the edge; he'd been forced to stand by and watch her grow weak and exhausted and afraid, and the predator in him had woken up. Just as it had with Ada, once upon a time.

She'd fared a little better than Ada, but she wondered now whether that was because Myrnin had stopped himself...or whether Oliver's presence had warned him off. Either way, it had been a near miss.

'Are you feeling sick?' she asked. She hadn't meant it to be quite that blunt, but she was too tired to be diplomatic. 'I mean, like you were before?'

'I can control myself. I just get in moods. You know that.'

'You'd tell me if you were in trouble.'

He smiled, and it didn't look right, somehow. 'Of course I would,' he said. 'Rest now.'

She wanted to talk to Shane, but she wasn't sure she could keep her eyes open long enough. Myrnin didn't wait for her to answer.

She was plummeting deep into sleep again as she heard the door close and lock.

The next time she woke up, she felt better. Fragile and hollow, but clear, and oh, *God*, she needed the restroom. Luckily, Myrnin had one very small toilet closet in the room; she got out of bed to head for it and groaned, because her legs felt like they'd been dipped in fire. The muscles were still trembling. She walked very carefully, bracing herself when she could, and while she used the toilet she took stock of how she felt otherwise.

Weak, sure. But it was so good to feel completely awake again.

Oh, and she also felt completely filthy. She needed a shower, a change of clothes, and about another week in bed, she decided. But since none of that was going to happen right at the moment, she splashed water on her face, finger-combed her hair, and went out to try the door.

It was unlocked.

The lab looked – well, exactly the same, except that there were more people there than usual. Myrnin, of course. Oliver had hung around, or come back; he was standing off to the side, arms folded, frowning with that 'convince me' look on his long, sharp face. She recognised another vampire, too, although she didn't know his name; he sometimes stopped in to visit Myrnin, and Myrnin had never introduced him.

On the other side of the worktable stood Amelie, immaculately dressed in a sky-blue suit and high heels. Her hair was up in the braided crown again.

Claire felt even grubbier.

They all stopped what they were doing as she came out of the door, and for a few seconds, no one spoke.

Then Myrnin smiled widely and stepped aside, and she saw that the machine they'd built was glowing with a soft, blue light.

Her eyes widened. 'It's working?'

'It is indeed working,' Myrnin said. 'Very good work, Claire. I've connected it to the interface. Look!' He turned a computer screen around towards her, and her artsy steampunky interface showed in rust browns and golds. Claire came forward to look closer. All the readouts she'd built in were measuring within normal levels.

She reached out and touched the STATUS button. A crisp computerised voice said, 'Morganville barriers are activated and within normal parameters.'

'But – wait, I didn't program it yet,' Claire said. 'The hardware is one thing, but you have to program it.'

'Oh, I did that,' Myrnin said, still smiling. 'Technically, you accomplished the goal Amelie set you. I saw no reason to torment you further with some simple instructions.'

'But…it needs to be tuned to a specific vampire brain, and you told me that—'

'It has been,' he said. 'It's been tuned to mine. Just as a template, mind you. I'll improve the programming as we go forward.'

Myrnin's brain. Myrnin's brilliant, fiery, half-insane

brain. Claire blinked and looked at Amelie, who was doing her best chilly ice-princess impression.

'Myrnin is the logical choice,' Amelie said. 'He has the greatest natural talent of any vampire in Morganville for influencing humans, although he rarely elects to use it. He won't be directing the machine's actions, only providing a type of baseline reading on which it will base its own calculations and decisions.'

Claire wasn't sure how to feel about any of this. Myrnin wasn't a programmer, and basing anything on Myrnin's brain seemed hinky to her. Still, the computer seemed pretty definite. Everything was working. The barriers were up. All the readouts were normal.

She was...finished?

It should have felt like a victory, but it felt instead like she'd missed something. Like something wasn't right, but she didn't know what it could be.

It was the voice, the computer voice.

It reminded her of...Ada. And that was extra creepy. It occurred to her that maybe Myrnin had done that deliberately, to bring her back to him, just a little bit.

It might have seemed romantic, if Ada hadn't done her level best to destroy them.

Amelie loosened up enough to smile at her, which was nearly a first. She looked a lot younger when she smiled, and even prettier. 'You did very well,' she said. 'I know that I asked much of you, and I know that you may not forgive me for offering such a difficult choice, but I had the town to consider, and there were pressures you cannot imagine that forced us to take these drastic steps. I had every confidence you would succeed.'

Claire felt awkward and a little flushed. She still resented being forced into this; she *really* hated the casual way Amelie had threatened her friends and family. And she didn't, at this moment, much care about being nice, so she said, 'Don't ever do that again. Don't ever threaten the people I love.'

The other vampires – even Myrnin – looked uncomfortable, shocked, or outright angry. Not Amelie, though. Her eyebrows rose. 'The people you love are constantly at risk, as are all people everywhere. Even mine. You should come to terms with that fact, Claire. I am only one thing that threatens their safety. As they occasionally threaten mine. It is the way of all life.'

Claire balled up her fists, but she wasn't like Shane. She couldn't lash out. She just had to breathe through the surges of anger that made red flashes across her eyes until it stopped.

Amelie must have known she wasn't going to get thanked; she nodded to the others, turned, and left. She hadn't been alone, Claire realised. Her two usual bodyguards were with her, standing just off in the shadows, and they followed her up the steps and out of the lab.

That left Myrnin, Oliver, and the other vampire, who now bowed stiffly towards her. 'Frederick von Hesse,' the vampire said, in what had to be a German accent. 'So nice to formally make your acquaintance. This is impressive work. Tell me, how did you come to understand so much of the hermetic arts?'

'I don't,' Claire said flatly. 'A lot of it doesn't make any sense at all.'

Oliver laughed – actually laughed. 'I like this new Claire,' he said. 'You should work her this hard all the time, Myrnin. She's interesting when she's forthright.'

Claire, possessed by the spirit of Eve, shot him the finger. Which made him laugh again, shake his head, and walk up the steps.

Gone.

Leaving her with von Hesse and Myrnin. Von Hesse had a little in common with Oliver in that he, too, looked like an aging hippie, but it was mostly the fact that his hair was shoulder length, blonde and frizzy. He looked older than most vampires, with a lined face and droopy blue eyes, but he had a nice, if tentative smile. 'I apologise,' he said. 'I did not mean to offend you.'

Claire sighed. 'You didn't.' For some reason, it was hard for her to stay mad at von Hesse. Oliver, no problem, but this vampire seemed a little...nervous? Fragile, maybe. 'I'm Claire.'

'Yes, yes, of course you are. You've done an amazing thing, Claire. Truly amazing.' He stood back from the table, admiring the glowing machine. 'I never thought it would be possible without the interface of an organic—'

'Please don't start with the brains again,' Claire said. 'I'm tired. I'm going home, OK?'

Myrnin, who hadn't said much, suddenly reached out and wrapped his arms around her. She stiffened, shocked, and for a panicked second wondered if he'd suddenly decided to snack on her neck...but it was just a hug. His body felt cold against hers, and *way* too close, but then he let go and stepped back. 'You've done very well. I'm extremely proud of you,' he said. There was a touch of colour high in his pale cheeks. 'Do go home now. And shower. You reek like the dead.'

Which, coming from a vampire, was pretty rich.

'Can I take the portal?' Claire asked. Myrnin moved the concealing bookcase and unlocked the door in the wall, swung it open, and bowed so low he practically scraped the floor. He also dug her cell phone out of the pocket of his baggy shorts and handed it over. Claire stepped up and concentrated until the living room of the Glass House was in focus. Nobody was up yet, it seemed. It was still dark outside the windows.

Before she stepped through, she looked at Myrnin and said, 'Thanks for taking care of me.'

He smiled faintly, but in a pained sort of way. 'I didn't,' he said. 'I put you at risk, all because I do what Amelie says. And I'm sorry for that. But she was right. It had to be done. And it had to be done quickly. I couldn't have done it alone, Claire.'

'Goodbye,' said von Hesse, waving. Claire awkwardly waved back, and stepped through the portal.

Home.

She took in a deep breath and looked behind her to see what seemed like a solid wall. She might have dreamt all of it, except that she was still shaky and felt oddly empty.

The house smelt so *good*. Chilli – that was normal – and somebody must have done laundry down in the basement, because she could smell the fabric softener. Too much, as usual. That was Shane's trademark.

She wanted to go straight up to him, but the stairs seemed like too much. *Way* too much. She could hardly stand up, much less climb.

She compromised by walking to the couch, moving the game controllers, and collapsing on the sagging cushions. There was a blanket draped over one end in an untidy mess, and she wrapped herself up in it and immediately felt better. Safer.

She wiggled around under the blanket and found

the cell phone she'd stuck in her pocket, and speed-dialled Shane.

''Lo?' He coughed and tried again. His voice was husky and low. 'Hello?' He must have looked at the screen, because all of a sudden he sounded wide awake – and alarmed. 'Claire? Where are you?'

'Downstairs on the couch,' she said, and yawned. 'Can't come up. Too tired.'

'Stay there.' He hung up, and she heard the thump of footsteps overhead. In just about a minute, Shane was coming down the steps at nearly a run. His jeans were on, but that was all – no shirt, and it made her warm all over to see him that way. He skidded to a stop next to the couch, staring down at her, then crouched to put their eyes on a level. 'Hey,' he said. 'You OK?'

'Sure. Just tired.' As proof, she yawned again. 'How long have I been gone?'

'For ever,' Shane said, and there was something wrong with his voice; it sounded strange and choked. 'Don't do it again, OK? Scared the shit out of me. Out of all of us.' He smoothed hair back from her face, and she reached up to do it to him, too. His hair really was getting emo-length, mainly from laziness and his never wanting to go get it cut.

'You didn't do anything crazy, right?' It was hard to keep her eyes open, but touching him felt so good. So amazingly good.

'Michael had to pound me a couple of times to convince me not to go stage a rescue.' Shane shrugged. 'He hits like a girl, for a vampire.'

'He was trying not to hurt you, dummy.'

'Yeah, I know. Scoot over.'

She did, and opened up the blanket. He slid in next to her, turned on his side, and kissed her before she could protest about needing a shower and toothpaste and all that stuff.

He wrapped her in his arms, so close, and she felt his breath stirring her hair. 'You're safe now,' he said. 'You're safe.'

She drifted off again in seconds into a deep, warm, dreamless sleep, feeling good for the first time in what seemed like years.

CHAPTER SEVEN

Eve woke them up when she clattered downstairs at ten in the morning. Shane groaned, rolled over, and fell off the couch with a thump, tangled in the blanket. Eve stopped on the steps and leant over the railing. 'Wow, Grace, that was impressive. You really stuck the landing... Claire?' She blinked, then practically flew down the rest of the steps. 'Claire! You're back! You're OK!' She stepped over Shane, who was still trying to get free of the blanket, and pulled Claire up to hug her like a rag doll. 'We were so scared; we didn't know how to get to you – everybody was looking—' She stopped and held Claire at arm's length. 'Ew.'

'Yeah,' Claire said. 'I need a shower.'

'I don't think a shower's going to cut it. Maybe fire hoses, and those brushes they use on elephants.' Eve stepped back and offered Shane a hand up as he finally got untangled.

'Speaking of elephants, you sounded like a herd of something coming down the stairs,' he said. 'What the hell are your shoes made of? Hooves?'

'And good morning to you, too, grumpy. Nice bedhead.' He flipped her off. 'No coffee for you.' Eve turned back to Claire and hugged her one more time. 'You're sure you're OK?'

'I'm fine,' Claire said, and yawned again. 'I will be once I get clean.'

'Yeah, big endorsement of that. I'll have breakfast ready for you!'

Shane grabbed Claire's hand. She smiled at him, oddly shy, because the glow in his eyes meant he was up to something, or *thinking* about being up to something. But he finally shook his head and said, 'Go on, before I do something I probably shouldn't.'

That sounded interesting. She wasn't *that* tired. But yuck, getting clean sounded even better. So she kissed him quickly and ran up the steps towards the bathroom.

'See?' she heard Shane yell at the kitchen. '*She* doesn't stomp around like a cattle stampede!'

'Bite me, Collins! No bacon for you, either!'

Things were back to normal. Claire breathed a huge sigh of relief, and felt something that had been completely knotted up in her gut start to relax.

The shower felt so good it was hard to actually get out again, but the creaky hot-water heater finally convinced her by spritzing in ice-cold bursts when it was about to give up altogether. The bathroom was wreathed in so much steam it was like a sauna, and Claire enjoyed the feel of it against her skin as she shaved her legs and underarms and applied lotion and generally felt human again.

Someone knocked on the door.

'Yeah, just a minute!' she called. 'I'm almost done!'

'Mom?'

Claire stopped in the act of finger-fluffing her hair and turned towards the door. All of a sudden, the heat of the bathroom faded away, and the knot in her stomach came back. 'What? Michael, is that you?'

Whoever it was, the voice didn't call out again, and when she went to the door and pressed her ear against it, she didn't hear anything at all. Weird. *Really* weird.

Claire put on her new, clean clothes – jeans, an orange camisole, and a pretty flowered sheer top that she'd scored at the resale shop. She unlocked the door and peeked out into the hallway.

Deserted.

She opened the door all the way and stepped out, accompanied by clouds of escaping steam. All the doors were shut, including Michael's at the end of the hall. She didn't see any sign of life up here, but Eve and Shane were still yelling back and forth downstairs.

Weird.

Claire left the door open and went to her room for her shoes. As she opened it, she found Michael standing there with his back to her.

'Michael?' Finding him in her room was more than a little shocking. He was really good about giving her privacy, even if it was technically his house; he always knocked and waited for permission before coming in, which he rarely did anyway. 'Something you wanted?'

He turned slowly to face her. She was blindly afraid for a second that something awful had happened to him, some kind of accident, but he looked...normal.

Just kind of dazed.

'What's happened here?' he asked her. 'It shouldn't be like this. Why is it like this?'

'I – I don't understand. It looks OK to me. I mean, sorry about the bed, I meant to make it up. What are you—'

'Who are you?' Michael interrupted her, and took a step back when she came towards him. 'Whoa. Stay right there. Who the hell are you and what are you doing in my house?'

Claire's mouth opened and closed, because she had

no idea what to say to that. Was he kidding? No, she didn't think so – there was real confusion in his face, real panic in his blue eyes. 'I – I'm Claire,' she finally said. 'Claire, remember? What's wrong with you?'

'I don't—' He pulled in a deep breath, closed his eyes, and clenched his fists tight. She saw something strange pass over his face, and then he looked at her again, and he was back to being the same Michael she knew. 'Claire. Oh, crap, Claire, I'm sorry. That was weird. I think...I think I was sleepwalking. I was dreaming it was three years ago, and my parents were still here. This used to be their room. I was thinking how weird it was that their stuff wasn't here.' He laughed shakily and wiped at his forehead like he was sweating, although Claire didn't think he was. 'Wow. Didn't like that much. It really felt wrong.'

She still felt afraid, for some reason. 'But...you're OK now?'

'Yeah, I'm fine,' he said, and gave her that dazzling Michael Glass smile that put girls on the floor from a distance. 'Sorry if I scared you. Man, I haven't sleepwalked in ages. So weird.'

'You knocked on the bathroom door,' Claire said. 'You...you asked if I was your mom.'

'I did? Sorry, that is super creepy. You're much shorter than my mom.'

'Brat,' she said, surprised into a giggle.

'That's no way to talk to a vampire.'

'Bloodsucking brat.'

'Better,' he said. 'I can't believe I just barged in here. I'm really sorry. Won't happen again.'

'It's OK; you couldn't help it.' But she still watched him all the way down the hall, until they were downstairs. Having a vampire do something that strange, even if it was Michael, gave her a serious case of the chills.

In the kitchen, when they were all together, everything seemed fine. Michael was the same, and Eve and Shane sniped back and forth at each other with the same casual sort of loving cruelty that they always had. Claire found herself doing nothing but watching them, looking for anything odd. Out of place.

'Hey,' Eve said as she set a plate of bacon and eggs down in front of Claire on the table. 'Space Ghost. You in there anywhere?'

Claire blinked and focused on her. Well, Eve would never freak her out, because Eve was always...Eve. Today's eyeliner was dark blue, and heavy, and her rice-powder make-up and navy lipstick probably *should* have looked weird, but instead, they just looked cute. And normal. 'Sorry,' Claire said. 'Still tired, I guess. That was really, really hard.'

'Spill. Tell me everything.' Eve was going through a phase where she wanted to eat everything with chopsticks. Claire watched her unwrap a set of cheap bamboo ones, scrape them together a few times, and dig into her eggs. 'Did you have to do anything gruesome?'

'Not unless you count sleeping in Myrnin's' – Oh, she realised right at the end of that sentence that she really shouldn't have gone there, because Shane and Michael both turned to look at her – 'uh, lab. No, not really.'

Eve stared. 'You were totally going to say "bed".'

'Wasn't!' Claire felt her cheeks flaming. 'Anyway, all I had to do was repair something. And then they let me sleep. No big deal.'

'No big deal? You were gone for almost five days without a word, Claire! You got *arrested*! Even our resident ex-con was impressed.' Meaning Shane, of course, who'd spent his share of time behind Morganville bars. He barely paused in chopping up onions for his eggs to flip her off. 'If it hadn't been for Michael and Myrnin...'

'Michael,' Claire repeated, and looked at him. He was microwaving his sports bottle, which held his morning O negative. 'I thought you might help hold him down and keep him from doing anything dangerous.'

'Wasn't easy,' Michael said.

Eve nodded. 'He stayed on Amelie until she told him what happened to you, and then he kept Shane from pretending he was a ninja and going to rescue you.'

'Hey, you, too!' Shane protested.

'Yeah, OK, me, too,' Eve said. 'Myrnin called, too. I guess he thought it would be reassuring or something to tell us you'd been standing up for forty hours, and not falling down. What a whack job. Oooh, was he wearing the bunny slippers? Tell me he was wearing the bunny slippers!'

'Sometimes,' Claire said, and dug into her breakfast. It was good, really good. Eve was developing a flair with eggs and bacon and morning-type stuff. 'You guys were really going to come get me?'

'Let's just say the boys got their fight on about it, and leave it at that,' Eve said, and winked. 'Tell me that doesn't make you feel all loved.'

Claire did feel loved, and it made her blush. She concentrated on her food as Michael, Shane, and Eve got their own and slid into the other chairs. At some point, Eve called Shane a tool. Shane called Eve a skank. Normal morning.

Michael, though, was quiet. He sipped his sports bottle and watched them all without saying much. There was something odd about him still, like he was standing a few feet outside of his body, observing. Claire got that feeling again, that gut-twisting one. *Something's wrong.*

But he seemed fine when they flipped for the

washing-up, and fine when he lost the coin toss. In fact, he was whistling as he scrubbed dishes, tossed them up in the air, and caught them with impossible vampire skill.

Show-off.

'Whoa, whoa, speedy, where you going?' Shane asked as Claire headed for the door. 'You just got here!'

'I need to talk to Myrnin,' she said.

'Not right now you don't. You need to go back to bed.'

'Thanks, *Dad*.' Which made her feel a horrible stab of guilt, because she hadn't even called her mom and dad, or gone to see them yet. 'Ah, about—'

'Yeah, I know, you need to see the 'rents. OK, but I go with.'

'Shane, you *know* how that's going to play out.'

He sighed. 'I really do,' he said. 'But I'm not letting you run around Morganville today all by yourself.'

She stopped and turned to him. They were alone in the living room, and she took his hands. 'You know about the frat guy? Kyle?'

Shane's face went completely still, but his eyes were hot. 'Yeah, I know. They've got him in the cage in Founder's Square. Word gets around, even if us mere mortals aren't getting tickets to the barbecue. People are angry. This could go bad, Claire. I don't think Amelie understands how bad.'

'You think someone might try to break him out?'

'I'm pretty sure someone will. Hell, I'd have done it myself, except I was more worried about you.'

'Shane, I heard what happened. He and his frat buddies pounded on a vampire, and then he killed his own Protector when he came after them.'

'Yeah, well, I'd kill any of them if he had his fangs up in my face, too.'

'But you wouldn't have let your friends kick some stranger's ass and rob them, either; I know you wouldn't. And Kyle was the ringleader. Truth is, I don't think it mattered to him who got hurt or killed. And I'm not sure it wasn't cold-blooded murder, with his Protector.'

'If you're not sure it *was*, then he shouldn't be in the cage,' Shane said. 'She's going too far. People in this town have a taste of freedom now, and they're not going to give it up that easily.'

'The vampires aren't going to give up being in charge, either. People are going to get hurt if both sides keep on pulling.'

Shane nodded slowly. His expression didn't change. '*Our* people get hurt here every day.'

There was no talking to him about this, Claire realised; Shane had come to terms with a lot of things, but he was never, ever going to believe that what the vampires did to humans for punishment was right.

And she couldn't blame him. She remembered how sick she'd felt, how horrified, when Shane himself had been in that cage, waiting to die.

Now Kyle was in there, and his family, the people who loved him, they were feeling the same awful horror. Even if he was a total tool, this was worse than punishment. It was cruelty.

'Maybe we should try to get him out,' Claire said. 'Does that sound crazy?'

'Only all of it. You know what the penalty is for breaking someone out of that cage?'

'Joining them in it?'

'Bingo. And sorry, but I'm not risking it. You're not exactly escape artist material.'

She was a little relieved, actually. 'Maybe I can talk to Amelie. Get her to change her mind.'

'See, that's much more you. Reason Girl,' Shane said. 'Parents?'

She nodded and grabbed her backpack from the corner – force of habit: she didn't have school today, but the weight of the books and all the assorted junk she kept in it made her feel steadier. Shane turned towards the closed kitchen door. 'Yo, undead-for-brains, we're heading to the Danvers House!'

'I heard that,' Michael yelled back.

'Whole point, bro.' Shane offered Claire his arm, and she took it, and they set out for her parents' house.

It was a nice day to walk, especially with Shane
next to her. Well, truthfully, if it had been forty below
and a blizzard, it still would have seemed like a nice
day with Shane, but it really was beautiful – sunny,
not too hot, a cloud-free, faded-denim sky that seemed
to stretch a million miles from horizon to horizon.
Wind, of course, like there always seemed to be in
Morganville, but more of a breeze than a gust.

It still tasted of sand, though.

'Want a coffee?' she asked. Shane shook his head
and kicked a rusted can out of their way.

'If I see Oliver I'm going to punch him right in the
face,' he said. 'So no. I'll skip the coffee.'

'Right, no caffeine for you at all.' There wasn't
much else to do in Morganville besides the coffee shop,
anyway. Movies weren't playing yet, and they were too
young for the bars, which also weren't open yet. She
was hoping to delay the inevitable bringing-Shane-to-
her-parents tension, but really, there was no getting
around it.

She was still working on what she was going to say
to her dad when Shane said, 'Huh. That's weird.'

There was something in his voice that made her
look up. She saw nothing out of place for a second, but
then she saw someone sitting on the curb a block up,
head down, shoulders shaking.

Crying.

'Should we...?' she asked. Shane shrugged.

'Probably couldn't hurt. Maybe he needs help.'

It was a he, after all, a college kid wearing a black knit shirt and scuffed-up jeans. Claire had seen him somewhere before...

It was the boy from the Science Building. The one who'd given her the rave flyer. Alex? She thought his name was Alex.

As they got closer, she felt that stab of anxiety again. Alex was not the kind of guy to be crying in public like some four-year-old, and besides that, he looked really, really upset.

'Alex?' Claire let go of Shane's hand and motioned for him to stay put while she crossed the last few feet to the boy. 'Hey, Alex? Are you OK?'

He gulped and swiped at his eyes, blinking furiously. Then he glared at her. 'Leave me alone.' There was so much ferocity in his voice that Claire instinctively held up both hands and took a step back.

'OK, sure, I'm sorry. I'm Claire, remember? From the Science Building? I just wanted to help.'

He looked confused then, as well as angry. He scrambled to his feet and looked around, then lunged for Claire and grabbed her arm. His eyes were wild. 'Who are you?' he said. 'Where am I?'

'Hey, man, let go!' Shane stepped in and batted Alex's hand away. 'Chill. She was trying to help, OK?'

That seemed to make him angrier. Alex shouted right in their faces, 'Where am I? How did you get me here?'

Shane looked at Claire and mimed drinking, then shook his head. 'Must have been one hell of a party,' he whispered. 'Who is this guy?'

'Just somebody from school.'

'Hey!' Alex was shouting again, getting red in the face. 'You tell me how I got here or I'm calling the cops!'

'Um...' Claire pointed behind him. One block away were the gates of Texas Prairie University. 'You're not exactly lost. I don't know how you got here, but all you have to do is turn around and go back to the dorm—'

Alex looked over his shoulder, then snapped his head back around to focus on her. 'I don't know what kind of sick joke you think you're playing, but you'd better tell me what's going on, *right now*.'

'Hey, enough. Back off,' Shane said, and pulled Claire out of easy reach. 'Go sober up, man. And find some kind of rehab, because, damn.'

'I'm not drunk!'

Shane steered Claire away, then across the street to the other sidewalk. Alex just stood there, shouting at them like a crazy man. Shane shook his head. 'Man. Frat guys. They really can screw up their lives.'

'I don't think he was drunk,' Claire said doubtfully. 'He didn't really look drunk.'

'Yeah, because you'd be the expert on that.' Shane sent her an ironic look, and she remembered, with a flash of shame, that he *was* the expert; his dad had been a drunk, and so had his mom, towards the end. Shane wasn't exactly a saint, either. 'OK, maybe he wasn't drinking, but he was definitely wrecked. What are the fratties taking these days? Maybe it was meth.'

Well, Claire really didn't know anything much about drugs. It wasn't that she was a prude; she just had a kind of ridiculous fear of anything that would screw up the way she thought. 'This is your brain on drugs' and all that. 'He probably needs help,' she decided, and pulled out her phone to dial Chief Moses. She told Hannah about the boy, feeling more than a little like maybe she ought to have minded her own business, but still. That had not been the Alex she'd met at school.

As she put the phone away, Claire remembered hearing that voice – Michael's voice – through the bathroom door this morning. *Mom?*

She shivered as a cool breeze skittered by.

But really, it was a beautiful day, and she didn't know why she was feeling so weird.

Visiting her folks was every bit as awkward as Claire had imagined. First, her mom opened the door, got a look of delight on her face as she saw Claire, and then immediately dimmed it down to a strained welcome when she spotted Shane standing behind her. 'Claire, honey, so glad you're here! And Shane, of course.' Somehow, that last part sounded like a total lie. 'Come in; I was just cleaning up the kitchen. I'm grilling chicken for lunch; can you stay?'

That was Mom all over, offering food in the second breath. It made Claire feel at home. She traded a quick look with Shane, and then said, 'Well, actually, we've already got plans, Mom, but thanks.'

'Oh. Of course.' Her mother was looking better these days – not as thin and haunted as she had been when they'd first come to Morganville. In fact, she looked like she'd gained a little weight, which was good, and she was dressing a bit less like a character in one of those black-and-white movies where women wore pearls to vacuum – more normal. Claire actually kind of liked her shirt. For Mom clothes.

'How's Dad?' Claire asked, as they followed her down the hall and turned right into the kitchen. It was the exact same layout as the Glass House, since they were both Founder Houses, but the Danvers House had an open entrance to the kitchen, and her mother had painted the room in sunny yellows that cheered it up a lot. Ugh, she still liked the ducks, though. Lots of ceramic ducks. Well, at least it wasn't the cheesy

ceramic roosters; that was an awful memory. Claire
and Shane took seats at the small kitchen table – a
lot nicer than the battered one they had back at the
Glass House – and Mom fussed around with cups and
saucers (Shane held the saucer up with his eyebrows
raised, like he'd never seen one) and got them coffee.

'Mom? How's Dad?'

Her mom poured coffee without meeting her eyes.
'He's doing all right, honey. I wish you'd come see us
more often.'

'I know. I'm sorry. It's been…kind of busy these last
few days.'

Her mom straightened up, frowning. 'Is anything
wrong?'

'No.' Claire slurped coffee, which was too hot, and
her mom never made it strong enough. It tasted like
coffee-flavoured milk. 'Not now. There was some trouble
in town; that was all.'

'Claire killed a vampire,' Shane said. 'She had to, but
it could have gone bad for her with Amelie. As it was, she
had to do a job for the vamps that almost killed her.'

She could not *believe* that he'd just blurted that out.
Shane raised his eyebrows at her again in a silent,
What? Like he couldn't believe she wasn't going to say
all of that herself.

Her mother just stood there, mouth open, holding
the steaming pot of coffee.

'It's not that bad,' Claire said in a rush. 'Really. I was just trying to help some people who were in trouble, including Eve. It just turned out...well, it turned out OK, in the end.'

Worst. Speech. *Ever.* And it didn't seem to reassure her mother at all.

'Mrs Danvers,' Shane said, and held out his cup for a refill on his coffee, with a smile that, Claire thought, he'd probably learnt from Michael; even her mother seemed to warm up to it. 'The point is, Claire did something really brave, and probably really important, so you should be proud of her.'

'I'm always proud of Claire.' And that, Claire thought, was true; her mother *was* always proud of her. Except maybe when it came to Shane, of course. 'But it sounds very dangerous.'

'Shane was with me,' Claire said, before he could open his mouth again. 'We look out for each other.'

'I'm sure you do. Oh, let me go see what's keeping your father. I can't believe he hasn't been down for coffee yet; that's a violation of the laws of physics. I know he's awake.'

Her mother set the pot back on the coffee machine and left the kitchen, heading for the stairs. Shane leant over to Claire and said, 'Does it give you déjà voodoo how alike the houses are?'

'That's déjà vu, and I hate you right now.'

'For narcing on you to your mom? Wait until you hear what I tell your dad.' From the sly grin on his face, she knew what he was thinking.

'Don't you *even* think about it.'

'I could tell him about that time we—'

'*Hell*, no.'

They were whispering, and on the verge of giggles, when a scream cut through the house like the sound of shattering glass. Claire dropped her cup and jumped to her feet, running for the stairs; Shane was just a couple of steps behind her, and caught up quickly on the stairs as he jumped them three at a time.

Claire's mom was nowhere in sight, but the door to her dad's office – which was Shane's bedroom in the Glass House – was open. Claire dashed for it and skidded to a halt in the opening.

Her mother was on her knees.

Her dad was lying on the carpet, looking small and weak and fragile, and she felt absolute terror shoot through her like lightning. Her knees went weak, and she felt Shane's hands close around her shoulders.

'Mom?' she asked in a small, shaking voice. Then she swallowed, got it together, and hurried the last few steps to drop down next to her parents.

Her mom had her hand pressed to her dad's neck, feeling for a pulse, but as badly as her hand was shaking, Claire was sure she couldn't tell even if she found one. She looked up miserably at Shane, who nodded and got on one knee next to her mom. 'Let me,' he said, and gently moved her mother's hand to feel for a pulse with his own, steadier fingers. It seemed to take for ever, but he finally nodded. 'He's OK. He's breathing, too. I think he just passed out.'

Claire's mother was crying, but Claire thought she probably didn't even know she was doing it. She had a frozen, blank expression that Claire thought was scarier that the scream had been. 'Th-thank you, Shane. I don't think we should move him.'

'We should turn him on his side,' Shane said. 'Recovery position.'

Claire's mother looked at him oddly, as if she wondered how exactly he knew all of this. Claire knew, all too well. He'd come home to find his parents passed out a lot, during that nightmare time when they'd been on the road, running from Morganville and memories. Checking for pulse and breathing and making sure they didn't choke on vomit was just a normal thing to do, for him.

Shane rolled her father onto his side and settled him as comfortably as possible, then sat back and said, 'Better call an ambulance. You'll probably want him to go to the hospital, right? Mrs Danvers?'

She blinked and slowly nodded, then got up and used the desk phone to call 911. While she did, Claire stared down at her dad's still, pale face. He looked *awful*. Now that the adrenalin shock was fading, tears were threatening to drown her, and she didn't want to cry, couldn't cry, not now. Her mom needed her to be strong.

Her dad opened his eyes. His pupils looked huge, but then they shrank back to normal size. Having his eyes open didn't actually make her feel that much better, because he looked at them like strangers.

Even Claire.

When he tried to sit up, Shane put a big hand on his shoulder and said, 'Sir, you'd better stay down until the ambulance gets here, OK? Just rest. Do you remember what happened?'

Her dad blinked, very slowly, and focused on Shane's face. 'Do I know you?' he asked. He sounded...confused. Claire's throat went tight and hot, and she choked back tears again.

'Yes, sir, I'm Shane, Claire's boyfriend. We had a talk last week about your daughter.'

Claire looked at Shane then, because that was the first *she'd* heard of any talk. Not that it was a bad thing, but she couldn't believe he'd gone off and talked to her dad without her. What a...medieval thing to do.

'Oh,' Dad said, and turned his head to look at Claire. 'You're too young to be dating, Claire. You should at least wait a couple of years.'

That was...random. And odd. She blinked and said, 'OK, Dad, don't – We'll talk about it later, all right?'

The response time of ambulances in Morganville was fast – after all, it wasn't that big a town – so Claire wasn't surprised to hear sirens already in the distance. 'You're going to be OK, Daddy,' she said, and took his hand in hers. 'You're going to be fine.'

He tried to smile. 'I have to be, don't I? I have to see you go to college.'

'But—' *But I'm in college.* No, she must have misunderstood him. He probably meant he wanted to see her *graduate* from college.

Because otherwise, what sense did that make? Anyway, it was probably normal for him to be a little confused. He'd passed out, and it was almost certainly his heart; she knew the doctors had been treating him for a while. Maybe this time they could fix it.

'I love you, baby,' he said. 'I love you and your mom very much; you know that, right?'

He put his hand on her cheek, and finally the tears just spilt over in a hot mess down her face. She put her fingers around his. 'I know,' she whispered. 'Don't leave, Daddy.'

The ambulance sirens were loud now, right in front of the house, and Claire's mom dropped down next to Shane again, touched his shoulder, and said, 'Would you go let them in, honey?'

He was gone in seconds, pounding down the stairs, racing to the front door. It didn't seem long at all before Claire heard the rattle of metal and heavy footsteps, and then the room was crowded with two big paramedics, one male, one female, who moved her and her mom out of the way so they could lay out all their kit. Claire backed up to the wall and, now that she had nothing to do, started to shake like she might come apart. Her mom put her arm around her, and they waited. Shane stayed out in the hall, looking in. When Claire wiped her eyes and glanced in his direction, he mouthed, *Hang in there.* She smiled weakly.

The paramedics talked to her dad, then talked to each other, and finally the woman got up and came over to Claire and her mom. 'OK, it looks like he's stable right now, but we need to get him into the hospital. I'll need somebody to come along to fill out the paperwork.'

'I'll...I'll get my purse,' Claire's mom murmured. The male paramedic had her dad sitting up now, and was taking his blood pressure. Shane moved out of the way as Mom headed out to get her things, and then came in to stand with Claire. He took her hand and held it tight.

'See, he's OK,' Shane said. 'Maybe he just passed out. Lucky he didn't hit his head.'

'Lucky,' Claire whispered. She didn't feel lucky. Not at all. Right now, she felt...cursed.

As they helped her dad to the waiting gurney, he looked over, and she was relieved when he said, 'Shane. Thanks for being here with my girls.'

'No problem,' Shane said. 'Feel better, sir.'

'Keep your hands off my daughter.'

The paramedics grinned, and the woman said, 'I think he's feeling better. You can meet us at the hospital if you'd like. Your mother may need you.'

'I'll go,' Claire said. 'Shane—'

'I'm not leaving you. You're going to need someone to fetch hamburgers, right? I'm your man.'

Yes, he was, she thought. Definitely her man.

The hospital wasn't Claire's favourite place, not ever, but now that it was her dad being wheeled into tests, it definitely was worse than usual. At least when she'd been the patient she didn't have to just...sit and wait.

She felt useless. Her mom had filled out all the sheets and sheets of paper, answered questions, made phone calls, done everything useful she could, but now she just sat, looking empty-eyed at a television playing in the corner of the waiting room. Claire kept bringing her magazines, and her mother glanced at them, thanked her, and put them aside.

It was awful.

Michael and Eve showed up a couple of hours later, bearing pizza, which by then was really welcome. Father Joe from the local Catholic church stopped in, too, and spoke to Claire's mother in private. They prayed, too. Claire wasn't in the habit, really, but she got up and joined them. Silently, her friends followed her, and it felt better having them with her. At the end, Michael crossed himself and hugged her, and Eve did, too. Shane just stayed with her, quiet and *there*.

Oliver showed up an hour later, and exchanged guarded nods with Father Joe; it looked like the two of them had one of those frenemy relationships that were so common in Morganville. Oliver didn't pray, at least not with the rest of them. He walked right over to Claire's mother and said, 'Your daughter has rendered the town a great service. There will be no charge for whatever treatments your husband may need. If it goes beyond what the doctors feel they can treat here, I will personally sign the paperwork to allow him to be transferred to another, larger facility out of town. And should one or both of you decide not to return, we will not object.'

That was...enormous, really. Claire sat, stunned, and just looked at him. He didn't so much as spare her a glance. His luminous eyes were fixed on her mom, and there was a strange kind of gentleness in the way he spoke.

'I don't know what to say,' Claire's mom finally said. 'I – Thank you.'

'My word is also the Founder's word. Should you need anything, get in touch with me immediately. I'll ensure it's done.' He hesitated, then said, 'Your daughter is impressive. Difficult, but impressive. I do not know you or your husband well, but I expect that you must be equally impressive to have such a child.'

Claire's mom raised her chin, looked him in the eyes, and said, 'What about my daughter?'

Oliver didn't hesitate. 'The offer doesn't extend to Claire. She must remain in Morganville.'

'I'm not leaving her here alone.'

'She's not alone,' Oliver said. 'We can hardly pry her from those who care for her even at gunpoint. And your daughter is no helpless child. You'll have to give her up to her own life, now or a year from now, what difference?'

Claire had never, ever seen her mother look like that – that focused, that fierce, that determined. Her mom put her arms around her, holding her in a tightly protective embrace. 'I don't have to give her up to *you*,' she said. 'I know Claire's capable of being on her own; I've known that for a long time. But she's our child, now and always, and once my husband is better we'll be back for her. You can't keep her here for ever.'

Shane took in a small breath, and Claire felt her

heart beat a little faster. *No, Mom, don't...* But Oliver didn't seem to take it badly. He inclined his head just a fraction and said, 'Perhaps not. Time will tell. But you must do the right thing for your husband, mistress. We will do the right thing for your daughter. For now.'

He took her hand, shook it, and walked out without ever saying a word to Claire, or anyone else.

Michael said, 'Anyone else think that's strange?'

'Well, I personally think it's awesome that he's letting them go, but strange? Not so much,' Eve said. 'Why shouldn't they leave? I mean, they shouldn't have really been here in the first place, right? Bishop moved them here, and then Amelie just didn't let them leave for her own reasons. They're not cut out for this town.'

'Nobody's cut out for this town,' Shane said. 'Nobody sane, anyway.'

'Says the kid who came back.'

'Yeah, kind of proves my point.'

Claire didn't say anything. She couldn't think *what* to say, actually. Yes, she'd wanted her parents out of this mess; it had been horrible when they'd been dragged into it in the first place, and not a day had gone by that she hadn't wished there were a way to smuggle them out to safety and get them a real life somewhere else.

But on the other hand, her mom and dad could be... *leaving.* And she wasn't going with them; she knew that. Even if she wanted to go, Amelie wouldn't let her go. That had already been made clear enough.

That her family might come *back* here, for her, when her dad was better – that was overwhelming and wrong. And, at the same time, weirdly comforting.

She and her mom didn't talk about it, not at all.

The rest of the afternoon passed slowly, and without anything in the way of excitement, or even new information. Claire fell asleep lying awkwardly in a chair, and woke up to find Shane draping a blanket around her. 'Shh,' he said. 'Sleep. You still need it. I'll wake you up if anything happens.'

She knew she shouldn't, but the past few days were crushing her hard, and she couldn't keep her eyes open, no matter how much she tried.

She woke up with a shock some time later – no idea when – to the sound of shouting voices.

Claire fought her way free of the blanket and stood, looking around for the danger, but there was nothing really visible in front of her. Oh, it was in the hall. She saw people running, including two security guards in full uniform, with guns.

'What the hell?' Michael had got up even faster than Claire. Shane and Eve were still trying to wake up from where they'd been dozing in their chairs.

Her mother was nowhere to be seen.

'It's in the hall,' Claire said. Michael moved to the doorway and looked out, then shook his head.

'Some crazy dude,' he said. 'He thinks he's a doctor here, I guess. He's yelling about how they're not following his orders. Security's got him.'

'Weird.'

'Well, it's a hospital. People aren't generally here because they're all good and normal.'

Michael had a point, but it still felt weird, again. That could have just been waking up like she did, of course, and the generally freaky nature of the past few days.

All Claire knew was that she was glad, so glad, that her friends were with her.

'Where's your mom?' Shane asked. Claire shook her head.

'Bathroom, maybe? Which is where I need to go.'

'Ooh, me, too,' Eve said. The boys rolled their eyes, like they'd planned it. 'What? It's what girls do. Get over it.'

'I was never on it,' Michael said, straight-faced. 'Don't take all day.'

Eve took Claire's arm as they walked down the hall towards the bathroom. No more shouting, so the crazy guy had been detained and taken off to the padded rooms, Claire guessed. There weren't very many people in the halls right now, and as she looked at the clock, she realised why; they'd been here for hours, waiting. She'd slept through most of it.

Mom wasn't in the bathroom, but Claire was relieved (no pun intended) to get there anyway. She and Eve chatted about nothing, really, during the entire process, and then Claire kept on talking while Eve checked her make-up, which took a lot longer.

Finally, Eve met her eyes in the mirror and said, 'You think your dad's going to be OK?' It was a direct question, an honest question, and Claire felt her breath catch in her throat for a second.

'I don't know,' she said, just as honestly. 'He's...he's been weak for a while. I hope this is just...something they can fix.'

Eve nodded slowly. 'Oliver said they could get the hell out of here. They should, Claire. They should go find one of those world-class heart places and never come back, like Michael's parents. Talk to your mom about it. Promise me.'

'I will,' Claire said, and sighed. 'Thanks.'

'For what?'

'For not just telling me everything's going to be all right.'

Eve paused in the act of fixing her lipstick. 'Are you kidding me? It's *Morganville*. Of course everything isn't going to be all right. We're lucky when *something* is all right.' She finished the lipstick, made kissy lips at the mirror, and said, 'OK, ready.'

As they left the bathroom, they saw Michael and

Shane in the hallway, and Claire's mother, and a doctor in a white lab coat with his name embroidered over the pocket. Claire hurried to join them, and Eve joined just a few seconds later.

'Dad?' Claire blurted out. Her mother took her hand.

'Your father is alive,' the doctor said. 'He's got a serious issue with his heart, and I've already spoken with Oliver to tell him we don't feel we can give him the care he needs here. I'd like to transfer him to a facility in Dallas. They've got the best possible specialists and facilities to treat him there.'

'But...is he going to be—'

The doctor – not one she was familiar with, from her various stays and visits here – was older, tall, with a long, mournful face and greying hair. He wasn't especially warm. 'I can't give you a good estimate of his chances, Ms. Danvers. I can only say that they're worse if he stays here.'

Claire's mom, who'd been taking it all in silently, said, 'When are you transferring him?'

'Early morning. You're welcome to ride with him.'

'I will. I have to...go home and pack some things. Claire—'

'Mom, if you want me to come with you...' Of course, Oliver hadn't said *she* could leave, but Claire wasn't in any mood to think about that.

'No, honey, it wouldn't be safe for you to try, we both

know that. I'll let you know as soon as we arrive, and I'll call every day. As soon as we can, we'll be back here. All right?' Her mother kissed her forehead and smoothed her hair back. 'Stay here. Stay safe, with your friends. He's stable right now, and I'll let you know if you need to come up and see him. There's no telling how long all this will take.'

'Can I see him? Before you take him?' Claire asked the doctor. He nodded.

'He's awake, but ten minutes only. Don't tire him out. He needs rest.'

'Want me to...?' Shane asked. Claire hesitated, but shook her head. She didn't think Shane would be especially restful for her dad, much as he meant well.

Her dad's room was quiet and very white, even though they'd tried to make it more cheerful with pictures on the walls. He was lying propped up on the bed, playing with a remote control, and he looked better. Not well, but better. 'Hey, sweetheart. Sorry I gave you such a scare.'

Claire laughed, but it tasted wrong in her mouth. 'You're apologising? Next thing, you'll be telling Mom you're sorry for messing up the carpet by falling on it.'

He acknowledged that with a wry little twist of his mouth. 'So, they're taking us to Dallas tomorrow. I hear they've told us we don't have to come back.' Her dad always seemed to see too much, Claire thought. Like he could see right through her. 'But you're going to stay here, aren't you?'

'I don't think they'll let me leave, Dad.'

Her father took her hand. His fingers were warm and strong, and she was so glad to feel that, after holding his limp, cool hand when he was lying on the floor. 'I want you out of here, Claire. I want you safe. I want you to get on with your life like you'd planned, to MIT. It's my fault you came here at all, you know; your mother and I wanted you to stay close, and – this is what happened.' He took in a deep breath. 'You're meant for something better. That's what I was trying to tell you before. It's what I told Shane, too.'

'You mean better than him,' Claire said.

Her father looked away. 'I know you think the world of him, but he's not the kind of boy who's right for you, sweetheart. I know he's got a good heart; I see it every time he looks at you. But he's going to hurt you, in the end, because he's not the kind of boy who stays. I don't want to see that happen. And I don't want you to stay here for him and destroy your chances.'

Claire raised her chin. 'I'm not, Dad. If I stay, it's not about Shane.' Well, it was, partly, but she wasn't going to say that *now*. 'I wanted to go to MIT because that was where I was going to find people who could teach me different ways to think, and would understand me, and work with me. I found that here, in Morganville. Myrnin does that. And he's got so much more to teach me. He's brilliant, Dad. He's not like anybody else.'

'Claire—'

'Dad, you're supposed to rest.' She put her head down, her chin on their clasped hands. 'Please. I need you to rest, and I need you to get better. I can do this. I know what I'm doing now, and I know it's not what other people might think is right, or popular. But it's right for me. I can make a difference. I can't just run away. I want you and Mom out of here, and safe, and trust me, someday I'll do all that stuff you talked about.'

He gazed at her for a long, long moment, and then sighed. 'That's my stubborn girl,' he said. 'Come see me in Dallas. Promise.'

'I promise,' she said. It felt like goodbye, and she hated it, but she knew she couldn't leave Morganville now. Even if Amelie wigged out and let her go...she couldn't just *leave*.

The time was up sooner than she expected, but a nurse came in and stood there, clearly waiting to hustle her out. Claire stood up and kissed her dad. 'I love you, Daddy. Please—'

'I heard you, you know,' he said. 'When you were talking to me, on the floor. You said, "Don't leave me." But I am leaving you, honey.'

'No, you'll be one phone call away,' she said.

'That's not leaving. That's just...transposition.'

She kissed him again, and then the nurse's glare sent the message that her time was definitely, completely up.

She left the room feeling lighter, somehow; he'd looked better, and he'd sounded clear.

He was going to be OK. She could feel it, deep inside.

They were all waiting for her, all her friends. Her mom went in, after a silent hug and kiss, to sit with her dad.

Shane looked at her with those warm eyes that – like her dad's – saw maybe a little too deeply. 'You OK?' he asked her quietly, as he took her hand.

'I'm OK,' she said, and took a deep, trembling breath. 'My parents are going to leave Morganville. That's what I wanted, to keep them safe.' The euphoria she'd felt on leaving her dad's room was fading now, and she felt shaky again. 'It's funny, I didn't think...I didn't think I'd miss them at all if they left. Is that awful? But I will. As much as I wanted them to go... Maybe I should ask Amelie if I can go with them.'

'You already know what she'll say. Look, if I thought you could leave, I'd be the first one stuffing you in the car and telling you to have a nice life,' Shane said. 'But I think we both know it's not that simple anymore.'

Nothing was, Claire thought. How had the world got so complicated?

CHAPTER EIGHT

Eventually, they all went home. Or at least homeward...Shane announced that he was starving, and Eve agreed, and Michael steered his car to one of Morganville's two all-night diners. This one was Shane's favourite, Marjo's, although Claire guessed that Marjo herself – the rudest waitress *ever* – was off duty, since a woman with the nameplate HELEN came to take their orders. She wasn't nearly as rude as Marjo, but she wasn't nice, either. Claire supposed that being nice was against the rules. Or maybe being on the night shift in an all-night diner in Morganville tended to make you bitter.

The food, though, was delicious. Juicy burgers, crisp fries, milk shakes to die for, although Michael skipped that and ordered something in a covered to-go cup that Claire thought was probably not ice cream. The diner was packed with late-nighters...college students, although they were pushing the curfew, as well as lots of quiet, pale people who sat in groups and, when they looked at the humans, had a special glitter in their eyes.

Marjo's, like Oliver's Common Grounds, was a place where the two halves of Morganville had a kind of unofficial truce. Besides, who didn't like hamburgers? Vegetarians, Claire supposed. But she didn't think there were any vegetarian vampires. That would be like an atheist priest.

Speaking of priests, Father Joe came in and looked around for a seat. Michael gestured for him to come over, and he did, stopping to say hello to people (and vamps) along the way. Father Joe wasn't a very large man, but he was...well, kind of cute. Eve had once had a monster crush on him (check that – from the wide-eyed look Eve was giving him now, she still had one). She'd claimed it was the cassock. Claire thought it was more the wavy red hair and cute smile.

'How's your father, Claire?' Father Joe asked, even before he'd sat down in the chair he'd pulled over to their table. 'I was planning to stop by again tonight before I went home.'

'He's doing better,' she said. 'They're taking him to Dallas tomorrow.'

Father Joe nodded and sat back as Helen came

over to take his order. Not surprisingly, he was having a hamburger, too. Claire wondered why they bothered to even have a menu, really. He favoured strawberry milk shakes, which put him in solidarity with Eve. 'I'll keep your father in my prayers,' the priest said, handing his menu back. 'And your mother, of course. And you. I assume you're staying in Morganville?'

Claire sighed. 'For now, anyway.'

'I hope to see you on Sunday, then, at the evening services. Amelie comes quite often.'

Huh, Claire had never considered that Amelie might be a churchgoer. 'And Oliver?'

Father Joe chuckled, then sipped on the strawberry milk shake Helen thumped down on the table before him. 'Oliver has...theological differences with the Roman Catholic Church. He attends a more nondenominational service we hold on Saturdays. Although he usually argues with me about formats.'

She could see Amelie in church, but *Oliver*? Really? That was...new.

Father Joe must have seen the confusion in her face, because he said, 'Most of them attend some sort of service. After all, in the times they were born and lived, religion was a vital part of life and society. It's a little less so today, but for many of them, it's hugely important to still feel they have a path to God.' He grinned. 'But I'm off duty right now. Seen any good movies lately?'

'Do *not* ask Shane,' Eve said. 'He's got awful taste.'

'Are you kidding? That last thing I took you to was totally sick!'

'If you mean, made me throw up, then yeah. Would it kill you to watch something where heads don't explode?'

'Probably not, unless it's one of those movies where everybody's wearing poofy skirts and corsets and nobody does anything. That might actually kill me.'

Eve looked at Claire. 'Really? Is he running for Worst Boyfriend Ever?'

'In the subcategory of Completely Awesome,' Shane said, and stole some of her fries. Eve stabbed at him with a fork, and missed.

The bell over the door chimed, and it wasn't that Claire was really looking, exactly; she was too busy laughing. But something about the woman who came in caught her eye. Maybe it was because she was clearly a vampire, and from the way she dressed and the hair, she'd probably last cared about fashion in the 1940s. She looked eerily out of place here, where most of the vamps were wearing casual, modern clothes, even if their hair styles seemed a little iffy.

She looked around the diner as if she were trying

to locate someone. The waitress, Helen, steered in her direction, and must have asked her if she needed help, because the woman focused in on her immediately.

And then she attacked her. Just...cold, flat-out *bit her*. It was so fast Claire couldn't react at all, at first; it seemed so totally random, so *wrong* that her brain kept insisting she wasn't seeing it.

Other people reacted, though. Father Joe, for one; he jumped up and raced to help. So did a tableful of vampires seated near the door. It took all of them to wrestle the vamp off of Helen, who collapsed back against the counter, holding a shaking hand to her bleeding throat. Her knees buckled, and she fell. Other diners bent down to check her as the vamps continued to fight with the stranger. She was acting crazy now, yelling in a language Claire didn't recognise at all. Finally, they got her out the door and off into the night.

For some reason, Claire hadn't moved at all. Most of the people hadn't. Maybe they'd been afraid to draw attention. She felt, suddenly, like a small, defenceless animal in a room full of predators.

'Uh, Mike?' Shane asked. 'What was that?'

'I don't know,' Michael said. 'But it was freaking weird.'

Helen was OK, it appeared, although she wouldn't have been if the vamp had been able to do her worst.

Father Joe offered to drive her to the hospital, and the cook came out of the back to keep order and make sure nobody ran out on their checks. He was a vampire, which for some reason struck Claire as immensely odd. A vampire fry cook just seemed...wrong. But then again, they were really *great* burgers. Being immortal gave you lots of time to perfect your grilling technique, Claire guessed.

As they paid their check and headed for the door, Claire overheard one of the vampires saying to another, 'Did you understand what she said?'

And the other vampire said, 'She was screaming that it was all wrong.'

'What was all wrong?'

'I don't know,' he said, and shrugged. 'The world? She's off her head.'

And once again, Claire felt that shiver.

Something wasn't right in Morganville.

She just knew it.

She woke up early the next morning, and felt as if she could've slept for a dozen more days. Nobody else was stirring, and Claire decided not to wake them up; she showered and dressed as quietly as possible, and sneaked out the front door while the mist was still on the ground outside, and the sun was just coming up.

Morganville was pretty at this time of day – still, quiet, cleaner somehow than it seemed in full light.

She'd always liked early mornings here better than any other time.

Mostly, though, she liked the fact that sunrise signalled most vampires to head for their beds. Except Myrnin, who hardly ever seemed to rest at all.

She walked the streets as lights came on in houses, cars began to move again, and people started their usual days. A construction crew had got busy early, lots of guys in flannel shirts, jeans, and work boots hammering and sawing in the clean morning light. It felt...new. And good.

There was a car parked in the middle of the street up ahead. Claire frowned and slowed, watching it – it wasn't pulled to the curb, it was just sitting there, blocking whatever traffic might eventually come by. As she watched, a girl only a little older than she was – maybe nineteen or twenty – opened the driver's-side door and got out. She stood there next to the car, looking around.

It was eerily familiar. It was like Alex, sitting by the side of the road, seeming so lost.

But this girl had clearly been heading somewhere. She was dressed for an office. Claire could see a laptop and a purse in the passenger seat. And there was a sealed cup steaming the aroma of coffee into the air from the cup holder in the door.

The girl caught sight of Claire, and waved her over.

Claire hesitated, remembering what kind of reception she'd had from Alex, but finally went. She stopped out of grabbing range and said, 'Are you having car trouble?' Because that made the most sense, obviously.

The girl looked at her and said, 'I can't find my mom's office.'

'I...Excuse me?'

'I know it's around here somewhere. My God, I go there all the time! It's ridiculous! Look, can you help me?'

'Uh...sure,' Claire said cautiously. 'What's the name of the office?'

'Landau Realty.'

Claire had never heard of it. 'You're sure it's around here?'

'I'm sure. It was right *there*. But the sign's gone, and there's nobody inside. I've been up and down the street. There's not even a note. It's ridiculous! I was there *yesterday*!'

A man came out of another building down the street, carrying a briefcase. The girl yelled at him. 'Hey, mister! Where's Landau Realty? Did they move?'

He hesitated, frowning, and then walked over, tucking his newspaper under his arm. 'Excuse me?'

'Landau Realty,' the girl repeated. 'God, really? Has everybody gone crazy?'

'You're...Laura, right? Iris's daughter?'

'Yes! Yes, Iris is my mom.' Laura breathed a huge sigh of relief. 'Now we're getting somewhere. Look, her office was right here, and I don't understand...'

The man was looking at her *very* oddly. He also looked at Claire, as if she ought to be doing something. She had no clue. Finally, he cleared his throat and said, 'Laura, look – I don't know what happened, but you *know* where your mom is. She...she died last year. The office was closed up. I attended the funeral. So did you.'

Laura stared at him, wide-eyed, and shook her head. 'No. No, that's not true. I'd remember—'

She stopped. Just...stopped. It was like someone hit a reset button in her head, because all of a sudden she looked older, and her face just crumpled with the weight of misery. 'Oh, God,' she said, and put both hands to her mouth. 'Oh, God, I remember that. I remember – What was I thinking? Why did I...? Oh, God, *Mom*...' She burst into tears and got back into her car, slamming the door as she fumbled for a tissue out of her purse.

The man hesitated, then decided he really didn't want to hang around to be a shoulder to cry on. He walked away quickly, like whatever had got into Laura might be contagious.

Claire hesitated. She felt like she *ought* to do something, but suddenly getting to Myrnin's lab seemed much more important.

Her conscience was cleared by Laura Laudau blowing her nose, wiping her eyes, putting her car in drive, and heading off down the street, still crying.

Something was very, very wrong.

It's the machine, Claire thought.

It had to be the machine.

When she went to see Myrnin about it, though, things didn't go as she'd planned. Not at all.

First, as she descended the stairs she found that the lights were all off. That wasn't like him; Myrnin had no real concept of energy conservation, and he couldn't be bothered to turn things off if they were already on. *Power failure,* Claire thought, but when she located a switch on the wall and threw it, all the sconces on the walls lit up with a reassuring golden glow, spilling colour and life through the room.

Myrnin was lying stretched out on one of the lab tables, wearing a crimson dressing gown that had seen better days at least fifty years ago. His eyes were closed, and he seemed...dead. Asleep? But Myrnin didn't sleep, not really. She'd seen him nap occasionally, but he'd wake at the slightest sound.

She'd just clomped down the steps and switched on the lights, and he hadn't moved.

'Myrnin?' She said it reasonably loudly, but he didn't stir. 'Myrnin, are you OK?' She was getting a sick, strange feeling about this. He looked...posed, almost. Like a corpse laid out for burial.

After what seemed like an eternity, his eyelids slowly raised, and he stared blankly at the roof of the lab. 'I think I was dreaming,' he said. His voice sounded drugged and slow. 'Was I dreaming?' He turned his head and looked at her with strange, luminous eyes. 'I thought you were gone.'

'I went home,' she said, and her uneasiness intensified to a prickling all over her skin. 'Don't you remember?'

'No,' he said softly. 'No, I don't remember. I've been feeling...tired. I wish I could sleep. Sleep must be a very nice thing.' In the same distant, contemplative voice, he said, 'I loved her, you know.'

Claire opened her mouth, then closed it without saying anything. Myrnin didn't seem to care either way. 'I loved her and I destroyed her. Don't you ever wish you could take something back, Claire? Something terrible that you wished had never happened?'

He *really* wasn't well. She just knew it. She could feel it. 'Maybe I should call Dr Mills,' Claire said. 'Or Theo. You like Theo. You can talk to him.'

'I don't need a doctor. I'm perfectly fine. I checked my blood for any signs of degeneration, and I'm free of any sign of the disease that afflicted us before.' He shut his eyes again. 'I'm just tired, Claire. Tired and...tired of everything. It's a mood. It will pass.' To prove it, he sat up and hopped off the lab table – from depressed to manic in one leap. His heart wasn't in it, but he rubbed his hands together and smiled at her. 'Now. What do you have for me, my little mechanic?'

She hated to say it now, because she knew it was absolutely the worst time to try to talk to him, but she had no real choice. 'I think there's something wrong with the machine,' she said. 'I think maybe we did something wrong.'

His eyes opened very wide. 'And why would you say such a thing? I've run all the tests, I tell you. There's nothing wrong.'

'It's not something that's obvious, it's just that—' She couldn't quite think how to phrase it, so she just blurted it out. 'People are acting crazy. I think it's the machine.'

'Don't be ridiculous. It's not the machine, it can't be,' Myrnin said. 'Don't be so overdramatic, Claire. People in Morganville regularly go around the twist, normally in fairly spectacular ways. It's really not all that unusual. Perhaps it's unusual to see so many acting oddly at once, but odder things have happened here.' He smiled and spread his hands. 'There. All explained. No cause for alarm.'

'Well – but there was this boy, Alex. I saw him this morning. He didn't know where he was. It was really weird, and he was really upset.'

'Don't young men these days constantly seek new ways to obliterate their brains? They certainly did in my day, although the most they had to work with were fermented beverages and exotic herbs. Young Alex almost certainly had a blackout that can be perfectly explained by drugs and alcohol.' Myrnin turned away to pick up his Ben Franklin spectacles, balanced them on his nose, and looked over them to say, 'Don't do drugs. I feel I ought to say that.'

'I *don't*,' Claire said, exasperated, and sat down across from him on a pile of boxes. 'OK, then, never mind Alex. Michael actually thought I was his mother! How weird is *that*?'

'Hmm. Less explainable, but when did this happen?'

'This morning.'

'Don't you ever wake up and think yourself in a different place, a different time? It happens to vampires fairly often, actually. It even happens to me occasionally, when I manage to sleep.' Myrnin studied her for a few long seconds. 'He's fine now, I assume.'

Claire hesitated, then had to nod. Michael had been absolutely normal ever since. So maybe she was putting things together that didn't belong. It might even explain the vamp in the diner, if vampires were prone to sleepwalking...'There was another one at the hospital,' Claire said. 'He said he was a doctor, but he wasn't. Michael said later that he used to be a doctor, before he had a breakdown.'

'Aha, a *breakdown*. I believe that might be called a clue.'

It was so *frustrating*. She just knew…but Myrnin's arguments were so logical and practical that she felt stupid. 'And this morning,' she said. 'Laura Landau. She was looking for her mom's office. But her mom's been dead for a year. And Laura went to the funeral and everything. It was like she just woke up and… forgot.'

That made Myrnin pause for a moment, considering. He touched his earlobe, tugged it, and finally said, 'I acknowledge that I have no explanation for that. I'll run another set of diagnostics and review the logs, I promise you, but I can see no way that these incidents could be connected with our efforts. The machine is designed to have an effect *outside* of town, not *inside*. I can assure you that, strange as this may seem, it could be complete coincidence.'

'Are you sure?' she asked. 'Are you really, totally sure?'

'Yes,' he said. 'I am sure. I double-checked everything after you went home yesterday. I even made a few improvements, just in case.'

The first part of that reassured her. The second part…not so much. 'What kind of improvements?'

'Oh, nothing, really. Mostly just streamlining. You really did very well, I certainly don't want you to think that I am one of those people who has to be in control all the – Oh, well, I suppose that's actually true, I do have to be in control all the time. But only because I am in charge, of course.' His manic chatter wasn't fooling her; there was a strange look in his eyes, and something was off about his behaviour, too. 'It's all fine, Claire. You should just leave it to me.'

She swallowed a mouthful of dread. 'Can I take a look? Not that I don't trust you. Only because I'm really worried about my friends.'

'Aren't I your friend?' he asked, very softly. There was a cold light in his eyes, something that seemed so alien to her it was like seeing him possessed. 'Friends trust each other. There's nothing wrong with the machine. In fact, for the first time in years, I actually feel...rested. I feel *better*.'

But five minutes ago he'd said he was tired. This was scaring her. 'Myrnin, you *are* my friend, but there's something not right about this. Please. Let me see it.'

He debated it for a moment, and then nodded. The cold light was gone from his eyes when he blinked, and his body language shifted back, subtly, to the Myrnin she knew. 'Of course you can, I'm sorry. I don't know what I was thinking. Well, I moved it downstairs and installed it below,' he said. 'I'll show it to you just this once. I put in safety protocols to protect it against any unauthorised tampering, so be warned, I don't want you down there alone, all right?'

'All right,' she said. The 'safety protocols' were, no doubt, something that would eat her or burn her face off. She wasn't eager to go poking around downstairs. 'I just won't feel good about it until I check for myself.'

He tapped his pen on his lips. 'I heard your father is unwell.'

'He's in the hospital. They...they were moving him and my mom today to Dallas, to a heart hospital.'

'And yet you're here, talking to me about all these vague suspicions,' he said. 'I would have thought that you'd be at his side, still.'

She felt terrible the instant he said it; she'd been feeling guilty about it all morning, but her dad had texted her at four a.m. and said, *No need to come, they're already getting me ready. Love you, sweetheart.* And she'd texted him back first thing when she woke up, but the ambulance had already left.

'He's already gone,' she said. 'And I want to make sure this thing didn't make him sick in the first place.' That was a little more of an attack than she'd planned, but she did mean it.

He stood there watching her in silence, and then bowed his head. 'Perhaps I deserved that,' he said. 'I haven't been myself, I know that. But I know the machine is working correctly. I can feel it. Can't you?'

'I can't feel anything,' Claire said. 'I wish I could.'

He led the way to the trapdoor in the back of the lab, and she stood back while he entered the code and pressed his hand to the plate. The hatch popped open with a hiss of escaping cool air.

'Right, down you go,' Myrnin said, and, without any warning at all, grabbed hold of her, wrapped his arms around her, and jumped into the dark.

It wasn't a long fall, but it was way longer than she'd ever like to jump by herself. Myrnin landed with hardly a jolt. For a second, he held on to her, which made her feel...weird, in a lot of wrong ways. And then all of a sudden he let go and was across the room, turning on overhead lights with the flip of a switch. 'I really ought to install one of those marvellous things. You know, the ones that turn the lights on when you clap?'

'You could get motion sensors.'

'Where would the fun be in that? This way. Stay close. There are a few new things lying around that it wouldn't be good for you to, ah, encounter.'

Right. Myrnin was the master of understatement, because from what Claire had seen of his downstairs playhouse, it was *full* of things that no sane person would want to run into. And now there were *new* things.

Claire stayed so close she might as well have been grafted to him. He seemed quite back to normal now, which was a relief.

At the end of a long, rough-hewn tunnel studded at not-very-regular intervals with lights lay a big, open cave that held the remains of the computer Claire had once known as Ada. Ada had been mostly machine, but partly vampire: Myrnin's former vampire lab assistant, and – although Myrnin never quite got around to telling the details – almost certainly his girlfriend, too, at some point. But Ada, like the rest of the vampires in Morganville, had contracted a disease that had made her slowly go insane – and unlike the rest of the vampires, they hadn't been able to treat her. It hadn't been so much the disease, Claire thought, as being stuck inside that mechanical *thing* without a body that had finally driven her completely crazy.

Ada was gone now, but the whole idea of her *still* scared Claire.

Her instant impression, when Myrnin turned on the overhead lights in the cave, was that Ada was back. The tangle of pipes, wires, hoses, screens, and keyboards that sprawled over half the cave was working again, hissing steam, clanking as its gears turned.

The screens on the sides of it were all dark. The one in the middle showed Claire's custom graphic interface, the one that had been hooked up to the parts on the lab table.

As she studied it, she realised that the parts she and Myrnin had developed and tested were actually welded into the machine, just below the big, clumsy typewriter-style keyboard. Liquid bubbled. Steam escaped in wisps of mist. She could see the clockworks turning.

'It's working just fine,' Myrnin said, and walked to the screen. It was a bizarrely out-of-place touch of high tech among all the retro brass and tubes. 'Here, I'll show you.' He deftly brought up the system logs and dials, and just as he said, there was nothing odd about how it was performing. Well, for a machine that killed car engines on command, and changed the memories of those who drove past the borders of town.

Changed the memories. Alex had forgotten where he was. Michael had called her his mom. Laura had thought her own mother was still alive.

Claire knew she was looking at the core of the problem, whatever 'the problem' really meant. But until she had proof, solid proof, there was no way Myrnin would believe her. He was feeling too fragile.

'Can you show me what improvements you made to it?' she asked. He gave her a frowning look, and she forced a smile. 'I just want to learn. You know, understand what it was I left out.'

That soothed him a little. He started to touch the mechanism under the keyboard, then pulled his hand back with a snap. 'Ah,' he said. 'Must deactivate the security... Turn around, please.'

'What?'

'Turn around, Claire. It's a secure password!'

'You have *got* to be kidding.'

'Why ever would I joke about that? Please turn.'

It was stupid, because she could *always* figure out Myrnin's passwords; she didn't think he ever used more than three, and they were all ridiculously simple. He didn't remember his own birth date, so he didn't use that, but he either used his name, Amelie's name, or Ada's.

She tried to count key clicks, but vampires typed really fast.

'Done,' he said. She turned; nothing looked any different. He pointed at a tiny LED diode on the corner of the keyboard. 'Green means it's off. Red means it's armed. Don't get them confused.'

She sighed and shook her head, then got on her hands and knees and crawled under the keyboard with him. It was murky underneath, but she could just make out what he was touching. 'It occurred to me that we could control the reaction in our departing guests more finely,' he said. 'I installed a variable switch. Should you wish to take more of their memories, you simply turn it up. It can be targeted to an individual, you see, or set as the general field around the town. But only outside of the borders.'

'What's it set on right now?'

'Three years. According to my research, most who leave Morganville do it within three years. We can, of course, exempt certain people from the effects if we choose.'

Claire's mouth went dry. 'What about my mom and dad? Did you—'

'Oliver brought me the waivers last night, and I programmed in their exceptions,' he said, and met her eyes in the dim, flickering light. 'Your parents will remember everything. That's a risk, a great risk. It would be safer, and kinder, if I had been allowed to take their burdens away.'

'They won't remember that I'm here if you do that. They'll think I—' She could hardly bear to say it out loud. 'They'll think I ran away. Or that I'm dead.'

He kept staring into her eyes. She couldn't read his expression at all. 'And you don't think that would be kinder, in the end?'

'No,' she snapped. 'Why would you?'

He didn't answer, just slithered out from under the console. Before she could get out, he'd tapped his password in again. The LED on the keyboard glowed red.

'Don't touch it,' Myrnin said, and there was a certain chill in his voice she hardly recognised. 'Only I can alter the machine from this point on. I don't want you down here. Do you understand?'

'Yes.'

'From this point on, the machine is *my* responsibility,' Myrnin said. 'Only mine.'

That did not make her feel any better. Claire swore to herself that she was going to figure out the password. She *had* to understand what was going on, and somehow, this machine was the key.

Everything seemed quiet the rest of the day. Claire walked home, after promising Myrnin she'd deliver doughnuts the next day. She didn't see any crazy people, or even confused people. Everyone seemed to have a purpose and understand where they were going.

Was it possible that she'd really just blown it all out of proportion because she was so scared by the fate of poor, doomed Kyle, and so tired from the brutal repair session on the machine? Things looked different today. Better, somehow. She felt a little foolish, really, after she'd stopped in a couple of stores and talked to perfectly normal (for Morganville) people, who didn't seem to have noticed anything odd at all.

Outside of the used bookstore, she ran into another familiar – and unwelcome – face. He stepped out of the mouth of an alley in front of her, keeping to shadows, and she pulled herself to a sudden halt as she realised that she was facing Frank Collins.

Shane's dad looked just the same as before – pale, with that scar disfiguring his face. She couldn't tell what he was thinking, or feeling, but he looked menacing as hell. It was his default expression.

'Stay away from me,' Claire said, and started to walk around him. He stepped in her path. She went off the curb into the sunlight, and that stopped him. 'Just leave us alone, OK?'

'I need to talk to my son,' Frank said. 'I need to explain some things. He trusts you.'

'Yeah, and I don't trust *you*. Why should I?'

'I saved your life,' Frank said. 'That ought to buy me a few minutes of your time.'

'Well, it doesn't,' Claire said, and kept on walking. 'Don't follow me anymore.'

He stood there watching her go, and when she finally looked back at the corner, he was gone. She shivered. There was something feral about Frank Collins now, something that made her hope she never ran into him in the dark.

She decided not to tell Shane about any of it.

She got a call from her mother just as she entered the swinging gate in the picket fence around the Glass House, and sat down on the steps in the warm morning sun to talk. Her dad was in the hands of some of the most expert heart doctors in the world, Mom assured her. He was resting comfortably, and she'd checked into a hotel nearby. Oliver had sent money to allow them to get an apartment until her father was well enough, and then he'd promised to refund the money they'd spent on the house in Morganville, although Mom was still hell-bent on coming back as soon as Dad was out of the woods.

It seemed very out of character for Oliver to do something that nice; Claire thought it had probably been an order, a pointed one, from Amelie, and she'd made Oliver do it because she wanted him to remember who was in charge. She and Oliver were often like that – Oliver wasn't a comfortable choice for her second in command, but he was good at it. He just didn't think he deserved to be only second, and Amelie had to watch her back with him, always.

It felt good to hear her mother's voice sound so strong and confident for a change. Her parents hadn't been right, here. The stress had hurt her dad, and her mom had...withered, somehow. She'd always been strong out there, but in here she'd seemed weak and lost.

This was better. Claire had to believe that it was better.

'Should I come this weekend?' she asked. 'To see Dad?'

'Maybe give it another week, honey; he's still going through a lot of tests with these new doctors. I'm sure he'd like to wait and see you once he's not being pulled away for new adventures in science every few minutes.'

'Are you doing OK?'

'Of course I am, Claire. This isn't the first time he's been in the hospital, and I'm booked in a very nice hotel. They even have a spa. I might just go get a massage later.'

'You should,' Claire said. 'You really should. You deserve it, Mom.'

Her mother laughed a little. 'Oh, baby, you are the sweetest girl in the world.' The laughter faded. 'I hate to see you stay there. You put yourself at so much risk. But I promise you we will come back for you. I'm not leaving you alone there.'

'I'm not alone; I have lots of friends. And I'd risk a lot more right now if I tried to leave; you know that. It's better if I stick it out here for a while. I can learn a lot from Myrnin, anyway. He's better than a whole roster of teachers at MIT.' *When he's sane,* she thought, but didn't say.

'And MIT doesn't have Shane,' her mother said dryly. 'Yes, I know. Believe me, I know. When I met your father I would have done anything to stay with him. Everyone thought I was crazy, too. But, sweetie, you have to promise me that you'll call me every day.'

'Mom! Every *day*? How many minutes do you think I have on this cell phone?'

'Well, then, at least every few days. And absolutely once a week, no matter what. If I don't hear from you—'

'I know, you'll send the National Guard.'

'That's my girl,' her mom said, and made kissy noises. 'I love you, honey. Stay safe.'

'You, too,' Claire said. 'I love you both very much.'

She hung up and sat there in the sun for a little while longer, thinking. She felt alone in a way that she hadn't before; although she'd worried about her parents, felt that they were a burden to her here, there had been something weirdly comforting about knowing they were only across town. That she wasn't on her own, not really.

She wondered if this was what it felt like to really, truly grow up.

Being alone.

Eventually, that feeling faded, mostly because the day felt wonderful sitting outside – it was deliciously warm in the sun. She thought about dragging out a lounge chair and reading in the glow, but that seemed like a lot of work. Instead, she leant back against a pillar on the porch, closed her eyes, and took a nap.

When she woke up, she smelt tacos. *Really* smelt them, as if she was sleeping in a taco store. She came awake, stomach rumbling, and opened her eyes to see a plate being held right under her nose.

When she reached for it, Shane snatched it back. 'Nuh-uh. Mine.'

'Share!' she demanded.

'Man, you are one grabby girlfriend.'

She grinned. It always made her feel so fiercely warm inside to hear him say that – the girlfriend part, not the grabby part. 'If you love me, you'll give me a taco.'

'Seriously? That all you got? What about you'll do sexy, illegal things to me for a taco?'

'Not for a taco,' she said. 'I'm not cheap.'

'They're brisket tacos.'

'Now you're talking.'

He held the plate out, and she took one. He took another, sank down next to her on the steps, and they munched in silence, enjoying the day. He'd brought cold Cokes, too. She popped the top on hers and tried to sneak a second taco – he'd brought *six*, after all. She managed, but just barely. When she went for the third one, Shane put down the plate and tackled her to the grass, and she used their momentum to keep them rolling until she came out on top.

He didn't fight, exactly. He looked surprised,

but pleased. 'Well,' he said. 'That's new. Now what, cowgirl?'

'Now I get the rest of your tacos,' she said, and leant forward to brush her lips teasingly against his. 'And maybe your Coke. And maybe something else.'

'What else? You've cleaned me out. I don't have dessert,' he murmured. The words were coming from somewhere deep in his throat, a kind of growling purr that made her feel nuclear hot inside. 'Unless you were thinking—'

'I don't know, what am I thinking?' She smiled slowly at the look in his eyes, and felt absolutely wicked. 'Any guesses?'

'I think I just became psychic,' he said. 'Holy crap.'

'Romantic.'

'You want romantic? Date—'

She put two fingers on his lips, hushed him, and then kissed him, long and warm, with tongue. When she was finished, she let him breathe. 'You were saying?'

'Not a damn thing,' he said, and used both hands to hold her hair back from her face. 'How'd you get to be so good at this?'

'I had a good teacher.'

'Better not have been Myrnin or I'll have to kick his predatory ass.'

'I mean you, dummy.'

'Oh.' He kissed her back, and somehow they rolled over again, and this time she was on the bottom. It could have felt like suffocation, but he was good at this. It just felt...sexy. 'How am I doing now?'

'I'm learning all the time.'

'Well, you're a scholar.' He trailed a finger down her neck, into the open part of her shirt, to where the first button held it closed. It felt like every nerve in her body paid attention to that, to the pressure, the slow speed at which his finger moved, the tug of fabric where he stopped. 'Oh, damn, sorry.' The button slipped out of the hole. 'You're undone.'

She looked down. The top of her cream-colored bra was showing, but only the top. It wasn't X-rated yet. It wasn't even PG, except that they were outside, and anybody could walk by and see them. Somehow it didn't feel like that, though. Here, with him, she felt like there was nothing else in the whole world except the two of them.

'Um, Claire?' Shane said. His finger had moved down to touch the skin right at the top of her bra. 'Maybe we should finish our tacos inside.'

'What about—'

'Eve and Michael are at work. I go in at two.'

Oh. 'That might be a good idea, then.'

He stood up and helped her rise, and they gathered up the plate and Cokes and went inside.

Best. Lunch. *Ever.*

Claire spent the rest of the afternoon humming around, ridiculously happy; when Eve came home and saw her, she put down her coffin-shaped purse and said, 'You look mussed. If I wasn't a total lady, I'd guess that you and Shane—'

'Excuse me? You're a *lady*?'

'I bought a title on the Internet. I own one square inch of Scotland, you know. And you're changing the subject.' Eve gave her a sharp grin and grabbed her hand. 'Give, already. Deets.'

'I'm *not* telling you details.'

'Sure you are. We're girls. It's what we do!'

'If we were guys, that would be gross.'

'Wait, checking...' Eve held an invisible phone to her ear. 'Nope. We're still girls, and the referee says that makes it OK. So give it up, Danvers. You look starry-eyed. It must have been fantastic.'

Claire *might* have actually told her, at least up to the parts that made her blush, but just then, Michael came in the front door toting his guitar, tossed his keys into the tray on the hall table, and yelled, 'Eve's got dinner duty!'

'Hey!' Eve yelled back, and stomped her foot. 'Your timing *sucks*, Michael!'

'Why, was there hot wild girl action—'

'Shut *up*, you perv.'

'Can't catch a break,' he said, and flopped down in the chair. 'I was just speaking for Shane, since he's off heroically chopping barbecue for money. Hey, you guys notice anything weird happening the last couple of days?'

Claire forgot all about the fun she'd just been having, and focused in on him with laser intensity. 'Other than the vampire going nuts at the diner, you mean?'

'Yeah, I see your point, but I mean...*more* people acting weird. More than usual. Two of my guitar students didn't show up. When I called one of them, he said he didn't know what I was talking about, and he wasn't learning the guitar. Which is definitely strange, because he's already paid me for the whole month.'

Michael had noticed it. It *wasn't* all in her head. Claire swallowed and glanced at Eve, who was frowning, too. 'I guess,' Eve said slowly, and crossed her arms over her black-and-pink-striped rugby shirt, with a skull where the logo should have been. 'When I got to the coffee bar on campus, there was this girl wandering around, asking everybody if they'd seen her roommate. Trouble is, she doesn't have a roommate. She hasn't for, like, years. But she was describing her like she actually existed.'

'That's what I'm talking about.' Michael nodded.

'Weird shit. I met at least two other people today who thought it was a couple of years ago. What the hell, right?'

'Right,' Claire said softly. Her good feelings, intense though they'd been, were officially gone now. Whatever was happening in Morganville, it wasn't in her head, and it was spreading.

She was going to have to go to Amelie if Myrnin didn't want to believe it. They had to take the system offline, run a full diagnostic. There was just nothing else to do.

Amelie wouldn't like it. Oliver *really* wouldn't like it.

'It's probably nothing big,' Eve said, and both Michael and Claire looked at her like they'd never seen her before. 'I mean, it's *Morganville*. Not like anybody here is ever far from the borders of Psychoville. I mean, I want to go nuts about twelve times a day.'

Michael stood up, facing Claire. 'You know something about what's going on, don't you?' he asked, and she saw a flicker of vampire red in his blue eyes – just a spark, but enough to let her know he was serious. 'Is it what you and Myrnin were working on? Is that it?'

'I don't know,' Claire admitted. 'But I'm going to find out.'

She just had no idea how to do that, without Myrnin's help.

When she got up, Claire checked the calendar and saw that there was another Elders' Council meeting scheduled for noon. That was the best time, she thought; she could probably get in, and once she laid it all out, Richard would be on her side, and Hannah. Hannah probably had more info about the weirdness than anybody else. Amelie and Oliver would have to act.

Going to the Elders' Council wasn't something Claire took lightly. She took a shower, fixed her hair carefully, dressed in her best black shirt and pants, and added the delicate cross necklace that Shane had given her, back when they'd first started all this. She had his mother's claddagh ring on, too. It made her feel stronger.

Downstairs, she turned on the TV while she ate her breakfast – eggs wrapped in a flour tortilla, with salsa. She tuned to the local Morganville station. Usually it was full of town propaganda about how great everything was, but not today; today, somebody had decided to put on some actual breaking news.

FAMILY OF FOUR KILLED IN MURDER/SUICIDE

Claire choked on her breakfast burrito. She didn't know the names that flashed on the screen, but it was awful enough, anyway; the kids were fourteen and twelve. The dad had freaked out yesterday, been hospitalised in the crazy ward overnight, then been sent home.

That had been a mistake, and now there were dead people. Dead *kids*.

Claire called up the Morganville Police Department and asked to be put through to Chief Moses. Hannah wasn't in the office, but the switchboard put the call through to her in her patrol car. She sounded stressed. 'What is it, Claire? It's a busy day.'

'I understand, but I need to get into the Elders' Council today. Can I go with you?'

'Why would you want to do that?'

'Because I need to tell them about what I think is causing these problems around town.'

Hannah was quiet a moment, then said, 'All right. I'll come get you in half an hour. Stay there. Don't go outside.'

Claire felt a stab of unease. 'Why?'

'Things are getting worse. We lost a whole family last night, and there are plenty of other problems. Just stay where you are, all right? This is important.'

'I'll be here.' Claire hung up and stared down at her blank cell phone screen as if it might contain the secrets of the universe. Then she went to the window and looked out.

At first, she couldn't see anything odd at all, but then she saw flashing police lights three streets over. She could just make out struggling shapes.

One of them was *on fire*. Like a vampire who'd

decided to stroll around in the daylight.

Claire stepped back from the window and ran into Michael, who was standing behind her. She whirled, slammed her hand into his chest, and pushed him back. 'Hey!' she said sharply. 'Creep much, Michael? Man, don't do that!'

He stared at her as if he'd never seen her before. 'What?' she demanded. Her heart was still pounding from the shock. She was waiting for him to say *boo* or laugh or shove her back, like they normally would.

He said, 'What are you doing here?'

'Looking out the window?'

'I don't know what you think you're doing, but you can't just...' He hesitated, and seemed to waver a little, as if he'd gone dizzy. 'Can't just—'

'Michael?'

'Can't just come in here and—'

'Michael!'

He put a hand to his head, as if he hurt, and squeezed his eyes shut. Then he took a deep breath, looked at her, and said, 'Oh, hey, you're up. Is there any coffee?'

She just stared at him, trying to see any more signs that something was going wrong with him. She remembered the vampire at Marjo's Diner – and how suddenly she'd flipped out on that poor waitress. Could it happen to Michael? Could she end up fighting him off any second? Not that she'd be *able* to fight him off. Michael was tall, strong, and very, very fast. She'd have a better chance of punching a speeding truck.

'I'll take that as a no,' he said. 'OK, I'll make the coffee. What's up with the window?'

She wordlessly pointed out to the flashing police car lights. They'd thrown a blanket over whoever was on fire. Michael looked, and then said, 'What do you think? International spy ring? Meth lab? People who pissed off Oliver this week?'

He sounded so *normal* now. And he obviously didn't even remember having that little...glitch. Claire cleared her throat and said, 'I'll make coffee.' It gave her an excuse to walk away from him, although he followed her into the kitchen. She got out the filters and the coffee and started loading the machine while Michael got down two mugs and put them on the table. 'Hannah's picking me up,' she said. 'I'll ask her about your international-spy-ring theory.'

'I'm betting on meth lab.'

Claire poured the water in and started up the machine, which hissed and gurgled and immediately reminded her of the gutted, reworked mechanical zombie of Ada under the basement of the lab. 'Did you sleep OK?'

'Yeah, why? Didn't you?'

She had, but now she wanted to crawl back in bed

and pull the covers over her head. 'Did...ah, did you have any dreams?'

Now he was really looking at her as if she was a mental case. 'Sure, I guess. Why do you want to talk about my dreams all of a sudden? What did *you* dream? Am I going to be embarrassed I asked?'

She'd been hoping maybe he'd casually say, *Yeah, I had this weird dream where I didn't know you,* but instead, she'd made him think there was something wrong with her. Perfect. The coffee machine started filling the pot, to her relief. Michael was easily distracted with coffee. Sure enough, as soon as there was enough for a cup, he got up, took it off the burner, and poured half in his mug, half in hers. That was nice of him. 'Claire?' he asked, as he slotted the glass carafe back in its spot. 'Anything you want to tell me?'

'Not...specifically.'

'Why is Hannah picking you up?'

Oh, *that.* She was almost relieved. 'I need to go to the Elders' Council today, that's all. Nothing dangerous, I promise.'

'You're not trying to get that kid Kyle out of the cage, are you? Because that would be dangerous on a lot of fronts.'

Well, she might try to talk Amelie out of it, but she didn't think Michael necessarily needed to know that. 'I'm not going to do anything crazy,' she said, which was safe, because *crazy* these days was definitely open to interpretation. 'I just want to talk to her about the machine. I don't think it's working right, Michael. And now people are—'

'Dying,' he said softly. 'I saw the news. You think he killed his family because of whatever's going wrong with the machine?'

'It's like the vampire in the diner who went crazy. I think that man knew something was wrong, and he couldn't deal with it.' Claire shuddered. 'It must seem like a nightmare, and you can't wake up. I tried to tell Myrnin, but he...he was weird about it. Weirder than usual, I mean.'

That made Michael pause in sipping his coffee. 'He's not doing anything he shouldn't be doing, right?'

'Like what?'

'Like hitting on you.'

'Ew. No, of course not. He doesn't see me that way.' Michael shook his head and went back to his coffee. 'What? You think he does?'

'Sometimes he looks at you a little – oddly, that's all. Maybe you're right. Maybe he just wants you for your blood.'

'Again, *ew*! What's with you this morning?'

'Not enough coffee.' The pot was filled now, so he got up and refilled his mug. She didn't get a second free service, but, Claire reflected, maybe she didn't need more coffee this morning. She was plenty jittery.

They got off of the subject of Myrnin, which was a relief, and onto things Michael liked to talk about, like the new songs he was writing. His demo CD was going to be out in the next two months, and he was supposed to see the packaging for it soon, too. That was cool.

He was telling her all about it when the doorbell rang. Hannah. Claire dumped out the rest of her coffee, told Michael she'd call if anything happened, and bounced.

Hannah was dressed in her cop uniform, looking serious and intimidating, even though she was lounging against a pillar on the porch with her arms folded. She turned her head as Claire came out and locked the door. She'd gathered up her braided hair, tied it, and put it up in a kind of bun; it looked cool, but then Hannah always looked cool. It was something she just radiated, like body heat. 'Morning, Claire.'

'Hey.' Claire nodded. 'Do you want some coffee? We just made a pot.'

'I've got some in the car. Let's go.' Hannah was already heading down the walk towards her cruiser, so Claire hurried after her, taking two steps for every one of Hannah's longer legs. 'Thanks for staying inside.'

Claire got in on the passenger side of the police car and put on her seat belt. As Hannah started the car, she said, 'What was happening?'

'Where?'

'Over there.' Claire pointed in the approximate direction where she'd seen the other police cars. 'Something happened.'

'Nothing you need to worry about right now.' That wasn't like Hannah Moses at all. She was usually relaxed, calm, confident, and she was hardly ever evasive. Now she sounded tense.

Claire tried for humour. 'Michael and I had a bet. He said meth lab. I say international spy ring.'

'Neither,' Hannah said, and pulled the car away from the curb. 'What are you going to tell the council?'

'I...don't want to talk about it yet.'

'You should,' Hannah said. 'My lover woke up this morning and didn't recognise me.'

Claire blinked. 'Your...what?'

'Yes, get over it, Claire; women older than you have boyfriends. But he didn't know who I was. He said he'd never met me.' Hannah was *crying*. Not a lot, just a shimmer of tears in her eyes, but it was chilling. Claire didn't know what to say. 'It lasted a while, and then he was fine. It's been happening all over town, but only to some people. For some it's worse than others, and it doesn't seem to go away. You heard about the murders?' Claire nodded. 'Do you know something about what's causing it?'

'I—' Claire swallowed hard. 'Maybe. Yeah. I think so.'

Hannah pressed harder on the gas. 'Then let's get you to the council, because I want this stopped. I never want to feel that again, and I never want to work another murder scene like the one I saw last night.'

Claire shuddered, and changed the subject. 'Is...is he human? Your boyfriend, I mean.'

'Yeah, he's human. Why?'

'It's not just humans who get it, whatever it is. Vampires do, too.' Claire hesitated, then plunged on. 'I think Michael forgot who I was this morning. Not for long, just for maybe a minute or two. But I don't think it's the first time he's forgotten.'

Hannah looked, if possible, even grimmer. 'That's not good news. Not at all.'

'I know.' Claire couldn't shake the memory of the vampire in the diner, who said the world was wrong, and then tried to kill the first person who came close. What if that happened to Michael? To Oliver? God, to *Amelie*? 'That vampire who went crazy, the one from Marjo's Diner the other night – how long did it take for her to come out of it?'

Hannah gave her a sideways look as she made the last turn towards Founder's Square, and slowed for the security station they had to pass. 'She didn't,' she said. 'Best we can tell, she never will.'

CHAPTER NINE

Kyle was still in the cage in the middle of the park, heavily guarded; Claire caught a glimpse of the barred square box and the heavy police presence as the car passed the borders of the square, and then took a ramp down to the underground parking beneath the buildings. Hannah had a reserved space, and as they walked towards the elevator it opened with a hiss. One of Amelie's black-suited guards – the woman – nodded to Hannah and looked at Claire with pointed intensity.

'She's with me,' Hannah said. 'I'll take responsibility.'

'Good enough,' the vampire agreed, and pressed the button for the meeting floor. 'I'll warn you, they're not in a wonderful mood.'

'They never are.'

The vampire chuckled, a very human sort of sound,

but somehow at least twenty per cent more sinister.
'Well, that's true. Good luck.'

Once they'd stepped out of the elevator, the vampire
was all business again, following Hannah and Claire
as they walked down the long marble hall to a set of
polished wooden doors that opened before they arrived,
from inside. Claire supposed that was intended to look
impressive, but it wasn't any big trick; the vampires
could clearly hear them coming.

There was only one guard in the room this time,
and their escort stopped outside and pulled the doors
shut behind them. Amelie was seated in her place, and
so was Richard; there were folders on the table, each
one neatly labelled.

Oliver was pacing, hands behind his back.

'You're late,' he snapped at Hannah. The guard was
right – he was clearly not in a good mood. Hannah
sat down beside Richard, leaving Claire standing in
indecision. 'And you've brought a friend. How...nice.'

Claire quickly sat down in the first available chair.
Oliver was eyeing her like a piece of trash he was
considering taking out.

'Claire,' Amelie said. 'This is unexpected.' Unexpected,
Claire thought, did not mean welcome. Amelie, like
Hannah, looked uncharacteristically tense.

'I needed to talk to you,' Claire said. 'Both of you.'

'*Must* we always be distracted by the yapping of

your favourite pet?' Oliver said, and crossed the room in a flash to slap both hands flat on the table, glaring at Amelie. 'Silence her until we're done. She shouldn't be here.'

That was...shocking. Claire had never seen him quite that aggressive towards the Founder before. It occurred to her, uneasily, that maybe she ought to have called Amelie first before showing up.

Amelie didn't flinch, blink, or react to Oliver's anger in any way. 'She's not my pet,' she said evenly, 'and I don't take orders from you, Oliver. Truly, you must try to remember that from time to time.'

He showed his teeth, but not his vampire teeth. Not quite. He pushed off from the table and paced again, moving like a lion who wanted a gazelle very, very badly.

Amelie turned her attention to Claire and said, 'You'll wait until our business is done. He's quite right. You shouldn't be here.'

Claire nodded. She didn't really want to wait – she wanted to blurt it all out – but there was a warning in Amelie's cold grey eyes that made it clear blurting was not a good idea.

'You are on edge, Oliver,' Amelie said. 'Sit, please.'

He threw her a filthy look and kept on pacing, back and forth. 'I had to put down one of my own last night, like a rabid dog. Do you imagine I should feel relaxed?'

Claire bent her head close to Hannah and whispered, 'What happened?' Hannah shook her head in warning. 'But I—'

Oliver rounded on her, eyes flaring red. 'Do you want to know what happened, Claire?' he said. 'Which part of it? The part where one of my oldest associates lost her mind and began to attack humans in the street? The part where I couldn't reason with her? Or the part where I was forced to kill her, on *Amelie's* orders?'

That met with ringing silence. Amelie continued to watch him, face calm and smooth, body very still. After a moment, she said, very quietly, 'You are overwrought. Sit down, Oliver. Please.'

'I will not,' he snapped, and turned his back.

After another moment of silence, Amelie went back to the open folder before her. 'Then let us move on to the business at hand. This request to expand the hunting permits is unacceptable. They're asking for four times the current limit, and they want to include the university grounds as well. This is highly risky to all of us. My proposal is that, rather than expanding hunting licenses, we discontinue the program altogether and seek another alternative. There are always a few humans who would willingly volunteer to be bitten.'

Richard started to say something, but he was crushed by Oliver. 'This is an old, tired argument. Are we vampires or not? We *hunt*. That's our nature.

Restricting it, even outlawing it, doesn't curb our instincts. It only makes us criminals for having them.'

'Oh, but I fully expect you to control your instincts, as I do. Unless you're unable to master yourself. Are you, Oliver?' Amelie's tone was sharper than Claire expected, almost...angry. It occurred to her, finally, that Amelie was upset, too.

Very bad combination, having both of them on edge, in a confined space.

This time, Oliver did flash fangs at her. 'You're on dangerous ground, woman. Don't push me.' Amelie's guard took a step away from the door. 'And don't presume to have your dogs threaten me, either. I've supported your rule in this town. I've even agreed to your experiments and social rules of behaviour. But I *will not* allow you to make us into pale copies of humans. It is not who we are, or who we should be, and you know that better than anyone.'

'I take it you will not entertain any alternative plans,' Amelie said after a moment. 'Then we will leave the program as it is, with a limited number of licenses, and the university remains protected ground.'

Oliver laughed. 'Are you *listening*? They won't obey you for much longer. They'll do as they choose, regardless of the law. They're angry, Amelie. You've allowed *humans* to kill vampires and walk away. If you choose to punish vampires for following their natures, you're as stupid as you were when you thought you could manipulate your way onto a throne as a girl of twelve. You never did reach that goal, did you? I'm sure dying a mere princess never sat well with you. That must be why you appointed yourself queen here.'

Amelie stood up, and the room went very, very quiet. Claire no longer felt the urge to try to talk. She felt the urge to crawl under the table. It was as if she, Richard, and Hannah no longer existed, at least to Amelie and Oliver.

'Are you telling me that you no longer want to serve as my second?' Amelie asked him. 'Because that is what I hear.'

'Amelie...' Oliver's voice was full of angry frustration. He, at least, hadn't forgotten the presence of others, and glanced quickly aside at the humans. 'Send them out. We need to settle this. It's been a long time in coming.'

'Richard and Hannah are equal members of this council. I will not dismiss them like servants.'

He laughed, and Claire saw the sharp glitter of his fangs. '*Equal?* How long have you been deluding yourself like this? You think any of them are ever *equal* to us? You are ceding control of this town to fools and mortals, bit by bit, and we are all going to suffer for it. *Die* for it. It *cannot* go on!'

'Sit down,' Amelie said. 'Now.'

'No. You are destroying us, Amelie, and I can't – I won't permit it to continue.'

They froze in place, staring at each other, and Claire hardly dared to breathe at all.

Oliver didn't blink. He finally said, 'Your human pets are turning on us. They're turning on *you*. The boy in the cage down there is proof enough of how much in contempt the humans hold your rules, and you. And they're not wrong, because we are killers, and they are our natural victims. If we let them have control they will destroy us. They have no choice.'

'That's not true,' Claire said. She hadn't exactly meant to say it, but now it was out, hanging in the air, and Oliver's attention was on her like a freezing blanket of snow. 'It doesn't have to be that way.'

He whirled to face her, and she wished she'd kept her mouth shut. 'So what is your solution, little Claire? Keep us in zoos, the way you keep other predators who threaten you? Exterminate those you can't control? That's what humans *do*. We know this. We used to be just as flawed, just as human.' Oliver looked back at Amelie. 'I'd have wiped all vampires off of the face of the land, in my breathing days. If I could have managed it.'

She smiled thinly. 'I know very well what you would have done,' she said. 'You did the same in your day with humans who worshipped differently from you and yours. But not all humans are as genocidally inclined as you.'

He hit the table so hard it vibrated. 'I did what was right!'

'You did what was right for those who agreed with you, and that is all in the past. We are talking about our *future*. Oliver, we cannot live as we did. We cannot hide in the shadows and run when discovered, like rats. In this modern age, there is no hiding among the humans, not for long. And you know it.' She hesitated, and then said softly, 'You must trust me, as you once did.'

He laughed, a rusty, raw sound, and turned to go.

Amelie flashed around the table in a white blur and put her back to the door before he reached it. He paused just a step away from her. Seeing them that close together, Claire realised how tall he was, and how he towered over her. Amelie looked fragile, suddenly. Vulnerable.

'Don't make me do this,' Amelie said. 'I value you. Don't destroy the peace we have.'

He reached out and fastened his hand on her arm. The guard moved towards them. Amelie shook her head, and the guard stopped, but stayed ready to jump. 'Out of my way,' Oliver said. 'This is useless. I've bowed to you for too long, and if I continue to do it, we will all suffer. You can't change us, Amelie. You can't change *me*. For the love of God, stop trying.'

'Sit. *Down*.'

'No. I've been your trained dog long enough.'

She broke free of his grip and slapped her hands on both sides of his face, freezing him in place. Her eyes…her eyes went *white*. Pure, cold, icy white. Claire looked away, because what howled through the room just then was a feeling of wild power nothing like she'd ever felt from Amelie before. Hannah and Richard had moved out of their chairs and were pressed against the far wall. Even the guard was backing up.

'Do *not* defy me,' Amelie said fiercely. 'I don't want to destroy you, but I will rather than allow you to hunt and kill as you wish. Do you understand me?'

It had to be impossible for Oliver to do anything but agree. Claire felt the pressure in the room increase, a kind of heavy psychic weight that made her gasp and want to curl into a ball – and it wasn't even aimed at her.

Amelie opened her mouth, and her fangs slid down, elegant and slow. She was no longer vulnerable. Not at all. She was…terrifying.

Oliver had to kneel to her. He *had to*. Claire could feel just the edges of what Amelie was doing, but the pressure on Oliver must have been like the weight of the ocean, driving him to submit.

He took a deep breath and brought his arms up sharply between hers, and knocked her hands away from his face. Amelie's eyes widened in surprise, and then he reached out and put *his* hands on *her* face.

Amelie's eyes faded back to grey, then turned very dark. 'No,' she said. 'No.'

'Yes,' Oliver said. 'I warned you before. I won't be ruled. Not even by you. I don't wish to do this, but you've left me no choice.'

Amelie was shuddering now. Power was pouring out of Oliver, and unlike Amelie's cold control, his felt hot, blood-hot, pounding like a pulse. Overwhelming. Claire's head was splitting from the pressure, and she saw Richard and Hannah were feeling the same pain.

'Submit,' Oliver said. 'Submit and I'll spare you the humiliation of kneeling.'

'No,' she whispered, but it was weak. Only a thread of sound. Her eyes had turned black. 'You will never have me, Oliver. Never.'

'I already have you,' he said.

'No.'

'This has been coming for so many years. You knew it. Let go. Amelie, I don't want to hurt you.'

It seemed to take everything Amelie had, but she struck his hands away from her face, just as he'd done to her. Her eyes paled back to grey. She was breathing, *visibly* breathing, which for a vampire meant she'd just done something extremely hard. 'I will never be your creature, Oliver,' she said, voice trembling. 'I will accept you as an equal. Never as a conqueror. You should know that by now.'

He stared down at her, and Claire felt the pressure in the room slowly bleed away. She should have felt relieved, but instead she just wanted to collapse and sleep. Hannah and Richard were holding hands, she noticed. That seemed odd. Maybe they were just as freaked out as she was.

'Equals,' Oliver said. 'How could we ever be equals, do you imagine? We aren't made for such things. We both need to rule. It's in our natures.'

'Then force me to submit. Or walk away.'

Oliver shook his head, and Claire thought he started to turn, but then his right hand shot out and closed around Amelie's throat, slamming her back against the wood. She tried to speak, but his grip was cutting off her voice.

'We can't be equals,' he said. 'I'm sorry. I never wanted it to come to this.'

And he *bit her in the throat.*

Claire screamed.

Oliver was drinking Amelie's blood. Amelie was fighting him, but he was too strong for her, and her guard...her guard wasn't moving.

'Do something!' Claire screamed at the guard, but

he just *stood there*. She dashed to the other door and threw it open. The female vamp was on guard there, and turned when Claire screamed at her, too.

But she didn't do anything, either.

Oliver suddenly let go of Amelie and stepped back, wiping blood from his mouth with the back of one hand. She stood there, eyes closed, and put a trembling hand over the wound on her neck. There was blood spilt on her immaculate white jacket. She didn't speak.

Oliver turned the guard and said, 'See her to a chair. Gently.'

The guard bowed his head briefly, then came towards her, but Amelie's eyes snapped open. 'Don't touch me,' she snapped, but he didn't obey her. Not at all. He took her arm and guided her back to a chair at the side of the table...not the head, where she'd been sitting before. Amelie shook free and sank down. She looked ill now, and angry, and humiliated.

Oliver stood where he was for a moment, then turned and addressed the other guard. 'Go get Ysandre and John,' he said. 'I want them here.'

The guard nodded and left. '*Ysandre?*' Claire said. 'You're bringing *her* in here?' Ysandre was a stone-cold menace. Amelie had kept her in prison for a while, and Claire hadn't seen her much recently. She'd hoped that someone had accidentally thrown her under a bus.

Ysandre had tried to hit on Shane. And that alone was reason enough to hate her.

'Quiet,' Oliver said. 'Sit down, all of you. You have no reason to panic. The situation is under control.' Under *his* control, which was in itself plenty of cause for panic, not to mention freak-out. But Claire didn't dare *not* obey, not until she understood what had happened, and why.

Richard looked at Amelie and asked, 'Are you all right?'

She opened her eyes and made her face into a smooth mask, showing nothing of whatever she was feeling now. 'I'm well enough,' she said. She took her hand away from her throat. The wound was already closed and healing. 'Don't interfere. This is an internal matter.'

'I know, but if you need me to help—'

'You can't help. I tried to keep my position. I failed.' She lowered her gaze to the table. 'Oliver leads the town now.'

'No,' Claire whispered. 'No, that can't be true. That isn't right. You're the Founder; you're—'

'Defeated,' Amelie said. 'Enough, Claire. There is nothing to be done now. He spared me some of the more humiliating aspects that could have accompanied the transfer of power. I won't disrespect that favour by rebelling now.'

Oliver didn't say anything. He took his seat at the head of the table, and a moment later the vamp guard came back, with two others – John, who owned the hospital and several clinics in town, including the blood bank. John had long blonde curly hair and a proud, sharp face. He looked like he'd rather be anywhere else. And next to him...Ysandre.

Ysandre was just exactly as Claire remembered her from her days as Amelie's father Bishop's follower. She was beautiful, and smoky, and sexy in a sleazy kind of way – that was mostly her clothes, because she loved low-cut crop tops and even lower-cut jeans. She trailed fingers over the back of Richard Morrell's neck, and he slapped them away with a glare.

'Temper,' Ysandre purred, and even in that one word Claire could hear the sickly sweet Southern accent. 'I'm just trying to be friendly. We're all friends here now, right?'

'Oh, for God's sake, do shut up,' John said wearily. He had an English accent that was a lot more charming than Ysandre's put-on drawl. 'Founder? You had something to—' Awareness dawned in his face, and Claire thought he must have sensed what had happened. His expression looked a lot like horror, and he stared at Oliver. 'No. No, that's not possible.'

'I'm afraid it is,' Oliver said. 'You command loyalty from many of Amelie's closest friends and supporters. I need you to spread the word. I am now in charge. You may hear it from her own lips.'

John definitely looked horrified now. Claire couldn't blame him. She was feeling pretty awful herself. 'Madam?' He went to one knee beside Amelie's chair. 'Command me and I'll obey.'

'There is nothing to command,' she said. 'You can feel the shift of power. It is a fact of nature, one none of us can fight. Obey him, John. I wouldn't wish to see you, or any of you, harmed.'

John took her hand and pressed it to his forehead in what looked like real grief, and then stood up and faced Oliver. 'No one will support this,' he said. 'Watch your back, Oliver. You were well treated, and you've betrayed her. We won't forget.'

'John, don't,' Amelie said. She sounded tired.

'I'm not threatening. I am stating facts. Which you know well, Oliver.'

Oliver nodded. 'I don't care how you feel about it. Bargain with yourself as you wish, but go and tell your fellows that I am now in charge, and I won't take any challenges to my power. I am not Amelie. Test me, and I'll destroy you.'

John's eyes flared a rebellious red, but he bowed stiffly and walked out of the room.

Ysandre laughed. 'What a sanctimonious old frog,' she said. 'Well, Ollie? I think I threw my lot in with the winning side this time. We're going to have a *wonderful* time. Where should we start? Let's just declare open season on the humans and kick it off right. I feel a good hunt coming on.'

Oliver looked at her with the same kind of distaste he'd just got from John. 'You're *not* my second,' he said. 'Don't presume to be informal with me. I spared your life for a specific reason, but don't think that it has anything to do with fondness.'

She frowned. 'What do you mean, I'm not your second? Who's going to challenge me for it, *John*?'

'There's to be no challenge. Amelie is my second.'

'*Amelie?*' Ysandre sounded furious, and Claire saw her hands clench. 'You can't be serious. You can't keep her around. She'll have a dagger in your back first chance she gets—'

'Like you would? I've seen how you treat your friends as well as your enemies, presuming you make any distinction between the two at all. Don't push me. I interceded for you when Amelie wanted to wall you up in a cell with Bishop. You can show your gratitude by remembering your place, which is definitely not at my side,' Oliver said. 'Go to my people. Tell them what's happened. Tell them I expect *nothing* to change until they hear differently, but that change will come. But it will be controlled, and measured, and I will look badly on any attempts to push it faster.'

Ysandre stared at him through narrowed eyes, and Claire thought she was just as angry as John, but for different reasons. She finally shrugged and said, 'Whatever you want, boss man. If you want to be a fool, go right ahead. You just got the big chair. Good luck holding on to it, with that kind of attitude.' She turned her attention to Claire, on the other side of the table, and smiled. 'Well, if it isn't the little bit of nothing. How's Shane?' She licked her lips. 'I've been missing him.'

Claire gave the vampire her best impression of Amelie's cold look. 'If I see you around Shane I'll stake you.'

Ysandre made a little *O* of her mouth, and then said, 'No empty threat, is it? I'll just bet you've got a stake somewhere, don't you? Bet you never go anywhere without it.'

Claire glanced over at her backpack. She'd brought it, but she'd set it in the corner, out of the way. It was on Ysandre's side of the table.

'I'd better go on and disarm her, boss,' Ysandre said. 'Security and all.'

Oliver looked irritated, but he didn't stop her. She went to the backpack, opened it, and dumped books and papers all over the floor.

A silver-coated stake tumbled out to thump on the carpet at her feet. Then a silver-coated knife.

'Well, well, well. I think these ought to be illegal, don't you?' Ysandre grabbed one of Claire's papers and wrapped it around the stake's handle, and one around the knife's, and strolled back to the table. 'Dangerous weapons, especially in council chambers.'

And before Claire or anyone else could suspect what she was going to do, she stabbed Amelie in the back, through the heart, with the stake. Amelie screamed and toppled out of her chair, limp, to the floor. Claire felt like the world was moving at nightmare speeds – Ysandre was too fast, Claire was too slow, she couldn't do anything to stop it as Ysandre yanked on Amelie's white-blonde hair and exposed her throat to the knife.

'No!' Oliver shouted, and sprang to his feet.

'*I'm* going to be your second whether you like it or not!' Ysandre yelled back, and put the knife to Amelie's throat. 'And the first thing is, get rid of the competition!'

Oliver lunged across the table. He hit her so hard he threw her into the far doors, which broke off the hinges, and Ysandre and the doors slid down the marble hallway for twenty feet before coming to a stop. She was still moving, weakly, but Oliver snapped his fingers and pointed the guards in her direction.

'No,' he said. 'You're finished. Amelie was right after all: you're too stupid to be allowed to live.'

He went to Amelie, kicked the fallen knife out of the way, and dropped to his knees beside her. She was frozen by the stake, and where the silver touched her, it was burning her. Ysandre's paper handle had fallen off, but Oliver didn't wait. He grabbed the silver and pulled it out of her back in one fast motion, and threw the stake into the corner. Claire caught a glimpse of his hand turning black from the contact, but he didn't pause, didn't seem to feel the pain.

He cradled Amelie's head in his hands. 'It's out,' he said. 'Can you hear me? *Amelie!*'

She still wasn't moving. Oliver pulled her into his arms. The female guard came back, pulling Ysandre's struggling body by the hair, and he snapped, 'Get Theo Goldman. *Now*. And put that one in a cage until I decide how we should be rid of her. Something painful, preferably.'

Amelie's eyes slowly blinked. She focused on Oliver's face. Claire had never seen her look so pale; her lips looked blue, and even her eyes seemed faded. 'You should have let her finish,' she whispered. 'Better death than dishonour, isn't that our code?'

'Hundreds of years ago it was,' he agreed. His voice was different now. Gentle. 'You're the last one to cling to the past. How bad is the pain?'

She seemed to think about it. 'Compared to what? To what you've done to me?'

He was holding her hand, and now he raised it to his lips. 'I wouldn't have acted unless you forced me. But we both know that I don't lose once I'm challenged.'

'You did,' she whispered. 'Once. To me.'

He kept her hand at his lips. 'So I did,' he said, so softly Claire almost missed it. 'I will never hurt you again. I swear it.' He hesitated, and then drew one sharpened fingernail across his wrist. 'Drink. I give it to you freely.'

A drop of his blood hit her lips, and she gasped, opening her eyes wide. She reached for his arm and pulled the cut to her lips, drank, and then let go. She sighed and went limp. Her eyes closed. Claire's throat closed up tight. She wanted to ask, but couldn't.

Richard asked for her. 'Is she dead?'

'Not yet,' Oliver said. 'A silver stake wouldn't kill her immediately at her age, even in her weakened condition with the loss of blood. But she needs additional treatment.' He looked up at Richard, at Hannah, and finally at Claire. 'No one speaks of this. No one.'

'You mean we don't say that you saved her?' Richard asked. 'Or that you love her?'

Oliver said, without blinking, 'Say it again and we will be electing a new mayor, boy. I'm not in the mood to tolerate more human nonsense today; do you understand me?'

'I understand that you want to turn this town into a cattle pen. That *my* people are going to be hunted and killed without mercy. So you know what, Oliver? If you want to run Morganville your way, you won't just be looking for a new mayor. You'll be looking for a place to hide while we tear this town apart.' Richard got up and just...walked out. Hannah sat for a moment, then got up and followed him.

Leaving Claire alone with him.

Oliver was looking down at Amelie's still, quiet face. He said, without raising his head, 'You should have gone with them. You have no part in this.'

'I can't go,' Claire said. 'I need to tell you something.'

'Then say it and leave.'

Her throat was dry, and she knew – *knew* – that he was ready to kill the next person who annoyed him just now. Amelie wouldn't, couldn't stop him. But she had to say it. She had to try.

'You said you had to kill a vampire last night,' she said. 'Not the one from the diner?'

'No,' Oliver said. He didn't look up at her. 'An old friend. I couldn't stop him any other way.'

'Did he say anything?'

'What?' Oliver looked up, frowning. 'No. He was beyond speaking anything like sense.'

'But he did speak.'

'Only to scream that nothing was right.'

That confirmed it, and Claire felt a cold, heavy sense of guilt. 'People are forgetting who they are. Or where. Or else they know something's wrong, but they can't tell what it is, and it's driving them crazy.'

'Then it's obviously not confined to humans,' Oliver said. 'Blood analysis on the affected vampires shows nothing. It's not the same as the illness we were enduring before.' So he *did* know. And he'd even done something about it, or tried.

'Then it's got to be the machine, the one Myrnin and I fixed. It started about the time we turned it on.' He raised his head and met her eyes, and her mouth, if possible, went even dryer. 'Myrnin doesn't think there's anything wrong with it. I…I wish that was true, but I think he's in denial. I think the machine is doing this to us, and it's getting worse the longer it's on.'

Oliver was silent for a moment, then said, 'And if we turn it off?'

'Then the barriers go down. But I think the memory problems stop, too.'

'You're certain of this.'

Was she? Because she knew she was staking her life on it. 'Yes.'

Oliver growled, low in his throat, and said, 'Then turn the damned thing off and fix it. Find what's wrong. We can't do without the barriers for long; our human residents are already defying authority, and once they realise the barriers don't function, we will lose control entirely, and this will become a true bloodbath. Do you understand?'

'Yes. I'll turn it off. We'll fix it.'

'Then you'd best get to it. Now get out.'

Claire scrambled out from behind the table and grabbed her backpack. She hesitated over the knife and stake, but scooped them up and stuffed them in before throwing it over her shoulder and running for the door. She looked back, once; Oliver didn't seem to have noticed she'd left. He was still holding Amelie in his arms, and for the first time, she saw real, raw emotion on his face.

Grief.

Dr Theo Goldman stepped off the elevator carrying his doctor's bag. He blinked at Claire as they manoeuvred around each other, him coming out, her going in, and said, 'I was told I had a patient. This is an odd place to find one.'

'It's Amelie,' Claire said. 'That way. Theo?'

He looked back, but kept walking.

'Please help her.'

He nodded, smiled reassuringly, and the doors closed on her before she could say anything else.

CHAPTER TEN

Myrnin wasn't at the lab when she arrived. That was unusual; she thought that maybe he might be sleeping, but when she checked his room at the back, it was neat and empty. He was just...out.

Well, that made things easier.

Claire called home and got Michael and Shane. 'I need you to come help me,' she said. 'And I need a ladder.'

'Tell me you did *not* volunteer us to paint somebody's house,' Shane said. 'That would be a lot like work. I'm already doing work way too much.'

Michael, however, got it immediately. 'You need to get through the trapdoor at the lab. Myrnin's not there?'

'No,' Claire said. 'Can you help?'

'Sure. Open up the portal and we'll come straight through.'

Claire hung up and rolled back the bookcase that blocked the portal – no easy job, because Myrnin hadn't balanced it for humans, although he'd at least removed the lead, which was nice – and unlocked the door from a set of keys she found in the mouth of one of Myrnin's discarded vampire-bunny slippers. She swung it open, concentrating on the Glass House, and the image flickered, wavered, and clarified into reality on the other side of the door.

Shane and Michael were carrying an extendable metal ladder. Claire reached through and gave Shane her hand, and he stepped over, pulling Michael after him along with the ladder.

'Wow,' Shane said, and shivered. 'That's not weird at all.'

'You've done it before,' Claire pointed out. 'When I first fixed the portal.'

'Didn't really think about it that time. Never gets any less strange, though. OK, where to?'

'Here.' She'd already unlocked the trapdoor at the back of the lab and opened it, and Shane leant over and peered down into the darkness. Michael pulled him back.

'What?' Shane asked.

'Better not to present a target before you know what's actually down there, hero. Let's get this ladder in, and then I go first, OK?'

'You bet, tough guy. Last time I was in a dark tunnel, I nearly got my face eaten. I'm a slow learner, but I do learn.'

They extended the ladder down, and Shane held it in place as Michael descended. Claire leant over and said, 'The light switch is at the end of the room.'

'Yeah, I see it – whoa.'

'What?'

Michael was quiet for a moment, then said, 'I'm thinking it's going to be better if I don't tell you. Just hurry.'

Shane went first, and then Claire; the ladder felt rickety, but it held just fine. She hopped the last couple of steps down to land on the cave floor. Michael had turned on the tunnel lights, so there was no risk of walking into an ambush by...whatever, but she was still wondering what he'd seen, exactly. If he wasn't just yanking Shane's chain, of course. He never got tired of that.

No sign of trouble all the way to the big cave, and Michael hit the main switch there to turn on the banks of lights. The machine – Claire hated to call it a computer, really – was sitting exactly as she'd left it, screen showing normal readouts. Nothing wrong at all.

'OK, I need to put in a password,' she said. 'Hang on a second.'

She thought about it, and tried Myrnin's name at the keyboard. No, the red light stayed on. She tried Amelie's. The red light stayed on.

She tried putting in Ada's name.

The red light stayed on.

Claire blinked at it. Myrnin didn't *have* more than three passwords. He couldn't even remember more than one at a time. He didn't have a birthday he could remember; he didn't have any family; what could he possibly use for a password?

Ah. She had it.

Claire.

The red light stayed on. Claire frowned at it. 'Seriously? *Now* you get security conscious?'

'Problem?' Michael asked.

'No. I'll get it.' She tried *Bob*, for Bob the Spider. Bob was busily spinning webs in a fish tank near Myrnin's chair. Myrnin fed him a steady diet of crickets and flies, which seemed to make Bob happy. That qualified as a pet, right? People liked to use pet names for passwords.

It wasn't Bob either.

She tried, in desperation, *Oliver*. Not it. She plugged in the names of every possible vampire she could remember, including Bishop.

None of them worked.

'At least he didn't put a lockout on it,' she muttered.

She'd tried at least thirty passwords, without success. 'Come *on*, I built you, you stupid piece of junk! Give me a break!'

'How about pulling the plug?' Shane asked. 'Just turn off the power.'

She thought about it, but shook her head. 'I don't know what everything does in here. I could shut down something vital. Or destroy something we can't rebuild easily.' She sighed. 'He won't be happy, but I'm going to have to ask Myrnin for the password.'

Michael's head suddenly turned, but before he could speak, a rich, slow voice from the darkness said, 'Ask Myrnin what, precisely?'

That was Myrnin's voice. His *hunting* voice. Claire had heard it before, and it gave her immediate, life-threatening chills. He stepped out of the dark. The cheerfully neon Hawaiian clothes were gone. He was dressed in elegant black, with a blood red vest, and his long hair was freshly combed and rippling in waves down to his shoulders, very old-school Gothic vamp. He was smiling.

Not in a nice way at all.

'Visitors,' he said, still using that creepy, oddly soothing voice. There was something about it that made Claire feel a little sleepy. A little...relaxed. 'So lovely to have visitors. I get them so seldom. Especially here.'

'Myrnin,' Claire said. He was steadily coming towards her, without looking like he was moving at all. His large eyes were fixed on her, luminous, *fascinating*. She couldn't blink.

'Yes, my dear. How surprising that you know.'

'Know what?' She felt stupid, almost drugged. He was close now, gliding up to her. She felt the cool brush of his fingers on her cheek.

'My name,' he said. 'How surprising that you know my name. Perhaps you should do me the courtesy of giving me yours.'

A rush of adrenalin spilt into her body. *He didn't know her.* Or Michael. Or Shane. He was acting like they were strangers.

To him, they were intruders.

She licked her lips and said, 'Myrnin, I work for you. I'm Claire. Remember? Claire.'

'Nice try, sweet one, but I already have an assistant. Maybe I'll save you for her. She'd like you.'

Ada. Claire's heart thumped painfully as she took it in. Myrnin had been sucked under by the machine, and he thought Ada was still here. Still alive.

'You're talking about Ada,' she said, and tried to keep her voice calm and even. 'She's not here, Myrnin. She's not coming back. Ada's dead.'

It was kind of cruel to say it like that, but she

needed to snap him out of it, and that was the verbal equivalent of a hard slap.

Myrnin pulled up short, dark eyes gone cool and unreadable, and then he slowly smiled. 'I'd know if she was gone,' he said. 'Can't you feel her? She's here. She'll be back. I know she'll be back.'

'Claire?' Shane said. He started to move towards them, but Myrnin suddenly backhanded him, and sent him rolling towards the wall.

'No interruptions,' he said. 'I'm *talking*!' He was suddenly, terrifyingly angry. 'Why would you say something like that, I wonder? Unless you'd done something to Ada?'

'Stop,' Michael said urgently. 'Claire, come over here.'

Myrnin made an exaggerated, annoyed motion with his hands and turned to face Michael. 'I *said* no interruptions! Oh – you're not human, are you? Hmm. One of Amelie's latest, I take it. I thought she'd sworn off of new fledglings, after that last disaster.'

Michael grabbed Claire's arm and pulled her close. 'Yeah, well, I'm Amelie's, and this one's mine. That other one, too.'

Shane, Claire thought, would punch him for that one. When he finally got up.

Myrnin's eyebrows slowly rose. 'Are you telling me that you brought snacks, and you're not going to share?

How rude. You're an intruder, too, you know. I don't have a taste for you just now, but these other two... well. I haven't drunk a good intruder in *ages*.'

'Myrnin, wake up!' Claire yelled. 'It's *Claire*! You know who I am!'

Myrnin shook his head sadly. 'You'd better eat her now,' he told Michael. 'She's far too loud. Makes my head hurt.'

And then he hit his forehead with the heel of his hand, again and again and again, frighteningly hard. Claire clung to Michael. She'd seen Myrnin do crazy things, but this was just...creepy.

He stopped. He'd opened up a cut on his forehead, and blood that was slightly paler than a human's trickled down towards his eyes. It closed in seconds. 'That's better,' he breathed. 'Now. You, new fledgling. You owe me a tribute, since you came here without permission. Choose.'

'Choose what?' Michael asked.

'Which one I will have.' Myrnin's fangs came down, lazy and terrifying, and he reached out for Claire. 'I think I like this one.'

Michael kicked him, right in the chest. It drove Myrnin back, but not very far.

Myrnin stopped smiling, and tilted his head forward. It made him look crazier. 'That wasn't wise, blood child. Not wise at all.'

'Run,' Michael said to Claire, and shoved her towards the tunnel. Myrnin snarled and jumped, but Michael got him in midair and pulled him down, hard.

Myrnin missed grabbing onto Claire's foot by about three inches. She hesitated at the base of the ladder. Shane was still in there, maybe hurt. She couldn't just run.

She heard Michael let out a muffled cry, and then Myrnin said, in a voice that echoed silkily off the tunnel walls, 'I like rats that run. Here, little rat. I'm going to save you for Ada.'

She swarmed up the ladder as fast as she could. She was halfway up when she felt it vibrate. Myrnin had jumped and landed on the rungs just a few feet below her. He was almost within grabbing range.

Claire kicked him in the face as soon as he was closer.

'Ow!' he yelped, surprised. She did it again. 'Ow, *stop*, you hellion! What do you think you're doing?'

She kicked him again, and he lost his grip on the ladder and fell. He landed on his back on the floor, looking surprised. His nose was bloody. He straightened it, and it snapped back in place with a soft crackle.

'Ow,' he said again, and shook his head. 'I won't let you live to regret that, you know.'

Claire raced up the last few steps and flung herself

out onto the lab floor, just as Myrnin tensed his legs and launched straight up, intending to grab her at the top of the ladder. He missed, hit the floor awkwardly, and rolled smoothly up to a crouch.

Claire scrambled up to her feet and ran for her backpack. She didn't want to use the silver, but she didn't know what else to do. She couldn't just let him eat her.

Myrnin seemed to have temporarily lost interest in her. He was standing now, looking around at the lab, mouth half-open. 'What...what in the devil happened? Did Ada do this? My. She's quite a good housekeeper, isn't she? I remember it being so much messier.'

Claire grabbed her backpack on the run and unzipped it. She cut her fingers on the knife she'd crammed inside, but groped around for the hilt and got it out just as Myrnin stopped looking at the scenery and started running for her.

He leapt from table to table, zigzagging as she did, eyes glowing dull red. She saw Michael climb out of the tunnel below, and then pull Shane up after him. Neither one of them looked very good.

Claire waited until Myrnin got close, and then slashed the knife across his chest. She just missed his face.

He stopped, looked down, and said, 'Oh, no, I *loved* this vest.' And then the silver started to burn him. His eyes went from dull red to bright, furious crimson.

He looked at Claire. 'No one fights back. That's strictly against the rules.'

'This isn't you,' she said. 'Please don't do this.'

For a second she actually thought she saw something surface in him, something she recognised...but then it was gone, and the old Myrnin, the cruel one, was back. 'If you come here again,' he said, 'I'll tear you apart. This is *my* home. You're not welcome.'

'Claire!' Michael yelled. 'The portal! Go for it!'

She wasn't far from it, but there was no way she'd be able to beat Myrnin. He was deadly fast, and very angry. She needed to hurt him enough to stop him, at least temporarily.

She lunged, buried the knife in his shoulder, and left it there. She didn't want to do it, but it was the only thing she could think of in that split second. Myrnin was old, maybe even older than Amelie; the silver would hurt him, but it'd take a long time to kill him. She had to take the risk.

It worked. Myrnin howled and grabbed at her, missed, and swatted at the knife, but it was all silver. He couldn't get a grip without burning himself. Claire didn't wait. She sprinted for the portal just as Michael arrived there and pushed Shane through ahead of him.

Claire looked back over her shoulder. Myrnin was

wrapping his torn vest around his hand to pull the knife out.

She plunged through and willed the network to lock down the entrance. She did it just in time; she felt the shock of Myrnin trying to drag it away from her, but she'd had practice at this now, and he was in pain.

His attempts to break through to the Glass House finally stopped.

Claire backed up until she bumped into the sofa, still staring at the blank wall. 'Hey, house?' she called. 'We have to keep Myrnin out. It's important.'

The Glass House had a weird kind of sentience to it – nothing she could name, exactly, but sometimes she asked it to help, and sometimes it even listened. Just now, she felt a rush of warmth, a kind of energy flow that moved through her and towards the portal, overlaying it.

A psychic lock, done better than she could have done it herself.

'Thanks,' she said. She wanted to collapse, but instead she looked around for Michael and Shane.

Shane was lying on the couch. Michael was still standing, but his shirt was shredded, and she saw the faint lines of injuries still healing up.

Shane had a cut on his head, and he still looked woozy.

'Right,' he mumbled. 'Hope somebody remembered

the ladder. That was a good ladder.'

Claire's knees wobbled, and she had to sit down, quickly. It was funny, and not funny at all. It was terrifying.

What had Hannah said about the vampire from the diner recovering? *She didn't. Best we can tell, she never will.* And Oliver had been forced to kill another vampire who went nuts, just last night.

Myrnin was the old Myrnin. The crazy Myrnin, the one he'd been when he'd been at his worst, before he'd killed Ada and put her brain into the machine. He'd been cruel. And he'd been insane.

He wasn't the man she knew at all. And now he knew what they were after.

'We have to get him back,' Claire said aloud, feeling sick and horrified. 'We have to.'

Because she cared about him...but also because Myrnin was the only one who knew the password to shut down the machine.

She tried calling Amelie, but got voice mail. She left a message to send someone to detain Myrnin – more than one someone, preferably heavily armed. Claire promised to try to shut down the machine in the morning, when the lab was Myrnin-free. If she couldn't crack his password, she'd do exactly what Shane suggested: she'd pull the plug. Better to destroy it all than to risk this continuing.

Getting Shane's head examined at the hospital was a little crazy, because of the number of strange incidents and injuries that were going on. Turned out he didn't have a concussion, but he did need stitches at his hairline. Again.

He wasn't too upset. 'Girls love interesting scars,' he said. 'Right? Girls? Are you with me?' Eve held up her hand. So did Claire. Michael and Shane high-fived, but not very hard, because Shane winced. 'At least whatever's going on hasn't hit any of us four. That's good.'

Claire looked at Michael, but he didn't seem to know why she was staring his way. He didn't remember. Or if he did, he'd chalked it up to dreams, the way so many people probably had.

Eve suddenly turned her head and watched someone walk by behind Claire. 'Wow,' she said. 'Can't even come here to get away from the bad elements. Monica on your six, CB.'

Claire looked. It was definitely Monica, heading straight for them. She was trailed by Gina, but not Jennifer – both dressed as if they expected a party to break out any moment, but in oddly out-of-date dresses. There was something strange about the way Monica moved, though. It looked less graceful than Claire was used to, almost awkward.

Monica went right past Claire without a glance,

glared at Eve, smiled at Michael, and focused on Shane. 'Oh, my God, you're here, too! I was wondering where you were. Didn't you get my texts?'

Shane looked at her, winced, and shut his eyes. 'Please make the bad thing go away.' he groaned. 'I've already got a headache.'

Monica's bright smile faltered, and Claire could have sworn she saw hurt flare briefly across her expression. Then the smile just got brighter. 'Oh,' she said. 'I guess you didn't get them. I e-mailed you, too. I'll send everything again.'

'Let's not,' Shane said. 'Are you kidding me? What are we, friends?'

Monica frowned at him. 'Quit being a little prick, Shane. Of *course* we're friends.' She giggled. *Giggled.* 'Well, you know. Kissing friends.'

Shane opened his eyes and stared at her. He opened his mouth, then closed it and looked at Michael, who was staring at Monica with exactly the same WTF look.

'Not that we couldn't be more,' Monica said, and winked at him. 'Remember that make-out session in the closet at school? That was hot, right?'

Shane actually blushed. Little red spots high on his cheeks. Claire stared at them, fascinated, and thought, *This is like watching one of those reality-show train wrecks.* It was almost...entertaining. 'Shut

up,' Shane said. He sounded like he was choking on
something.

'Oh, relax. It's not like we did it or anything. Yet.'

'Seriously. Shut. *Up.*'

Monica must have finally got the idea that Shane
was really not joking, because she looked a little
thrown, then hurried on to another topic. 'So what
happened to you? Oh, we're here because Jennifer
got into her mom's gin or something and forgot how
to drive, even though she just learnt. So funny! She
totally destroyed her mom's car – at least, I think
it was her mom's car. Some kind of red convertible.
Tacky! So she's a couple of rooms over. You?'

'Just do me a favour and leave, Monica. I don't need
the aggravation right now.' When Shane wanted to
be, he could be blunt and kind of mean, and Claire
actually felt a twinge of sympathy for the way Monica's
smile collapsed.

'Jeez, I was just trying to be nice, Collins,' Monica
said. 'You don't have to be such a toe rag *all* the time.
You're not *that* cute, you know. I can do better. Lots
better.'

She flounced off. Literally flounced, with her hair
bouncing. *So* odd.

Shane said, finally, 'Did that remind anybody else
of something?'

'Yes,' Eve said, tapping her lower lip with a blood

red fingernail. 'How much I need to shave her head while she's sleeping.'

'That's not what I meant. Mike?'

'School,' Michael said instantly. 'That's what she was like in school when she was coming on to you.'

'Speaking of school,' Eve said. 'What the hell was this about the closet make-out session?'

'Nothing.'

'Did you seriously tongue-wrestle Monica in the—'

'Eve, *shut up.*'

'No, seriously, I have to know this. Were you high? Because that is honestly the only excuse I can think of.'

'It wasn't my fault. She grabbed me and pulled me in.' Shane got that flush in his cheeks again. 'Once. It was once. And I told her to fuck off the next day.' Shane's eyes widened, and Claire saw his expression change. 'The next day. That was the day she...the day she told me she'd make me sorry.'

'Oh, man,' Michael said. 'It was only a couple of weeks before—'

Shane shut his eyes again. 'Don't want to talk about it.'

Even Eve let that one go, because what was going unsaid was that two weeks later, the fire had started at Shane's house, and Monica had been to blame. Maybe.

And Shane's sister had died.

'She didn't even look at me,' Claire said. 'She *always* looks at me.'

'What?' Michael asked, distracted.

'Monica. She never lets a chance go by to say something rude to me. But she didn't. It was like she didn't even know I existed.'

That was why Monica had ignored her, Claire realised. She wasn't her enemy. She didn't even know her. Monica was mentally back in...what had it been, tenth grade? Before Shane's house had burnt, and his family had left town.

Monica thought they were all still in *high school*.

'Creepy,' Claire said.

Shane swallowed. 'You have no idea. Monica used to follow me everywhere. Send me porn notes and texts. She told people she was my girlfriend. She beat up any girl I talked to. It was miserable.'

Wow. Monica had been Shane's *stalker*. That put a whole different light on things. 'How long did that go on?'

'I guess about three months, maybe. Michael?'

'Yeah, that sounds right. It was after she decided I was off-limits.' He shook his head when Claire opened her mouth. 'Don't ask. She was a serial stalker. Worked her way through most of the jocks, but I don't know why she picked on the two of us.'

'Well, how about you're adorably cute and talented?' Eve said. 'I crushed all over you, too. Not you, Collins. You, Glass.'

The doctor came in around then, and expelled them while Shane got stitches. Claire was happy enough to miss that part. Stitches were painful; she knew that from experience.

Monica and Gina were sipping cans of cola from straws and giggling while they checked out the butts on the interns and doctors. It was so...*not* them. And yet, it was, at the same time. Monica kept looking towards the curtain that hid Shane from view with hungry, fascinated eyes, and that made Claire feel hot and furious and filthy.

Monica still thought Shane was interested in her. All evidence to the contrary.

'This isn't right,' Michael said, looking around. 'It just doesn't feel right. You know? It's like everything's just...out of tune. I don't know if you feel it the way I do. Vampires sense things differently.'

'That may be why some get violent,' Claire said. 'We have to fix it. Somehow. It can only get worse.'

'Well, you can't go back to Myrnin. Not after—'

'Michael, I have to! This thing comes and goes, right? People snap out of it. He'll come back, and when he does I have to be there and find out what to do.' She took a deep breath. 'Or, like Shane said, we have to pull the plug. That's the only other solution.'

'Nuke the site from orbit,' Eve said. 'It's the only way to be sure.'

'Do *not* quote *Aliens* at me; I'm freaked out enough already!'

'Sorry. But it's always good advice.'

'It actually *is* good advice,' Michael said. 'I can go pull the plug. Myrnin won't come after me—'

'He would,' Claire said. 'Myrnin used to bite other vamps, too, in case you forgot. You can't assume just being in the blood club is going to get you through. And he's strong, and really fast. Don't. Make Amelie go, or Oliver. I don't think he'd bite them.'

'You don't *think*?'

She shrugged unhappily. 'I don't know him anymore when he's like this. I don't know what he's going to do.'

'We are so screwed,' Eve said. 'What about Amelie? What's she doing?'

That opened up a whole can of worms that wriggled unpleasantly in the pit of Claire's stomach. She was absolutely sure that Amelie and Oliver wouldn't want her telling anybody about what she'd seen earlier, not even – or maybe especially – Eve and Michael. She decided to hedge. 'I don't know. Oliver told me to take care of it, but...' Claire was forced to shrug again. 'Maybe by now they've both got it, too.'

'Well, that would be bad. Epically bad.'

It would, Claire thought. 'I should check in with them and see what they want to do. It's weird nobody's called me back,' she said. 'Michael, could you stay and wait for Shane—'

It turned out, as the curtain whipped aside, that there was no need to wait. Shane joined them, moving slowly. The stitches were in, but he had a white bandage taped over them. Claire took his hand, and he smiled. It looked a little pale. 'I'm good to go. What are we doing?'

'Taking you home,' Claire said.

'Not if you guys are going somewhere else.'

'You're walking wounded,' Michael said. 'I'm pretty sure this isn't optional.'

'Oh, yeah? You want to try to stop me, tough guy?' Shane said, and grinned. 'I know you better. You wouldn't hit a guy who's down.'

Eve held up a hand for a high five with him. 'Give it up for Shane Collins, master manipulator!'

He smacked it, and winced a little again. 'Yeah, well, you don't grow up with my dad without knowing a few things. So where are we going?'

'To Amelie,' Claire said. 'She can go with us to the lab and keep Myrnin pinned down while we pull the plug, if he's not...you know, better.'

'Define *better* with that guy.'

'Not all fangs and *raaaaar.*'

'Oh. OK. Quick stop at the house. I want to load up on the good stuff.'

If Shane expected an argument, he didn't get one. Claire was thinking the same thing.

When you were going into a war zone, you didn't go unarmed.

CHAPTER ELEVEN

Eve had ordered something special off the Internet, which had arrived by mail, Claire discovered. She'd got three of them, and Claire put hers on with a whoop of delight.

Getting two-inch silver chain chokers around the neck of a guy, especially Shane, proved to be more of a problem.

Shane held the jewellery at arm's length, dangling it like a dead rat. 'No way in *hell* am I caught dead or alive wearing that.'

'Oh, come on, just this once,' Eve said. 'Protects your neck. As in your arteries and veins? That's kind of crucial, right?'

'Thanks for the thought, but it doesn't go with my shoes.'

'You're seriously going to worry about what people think right now?'

'No, I'm worrying about people taking pictures and putting them on Facebook. That crap never dies. Kind of like you, Mikey.'

Michael, straight-faced, said, 'He's got a point, because I would definitely take pictures. So would you.'

Eve had to grin. 'Yeah, I would. OK, then. But you'd look glam. I could fix you up with silver eye shadow to match.'

'Tell you what: you can be Glammera the vampire hunter. I'll stick with being manly and heavily armed.'

Michael snorted and picked up some wooden – i.e., mostly nonlethal – stakes, which he stuffed in his jacket. 'You guys ready?'

'Guess so.' Shane gave his small crossbow another once-over, then put it in the carry bag. Eve had packed a (for her) huge purse full of stuff. The purse, of course, had a shiny yellow happy face on it – with fangs. Claire stuck with her unfashionable, but useful, backpack. She'd emptied out all of her books and left them stacked on the table. She had no idea when she'd actually get back to school, but it certainly wouldn't be today.

Shane dropped the silver choker to the table, shuddered, and led the way out of the Glass House to the car. Michael locked up behind them, and Claire thought about how natural it was now for them to watch one another's backs. There wasn't even any discussion. Shane went first, keys to Eve's hearse in hand; Eve had, of course, called shotgun, so she was heading straight for the passenger side. Claire was checking shadows and heading for the back of the long black coach, and Michael zipped down fast and joined her as she opened the back. He was the last one in, and smacked the roof to signal Shane as he and Claire sat down on the long bench seats in the back.

Eve had added some kind of colour-changing strips along the inside of the roof. 'What's with the disco lights?' Michael said, rolling down the window between the driver's compartment and the back.

Eve turned around, and her face brightened. 'You like it? I thought it looked really cool. I saw it in a movie, you know, in a limo.'

'It's cool,' Michael said, and smiled at her. She smiled back. 'Can't wait to lie here and watch it with you.'

Claire said, 'You don't have to wait, it's working now, look – Oh. Never mind.' She blushed, feeling stupid that she hadn't got that one in the first second. Eve winked at her.

'Shouldn't you be calling Amelie and getting us some kind of parking permit?' Eve asked. Claire nodded, glad to be off the hook, and made the call. It rang to voice mail, and Claire left her a message. She was just hanging up when she spotted a parked police car out of the window.

Hannah Moses was standing alongside it. Just... standing. Looking around.

'Wait,' Claire said, and leant over to grab Shane's shoulder. 'Stop. She can get us in; she's got permission to go to Founder's Square anytime she wants.'

Shane pulled in behind Hannah's cruiser, and Claire got out to talk to her. She moved fast, because this wasn't a well-lit area, and everything seemed really dark tonight anyway. Even with the hearse's headlights shining, it felt shadowed.

'Hannah!' she said. 'We need some help. Can you get us in to see Amelie?'

Hannah turned to look at her, and there was something odd in her body language. She seemed tense and ready to react. She kept her hand near the gun in her holster. 'Who are you?' she asked. 'Name.'

'Oh, crap,' Claire said. 'You've got it, too.'

'Name!' Hannah snapped. 'Now!'

'Uh, OK, I'm Claire. Claire Danvers. You know me.'

Hannah shook her head. 'This is Morganville,' she said. 'I can't be in Morganville. I was in...I was in Kandahar. I was *just there*.' She looked down at her police uniform and shook her head again. 'I wasn't wearing this. I'm not a cop. I'm a marine. This can't be happening.'

'Hannah, you're having a...a flashback, that's all. You're not a marine; you're not in Afghanistan. You're here, in Morganville. You're the chief of police, remember?'

Hannah just looked at her as if Claire were crazy.

'Look at what you're wearing,' Claire said. 'Police uniform. Why would somebody kidnap you, bring you here, and change your clothes? What sense does that make?'

'It doesn't,' Hannah admitted. 'None of this makes any sense. I need to call in.'

'Call in *where*?'

'To my commanding officer.'

'Hannah, you're not *in* the marines now! You don't *have* a commanding officer!'

Hannah didn't seem to hear her this time. 'They'll think I'm AWOL. I need to tell them what happened.' Then she looked around again, and the look in her face was a little desperate. 'Except I don't know what happened.'

'I just told you! Flashback!'

'This isn't a combat flashback!'

'No, it's...' Lying, Claire figured, was now the only way to go. 'You've been drugged. You have to believe me. You live here, in Morganville. You're the chief of police.'

Hannah was shaking her head – not as if she didn't

believe it, but as if she didn't *want* to believe it. 'I'm
not going back to Morganville. No way in *hell* am I
signing up for that.'

But you did, Claire started to say, then held it back.
She didn't know why Hannah had changed her mind;
maybe something had happened to her while she was
in Afghanistan, or since she came back from there. But
whatever it was, in Hannah's mind, it hadn't happened
yet.

'I know this is hard,' Claire said. 'But we need your
help. Really. All you have to do is call in permission for
us to go into Founder's Square. Would you do that?'

'I don't know you people,' Hannah said. 'And you're
driving around in a damn *hearse.* It doesn't exactly
make me want to trust you...' Her voice trailed off, and
she blinked as the hearse's doors opened, and Michael
and Eve got out. 'You're...you're the Glass kid. The
guitar player. I remember you. And—' Hannah did
an absolute double take, the most surprised Claire
had ever seen her. 'Eve? What the hell did you do to
yourself? Have your parents seen how you look?'

Claire exchanged a mute second of stares with her
friends, and Eve finally said, 'Ah, yeah, they've seen
it. I've been dressing like this for about three years;
don't you remember?'

'No,' Hannah said, and suddenly sat down on the
sidewalk. Just...sat. She put her head in her hands.

'No, I don't remember that. I remember…you were in school with my brother Reggie, before he…I saw you at the funeral…'

Eve crouched down next to her and put a hand on her shoulder. 'I know,' she said. 'But then you went to Afghanistan, and then you came back, and now you're the head police chick. You have to remember that!'

'I don't,' Hannah said, and Claire realised with a shock that she was crying silently, tears running down her face. 'I don't remember that at all.' She pulled in a deep breath, wiped her face, and let Eve help her to her feet. 'All right. Let's say all that's true, even if I don't believe it. What do you want?'

'Just…we need you to call in to the guard post at Founder's Square and give us a pass to see Amelie,' Claire said. 'Please. I've tried phoning. She's not answering.' And Claire found that she was really, truly worried. Not that Amelie was a friend, exactly, but the idea of a Morganville without her was…unthinkable. She couldn't get the image of Amelie lying limp on the floor in Oliver's arms out of her head.

Hannah stared at her like she was even crazier than before. 'We don't *ever* call the Founder by name.'

'We do now,' Claire said. 'I do. We all do. You have to believe me, things around here are different now. Please, Hannah. We really need this if we're going to help people.'

Hannah took another look around at the town, at them, and finally nodded. 'All right,' she said. 'You tell me what to do and I'll do it. Anything to make this all...stop.'

Claire got into the police car and found Hannah's cell phone. Sure enough, it had all kinds of numbers plugged in, and one of them was to the guard station at the entrance to Founder's Square. She dialled it for Hannah and held out the phone.

'Guard post?' Hannah said, and here, at least, she seemed to be on familiar ground. Marine training did that for you, Claire guessed. 'This is Lieut— This is Hannah Moses. I've got four kids in a hearse who are cleared for admittance to Founder's Square.' She covered the phone and looked at Claire. 'Anything else?'

'Um – they should let us in to see Amelie.'

Hannah took in a deep breath and nodded as she uncovered the receiver. 'Yeah, and they'll need unescorted access to the Founder's office.' She listened, and her eyes widened a little. 'Great. Thank you.' She passed the phone back to Claire, who hung it up and put it back in the car. 'They said they'd put you on the list. Just like that.'

'Thanks, Hannah.' On impulse, Claire hugged her. Hannah was a solid block of muscle, but then she softened a little and hugged her back. 'Go home. Don't go out again until things stop feeling weird, OK?'

'Home?' Hannah echoed, and looked haunted again. 'I've got no home here.'

Well, she probably did, but Claire didn't know where it was. She thought for a second, then said, 'Go to Gramma Day's house. You used to live with her, right?'

'When I was a kid, yeah.'

'She'll help you,' Claire said. 'Tell her I said hello.'

'She's a tough old lady,' Hannah said, but it sounded fond. 'Yeah, I'll go there. But you owe me explanations, Claire. Real ones.'

'If this goes right, I won't owe them anymore,' Claire said. 'Be careful, OK?'

Hannah smiled faintly. 'I'm from Morganville,' she said. 'I'm always careful.'

They left her behind, still standing beside her patrol car, and headed for Founder's Square.

The guards looked inside the car, but didn't search; Claire supposed they had no real reason to, with Hannah approving their visit. Eve looked nervous, but not *too* nervous, and having Michael with them guaranteed that the vamps would keep their hands off, anyway. The guards waved them on, and Eve guided the big car down the ramp and into the underground parking area. 'Damn,' she said. 'I hope I can park this thing in here.'

In the end, she wedged it sideways in two spots, but since the garage was mostly deserted, Claire supposed nobody was going to complain. 'OK, we're here,' Shane said. 'What now?'

'Let's do this smart,' Michael said. 'Shane, you and Eve stay here with the weapons. I'll go up with Claire. If we don't come back in ten minutes, load up and come running.'

'You're taking weapons,' Shane said.

'Just what we can conceal,' Michael said. 'If we go in there with crossbows, Amelie will kill us all just for doing it. She'll overlook personal defence. Not armed assault.'

Claire lifted her backpack. People were so used to seeing it on her that it didn't matter what she carried inside. She knew Michael had stakes on him. It would have to be enough. 'I'll call you if it's OK,' Claire promised, and kissed Shane quickly. He grabbed her hand when she tried to leave the car, and pulled her back for another kiss, a longer one. He didn't want to let go, and neither did she, but he finally sighed and nodded, and she opened the back door.

'Hey, Mikey? You get her hurt and I'll end you.'

'You let anything happen to Eve and I'll do the same,' Michael said. He'd just finished kissing Eve, too. 'While you're at it, don't get yourself killed either, bro.'

'Ditto. And don't kiss me.'

Claire cocked her head at him, exasperated. 'Seriously, Shane? *Ditto?* That's the best you can do?'

Shane and Michael exchanged identical looks and shrugs. *Guys.*

'Let me show you idiots how it's done,' Eve said, and hugged Claire fiercely. She kissed her on the cheek. 'I love you, CB. Please take care of yourself, OK?'

'I love you too,' Claire said, and suddenly her throat felt tight and her eyes burnt with tears. 'I really do.'

Shane and Michael watched them with identical expressions of blank bemusement, and finally Shane said, 'So, basically, it's what I said. Ditto.'

Michael grinned and headed for the elevator that would take them up to the Elders' Council level. 'Coming?'

Claire picked up her heavy backpack and ran to join him.

The elevator was empty and cool, the metal gleaming as if someone had just finished polishing it. Michael pressed the button and looked down at her. 'You OK?'

'Fine.'

'Your heart's beating really fast.'

'Gee, thanks, that's very comforting that you can hear it.'

He smiled, and it was the old Michael, the one she'd

first met before all the vamp stuff. 'Yeah, I know it is. Sorry. Just stay behind me if there's trouble.'

'You sound like Shane.'

'Well, he did say he'd kill me if I got you hurt. I'm just looking after my own neck.'

'Liar.'

He ruffled her hair, like an annoying big brother, and stepped in front of her as the elevator dinged to a stop, and the doors slid open. She couldn't see anything, but evidently the coast was clear, because Michael stepped out and walked down the hallway.

'There's usually a guard there,' Claire said, peeking around him at the double doors of the council chamber.

'When they're meeting,' Michael agreed. 'No reason to guard an empty room. It's this way.'

He turned at a T intersection and went right down another identical hallway, all panelling and marble floors and steadily burning dim lights. It *still* reminded Claire of a funeral home. No sounds in the building except for the muted sighing of central air. The air was cool, verging on cold. All the doors were unmarked, at least to human eyes.

'Up there,' Michael said. Claire nodded. She could see a vampire guard in black stationed outside of one of the doors – the woman who'd been one of the guards at the council chambers. She was sitting in a chair reading a magazine, but as Michael and Claire approached, she stood up and assumed her usual at-rest position.

'Michael Glass and Claire Danvers for Amelie,' Michael said.

'You don't have an appointment.'

'No,' Claire said. 'But it's important. We need to see her.'

'My instructions are that she isn't to be disturbed,' the guard said.

'But it's an emergency!'

'I have my orders.'

'Amelie will want to see us,' Michael said.

The other vampire raised her eyebrows, just ever so slightly. 'It doesn't matter whether she would or not,' she said. 'Amelie no longer gives the orders. Oliver does, and his orders are that she should rest undisturbed. Now go or I'll have you removed.'

'Maybe we should see Oliver,' Claire said, doubtfully.

That made the vampire guard smile, with the tips of fangs showing. 'An excellent idea, but again, you have no appointment. Oliver sees no *human* without an appointment.'

'What about me?' Michael said. They got into a staring match.

'I'm afraid Oliver is not available to anyone at the

present time,' she finally said. 'Orders.'

'Then we'll just see Amelie,' Michael said, and reached for the doorknob. The guard's hand flashed out and closed white and hard around his wrist, stopping him an inch from the metal. 'Really? You're sure you want to do it this way?'

The guard smiled, with vamp teeth showing fully now. 'You're the one pushing the issue, New Guy. I told you, go away. There's no more discussion – ' Her expression suddenly altered, and even Claire felt some kind of force sweep past them, a kind of pressure wave that made both the vampires turn towards the Founder's closed door.

Claire found she was holding her hands to her head, and couldn't remember doing it. She looked up at Michael, who looked just as shaken as she felt. The vampire guard looked just as surprised.

'What was that?' Claire asked.

'Amelie,' Michael said. He reached again for the doorknob, and the vamp blocked him. He grabbed the vamp's arm above the elbow with his left hand, and tipped her over his head in a sudden, shocking movement. She should have been down on the floor at the end of it, but instead she twisted in midair and came down lightly on her feet, got her balance, and slammed *him* against the panelled walls with her clawed fingernails at his throat.

Claire grabbed the doorknob and plunged inside the office.

Inside, it was dark. Pitch dark. She couldn't see a thing, and for a second she just stood there, hoping her eyes might adjust. Nothing. It was like swimming in ink. Claire groped along the wall for a switch, and found one.

When she flipped it on, she found Amelie standing about one foot away from her, staring at her with wide, ice-grey eyes. Claire yelped and flinched back against the door. Amelie leant forward, one palm against the wood to the side of Claire's head. With her right hand, she reached over and turned the bolt to seal them in.

'Now,' she said softly. 'Who are you, little soft girl? Some novice vampire slayer who thinks she will free the town and become a hero of the people? Do you really think you have the courage to put a stake in my heart, child?'

Amelie didn't know her. At all.

Worse, there was another vampire in the room. Oliver.

And he was lying unconscious on the floor, with blood streaming from two puncture wounds in his throat.

In retrospect, it was fairly obvious what had just happened; Claire had seen the reverse of it earlier, in the council chamber, when Amelie and Oliver had struggled for control of the town, and Amelie had lost.

It had happened again, and this time she'd *won*.

Claire looked at the hot, alien light in Amelie's eyes, and thought, *Yay?* It was a crazy thing to think, especially since the thought sounded like Eve's voice inside her head, but somehow it made her feel a little steadier. A little stronger.

'Don't mind the intruder,' Amelie said, glancing aside at Oliver, who was showing no signs of moving. 'I've put him in his place. As I assure you I will do for you, little slayer girl.'

Claire swallowed hard and tried to regulate the racing beat of her heart. Showing fear wasn't going to help. 'My name is Claire Danvers,' she said. 'I'm Myrnin's apprentice.'

Amelie smiled. Not a nice smile. 'My dear, Myrnin would devour you for a morning snack,' she said. 'He's done it before, to those more capable and better loved by him.' The smile died. 'Now. Who are you?'

'Claire! My name is Claire! You know me!'

'I do not. Nor do I see why I should bother. You shouldn't have come here, little girl. I don't tolerate these kinds of rebellions.'

Claire had no idea why she thought of it, but suddenly, a page from the history book that she'd bought at the used bookstore flared in front of her brain, clear as if it had been pasted on. She could see every detail of the type, even down to the water stains on the paper. 'But you did,' she said. 'About a hundred years ago. You let Ballard Templin go free after he took a shot at you on the street.'

That surprised Amelie enough to make her cock her head and frown, just a little. 'Ballard Templin,' she repeated. 'How would someone of your age know of Templin?'

'He was a gunfighter,' Claire said. 'And he was hired to kill you. You took his gun away and told him to go kill the man who'd hired him. He did. It was the bank manager.'

'These are things you should not know, girl. Things that were never made public.'

Claire called up another page in her memory. 'You bought the land for Morganville from a farmer named Roger Hanthorn, for about a hundred dollars. The first barrier around it was made out of wood, a big fence, like a stockade. And you used to play the harp. People said you played like an angel.'

Amelie had gone very still, and the bafflement in her face was almost human now. 'You *cannot* know these things.'

'Your father was Bishop,' Claire said. 'And you were in love with Sam Glass—'

She didn't know what she'd said wrong, but Amelie

bared her fangs and grabbed Claire by the arm. She threw her across the room in a weightless rush, and Claire lost the backpack along the way as she tumbled over and over, until she came to a hard, sudden stop against the wall.

Things went fuzzy then, and she felt weirdly hot. She blinked a few times, and Amelie's face came into focus right above hers. 'Who are you?' Amelie said. 'What do you know of Sam? *Where is he?* He can't hide from me, but I can't sense him! Who has taken him?'

Claire snapped back to instant clarity. She was hurting, but she didn't think anything was broken. There was a hot, throbbing spot on her head where she'd hit the wall, though.

All of that faded to the background as she realised what Amelie was asking.

She thought Sam Glass was alive.

She thought Sam was *missing*.

And she thought Claire knew where he was.

That was bad, but what was worse was that there wasn't any good answer. What was she going to tell her? *Sam's dead? You buried him? I can show you his grave?* How horrible would that be? And besides, Amelie would probably kill her for it, even if she believed it, which she probably wouldn't. Hannah hadn't believed she was back from Afghanistan. This would be a lot harder to accept.

'Well?' Amelie whispered, and pressed her fingernails gently into Claire's neck so she could feel the sting. 'I won't kill you, girl. Not yet, and not quickly. If you've done anything to Sam Glass, I will see you destroyed slowly, in the old ways. You can save yourself by telling me where to find him, *now*.' Her eyes widened. 'Was it Oliver who took him?' She let go of Claire and whirled to stalk over to Oliver, who was just opening his eyes as she bent to grab him by the shirt front and drag him up to a sitting position. The wounds on his throat were almost closed. 'You.' Amelie's voice dripped with scorn and venom. 'Is this how you repay my kindness to you? I let you live the last time you challenged me. Did you take Sam Glass to ensure your victory this time?'

Oliver blinked, and Claire was sure she saw bafflement in his eyes, and dawning realisation. 'She doesn't remember,' Claire said. 'It's got her too.'

'So I see,' he murmured, and shut his eyes again. 'I can't help you, Claire. I can't help either of us.'

Claire's mind wasn't blank, exactly; it was whirling with ideas and thoughts and schemes, and the problem was that none of them would save her, and she knew it.

Amelie stared down at Oliver with ice-cold fury, and said, 'Tell me where he is, now, or I will destroy you.'

'I can't tell you anything,' Oliver said. 'I'm sorry.'

She was going to *kill him*. And Oliver wasn't going to make a move to defend himself – or maybe, Claire realised, he couldn't. She'd weakened him too much already. 'The machine's malfunctioning!' Claire blurted, as Amelie pulled back her hand with claws extended to rip out his throat. 'That's why you're confused! That's why you can't remember where Sam is! You know where he is, Amelie. You know me, too. You gave me a gold bracelet for a while, and now I have a pin. You gave me a pin! You have to believe me!'

That was not what Amelie was expecting her to say, obviously, because she drew back, just a little. She let go of Oliver and came back to Claire, and Amelie's fingers touched the small gold pin, with the Founder's symbol, that Claire had on her shirt. 'Where did you get this?' she asked. 'From whom did you steal it?'

'I didn't steal it,' Claire said. 'You gave it to me. How could I know the name of Myrnin's computer if I wasn't who I say I am? How would I know any of what I said to you?'

She thought for a second that she'd gambled all the wrong way, because Amelie looked so angry, and so... confused. All she had to do was hit her, and Claire was going to come to a very messy, unpleasant end.

'A good question,' Amelie finally said. 'How do you know these things? Only Myrnin and I know of the machine. No one else. No one alive. Did he tell you?'

'I work for him,' Claire said again. 'I work for *you*. And there's something wrong with the machine. That's what's wrong with you. Don't you *feel* something's wrong?'

Amelie kept watching her for a moment more, then frowned down at Oliver, who was propped now against the wall, still making no effort to rise. She turned and walked back to a big, polished desk. Claire looked around and realised that she recognised this room; she'd been in it before, but by portal rather than the front door. There were a lot of old books in built-in shelves, and beautiful old furniture, and soft lights. Large windows that were, just now, uncovered to show Founder's Square at night.

The cage in the middle of the park was lit up like an exhibit. Claire wondered if the boy was still in there, or if somehow he'd managed to take advantage of the confusion and get out. She kind of hoped so. What if *Kyle* didn't remember why he was in that cage? How awful would that be?

Claire limped over to a chair and fell into it. Her head was spinning, and she felt like she wanted to throw up, but there was no way she was going to do that on Amelie's fancy carpeting. Oliver had already bled all over it.

Outside the room, there was sudden silence, and then the door banged open with a crash that sent the lock flying right out of the wood. Michael came inside, dragging the guard along with him. She'd been tied up with what Claire realised were strips torn from her coat, and he'd added a gag. Both of them looked ragged and worn-out.

Amelie stood up, mouth open, and cried, 'Sam?' just a second before she realised she was wrong. Not Sam Glass. His grandson. They looked a lot alike, except for their hair colour. Sam's had been more red. 'Michael. But you...you can't be...' Her expression changed, slowly, and she breathed out, 'No. Not possible. You can't be any get of mine. I would know this. I would *remember*.' But Claire could tell that she could feel it was true – and that made Amelie even more confused.

A confused Amelie was very dangerous.

Michael dumped the guard in the corner and came to Claire. 'Are you hurt?'

'No, I'm OK.'

'There's blood on your shirt.'

Oh. Yeah, her neck was bleeding a little. Not enough to worry about. 'I'm fine.' Except for the headache, which was bad, but that wasn't something she wanted to go into. Michael looked doubtful, but he turned from her to look at Oliver. 'What happened to you?'

'Complacency,' Oliver murmured. 'I thought she was under my control, and then – she changed.'

'She lost her memory,' Claire said. 'She forgot

you'd taken over. So she attacked you.'

Oliver lifted a weak hand in agreement, and they all looked at Amelie, who was white as a marble statue now. 'How can this be? You were...I remember you, Michael. You should be younger...thinner—'

'And not a vampire,' Michael said. 'But I am one. And you made me one.'

'Yes,' Amelie whispered. 'I can feel that. But *how*... how can this be true when I don't—'

'It's the machine in Myrnin's lab,' Michael said. 'We need your help to stop it before it's too late. Myrnin doesn't remember things, either. He won't let us get close without a fight. You're the only one he'll listen to.'

'I must think,' Amelie said, and sat down as if she'd lost all strength. 'Leave me.' She didn't seem to care about them anymore, any of them. There was a deep, miserable confusion in her eyes, and Claire remembered how the vampire in the diner had snapped. Surely that wouldn't happen to Amelie.

Not to Amelie.

Claire turned to Oliver. 'Help us,' she pleaded. 'We need your help. *You* still remember.'

'For how long?' Oliver asked. He, too, sounded weak and odd. 'I saw it overtake her. It will do the same to me, and I'll be of no use to you then.'

'Convince her to come to Myrnin's lab,' Michael said.

'That's how you can be of use to us. We need you there. Both of you.'

Amelie looked up sharply. 'No one convinces me. Leave now, or I'll destroy both of you. If there's action to be taken, I will take it, but you *will not* stay here and insult my authority by appealing to *him*.' She pressed a button on her desk, and an alarm began to sound out in the hall. 'I must have time to decide what to do.'

Michael pulled Claire out of the chair, grabbed her backpack, and said, 'We're going.'

'Then run,' Amelie said. 'Because if my men catch you, I will have them kill you.'

Michael nodded, and practically dragged Claire at a run out of the office.

'I can't!' Claire panted. Her head was pounding, and she couldn't keep her balance. Michael didn't hesitate. He grabbed her and threw her over his shoulder, and kept running. She could see behind him.

Vampires were coming out of the doors and running after them. *Jumping* after them, eating up the corridor in big bursts of movement. 'Faster!' she screamed. He got to the intersection of hallways and raced so fast that she felt even dizzier from the rush of wind and blurring panelling. OK, she was *not* going to throw up on Michael's shoulder. She just couldn't.

Michael banged through a door, and suddenly she

was airborne. That didn't help the disorientation *at all*, but at least it was fast, and she felt the impact when he landed – where?

Oh, at the bottom of the stairwell. She craned her neck and looked up three stories, where the vampire pursuers were jumping after them, and one of them was on the railing, readying to leap right on top of them.

Michael didn't wait. He threw open the door to the parking garage and the next thing she knew, she was being tossed into the back of the Death Limo and Eve was peeling out of the garage like her tailpipe had caught fire.

Claire breathed as deeply as she could, and in a few seconds, the world stopped twisting around quite so badly. She opened her eyes and looked up at Shane, who was holding her in his lap.

'You were supposed to call,' he said. He sounded angry.

'Sorry,' she said. 'We were busy being almost killed.'

Eve screamed through the window at the front, 'Michael? Michael, what happened; are you all right?'

'I'm OK,' he said. He must have been, because Claire couldn't imagine how he'd outrun all those vamps if he hadn't been. He was lying down, though, on the other bench seat in the back. 'They won't chase us outside of the square.'

'I'm not taking any chances! We are going straight home!'

Nobody had any argument for that. Claire was thinking, *But we have to do something. Anything.*

The problem was, everything she could think of ended with them getting killed.

She *had* to think of something.

Only she didn't. It was late, and they were all tired, and her head hurt. She fell asleep on the couch, and Shane finally woke her and told her to go to bed. She wanted to stay with him, but she knew she shouldn't, not when she was trying to think, and her head hurt so badly.

She didn't remember getting upstairs to her room, but she must have, because when she woke up, sunlight was streaming through the curtains and laying a warm blanket across her bed. She felt better, until she poked at the bump on her head; that still hurt. But it was healing, she could tell.

She still hadn't thought of what she was going to do, except that she needed to get to Myrnin, convince him to help, or else she needed to take down the computer's power. *Maybe the power station*, she thought, but she'd been there once, and unless she was planning to get a full Navy SEAL team and maybe Hannah's old marine buddies, there was no way she could take out the power there.

It had to be done in the lab. Which left the problem of the crazy vampire who didn't remember her, and wanted to have her for lunch.

There was nothing coming to her, nothing at all. Amelie might help, or she might not. There was no telling what she, or Oliver, would do.

It was still early enough that Michael was probably home, but Claire thought today was Eve's early day at Common Grounds; she put in only about sixteen hours a week there, but she tried to do it early mornings, because she *really* didn't like spending evenings there anymore. So she'd probably already been up and gone, if she was intending to work at all. Shane would be in bed. He never got up before ten unless he had to.

Sure enough, when Claire went into the bathroom, there was fog on the mirror, and still-warm drops in the shower, and Eve had left her make-up scattered all over the counter. Claire put it back in the bag and got out her own, which wasn't much beyond an eye pencil and some mascara. She showered and dressed fast, and had her mind on what she was going to say to Oliver when she opened the bathroom door, and ran straight into Michael.

He looked at her in shock – so much shock, in fact, that she checked to make sure she'd remembered to put her pants on. She had. 'What?' she demanded. 'Do I have something on my face?'

'What are you doing in my bathroom?' Michael asked, and took a giant step back. 'How did you get here?'

Oh, *crap*. She'd been afraid Michael was susceptible to whatever was going on, and now here it was again. Just like Amelie. Just like Myrnin. Just like Monica, for that matter.

He didn't wait for her answer. He ran to the end of the hall, to *her* room, and threw open the door. 'Dad...' He fell silent, staring at the room. 'Dad?' He backed up slowly. 'What the hell is going on?'

Claire sighed. It seemed like her whole life was being spent telling people the bad news. 'I know you're not going to believe this, but I live here, Michael. I've been here for a while now.'

He turned back on her, fists clenched. She'd never seen that look on his face – scared and desperately angry. 'What did you do with my parents?'

'I promise, I didn't do anything! Look, you can ask Eve if you don't believe me, or Shane—'

'Did Monica put you up to this?' Michael asked, and pushed her. That was a shock, and the grim, furious expression he had made her feel cold inside. 'Just get out. Get out of our house!'

'Wait!' It was no use; he wasn't going to believe her any more than Hannah had, or Amelie, or Myrnin. 'Wait, don't—'

Michael pushed her again. With vampire strength.

Claire flew backward, fell, rolled, and almost slid down the stairs before she grabbed hold of a banister railing to pull herself to a stop. Michael stood there, looking utterly astonished; he stared at her, down at his hands, and back again.

'You're a vampire, Michael,' Claire said, and scrambled up. Her head was hurting again. No surprise there. 'If you don't remember anything else, remember that. You can hurt people, even if you don't mean to do it.'

'Get out!' he yelled. He looked really upset, and very, very angry. Bad combo for a vampire. His eyes had taken on a wicked crimson shimmer.

Claire went down the steps, grabbed her backpack from where it was leaning against the wall, and dashed out the door. Once she was outside in the sun, she stopped and pulled out her cell phone, and dialled Shane's number. It rang and rang and rang, and finally he picked up and mumbled something that didn't really sound like a word.

'Wake up! Watch your back,' she said. 'Michael doesn't remember who I—'

She didn't have any time to say more, because Michael had followed her out onto the porch, and as she started to turn, she saw that he was coming after her.

In the sunlight.

'No!' Claire yelled, and dropped her phone and the backpack to the ground. Michael's skin started to sizzle and smoke instantly on contact with the sun, and he just *stood there*, staring down at himself, as if this was some horrible dream, and he was waiting to wake up. 'Michael, get back! Get in the shade!'

'I'm not...I'm not a...' He staggered and fell to his knees. 'I'm not a vampire.'

'Michael!'

She didn't have a choice. She'd have to risk him turning on her, like Myrnin; she couldn't leave him out here to fry. He didn't seem to understand that he had to move – or maybe he wasn't able to. She couldn't tell.

'Shane! Shane, get your ass down here!' she screamed, loud enough that she hoped he could hear it over the still-on cell *and* through the windows. She couldn't wait for him, though.

She dumped her backpack and raced back to grab Michael under the arms. His shirt was on fire, and she batted it out before trying to drag him, but as soon as she did, the shirt burst into flames again, singeing her own clothes. The shadows were still three feet away. If she got him there, he'd be all right, she knew he'd be all right...but he was struggling now, and she kept losing her grip.

Do it, just do it! Claire took a better hold and gritted

her teeth and pulled with all her might. He was heavy, really heavy, and it hurt trying to hold on while he thrashed. She towed him another foot. It seemed to take for ever.

'Move!' Shane yelled from behind her, and jumped down the steps with a heavy quilt in his hands. He threw it over Michael and started slapping out the flames. 'What the hell *happened*?'

'He...he forgot he...' Claire couldn't get her breath. 'I couldn't get him to go inside.'

'Jesus, Michael...Claire, go call an ambulance. Hurry.'

She stumbled up into the house and made the call as Shane dragged their friend back up the steps and onto the porch. She hoped she made sense to the emergency services person on the other end. She honestly didn't know. All she could think about was getting back out there and helping Shane.

It was only as she hung up the phone that she realised her own hands were burnt, too. She tried not to look too closely. They didn't hurt yet, exactly. That was probably shock. She went back out to the porch, and saw that Shane had peeled away the quilt.

Michael was alive, but he didn't look good. His shirt was covered with burnt holes, and the skin underneath looked horrible. So did his face, his hands, his arms — every part of him that hadn't been fully protected. He was still awake, and his eyes had turned a brilliant ruby red. 'I'm not,' he was saying. 'I'm not one of them. Shane, tell me I'm not!' He sounded so afraid. His whole voice was shaking.

Shane's expression made Claire's heart ache, and his voice came out rough, but oddly gentle. 'You're not one of them, bro,' he said. 'You're one of us. You'll always be one of us.'

Michael was crying now. 'Get my dad. I need my dad.'

Shane pushed his hair back with one hand, clearly not sure what to say, and then shook his head. 'I can't. He's not here, Mike. Just stay still, OK? You're going to be OK. They'll fix you up.'

'Get Sam,' Michael pleaded. 'He'll tell you I'm not... I'm not...'

It was *awful*. Claire wanted to cry too, but she knew if she started she wouldn't be able to stop. Why Michael? God, it was *her fault*. Hers and Myrnin's. This was happening to so many people, and she couldn't take it; she really couldn't. Michael didn't deserve this. *Nobody* deserved this.

'Claire, your hands...' Shane was looking at her now, and he seemed pale. 'You burnt your hands.'

'I'll be fine,' she said. It seemed the thing to say. It didn't look so bad now, in the sun. Mostly they were red and angry-looking, like a terrible sunburn.

Well, she'd had those before. 'Is he in pain?'

'I'm right here,' Michael said. He was getting hold of himself, a little. 'It hurts. Not so much now, though.'

'He's healing,' Shane said quietly. 'He'll be all right.'

But Michael was staring at Claire now, and suddenly he said, 'You...you did something to me. Poured gas on me. Something. I'm not a vampire. I didn't just catch fire.'

'No!' Claire was appalled he even *thought* it. 'No, Michael, I didn't—'

'Get her away from me,' Michael said to Shane. 'She's crazy. She was in the house. She's one of Monica's friends. You know how they are with fire.'

'Mike...' Shane hesitated, then plunged on. 'She lives here, man. She's got the room at the end. Your parents' room. She's OK. Really.'

Michael didn't say anything to that, just shook his head and closed his eyes. Shane looked at Claire, and lifted his hands in a silent apology. She nodded.

It was a relief hearing the ambulance come screaming towards them.

Shane went with Michael to the hospital, and the paramedics looked Claire's hands over, gave her some kind of cream, and told her she'd be fine. She didn't feel fine, but she ignored it. Somebody had to tell Eve, and she didn't want to do it over the phone. There were some things that just didn't sound right, and this was a big one.

Backpack and phone back in place, Claire ran the blocks to Common Grounds. Along the way she saw plenty of evidence that things were going even farther off the tracks – lots of police out, people wandering the streets looking lost and upset, people fighting. One woman kept trying to get into a house, and she was scaring the people inside.

Claire didn't stop for anything.

Common Grounds, on the other hand, was weirdly normal. The overwhelming aroma of coffee hit her like a wake-up call as she came in the front door, and there were plenty of people here, huddled over their mochas and frapps and lattes as they studied or chatted or phoned.

Everybody seemed to be from TPU today. She couldn't spot a single Morganville resident – but then, it was the middle of the morning, and most people had already left for work, unless they were out wandering the streets, confused.

There was no sign of Oliver in the place, and no sign of Eve, either. There was some other girl working the register. Claire hurried up, breathless, and said, 'Where's Eve?'

'Who?' the girl asked. She looked new. And clueless.

'Eve,' she said. 'Tall girl, real Goth? She works mornings. I need her.'

The girl gave her a harassed look as she added milk and stirred, added whipped cream, and handed a cup over to one of the two boys Claire had displaced. 'Are you deaf? She's not here. I don't know any Goths around here.'

'She *works here*!' That got nothing but a shrug. Not a very interested one. 'What about Oliver?'

'You mean George?'

'George?' Claire stared at her, a sick feeling growing in her guts.

'Yeah, George, the owner. Not sure where he's got to today.' The girl went to ring up someone else. Claire hissed in frustration and tried to think what to do next; it was clear that whatever memory reset the counter queen had undergone had erased Oliver, too.

Claire headed for the door. She was surprised to hear the girl call after her. 'Hey!' she said. Claire looked back. 'Some girl came in today and tried to put on an apron. I guess she was kind of Goth; she had black hair, anyway. I told her to go home.'

Claire caught her breath. 'Home,' she said. But if Eve had it too, she might not remember the Glass House as home. Like the woman she'd seen down the street, trying to unlock a door that wasn't any longer her own.

She'd have gone *home* home. To her parents' house. That could be – well, either good or bad, depending. Claire wasn't really sure. She'd been under the impression that Eve's dad, who'd passed away last year, had been the real trouble in Eve's home life, but what about Jason, Eve's brother? Three years ago, he'd probably been a dangerous little creep. It might not be safe for Eve at all.

'The Rossers,' she said. 'Where do they live?'

'No freaking idea,' the counter girl said, and turned to the next customer. 'Yeah, what do you want?'

Claire was ready to interrogate everyone in the shop for answers, but she didn't have to after all, because a door opened at the back of the shop, and she saw Oliver in the shadows. He looked odd – tired, wary, and very paranoid. He looked around the coffee shop, frowning, and his eyes fixed on her.

He nodded, very slightly.

He knew who she was. That sent a wave of relief flooding through her, all out of proportion to things. She wanted to lunge over and kiss him. Well, ew, not really, but maybe a hug. Or a handshake.

What she did do was walk slowly and calmly over to him. 'Are you OK?' she asked.

'Why?'

'I don't know, because the last time I saw you, you had bite marks in your throat?'

He grabbed her wrist and held it very, very tightly. 'You'd do well to forget you ever saw any of that.'

'There's too much forgetting going on already.'

'Certainly true,' he said, and let go. 'Were you concerned for me?'

'Not exactly.'

'Wise answer.'

'Michael has it. The memory thing. He doesn't – he doesn't remember who I am.'

Now she had Oliver's full attention. He looked at her for a moment, then turned and walked away. She hurried after him to his office. Oliver closed the door behind her, leant against it with his arms folded, and said, 'I thought you and Michael were going to shut down that cursed machine. Haven't you done so?'

'No, we – I—' She had no excuses, really. 'Not yet. I was going to try this morning, but I really need help. Michael's – Michael's not it. What about Amelie?'

Oliver took in a deep breath that, as a vampire, he didn't really need except for talking, and then let it out. 'Amelie is – struggling to understand, but she's having a difficult time accepting the world as it is, when part of her is insisting on seeing the world as it was. She let me go. I'm not sure how long that will last.' He shook his head, as if pushing all that away. 'Tell me what you think the machine is actually doing.'

'Instead of wiping memories of people leaving town,

it's broadcasting a wider field, and it's affecting people *in* town. I think it's wiping out at least three years of memories. Maybe more for some people; I don't know.'

'And how do you come by this startling calculation?'

'Hannah says she was in Afghanistan yesterday,' Claire said. 'Michael talks about his mom and dad as if they were still living in the house. Amelie acts like Sam Glass is still alive, but missing. Monica thinks she still has a shot at dating Shane. And Myrnin... Myrnin isn't at all like the Myrnin I know.'

'No, he wouldn't be,' Oliver said, thoughtful. 'When I came to town he was already far gone. He would have been completely unpredictable three years ago. Amelie doesn't remember Sam's death, you said. She certainly doesn't remember my arrival, either. It's a complete puzzle to her as to how I came to enter Morganville without her knowledge. I guarantee that she's well on the way to blaming me for this entire disaster.'

'Why you? Why not Myrnin?'

'When I came to town, Amelie and I...we had a great deal of history behind us, none of it good. It took us work to reach the understanding we have. If she doesn't remember that, it will be war all over again.'

'It's worse than that. Michael walked out into

the sun,' she said flatly. 'He doesn't remember he's a vampire.'

Oliver's eyes widened just a bit, and then he said, deliberately neutral, 'I hope that the sun convinced him otherwise. And I trust you called for help.'

'He's on his way to the hospital. I came to get Eve, but I think she's gone to her parents' house. She won't remember me, either.'

'If Michael's been injured, they won't take him to the hospital; they'll take him straight to the blood bank. He'll be all right, as long as he wasn't in the sun for long. Some blood, a little rest, he'll heal fine. The bigger issue is that if he refuses to believe in his current condition, he'll lose control and feed recklessly. Probably on one of his friends, because you're all too thick to take proper care.'

'I know,' Claire said, and leant wearily against Oliver's desk, which was loaded with papers, unopened mail, pens, paper clips...messy. That made her feel better about him, somehow. 'We need to stop this, but Myrnin put a password on the computer. I can't shut it down by myself.'

'Pull the plug,' he said. Funny. Oliver and Shane thought alike, and just about at the same speed. Claire didn't imagine either one of them would like that comparison, though.

'I can't do it with Myrnin trying to snack on me. I'm

kind of tired of just about getting killed for now. If you go with me and keep him off of me—'

Oliver, at least, had a sense of urgency. He grabbed his long leather coat, hat, and gloves, and dressed for the sun. 'Then let's go,' he said. 'The sooner, the better. I can't guarantee how long Amelie will allow me to operate freely.'

'But Eve – I was going to get her. Let her know about Michael.'

'We'll go by the Rosser house on the way, if you insist,' he said. 'But if she's not there, we go on. No arguments.'

That was fine with Claire. She was too tired to argue. As she tried to pick up her fallen backpack, she winced. Oliver grabbed her wrist and looked at her hand. 'You're burnt,' he said. He sounded surprised, and continued, 'You tried to pull him out of the sun. With your bare hands.'

'I had to try,' she said. 'He's my friend.'

Oliver gazed at her for a few seconds, then shook his head and let go. 'Just don't let it slow us down.'

CHAPTER TWELVE

Oliver had a limo, but no driver. His vampire driver had wandered off, leaving the car open and the keys in the ignition. Oliver cursed under his breath in some language Claire didn't recognise – she knew it was cursing; it just sounded that way – and got behind the wheel. Claire got in the passenger seat.

Eve was right: limos felt a whole lot like hearses, when you got right down to it.

Oliver drove fast, which was alarming, because Claire of course couldn't see a thing through the extremely dark windows. She concentrated on air bags and seat belts and all the nice safety features that car manufacturers built in these days. Vamps couldn't opt out of air bags, could they? Well, at least there were seat belts. That was something.

'Why not you?' Oliver asked.

'What?'

He glanced over at her. 'Why not you, or me? What keeps us from being affected by this miasma?'

'What's a miasma?'

'A fog,' he said. 'An influence.'

'I don't know,' Claire said. 'To be honest, I don't know if we're immune, or if it just takes longer for some people, or if it's just completely random. But it could be that because we weren't here three years ago, it doesn't affect us.'

'Hannah Moses wasn't here, either.'

'Yeah, but she's *from* here. Maybe there's a connection. We're both—'

'Outsiders,' Oliver finished. 'Interesting. I'm not certain how that would work.'

'It might not, for much longer,' Claire said. 'It hit Myrnin sooner than Amelie. It hit some people right off the bat, and others days later. I don't think it's following any kind of pattern. Maybe we're going to get it after all.'

'Are you armed?' Oliver asked her.

She glanced down at her backpack and instantly, instinctively held back. 'No.'

'Lie to me again and I'll put you out on the street and do this myself.'

Claire swallowed. 'Uh, yeah.'

'With what?'

'Silver-coated stakes, wooden stakes, a crossbow, about ten bolts…oh, and a squirt gun with some silver-nitrate solution.'

He smiled grimly at the dark windshield. 'What, no grenade launchers?'

'Would they work?'

'I choose not to comment. Very well, I will take your crossbow. Try to use nonlethal methods, if you please; there's been enough disaster in this town recently. Also, I assume you're still fond of Myrnin, in some way.' He said that as if he had no clue why that might be the case. Well, she could understand that, from his point of view.

'I won't kill him,' she said. 'But I'll hurt him if he tries to hurt me.'

'An excellent strategy, except that if you hurt him he *will* kill you, most likely. So leave Myrnin to me. You do your job, and this will soon be over…' His voice faded as he made a turn, and Claire saw something happen in his face, which was an eerie blue-white in the car's dashboard lights. She just wasn't sure what it was. 'Get down, Claire.'

'What—'

He didn't tell her again, just reached over, grabbed her head, and pulled her sideways on the seat, then pushed her down into the wheel well.

The windshield rattled, and all of a sudden there

were holes in it, sunlight streaming in. No, that hadn't
been the windshield rattling. Something had hit the
car.

Bullets had hit the car.

Oliver swerved the limousine and accelerated, but
there was more noise, and this time Claire realised it
was gunfire. The entire windshield fell out, and Oliver
made a choked sound as he got a faceful of blazing
sun.

But he kept driving, until they hit something with
a crash. Above her, Claire saw a flash of white as she
was thrown forward against the carpet.

Great, the air bags had deployed, and she was in the
wheel well. But at least she hadn't had far to go, and in
fact, she didn't think she was hurt at all, though there
was some glass that had fallen on her.

Oliver was fighting to get free of his seat belt and
the deflated air bag, but he didn't make it. Someone
yanked open his door, and Claire guessed they cut the
seat belt, or broke it, because they dragged him out of
the limo. He was struggling, but their attackers must
have been vamps, because he wasn't getting away.

They don't know I'm here, Claire realised, and
stayed where she was, curled into a very small ball in
the shadows under the dash. Her backpack had slid off
the seat and was next to her. She carefully unzipped
it and pulled out the small, folding crossbow, cranked

it open, and got out the bolts. She did it very carefully, hoping the noise of the fighting outside would cover up any sound of what she was doing. It must have, because nobody reached into the car to grab her.

She heard Oliver being dragged off, and finally risked slithering out of her hiding place to peek over the dashboard, out the sharp-edged hole where the windshield had once been.

There were vampires out, all in their heavy coats and hats and gloves. Some carried umbrellas, which was surprisingly practical of them. A whole group of them, maybe twenty in total, were standing in the shade of a building.

Amelie had an umbrella, but she didn't carry it herself. She had a minion for that. Her umbrella, like all the others, was black, but the silk suit she was wearing was icy white, with hints of blue. The colour of dead lips, Claire thought, and wished she hadn't. Amelie looked *dangerous*, even though she was just standing there, hands folded, watching as Oliver was dragged over and dumped at her feet.

'I knew it was you,' she said. She sounded viciously angry. Claire could just barely hear her, but she certainly didn't want to try to get any closer. '...think you wouldn't be suspected? Such an obvious...'

The wind kept blowing, and it made it harder for Claire to hear what was going on. Oliver said something, and it must have not made Amelie happy, because she snapped her fingers and a couple of other vampires grabbed his arms and raised him to his knees. Claire couldn't help but think how wildly all this had reversed; first Amelie had been at his mercy, then he'd been at hers, and now she had him once again.

That wouldn't make Oliver happy. Not at all.

'Don't spin your tales with me,' Amelie said. 'I don't believe we were ever...' More wind, and Claire lost the words. '...coming here. You were invited, once. You refused. Now you think you can just come here and scheme to take over—'

Oliver laughed. It had a raw, desperate sound to it. Whatever he said then, Amelie drew back a step, and then she shook her head. 'Useless,' she said. 'Take him to the cells. I'll decide how to deal with him later.'

There were way too many for Claire to even *think* about staging any kind of rescue. Oliver was clearly hurt, and she didn't think he'd appreciate any Rambo-style heroics, anyway.

But she'd just lost her chance to stop all this. Without Oliver, she had almost no chance of getting past Myrnin.

Unless Myrnin was more himself this time.

The vamps melted into the shadows, taking Oliver with them, leaving Claire and the shot-up limo where it sat, in the middle of the road. She sat back and dialled her cell phone, but the lab number kept ringing, and ringing, and ringing. Just as she was about to hang up, there was a click, and Myrnin's voice said, 'Hello?'

'Myrnin, it's Claire. Claire Danvers.'

Silence.

'Myrnin, do you know who I am?'

More silence, and then Myrnin said, very softly, 'My head aches.'

'Myrnin, do you know who I am?'

'Claire,' he said. 'Yes, Claire. I know you. Of course I know you.'

A feeling of hot relief made her just about melt into the seat cushions. Oh, thank *God*. She'd caught him at a sane moment. 'Myrnin, you have to do something for me. It's really important, OK? I need you to go down to the machine in the basement of the lab. Do that now, OK? Right now.'

'My head aches so. Do I have to?'

'I'm really sorry, but this is going to help. Please. Just go now.'

She heard noises that she assumed meant he was unlocking the trapdoor, jumping down, walking through to the cavern, and then he said, 'All right, I'm here. Claire? Could you come here to help me? I really don't feel at all well.'

'In a minute,' she promised. 'Right now, I need you to go to the keyboard and enter the password you put on the system so we can turn it off. Can you do that?'

'Password,' Myrnin said. 'I don't think...I can't remember any passwords with this headache. Could you come help me?'

'I can't until you do this. Just concentrate. Remember the password, OK? Put it in and then I can come help you.'

'Oh, all right...I think maybe – yes, I think that's it. I'm turning it off now.' She heard sounds of clicking, of what sounded like switches being thrown, and then Myrnin said, 'All right. It's safe. You can come back now, Claire.'

There was something strange about his voice. It wasn't right. 'Myrnin? Did you turn it off?'

'Of course. I did just as you asked. Now come.'

That *really* wasn't right, and Claire felt a shiver working its way up her spine. 'Myrnin, are any of the lights still on? Are you sure you turned it off—'

'*Come here right now!*' Myrnin roared, and she was so shocked she dropped her phone and scrambled away from it in panic, as if it had grown teeth. 'Come here, little Claire. Juicy, sweet little Claire who thinks she can fool me into destroying Morganville. Come and get your reward!'

Claire folded up the phone and ended the call. She

sat clutching the crossbow, feeling cold even in the sunlight.

She'd never felt so alone, never. Not even when she'd first come to Morganville.

She couldn't stop this. She was helpless. Completely helpless.

She put her head on the deflated air bag and cried.

Eventually, crying wore off, but the feeling of overwhelming failure didn't. She kept the crossbow ready, just in case. She thought she'd go to Eve, find her...but then she realised that although Oliver had known where they were going, she had no idea where Eve's house might be. The only thing she could think of to do was...go back to the Glass House. It seemed like a long, scary walk. There were lots of people roaming around, mostly confused, angry, or terrified. She tried to avoid them, but sometimes they confronted her and wanted to know where their wives, husbands, sons, daughters, moms, dads were. Or what had happened to their houses. Or their cars. Or their jobs.

She could have sworn someone was following her.

She finally just started running, running as if her life depended on it, and there was such a surge of pathetic hope when she saw the Glass House up ahead that she felt sick. She unlocked the door and slammed it behind her and slid down against it, holding her head in her hands.

It'll happen to me, too, she thought. *Maybe in an hour. Maybe tomorrow. But I'll forget, too. And when I do, nobody will be able to stop this.*

She felt a rush of warmth around her, almost of comfort. It was the house, trying to respond to her misery. She wiped her eyes and sniffled and said, 'That doesn't help. Nothing helps.'

But somehow, it did help a little, even though she knew it was as useless as a hug during an earthquake. She sucked in a deep breath and got up to go upstairs. No Michael, of course. Not yet. And no sign of Eve, so she probably was at her parents' house, after all. Her door was open, and her clothes were all thrown around. It was impossible to tell whether that was panic or just natural behaviour with Eve.

Claire's room was neat and just the way she'd left it. She got into bed and pulled the covers up, keeping the crossbow with her, and curled onto her side. She still had her phone with her, and she paged through the contacts list, feeling miserable and alone. Finally, she tried to call Eve's cell. She didn't know why, but maybe Eve had snapped out of it. Maybe she—

'What?'

That sounded like the Eve she knew. Claire slowly sat up in bed, clutching the phone like a lifeline. 'Eve? Oh, thank God. Eve, where are you?'

'Home, duh. Who's this?'

Her heart sank. 'C-Claire.'

'From school?'

'Uh – yeah. From school.' She only lied because she felt so bad, and she needed to just hear a friendly voice. Even if that person didn't know who she really was. 'In math.'

'Oh, yeah, you sit at the back, I remember.'

Claire cleared her throat, because her voice sounded thick and teary. 'What are you doing?'

'There is some weird shit going down in Weirdsville, let me tell you. I came home and my mom won't talk to me, which is actually nice for a change, but my room is *gone*. I mean, it's here, but it's full of junk. I had to move stuff to get to my bed! It's like they didn't care if I ever came back.' Eve sounded manic, and nervous. 'It's weird, I mean, my stuff...I think she trashed everything. I can't find my clothes. I think my parents are trying to make me leave. Which, fab, I'll go, you know? I hate it here. Don't you?'

Claire sniffled and wiped her nose. 'Yeah,' she said faintly. 'I do. Where would you go?'

'I don't know. Away, you know? Away from all this crap. Someplace sunny, if you get me.'

'What about Michael?'

'Michael? *Glass?*' Eve laughed, but it sounded edgy and strange. 'Like he knows I live at all. I mean, he's hella cute, but he's not ever going to notice me.'

'I think he will,' Claire said. 'I mean, I think he thinks you're cute.'

'Really?' Eve's voice sharpened and got suspicious. 'You think I'm really going to fall for that? Am I supposed to go up and fall all over Mr Perfect Glass and get humiliated; is that what this is about? Who are you, one of Bitch Queen Monica's posse? Because if you are—'

'I'm not! I promise!'

But Eve's paranoia switch was well and truly tripped now. 'Yeah, well, nice talking to you. Have a great life.'

And she hung up.

Claire clutched the phone to her chest, hard, and tried not to scream out her frustration. When the phone rang, she thought it would be Eve calling back, maybe to give her more attitude. 'Yeah?' she said miserably.

'Claire?' *Shane.* 'Claire, are you OK?'

She almost started crying again. 'I'm home; I'm at the Glass House. Where are you?'

'On my way there now,' he said. 'Stay put. It's not safe out here.'

'I know.' She sat up and hugged her pillow. 'Oliver wasn't affected; he was going to help me get to Myrnin.'

'Claire, I *told* you not to—'

'It doesn't matter. We got ambushed on the way.

Amelie hauled him off. I think she thinks he came
to kill her. She doesn't remember him living here, or
that he was her...friend.' *Friend* didn't sound right,
especially given what had gone on between them. 'I
don't know what happened to him.'

'Well, sorry to say this, but if she kills him, boo-hoo,
and I'll get counselling. Look, just *stay there*. I'll be
home in about ten minutes. I'm bringing food.'

'What about Michael?'

Shane was silent for a long few seconds, so long
Claire checked the screen to see if she'd lost the
connection. 'I couldn't get him to remember,' he finally
said. 'It was safer to leave him with the vamps. He
nearly took my throat out, and he kept screaming he
wasn't...you know. It was bad.'

'It's all bad,' Claire said. 'And it's all my fault. I can't
stop it, Shane. I can't do anything to stop it.'

'Hey, hey, stop that. We're going to figure this out,
OK? We'll find a way. But first, we eat, we get some
rest, and then we save the world. Right?'

'Just hurry,' she said. 'Nothing bad can happen
when I'm with you.'

'Wow. I'm not sure if I feel shiny or scared.'

'Scared is useful right now.'

'Good point. I'm coming, OK? I'm running.'

She was smiling, though faintly, as she hung up.
She stayed in bed, crossbow at her side, until she heard

the front door downstairs open and close, and Shane's voice called her name. Then she got up and took the crossbow and phone downstairs to meet him.

He looked a little worried about the crossbow as he set a grease-stained bag on the dining table in the corner. 'Expecting somebody else?' he asked. 'Because I hope that's not for me.'

She put it down, ran to him, and kissed him frantically. He held her close and kissed her back, warm and sweet and soft, and just the fact that he was *here* with her made things so, so, *so* much better.

She finally broke free of the kiss and put her head on his chest. 'Thank you,' she said. 'Thank you for remembering.'

'Yeah, no problem,' he said. He sounded amused. 'You may not thank me for the burgers and fries, though. I don't think Dan's Drive-In is doing its best work today.'

'Anything,' she said. 'As long as you're here.'

'Claire.' He pushed her away a little, and tilted her chin up. He looked tired, and worried, and she thought he was, deep down, just as freaked out as she was. 'Don't forget me, OK?'

'I won't,' she promised. 'I don't think I ever could. Not even...not even if...'

He hugged her, and they really didn't need to finish that conversation at all. It was all...better.

Eventually, he said, 'The burgers are getting cold,' and Claire let go and went into the kitchen to retrieve the all-important drinks to go with dinner. And yeah, the burgers were kind of gross and the fries were a little cold, but she savoured every bite. It tasted like normal life, and she needed every bit of that she could get. They cleaned up afterward, and Shane decided that he'd better wash the dishes, because it was Eve's turn and she wasn't going to remember anyway, even if by some miracle she found her way back here. And that felt good, too.

It felt like being in control, at least of the kitchen.

Claire called her mom, who talked about the tests they were running on her dad, and how they planned surgery to fix the valve in his heart, and how he was doing so well, really, all things considered. Claire said very little, because she was afraid she'd just start crying hysterically if she did. Mom didn't seem to notice; her focus was on Dad, of course. And that was OK.

The last thing her mother said to her was, 'I love you so much, honey. Be safe. And call me tomorrow.'

'I will,' Claire whispered. 'Love you too, Mom.'

She hung up before her voice could tremble, and saw Shane watching her with a kind of warm understanding in his face.

'That was hard, huh?' he asked, and put an arm around her. 'Your dad's OK?'

'Doing better than they expected,' Claire said, and took in a deep breath. 'Unlike us, I guess.'

'Hey, don't count us out yet.'

'I don't,' Claire said. 'But it's bad, Shane. I feel like we're really alone this time. Just the two of us.'

He hugged her closer. 'And that's not all terrible. Tomorrow we're going to get this handled, all right? You're too shaky right now, and going out in the dark isn't a fabulous plan. We'll fight monsters in the morning.'

The Morganville TV station was showing reruns of shows from three years ago. Shane put in a movie, and they talked about...well, nothing, really, and kissed and stayed together until finally, there was nothing to do but go to bed.

Shane walked her to her bedroom door, and before he could say anything, she said, 'Stay, OK? I want you with me.' He just nodded, and she saw relief on his face. He'd been going to ask, anyway.

They got undressed – mostly – in silence, and slipped under the blankets to hold each other. Claire was too worried and scared to want to do anything else, and she thought he felt the same, really; it was more holding on for comfort right now. And that was good. That was really good.

'I don't know what I'm going to do tomorrow,' Claire said finally, into the dark. Shane's arms tightened around her, pulling her closer against his chest.

'Tomorrow, we've going to find out who can still fight, and get down there and pin Myrnin down and fix this,' he said. 'I swear. We're going to make this work.'

'The two of us.'

'Yeah, the two of us, and whoever's left who's not bug-eyed crazy.' He kissed the back of her neck, very gently. 'It's going to be OK. Sleep.'

And she did, warm in his embrace, and dreamt of silver rain.

CHAPTER THIRTEEN

Claire woke with the sun in her eyes, again, and for a precious, sweet second she just savoured the warmth of it on her body, and the fact that Shane was still curled up against her back, one heavy arm around her waist. Then, regretfully, she turned over to face him. 'Hey,' she said. 'Wake up, sleepyhead; we overslept.'

Shane mumbled something and tried to put a pillow over his head. She pulled it off. 'Come on; get up; we've got things to do!'

'Go 'way, Lyss,' he moaned, and opened his eyes, blinked, and finally focused on her.

And then he completely, totally freaked out.

He actually flailed around, got caught in the covers, and when he tried to get free, fell out of bed onto the floor. Claire laughed and leant over the side, looking down at him. 'Hey, are you...OK...'

The words died in her mouth, because he was *still*
freaking. He writhed around in the covers, grabbed a
blanket, and wrapped it around his body as he climbed
to his bare feet, backing away from the bed.

And her.

He held out the hand that wasn't holding up the
blanket, palm out. 'OK,' he said. 'OK, think, Collins,
think – yeah, OK, this is awkward, and I'm really
sorry, because I'm sure you're really— Oh, man. What
the hell did I do? Was there drinking? There must have
been drinking.'

'Shane?' Claire still had a sheet, and now she pulled
it over herself, suddenly cold and feeling very exposed.
'Shane—'

He was *still* backing away, looking panicked and
deeply uncomfortable. 'So, we've obviously been formally
introduced at some point in my insane drinking binge.
Uh, hi. Look, you've got to keep it down, OK? My
parents will *kill* me if—' He stopped and looked around
the room. 'Oh, *shit*. This is not my room, is it? This is
yours. As in, I never went home, all night. My dad is
going to—' He squeezed his eyes shut. 'Pants. I need
pants. Where are my pants?'

Claire felt like her heart was breaking. Really,
truly shattering into sharp, jagged, bloody pieces.
She wanted to scream, and cry, and most of all, she
wanted this *not to be happening*. She couldn't bring

herself to say anything, and he ignored her totally
to look around. He found his pants and T-shirt, and
awkwardly put on his pants under the cover of the
blanket before dropping it. Before he got his shirt on,
he turned back to look at her, and it *hurt*, it hurt so
badly to have him see her like that and not know her
at all.

Her utter, horrified misery must have shown in her
face, because his expression softened a little bit. He
took a couple of steps towards the bed and said, 'Um,
look – I know... I'm sorry; I'm probably a complete
douche bag for doing this to you, and I promise, this
isn't...I don't really get drunk off my ass and hook up
like this, and you seem...you don't seem like the type.
I mean, you're pretty; I don't mean you're not – I'm
sorry; I suck at this. But I have to get home, right now.'
He pulled his shirt on and looked for shoes, which he
slipped on without socks or even bending over to tie
them. 'Look, I'll call you, OK? Uh...your name is...'

'Claire,' she whispered, and tears broke free and
started streaming down her face. 'My name is Claire.
This is my fault.'

'Hey, don't do that, don't – I'm sorry. It's not your
fault. You seem' – he bent over and awkwardly kissed
her, and it felt like he was a stranger – 'nice. I promise
I'll talk to you later. We'll figure this out. Oh, Jesus,
did I have a...Did we take precautions or...' He shook

his head. 'Not now, I can't think about this right now.
I have to go. Later.'

'Wait!' she wailed, as he opened her bedroom door
and ran out down the hall. 'Shane, *wait!*' He didn't.
She grabbed up her jeans and shirt from the floor,
threw them on, stepped into her shoes, and ran after
him. 'Shane, please don't—'

He was standing in the living room, staring around,
and when she came clattering breathlessly down the
steps, he turned to look at her again. This time he
didn't seem as confused. But he didn't seem to be back
to himself, either. 'This is Michael's house,' he said.
'What are we doing here?'

'Shane — Shane, please listen to me; we *live* here!
With Michael! And Eve!'

'Keep your voice down!' He made frantic shushing
motions at her, and lowered his voice even more. 'OK,
you seemed nice, and now you seem a little bit whacked.
We don't live here. Maybe *you* live here — maybe you're
some cousin or something; I don't know — but *I* live
with my parents and my sister. Not here.'

'No! No, your parents—' Oh, *God*. What was she
going to say? What *could* she say? Her mind went
completely blank. He waited, then held up both hands
and backed away.

'Whatever, crazy chick who maybe lives here and
maybe also breaks into Michael's house when they're

all gone. I'm out. Have a nice delusion.'

She couldn't let him go; she just couldn't. As he walked down the hall, she ran after him. 'Shane, don't. Don't go home. You *can't*!'

He didn't even argue with her at that point; he just opened the front door and walked out into the morning sun. She hesitated in the doorway, wondering if she should go back and get her backpack, get *something*, call *someone*, but he was walking fast, and she had no idea where the old Collins house had once been. He'd never once told her, or pointed it out to her.

She locked the door and started following him.

Shane never looked back; maybe he knew she was there and was determined to ignore her – she wasn't sure. She kept a good distance between them, careful not to look *too* creepy and stalkery, but it couldn't be helped. If she let him out of sight...

He turned the corner up ahead, and when she hurried to catch up, she saw him sprinting, putting a lot of distance between them, fast. *No, no, no!* If she lost him now she might never find him again. It was too terrifying, not only for her, but for him. He just didn't know it yet.

She was passing an alley, sure he was still up ahead, when Shane grabbed her and slammed her hard up against the side of a building. She hadn't realised in a long time just how big Shane was, or how strong. Or how he usually didn't show it, unless he wanted to. Like now. There was a fire in his eyes, and an angry, stubborn set to his jaw. Shane in fighting mode.

He pinned her in place for a long moment, as if he were trying to decide what to do.

'Enough,' he said then, and let go. 'Look, I don't want to hurt you, but you need to stop following me. It's creepy and weird. Walk away, or next time I'm not going to be so nice about it.'

'You wouldn't hurt me,' Claire said. 'I know you wouldn't.'

'Yeah, well, don't count on it. I don't like hitting girls, but it doesn't mean I won't hit back if you start the fight. Ask Monica.' He frowned then, and she saw real anger in his eyes. 'Monica. Did she set this up? What was it, some kind of roofie thing; she took pictures? She's going to Facebook the hell out of it? Blackmail me?'

'No. I don't have anything to do with Monica.'

'Bullshit,' Shane said bluntly. 'Stop following me. I mean it. And quit crying; it's not going to work.'

He walked out into the sunlight and kept going. She didn't know what to do. She knew he meant it; she *was* acting weird and crazy and dangerous, and in Morganville, nobody could afford to ignore that. So he'd probably do something if she followed him. Maybe even get her arrested.

She didn't care, but there had to be some other way. *Something.* She couldn't just let him go.

A woman passed by on the street, looking confused and checking the addresses of buildings. Probably trying to find a store that wasn't there anymore. Claire waited until Shane was out of sight around the corner, and then walked up to the stranger. 'Hello,' she said, trying desperately hard to sound polite and helpful, and not as deeply freaked out as she felt. The woman gave her a distracted smile. She had on a bracelet, so she was a Morganville native, which was a relief. 'Um, are you looking for something?'

'Oh, it's so stupid. I think I got turned around,' the woman said. 'Can't understand how, I've been working here for years – Grant's Dry Cleaner's. I could have sworn it was...right here...'

'Oh, I think it moved,' Claire said. 'Isn't it one block over now?'

'Is it?' The woman frowned, and Claire saw fear and confusion in her eyes. She wished she could help her, but she didn't know how, really. 'Oh, that must be it. I can't imagine why I...Guess I'm losing my mind. Isn't that odd?'

We all are, Claire thought, but she said, 'I can't remember anything before I have coffee,' and smiled. The woman looked a little reassured. 'Um, maybe you can help me? I was looking for Frank Collins's house; I think it's around here somewhere?'

'Oh, Mr Collins.' The woman didn't look as if she was very fond of him, but she nodded. 'Yeah, he and his family live two blocks over, then one block to the left. It's on Helicon Drive. Big two-story house.'

'Thanks,' Claire said sincerely. 'I hope you get to work OK.'

'Oh, I will. Maybe I'll just stop for coffee first, though.'

Claire gave her a little wave and took off running. The lady called after her, 'Dear, you're going the wrong way!'

'Shortcut!' Claire yelled back.

Now that she knew where the house should be, she cut along a side road and through a couple of alleys – dangerous, but necessary if she wanted to avoid looking like she was following Shane again. She ran hard, and came out on the right road, and a block farther over, just as he came walking from the other direction.

There was a big, ugly empty lot in the middle of the street between them, with a rusted, leaning mailbox. The lot was overgrown with weeds, but the remains of a house were still there...cracked concrete foundations, some steps leading up to a door that wasn't there. Nothing else but some burnt pieces of wood too big to haul away easily. Claire stopped and stood where she was, watching as Shane came towards the lot...and stopped.

He looked at the ruins, then at the mailbox. Then at the cracked foundation again. Finally, he opened the mailbox to look inside. The door fell off of it, but he found some aging, yellowed papers inside.

Bills. With his family's name on them, Claire guessed. He stared at them, shook his head, and slowly put them back into the box.

She saw it hit him, the same way it had hit all the others – the knowledge that things weren't like they were supposed to be. That time wasn't where it should have been. That everything was wrong.

He staggered and tried to catch himself against the mailbox, and knocked it over into the weeds. Shane frantically tried to pick it up, fix it, make it right, but the post was rotted through, and he finally had to lay it down and then sat beside it, holding his head in his hands, shaking.

Claire walked over, very slowly. 'Shane,' she said. 'Shane, I'm so sorry. I didn't know how to tell you. I'm so sorry.'

'My house,' he whispered. 'It's here. It's supposed to be *here*.' He looked up at her, and there were tears swimming in his dark eyes. 'Something happened. What *happened*?'

She felt sick, and she loathed every second of what

she knew she was about to do to him. 'There was a...
an accident.'

'Where are they?' Shane asked, and looked at the
devastation where his life had once been. There was a
rusted swing set in the back, bent and broken. 'Alyssa.
Where's Alyssa? Where's my sister?'

Claire reached out a hand to him. 'Get up,' she said
softly. 'I'll take you.'

'I want to see my sister! I'm responsible for her!'

'I know. Just...trust me, OK? I'll take you.'

He wasn't in any shape now to be angry, or even
suspicious. He just took her hand, and she pulled him
up to his feet and held on, leading him down the street
and on. The sun blazed down warm, but the breeze felt
colder, bringing winter in short, sharp bursts.

'Where are we going?' Shane asked, but not as if he
cared much. 'I can't believe...It must have happened
last night when I—'

'Shane, you saw that. The weeds are waist-high.
The mailbox was rotted out. There's nothing there.'
Claire pulled in a deep breath. 'It's been years since
that happened. It didn't happen overnight.'

'You're cracked.' He tried to pull free of her, but she
held on. 'It's not true. I was there *yesterday*!'

'Listen to me! God, Shane, *please*! I know you think
it was yesterday, but it's been a long time. You've
been...other places. You just don't remember right now.'

She swallowed a lump in her throat and tried to go on sounding brave and calm. 'You'll be fine. Just...trust me.'

'Take me to my family.'

'I'll take you to Alyssa,' she said. 'Please. Trust me.'

She knew the way.

The graveyard was cold and silent, and the wind felt even more like winter here, even with the sun sparkling off of granite headstones and white marble mausoleums. The grass was still a little green, but mostly brown.

The headstone read, ALYSSA COLLINS, BELOVED DAUGHTER AND SISTER, and it gave her dates of birth and death.

Shane read it, and his face went white and very still. His eyes seemed strange when he looked at Claire. 'It's not true.'

'I'm sorry,' she said. 'But it is.'

'It's a sick joke.'

'No,' she said. 'Shane, Alyssa died in the fire. She died three years ago, before you left Morganville with your mom and dad. Before I ever came here. I know you don't remember that, but it happened. You left town, and you came back, and you moved into Michael's house with him and Eve. Then I came and moved in, too.'

'No,' he said, and took a big step back, then another one. He almost ran into another headstone, and braced himself when he staggered. 'No, you're lying, this is some sick little game of Monica's, but this is low even for her—'

'Shane, Monica didn't do this, and it's not a game! Shane! *Listen!*'

'I've listened enough to you!' he yelled, and shoved her so hard she fell and almost cracked her skull on Marvis Johnson's memorial stone. 'You stay the hell away from me and my family, you crazy bitch! This is *sick*! This is *fake!*'

He tried to push over Alyssa's tombstone. It didn't move. He kicked at it, panting, and Claire lay where she was, watching him, heartsick. She'd thought maybe this would convince him, maybe it would force him to remember...but he didn't. He couldn't.

'Please,' she whispered. 'Please stop, Shane. Stop hurting yourself; I can't stand it.'

He collapsed against his sister's tombstone and just sat there, his back to Claire. His shoulders were shaking. She got up and went to kneel beside him. He looked destroyed, just...broken. She put her hand on his shoulder.

He didn't hit her, at least. He didn't seem to notice she was still there. He was pale and shaking and sweating, and hunched in on himself as if somebody had punched him really, really hard. 'She can't be,' he said. 'She can't be dead. I just...I just saw her. She was making fun of my shirt. My shirt...' He looked down at himself, pulled his T-shirt out, and said, 'I wasn't wearing this. This isn't even my shirt. This is wrong. This is all wrong.'

'I know,' Claire said. 'I know it feels that way. Shane, please come back with me. Please. I'll show you the room you have in Michael's house. You'll recognise some of the things in there; maybe it'll help. Come on, get up. You can't stay here; it's cold.' He didn't move. 'Alyssa wouldn't want you to stay here.'

'Why didn't she get out?' he asked. 'If there was a fire, how did I get out if she didn't? I wouldn't leave her. I wouldn't do that. I couldn't...just...run—'

'You didn't,' Claire said, and put her arm around him. 'You tried to save her. You told me, Shane. I know how hard you tried.'

He finally swiped at his eyes and looked at her. 'I don't even know you,' he said. 'Why are you doing this?'

There it was again. How could her heart keep on breaking? Why didn't it just do it once and get it over with? Claire struggled to keep the hurt she felt from echoing in her voice. 'I know you think you don't,' she said. 'But honest, Shane, you do know me. We're... friends.'

He stared at her for what seemed like the longest time, and then he said, 'I'm sorry I pushed you. I don't...I don't do things like that.'

'I know.'

'Is it true? Is Lyss really...'

Claire just nodded without speaking. Shane's hair blew in his face, but he didn't blink. She reached over without thinking and moved it back. He caught her hand against his face.

'You touch me a lot,' he said. 'Don't you?'

She looked down and felt the blush mounting in her face. 'I guess I do,' she said. 'I'm sorry.' She risked a quick look up at him. He was studying her, as if he were really seeing her for the first time. 'What?'

'Are we going out?'

She nodded. He didn't say anything at all. She didn't know how to feel about that. Before she could think how to ask what he was feeling, he stood up, and she hurried to do the same.

'So I have amnesia,' he said. 'That's what you're telling me. I got some kind of kick in the head and I lost a bunch of time and forgot all this. And you.'

That was...*so* much easier than what she'd been trying to say. 'Yes.' She nodded. 'Amnesia. That's why you need to trust me, Shane. It's dangerous out here. You don't know how dangerous.'

For the first time, he gave her an ironic expression

she recognised – classic Shane. 'It's Morganville. Of course it's dangerous.' He glanced back down at Alyssa's headstone, and that moment of the Shane she knew flickered and almost disappeared. Almost. 'She wouldn't want me moping around the cemetery like some dumb-ass. Alyssa wasn't like that. She'd make fun of me if I did.' Shane took in a deep breath. 'So I guess...I guess I can go to Michael's house. At least I know him, even if I don't know you.'

She smiled a little. It felt forced. 'We'll work on it.' She held out her hand, but he put his in his pockets.

'No offence,' he said, 'but I've got a lot to think about, here. I need some time.'

Her shattered heart broke all over again.

It felt just as bad this time.

'Sure,' she managed to say. 'I understand.'

There was still nobody at the Glass House when they returned, but Claire still shuddered in relief at just being home. Shane looked a little mistrustful, but he came inside and didn't protest when she locked up behind him. 'Do you want to see your room?' she asked. He shook his head, hands firmly in his pockets. 'Do you want coffee?'

'I hate coffee,' he said. 'Never touch the stuff.'

'Really?' Maybe that had been something he'd learnt on the road, with his mom and dad. 'OK, how about... Coke?'

'Sure. Who doesn't love Coke?'

She left him looking at the TV and the game controllers, and went to pull the last two cans out of the fridge. Somebody was going to have to go shopping. She supposed she'd better do it soon, before she lost her mind, too. Even in an apocalypse like this, surely running out of Cokes qualified as a disaster.

Shane was sitting on the couch when she came back, and she handed over the can and sat on the other end, leaving plenty of comfort space between them. He nodded and popped the top. 'So, I live here?'

'Yeah. Right up there.'

'That's Michael's room.'

'No, he's over there now.'

'Huh, he always liked that room better.' He poked at the controller. 'And we have an Xbox.'

'Actually, you've got an Xbox 360,' she said. 'You bought it last year.'

'Sweet. What's the difference?'

'Do you really want to talk about games right now?'

He stopped fiddling with the controller and put it down. 'I guess not. Those other people out there, the ones acting so weird – they've got what I have, right? This memory problem. I didn't just get kicked in the head or drugged or something.'

'No,' Claire said. 'There's a machine underground;

it's what wipes people's memories when they leave town. But it's not working right. It's wiping memories inside town.'

He stopped to think about that. It said something about his childhood in Morganville that he didn't, in fact, find that unbelievable at all. 'How many people have it?'

'A lot. Maybe all of us, eventually. Michael got it yesterday. So did Eve. So did Amelie.'

Shane looked at her sharply. 'Who?'

'You know. The Founder.'

'You know her by *name*?'

'So do you. But right now, she's stuck in three years ago, just like you. She doesn't remember me. She doesn't remember Oliver or—'

'Who's Oliver?'

This was going to be harder than she'd expected. 'Never mind. The important thing is that before we went to sleep last night, we agreed we were going to find other people who could help us and we were going to try to turn off the machine.'

'We went to sleep together,' he said. 'Without clothes.'

'Uh...yeah. We had underwear on, though.'

'Right. Why do I think that maybe it's come off before?' He stared at her for what seemed like an uncomfortably long second, as if he were remembering her almost naked. 'OK, sounds easy enough. Let's do it, if this is going to fix things.' He watched her expression, and said, 'But it isn't that easy. Is it?'

'The vamps won't let us anywhere near where we need to go,' she said. 'I can't think of any of them we can count on now. Not even Michael.'

'Wait a second, *what*? Michael *Glass*? He is *not* a vampire. I think you mean his granddad, Sam. Are you sure you really live here? Because that's a pretty gigantic mistake.'

'I'm not talking about Sam,' Claire said. 'Michael... Michael got bitten. And now he's a vampire. But he doesn't remember becoming one, and that's a big problem. So if you see him, don't, you know, hug. He bites. He doesn't mean to, though.'

'You *are* freaking insane; I was right the first time about you. Michael, a vampire? Never happen.' But even though he said it, Shane didn't try to get up and leave. 'You're not from Morganville. If you were, I'd remember you, right? So who are you, exactly?'

'I came to the university. That's how I met you guys.'

He laughed. 'Me? In college? Yeah, make up another one. Look, I barely got through last year in high school. I don't think anybody's going to be giving me college admission, not even to TPU, the crappiest school in Texas.'

'It's not that bad,' Claire said, although she had no idea why she was trying to defend the place. It hadn't done her many favours. 'I didn't meet you *in* college. I met you *because* of college. Because of Monica.'

'Morrell.'

'Bitch queen of Morganville,' Claire said. 'Well, she's still all that, and more. I guess she was pretty bad in high school, but trust me, she's worse now.'

'Nice to know some things haven't changed.' Shane pulled in a deep breath. 'OK, I didn't want to ask, but...what about my mom and dad? Where are they?'

She just looked at him, and he finally turned his head away. 'OK,' he said. 'I get it. They're dead, too.'

'Your mom...your mom is,' Claire said. 'I don't know where she's buried. Your dad's...well—'

'Still an alcoholic jerk? Big shock.'

'No,' she said. 'Your dad's a vampire.'

Shane froze, eyes wide, and then laughed in a bitter, shocked kind of way. 'Like hell he is. He'd kill himself first.'

'Trust me, I think he thought about it, after it happened. But I guess he's decided to hang around after all. Wait...maybe we can find him. Maybe he's not affected yet. He might help us.'

'*My* dad? Even if he wasn't a vampire – and I'm not buying that he is, by the way – he wasn't big on doing favours for anybody. Not even his own kids. Maybe we'd better skip the family reunion.'

Claire wasn't so sure, but she didn't want to freak Shane out any more than she had to, and Frank Collins as a vampire was enough to freak *anybody* out. Much less his own son. 'OK,' she said. 'But we have to find a way to get to that machine and shut it off. And we need help. *Any* help.'

'I'm glad you said that,' said a voice from behind them. 'Because you've got no idea how much help you need.'

Claire and Shane both jumped off the couch, suddenly and completely on the same side; he even got in front of her, the kind of protective instinct Shane had always had, since the first time she'd met him. He might not believe her, or trust her, but he'd still fight for her.

Maybe because somewhere, deep down, he *did* remember.

Claire realised who was standing there, in the shadows by the stairs, about the same time that Shane did. It was the scar on his face that registered first, and then the rest of it...long, tied-back hair, a hard, unforgiving expression, a tough, thin body. He was wearing a leather vest over a Harley T-shirt and old jeans, and combat boots. He had a big, scary knife in a sheath at his waist.

Frank Collins.

Vampire.

'Dad,' Shane whispered.

'Hello, son.'

'How did you get in here?' Claire blurted, because she knew, *knew* that the house itself had been on guard for Frank. But she hadn't felt anything when he'd entered, no warnings, nothing.

Maybe the house thought they needed his help, too. Or, more worryingly, maybe the machine had robbed the house of its protective ability. It was slowly destroying everything good in Morganville.

Frank shrugged. 'I've been following the two of you around for a couple of days. Had to know what you were planning to do about all this,' he said. 'Not too surprised about what my son said about me, if that's what's worrying you. I deserved it. Still do.' He looked over at Shane. 'But I don't drink much anymore. Well, not booze, anyway.' He smiled and showed vamp teeth.

Shane backed up a step and ran into Claire. She steadied him and whispered, 'I told you.'

'It can't be,' he said. 'There's some kind of—'

'Mistake?' Frank said, and jumped over the couch in one smooth, ominous vampire move to land right in front of them. They were up against the wall now, next to the TV. 'Only mistake I ever made was coming back to this cursed town in the first place, Shane.

And sending you back here to help. If we'd stayed on the road, we'd still be running, but at least we'd be together.'

'Running. Running from what?'

'Oh, come on, son. You think they really let us leave, just like that? We had help getting out, but they'd have brought us back, or killed us, if they'd caught us. Just like they killed your mother.'

Shane's breath went out in a rushing moan, as if his dad had punched him. Claire put her hand on his shoulder and glared at Frank. 'Stop it,' she said.

'You started it,' Frank said. 'You told him part of the truth, didn't you? Told him about Alyssa? Well, he needs to know everything. He needs to know how his mother got into drugs to forget the pain. He needs to know how we got chased from one ratty motel to another across the state. He needs to know those bastards cut her wrists and dumped her in a tub to pretend it was suicide—'

'Stop it!' Claire screamed, and put herself in front of Shane, like she could protect him from the words the way he protected her from fists.

'And how he found her,' Frank finished, softly, 'floating there. Dead. I thought I'd lost you too, son. You didn't talk for days, didn't sleep, didn't eat. But then you told me you wanted to come back here, to Morganville. To make them pay.'

Shane had gone almost as white as his vampire father now, and his eyes were huge and dark and empty. Claire turned towards him and put her hands on his cheeks, trying to make him look at her. He didn't. He couldn't look away from Frank. 'Shane, Shane, listen, he's trying to hurt you; he *always* tries to hurt you—'

'Not always,' Frank said. 'Somebody's got to tell the boy what he needs to hear, even though it hurts. He needed to know what happened to his mom. You weren't going to tell him, were you?'

'There wasn't any reason! You just like to watch him suffer!' Claire snapped. 'You're a mean, vicious, evil—'

'I love my son,' Frank said. 'But he had to grow up in those three years after Alyssa died. And he has to do it all over again, now, even faster. Can't sugar-coat that, Claire.'

Shane put his hands on Claire's shoulders – the first time he'd actually touched her gently, she thought, since waking up this morning – and moved her out of the way. 'So I'm what, eighteen now? Not fifteen?'

'Almost nineteen,' his dad said.

'Good.' And Shane punched him in the face.

Well, he tried to. Frank caught his fist about an inch away from landing. He didn't punch back, or shove, or squeeze Shane's hand into a mess, although Claire knew he could have. He just held it there, even though

Shane tried to pull back. 'Son,' he said, 'I was bad at being a father, just as bad as I was at everything else. You were the one who took care of your mother and Alyssa. You did the job I was supposed to do, being the man of the house, from the time you were eight years old. And I'm sorry for that.'

He pulled Shane forward and hugged him. Shane was stiff as bundled wire, but after a moment, he relaxed a little, and then stepped away. Frank let him go.

'So now you want to make it up to me,' Shane said. 'Well, you can't. I didn't trust you before. I damn sure don't trust you as a bloodsucker.'

'Right now, you two need a bloodsucker,' Frank said. 'At least, that's what I heard the girl saying. Isn't that right, Claire?'

She didn't like agreeing with Frank Collins, ever, but she had to nod. 'You aren't affected yet.'

'There are a few who aren't,' Frank said. 'Don't know why; maybe our brains are just wired different, or maybe it's just random. Most of the others are hiding out; can't say I really blame them. I might be able to get a couple of people on board if we need them.'

'Vampire people.'

Frank bared his fangs. 'I've still got friends on both sides of the bloodline. You want 'em or not?'

Claire and Shane exchanged a look. He still didn't

know her, she thought. He still didn't really trust her. But clearly, next to Frank, she had got a major boost on the cool scale.

'Up to you,' Shane said. 'You're the one who knows what's going on. I'm just the muscle.'

'That's not true. You're smart, Shane. You just hide it.'

Frank smiled. 'You never had to sign his report cards.'

'Shut *up*, Frank; I wasn't talking to you,' Claire said sharply. 'Go...lurk, or something. I need to talk to Shane alone.'

Frank shrugged and walked away. He picked up Shane's Coke can and drained it as he toured the living room, messing with things.

'And don't you dare touch Michael's guitars.'

He waved without looking back.

Claire grabbed Shane by the shirt and towed him with her into the little-used parlour at the front of the house, the farthest she could get from Frank, although she knew it really wasn't any use. He was a vampire; he could probably hear ants walking. Well, at least it *felt* like privacy.

She let go of Shane, who looked down at her with what seemed like a kind of amusement. 'You know,' he said, 'most people were scared to death of my dad, at least when he was drinking. Including me, mostly.

Now he's a vamp, and you just ordered him around like you don't give a crap.'

'I don't like him very much.'

'Yeah, got that. You look like a strong wind will snap you off at the knees, but you're a tough little thing, aren't you?'

She smiled and wished that for once she wouldn't blush at a compliment, but that was a lost cause. 'I guess,' she said. 'I'm still here. That counts.'

'Yeah,' he said, and moved a strand of hair back from her face. 'That counts.' He suddenly realised what he was doing and cleared his throat. 'OK, so what's the plan? We get Frankenstein and his friends to back us up?'

'I heard that!' Frank called from the living room. Shane silently shot him the finger, which Claire slapped down.

'Don't do that!' she whispered.

'What, you think he can sense it with his magic vampire powers?'

'We need him, Shane.'

He smiled bleakly. 'Yeah, well, Frank's never been around when I needed him, so don't put a lot of faith in that.'

'We need to come at this two ways,' Claire said. 'First, you and I are going to go in the front entrance to the lab. Second, right about the time we get Myrnin distracted—'

'Who's Myrnin?'

Claire controlled an urge to roll her eyes. 'Badass crazy vampire scientist who's my boss.'

'You realise no part of that sentence made sense, right?'

'Just stay out of his way. Don't let him get close.'

'Yeah, that's easy.'

'If you can get a crossbow bolt or a stake in him, do it,' Claire said. 'It won't kill him if you don't use silver, but it'll put him down and out of the way until we're finished.'

'What if he has friends? You know, back-up?'

'We do the same thing to them.'

Shane pointed a thumb at the living room. 'And what about *him* and *his* friends?'

'They come in the back way,' Claire said. 'Through the portal.'

'Good plan,' Shane said, and then paused. 'What's a portal?'

Claire sighed. 'We've got work to do.'

CHAPTER FOURTEEN

Frank's friends turned out to be – no surprise – kind of the dregs. A couple of vampires whom Claire absolutely didn't trust around her veins, and who had a disturbing tendency to flash fangs at her when they thought she wasn't looking. One was named Rudolph (and she had to resist the temptation to laugh), and the other just went by West. They looked exactly like the kind of friends she'd have expected Frank Collins to have – greasy, shifty, and tough. Oh, and West was a woman, a tough blond biker-type chick who wore a muscle tee to show off her biceps, which even Shane agreed were impressive.

He'd also brought in some humans – again, biker types, who were big on muscles and (Claire thought) not so much with the brains. But they were going to help, and for their own reasons – mainly because their family or friends or girlfriends had forgotten all about them. They weren't the kind of people who liked being overlooked.

The Glass House filled up pretty quickly, and Claire had to send people out for supplies; she broke out all of the vampire-fighting equipment she knew about in the house, which was considerable, but it still wasn't enough to equip what was shaping up to be a small army. She gave her recurve bow – a souvenir of her last trip outside of Morganville – to West, who said she used to be a competition archer, back in her day. Which was, apparently, back in the day when people wore armour. Claire kept a small folding crossbow for herself.

By the time the human bikers came back with more wood for stakes, and cases of beer and Cokes, the day was half over.

'Do they have to drink beer before we do this?' Claire complained to Frank, who was looking over a selection of stakes and testing them for sharpness on the end. He had a can in his hand, too. 'Correction, do *you* have to drink beer before we do this?'

'You get ready your way,' he told her, and chose his weapons. 'We'll get ready ours.' She started to leave him to it, and got only a couple of steps away before Frank said, without looking up from the stakes in his hand, 'How is he?'

'Who?'

'Your father.'

Of all the things Claire had expected, that wasn't it, and it took her a minute of honest puzzlement to try to work out why someone like Frank Collins would even care. She finally said, 'He's doing OK. I talked to my mom yesterday; the doctors think they can fix his heart problem. He's feeling a lot better.'

Frank nodded. 'Good. Family's important,' he said. 'Maybe too important, sometimes. I know how much I screwed it up with Shane. Can't blame the kid for hating me now.' It was almost a...question? And if it was a question, what could Claire say? *Yeah, he hates your guts.* That probably wasn't what Frank was hoping to hear.

'Just take care of him,' she said. 'That's what you're supposed to do. Stop using him, and start protecting him. I know he thinks he doesn't need it, but sometimes he does. Sometimes we all do.'

Now Frank did look up, and Claire felt a blush building in her face as he stared at her like he was actually *seeing* her for a change. 'He did OK,' Shane's dad finally said. 'Picking you.'

She wasn't sure how to feel about earning the worst dad in the world's approval, so she just smiled weakly, and headed for another room – any other room.

The bikers finally drained the beer and got

themselves loaded up in other ways, and they were just finishing with the preparations when the front door rattled.

Claire hushed everybody, and went to look out the window. There were two people on the doorstep. One of them was wearing a big, floppy black hat and coat, and the other one was completely shrouded in a blanket.

'What do you think, should we let them in?' Shane asked. He'd come up behind her, as close as if he actually remembered who she was. That felt...weirdly good, that he wasn't trying to stay out of her space. That he trusted her that much.

'I think that they probably have a key anyway,' Claire said, as she heard the lock turn. 'Let me take care of this.'

She got to the hall just as the door swung open, and the figure in the blanket came over the threshold. Behind it, the one in the hat came in and shut the door and locked it.

'I'm telling you,' Eve was saying, 'something is totally *wrong* around here. My mother is completely mental. More mental than she was before, and that is at least ten trailer trucks of crazy—' She stopped when she saw Claire standing there, and pulled off the hat. Her look of surprise turned to calculation, and then an outright glare. 'OK, who's this? Michael? You have a *girl* in your house? You could have told me!'

'Who's *what*? What girl? Get this off of me!'

Eve grabbed one end of the blanket and unwrapped, and Michael stumbled out of it, looking lightly broiled but nowhere near as bad as the last time Claire had seen him. She smiled in delight and moved towards them, then realised it wasn't a good idea, because they both looked immediately on guard.

Crap. They didn't know her. Once again, it hurt.

'Hi, Michael, Eve,' Claire said, and tried for a reassuring smile. 'You're right. There's something really wrong in Morganville, no doubt about it. Eve, I'm Claire. I talked to you on the phone, remember?'

Eve let that process for a second, then turned to Michael. 'Is this your *girlfriend*?'

'What? No! No, I never saw her before!' Michael said. 'I told you, I don't have a girlfriend! Ah, right now, I mean. Not that I never have. Or will.'

'He's kind of between girls,' Shane said, stepping up behind Claire. 'Hey, Mikey. Eve.'

Eve squealed. 'Shane? Thank God, somebody sane. Well, sane-ish.' She didn't give him a chance to answer, just threw herself at him and hugged him. 'I looked for you at school. Figures you'd be skipping.'

'Don't get all handsy, Gothica; I was busy.' Eve backed off, smiling, and Shane exchanged a manly fist-bump with Michael. 'Hey, man. You've looked... better.'

'I know. I'm...I'm sick, that's all,' Michael said. 'What are you doing here? Wait...' He looked past them to the living room, where the bikers were crushing beer cans and checking weapons. 'OK, I think I have a better question. What are *they* doing in my house? And where are my parents?'

'Long story,' Shane said. 'You guys had better sit down.'

In the end, Claire was pretty sure Eve believed it, and Michael really didn't; he seemed firmly set on denial of everything that didn't fit his sixteen-year-old-logic framework, including the fact that he was a vampire. He also couldn't get used to the idea that his parents had moved away, or that his grandfather was...gone.

Shane had adjusted pretty fast, but Michael...not so much. Claire wondered if that had something to do with their personal histories; Shane had grown up adapting to whatever mood his father might have been in, learning to be on his own, learning not to assume that everything was as it seemed. Michael must have had just the opposite kind of life – stable, quiet, with parents who loved him.

Oddly, that seemed to hurt, not help, when it all got taken away from him. Claire was afraid that it was going to drive him crazy, like some of the other vampires, if they didn't fix this soon.

'Wicked crazy stuff you're telling us, you know,' Eve finally said, sipping her Coke. 'Not that I don't believe you. Morganville's always running on Standard Insane Time. So. What do you want us to do, exactly?'

'Ah...nothing?'

'Nothing? Oh, come on, you're going to go all *Mission: Impossible* and I don't even get to wear a fake face or pose as a spy or *anything*? This plan sucks. I am not the friend who holds the purses.' Eve leant forward. For Eve, she was dressed kind of plainly – a black, tight T-shirt, a silver skull necklace, the silver choker that matched the one Claire was wearing, and some temporary tattoos of roses that ran up her arms. Plain black jeans and heavy boots. 'Look, I'm all Action Goth! Give me a job! I live here, too, you said. Don't I? Doesn't that mean I have as much to lose as anybody else?'

'Uh...yeah, you do. OK, you come with me and Shane. But remember – the idea is to distract Myrnin, not kill him. And don't put yourself in more danger than you have to.'

'If she's going, I'm going,' Michael said. Eve looked at him, surprised. 'What? I'm not letting you girls have all the fun.'

'Hey!' Shane said. 'Shut up, Goldilocks.'

'I'm going,' Michael snapped back. 'If this needs doing, my family's always been the ones around here to step up and get things done. If...if there's nobody else, then it's just me. So I'll help.'

'Just don't vamp out on me, man.'

'I'm not a fucking *vampire*, Shane!'

That argument had been going on for about an hour, and evidently, Frank was really tired of it. He walked out of the living room and into the parlour, pulled the knife from his belt, and sliced Michael across the arm.

Eve screamed, and Shane jumped up and shoved his dad back. Michael stared down at his arm in shock. It was a big, ugly cut, and it bled...and then it stopped.

And then it slowly closed up.

Eve sat down so suddenly it was as if she'd fainted, except her eyes were still open. Shane froze, staring at Michael's arm as it healed up.

Michael looked like he'd seen a ghost. His own ghost. 'No,' he said. 'No, it's not...I'm not—'

'Oh, shut up,' Frank snapped. 'You're a vampire. Get over it, kid. Move on. Claire, if you want to get this done, let's go. Seems like most people who forget things do it overnight. We can't wait for tomorrow. Chances are, some of us standing here won't remember what the hell we're supposed to be doing by then. We can have your therapy session later.'

He put his knife back in the sheath and stalked away. Claire cleared her throat. 'Michael? You all right?'

He ran his fingers over the smooth skin where the cut had been, wiping away the blood. Then, as if in a dream, he put his fingers in his mouth.

'It tastes good,' he said. 'Eve, it—'

'Yeah, I get it; you're a vampire,' she said. 'Creepy. And OK, a little hot, I admit.'

'You don't mean that.'

'Come on. I still like you, you know, even if you... crave plasma.'

Michael blinked and looked at her as if he'd never seen her before. 'You what?'

'Like. You.' Eve enunciated slowly, as if Michael might not know the words. 'Idiot. I always have. What, you didn't know?' Eve sounded cool and grown-up about it, but Claire saw the hectic colour in her cheeks, under the make-up. 'How clueless are you? Does it come with the fangs?'

'I guess I...I just thought...Hell. I just didn't think... You're kind of intimidating, you know.'

'*I'm* intimidating? Me? I run like a rabbit from trouble, mostly,' Eve said. 'It's all show and make-up. *You're* the one who's intimidating. I mean, come on. All that talent, and you look...well. You know how you look.'

'How do I look?' He sounded fascinated now, and he'd actually moved a little closer to Eve on the couch.

She laughed. 'Oh, come on. You're a total model-babe.'

'You're kidding.'

'You don't think you are?' He shook his head. 'Then you're kind of an idiot, Glass. Smart, but an idiot.' Eve crossed her arms. 'So? What exactly do you think about me, except that I'm intimidating?'

'I think you're...you're...ah, interesting?' Michael was amazingly bad at this, Claire thought, but then he saved it by looking away and continuing, 'I think you're beautiful. And really, really strange.'

Eve smiled and looked down, and that looked like a real blush, under the rice powder. 'Thanks for that,' she said. 'I never thought you knew I existed, or if you did, that you thought I was anything but Shane's bratty freak friend.'

'Well, to be fair, you *are* Shane's bratty freak friend.'

'Hey!'

'You can be bratty and beautiful,' Michael said. 'I think it's interesting.'

Shane cleared his throat. 'Look, could we get moving? You two are giving me diabetes. And if we're going to get this done—'

'Oh, chill out, Collins; we're bonding, here.' Eve met Michael's eyes squarely. 'So we're good?'

'Ah...I guess.'

'Don't bite me.'

He smiled faintly. 'I won't.'

'Then let's go save this stupid town so I can ask you out on a date already.'

'Well, you don't actually have to wait,' Michael said. 'This is kind of a date.'

'Hmm.' Eve thought it over. 'Potentially fatal, dangerous – yeah, it does sound like a lot of the dates I've had, come to think of it. Only with at least twice the hotness.'

Shane looked at Claire and made a gagging sound, which made her laugh. That made *him* smile, and for a second there it was, that connection, that feeling that took her breath away, like she was flying all the way up into the sun's warm glow.

Shane hesitated, then held out his hand to her. 'We do it together,' he said. 'The four of us. Right?' His fingers felt warm on hers, so familiar it almost brought tears to her eyes.

'Right,' Claire said. 'Michael, just because you're a vampire doesn't mean you shouldn't watch out for Myrnin. He's killed other vampires before. Just... everybody, watch out for each other.'

'Hey, we're Morganville kids,' Eve said. 'That's what we do.'

'If you'll all done kissing and exchanging class rings, let's go,' Frank said from the doorway, and tossed Eve a wooden stake, which she snatched out of the air. Michael got a crossbow. They looked at each other, and then exchanged the weapons without saying a word.

'We'll take Eve's car,' Claire said.

'I have a car?'

'It's the hearse out there.'

'But...I don't even have a driver's license!'

Claire went out to the skull-shaped purse sitting on the table in the hall, opened it, and combed through stuff until she found Eve's ID. She handed it over. Eve looked at it, open-mouthed, and showed it to Michael. 'That is a *wicked* bad picture, so don't judge,' she said. 'But look. Eighteen. I'm eighteen!'

'Come on, I've seen you with fake IDs since you were twelve,' Michael said, and looked at Claire. 'Is it real?'

'It's real. She's eighteen. You're nineteen, by the way.'

'Huh.' Michael said that like he wasn't sure how to feel about it.

'You're going to let her drive?' Shane asked Claire quietly. 'Really? Even though she doesn't remember how?'

'Think of it as on-the-job training,' she said. 'You can co-pilot. She'll be fine.' Claire left them and went to Frank and his group. 'Move this.' She pointed to the bookcase Michael had put in front of the portal for extra protection. The bikers shoved it out of the way, with a lot of enthusiasm that sent books tumbling to the floor. 'There'll be a door here at some point. Whenever there is, get through as fast as you can. I don't know how long I can keep it open.'

Frank frowned at her. 'Why don't we just all go the same way?' he asked.

'Because the door's locked on the other side, too,' she said. 'I need to unlock it before you can get through. Trust me: this is better.'

'Well, hurry up,' he said. 'Getting dark out there. You don't want to be on the streets at night.'

'Thanks, *Dad*,' Shane said. 'Great advice. Never would have thought of that on my own, what with all the vampires and crazy people and everything.'

Frank just shook his head and said, 'Be careful. All of you. I get the feeling this one ain't gonna be no walk in the park.'

That, Claire thought, was probably an understatement.

The streets were a mess. People had abandoned cars and left them; they passed the wreck of Oliver's limousine, too, which, now that Claire took a good look from the outside, seemed even more terrifying. Eve drove with extreme caution, steering with both hands rigidly on the wheel in the driver's-education-approved ten and two positions. She looked petrified, and that didn't get any better the farther they got from the Glass House, and the closer to their destination.

By the time they'd pulled to a stop where Claire said, next to the entrance to the alley by the Day House, Eve looked ready to collapse.

Claire looked over at her from the passenger seat and said, very softly, 'Eve, are you sure you can do this? You could stay here. In case we need to get away quick.'

'That's true,' Michael said. 'We could use a reliable getaway driver if this doesn't go well.'

Eve was breathing too fast, and even with the make-up, her face was flushed, but she shook her head. 'No,' she said. 'No, I can do it. I want to stay with you guys. Besides, Collins might do something stupid if I'm not there to tell him different.'

'Bite me, Goth princess,' Shane called from the back. 'Not literally or anything.'

'Maybe you should say that to Michael.'

'Not funny, Eve,' Michael said.

Eve raised her eyebrows and held her fingers up, measuring off about an inch. 'Little bit,' she said. Claire smiled. 'So. We're going, then.'

'Yeah, we're going.' Claire opened her door and got out. The sunset was beautiful tonight, all oranges and deep reds against a dark, endless blue. She stared at it, because the thought crossed her mind that if this didn't work, if she couldn't pull this off, it might be the last sunset she'd ever see.

Or any of them would ever see.

This is my fault, Claire thought, as she did about every minute of the day. *And it's my responsibility.*

Michael was holding Eve's hand, Claire saw, or at least, Eve was holding his for dear life. They joined her. Eve still looked petrified. After a second's hesitation, Michael put his arm around her shoulders. 'Hey,' he said, and leant closer. 'You're going to do OK.'

'Really? How do you know?'

'Because I know you.'

Eve smiled faintly, and then grabbed him by the shirt and pulled him close. They stood that way for a second, Michael staring down into her eyes, and then she stood on her tiptoes and kissed him.

'Whoa,' Shane said. 'Really? *Now?* Seriously?'

Fifteen-year-old Shane was no kind of romantic, Claire thought, and wanted to smack him in the back of the head. Michael and Eve ignored them, and just kept on kissing until finally Eve pulled back and took in a deep breath. The white make-up really wasn't doing much to tamp down the brightness in her cheeks.

Michael had black lipstick smeared all over his mouth. Eve reached in her pocket and dug out a tissue, and wiped it away. It was sweet and sexy at the same time, the way Michael watched her, as if he couldn't believe his luck.

'Sorry,' Eve said. 'I needed to do that. In case I die or something.'

'It's OK,' Michael said. 'Really. Anytime.' He sounded like he meant it, too.

Shane looked at Claire, and for a second she thought – but no. He said, 'Don't expect me to go all Romeo on you or anything.'

She swallowed a little bubble of disappointment. 'I don't,' she said, and kept her voice cool and level. 'Just watch my back.'

'Uh...OK.' He sounded a little disappointed, too. What was she supposed to have said? Guys.

'Let's go,' she said. 'We're sitting ducks out here.'

Shane stuck next to her, and Michael and Eve followed behind, still holding hands. Claire glanced over at him as they walked down the narrowing, high-fenced alley. 'You scared?'

He shook his head. 'Weirdly enough? Not really. It feels...like I've done this before. Or like it's just a dream, and I'm going to wake up. I can't tell which.' He made a fist and looked at it. 'I'm bigger than I feel like I should be. Three years of growth, I guess. I feel stronger. That's good.'

'Shane, in case we don't...don't come out of this, I wanted to say...'

He glanced over at her, and she felt her whole body warm from it. She remembered that look. It made her feel naked inside and out, but not in a creepy kind of way. In a way that felt...free. 'If what you say is true, and I guess it has to be, I think I know why we're... together,' he said. 'I think I'd fall for you no matter what, Claire. You're kind of awesome.'

She grinned. 'You just like older women.'

'Damn straight,' he said, and spun a stake in his fingers as if he'd been doing it all his life. Which, she thought, maybe he had, really. 'So what were you going to say, before?'

She sighed. 'Nothing.'

'No, really.'

'I was going to say that I love you.'

He didn't know what to say to that, she could tell, and for a few steps there was dead silence. 'I knew I didn't just hook up with you,' he finally said. 'You know I can't say it back, right? Because I just met you and everything?'

'I know,' she said. 'But I had to say it anyway. Kind of like Eve, with the kissing.'

The shack was up ahead. Once they were inside, there would be no going back. Claire had a terrible premonition, a black, suffocating feeling that this was the last moment for them, that one of them, maybe both of them, wouldn't come through this alive.

She was going to lose him, and to make it worse,

she didn't really even *have* him anymore. That hurt so badly it almost made her cry.

Shane suddenly stopped, turned to her, and grabbed her. She didn't know why at first, and then he bent his head to hers and *oh*, he was kissing her, and it was tentative at first, and then sweet, and then it was…incredibly hot and tender and lovely and it made all those broken-hearted moments vanish like snow under the sun.

He let her go, finally, and stepped back, eyes glittering, lips damp, spots of colour high on his cheeks. He didn't say anything. Neither did she.

Finally, Michael leant over and said, 'If you're done, shouldn't we be moving or something?'

'Oh,' Claire said, and almost laughed. 'Yeah. Let's get this over with, because I want to do *that* again.'

The moment of golden joy that kiss had sparked inside her stayed with her as she unlocked the shack's door, and even as they started down the steps towards Myrnin's lab.

It lasted right up until they were about halfway down, and she heard Myrnin say, in a silky, dark voice, 'I do believe I have visitors.'

Well, it wasn't as if she'd expected him not to notice, but there was something alien in his voice, something that made her completely go cold inside. 'Keep going,' she whispered. 'Spread out. Pretend it's vampire dodgeball.'

'Oh, *now* you tell us,' Eve whispered back. Her voice was shaking. 'I frickin' hate dodgeball. Good luck, new girl.'

'You, too.'

'I'm faster than the rest of you, if — *because* I'm a vampire,' Michael said, and it was some kind of breakthrough for him to say that. 'If you get in trouble, I'll be there.'

'Nice,' Shane said. 'I'm warming up to this bloodsucking thing, Mikey.'

'No, you're not.'

'OK, no, I'm not, but right now let's pretend I am.'

Claire stepped down to the floor of the lab. It was silent now, and it looked deserted. The lights were burning, but somehow it seemed very dark, and very scary. She reviewed what she had to do: get to the bookcase, move it aside, unlock the door that covered the portal, concentrate, get the portal open, and hold it while Frank and his people came through.

Yeah, that was going to be easy.

Shane, Michael, and Eve were moving farther from her, leaving her on the far right side. That was good; she had a straight shot to the bookcase from here.

Too easy.

'I warned you,' Myrnin's voice said, echoing from the corners of the room. 'I told you that if you came here, you were mine. *Why* wouldn't you listen?'

'Because we can't,' Claire said. 'I'm sorry, but we have to do this. I don't want you to get hurt.'

'That's sweet. And very unlikely, because I'm going to eat you and your friends, little Claire, just as soon as you tell me *what you've done with Ada.*'

The vicious darkness in his voice took her by surprise, but she should have known it was coming; she should have known that just as Amelie had assumed that Sam was being held captive, Myrnin would think the same thing – or worse – about Ada.

He loved her, and he thinks we have her, hurt her, or killed her. Myrnin wasn't going to help them. He'd do everything he could to stop them.

'We have to move,' Claire whispered to Shane. He nodded.

'Are we playing a game?' Myrnin asked. Well, of course he could hear her. 'I like games. This looks like...chess.' And he leapt out of the shadows and up on top of one of the granite worktables towards the back of the lab. 'Your move, little pawns. But do try to play well. It's no fun, otherwise.' He was wearing a black velvet coat that reached down to his ankles, a bright red silk vest, black pants, and high boots, like some escapee from a pirate movie. He crouched down on the table, watching the four of them as they slowly spread out. 'So many choices. I think I'll move...*this way.*' And then he leapt.

For Eve.

She screamed and dived forward, rolled, and he missed her by about a foot where he landed, but he was already turning and grabbing at her, so fast that it was a blur...

And another blur hit him from the side and knocked him into an uncontrolled slide across the floor towards the other side of the room. Michael, who stood there over Eve, fangs down, looking pale and dangerous and angry. 'Your move,' he said. 'You hurt her, and I'll take your arm off and feed it to you.'

'Oh, it's the littlest vampire,' Myrnin said, and rolled to his feet. 'Really? You're already in love with one of them? That must be some sort of record, boy. Don't worry. It'll wear off by dinnertime.'

'Would you *stop*?' Claire yelled at him. 'Stop with this cape-twirling stupid *act*? This isn't you, Myrnin! You're a good person!' Even as she said it, though, she kept moving towards the bookcase – careful not to look like she had a purpose.

He got to his feet and dusted himself off, with special attention to a spot of dirt on his coat. 'Am I really?' he asked. 'And how would you know? Oh, yes, you think you know me. I assure you, you don't. Not at all, little girl.'

'You bit me, once,' she said, and showed him the healed scar on her neck. 'And you cared enough to stop.'

'Oh, I think I'd remember something like that. And I can't think why I'd ever decide to stop drinking from such a delicious fountain,' he said, and without a flicker of warning, he was suddenly coming towards her, a shape that almost disappeared in the dark as he moved between the wall sconce lights.

She didn't wait. She whirled, grabbed a glass beaker of something from the worktable next to her, and threw it right in his face. Whatever the liquid was, it surprised him, and it must have hurt, because he gave a choked cry and veered off course to slam into the table and send it, and the glassware on it, crashing to the floor.

'Go!' Shane yelled to Claire, and jumped on Myrnin's back, trying to pin him down. She couldn't watch, couldn't afford a second's hesitation. She ran for the bookcase, hit it at speed, and sent it squealing out of the way. She already had the keys in her hand, but adrenalin was making her shaky, and it took two tries to get the key into the silver lock on the door. She finally got it open and threw the padlock aside, swung the door open, and stared into the darkness on the other side.

Concentrate.

It was so hard, because she could hear the fighting behind her. Michael and Shane had Myrnin, but he was throwing them all over the place, and glass was breaking, and Eve was screaming, and she had to look back; she *had to...*

Claire closed her eyes and visualised the living room of the Glass House: the sofa, the TV, the table, the bookcases, the guitars, everything all in a rush. When it was stable in her mind, she opened her eyes and sent the image out into the dark.

Yes!

Colours swirled like ink in water, and started to make an image in the darkness. It was the Glass House. She'd got it right.

Frank Collins was standing on the other side. She raised a hand to tell him to come through. He jumped, and she felt the stir of air against her face as he passed her, heading for the fight. Then West came through with the bow. Rudolph was following her—

Something hideously strong grabbed her from behind, and she lost control of the portal. Rudolph screamed, and something terrible happened to him as the opening snapped shut – she didn't know what; she couldn't see; there was a hand over her eyes and her mouth; she couldn't breathe, and the hand was cold, very cold...

Myrnin's voice whispered in her ear, 'Checkmate, little pawn. Your move.'

CHAPTER FIFTEEN

He took the hand off her eyes and wrapped his other arm around her waist, holding her tight against him. 'Stop,' he said to the others. Claire opened her eyes to see Shane getting up from the floor, wiping blood from his eyes. He looked dizzy, but focused. Eve was standing frozen about twenty feet away, terrified and unsure. Michael was down with a wooden stake in his chest – *oh, God*, that could kill a young vampire if it was in long enough – and Frank Collins was slowly circling around, staring at Myrnin and Claire with the intensity of a hunting tiger.

West, the only other member of their back-up who'd made it through alive, had her bow drawn and was standing with an arrow pointed at Myrnin's chest. The only problem was that Claire's own chest was actually in the way.

'Help Michael,' Claire said. Myrnin's hand closed around her throat, choking off her words, but Shane seemed to understand, and went to pull the stake out of Michael's chest. Their friend rolled on his side, coughing, weak and not able to even try to get up.

Shane held the stake in his fingers and twirled it restlessly, staring at Myrnin now with the exact same expression his father had.

'Let the kid go,' Frank said. 'You know how this is going to end. It's just a matter of how bloody you want to make it.'

'Well, friend, I don't know about your tastes, but I tend to like it *very* bloody,' Myrnin said. He shifted position, dragging Claire along like a rag doll without any effort at all. 'Have we been introduced?'

'Probably not. Why, you asking me out, sweetheart?'

'You're not my type, darling. Is this one yours?'

'No,' Frank said, and looked at Shane, just in a quick flicker. 'Let's say she's a friend of the family.'

'That'll do. Now, if you want to keep her breathing, you'll take all these children and your woman-at-arms – hello, West, how have you been, my dear? Haven't seen you since Richard was king – and depart gracefully, while you still have the chance, and bring Ada to me. If you do, I may let this one go.'

'Nice offer,' Frank said. 'Why exactly should I take it again?'

'Because the boy there wants you to,' Myrnin said. 'I can tell. Can't you? He's just dying to come over here and save her from the evil, wicked vampire. Well, boy, why don't you? Don't you like her?' Myrnin's hand tightened on her neck. 'Come on, tell her how you feel. It's your last chance, you know, before she dies.'

Don't, Claire tried to say, but all that came out was a squeak. She felt a little sick, because she knew what Myrnin was doing, and she hated it.

'Sorry, freak,' Shane said, 'but you've got a wrong number. I don't know that chick at all. And the second you kill her, we'll take you down, so maybe you'd better find a new plan.'

That stung a little, but Claire could see that he was lying, at least about that first part. She could see it in his eyes. It hadn't been long, but he felt something for her, even if it wasn't maybe what she felt yet – and she knew Shane. He'd never, ever stand by and just let her be hurt. He wouldn't do that even if she was a total stranger.

'I think your friend has a hero complex,' Myrnin said in a whisper, right into her ear. 'That makes this even more interesting, doesn't it, *Claire*?'

She felt her heart stutter in her chest. *He knew her.* No – no, wait, he didn't; he just knew her name. It wasn't the same Myrnin, not at all.

The grip around her throat eased just a little, and

she was able to gasp out, 'Myrnin, please stop. Please. You know this isn't right.'

'You know what isn't right? Waking up to find everything changed, to find Ada missing, to find humans breaking into my last safe haven intent on destroying what I hold dear. Does that sound right to you?'

'It's not what you think,' Claire said desperately. 'Ada's not here. She's not coming back. You have to understand, what's down there isn't something you should be protecting, it's something you have to *stop!*'

He was silent. Frank Collins took a step forward, then stopped, watching Claire's face. She frantically shook her head.

'You do sound convincing,' Myrnin said. He put his head down, mouth *very* close to the side of her throat, and took in a deep breath. 'You do smell familiar, I admit. Your scent is all over the lab, and I confess, I have no explanation for that.'

'Because I work here. For you,' Claire said. 'You know that. Myrnin, you have to remember. Please try.'

All of a sudden he let her go and shoved her forward, hard – straight into Shane's arms. Shane dropped the stake to grab her as she fell, and held on.

Myrnin stood there for a moment, head cocked to one side, staring at the two of them. 'I have the oddest feeling,' he said, 'that I've seen this before. Seen *you* before.'

'You have,' Claire said, and cleared her throat, trying to ignore the ache. 'Myrnin, you know us. Stop. Just stop and think, OK?'

He stared at her, and she saw that he was trying – groping for the lost threads of his life. She saw how it frightened him to feel this way, too. Maybe he'd enjoyed it, on some level; maybe it had felt like freedom, not worrying about anyone but himself, and Ada.

But that wasn't him. Not anymore. It hadn't been for years.

'Claire,' he said, and took a step forward. 'Claire, I think...I think I...forgot something...about – I don't think this is right. I don't think any of this is right. And I think I know – I think I know Ada—'

He stopped and turned to look at the portal an instant before Claire felt the flash of power from it. 'No!' he snapped, and stretched out a hand towards the doorway, which was starting to spark and flicker with colour. 'No one else comes in!'

She couldn't let him stop this, no matter what happened, but she felt sick about it. She'd been close, so *close* to breaking through...and now it was gone again.

Claire scooped up the fallen stake and lunged for his back.

She didn't make it, of course; Myrnin was too fast, and too alert. He whirled, grabbed her arm, and held the point of the stake an inch from his chest, staring right into her eyes.

'Oh, child,' he said. 'You shouldn't have done that.'

But she'd done exactly what she'd meant to do, and in the next second, power rushed through the room, crackling along her skin, and Amelie stepped through the portal behind Myrnin, shining like a white diamond in the dim light. Behind her came two more vampire guards, and Oliver. But Oliver wasn't going to be any help, because he was wearing silver chains on his wrists and ankles.

He could hardly stand, Claire realised. He looked *terrible*.

Myrnin forced Claire to drop the stake, and held on to her wrist as he turned to face Amelie, bowing low from the waist. 'Founder.'

'Myrnin,' Amelie said, as the portal dissolved into black behind her party. 'I seem to have interrupted. I recognise the girl you have in hand, and West, of course.' West, looking very unhappy, loosened the bow and removed the arrow from the string, bowing to Amelie. With a glance at Frank, she walked over to stand with the new arrivals, signalling a change in her allegiance. Amelie fixed her attention on Frank, and then Michael, who was still on the ground. Eve was kneeling next to him, trying to help him get up. 'This doesn't seem to be going well for you, Mr Collins,' she said. 'I suggest you take these children and withdraw while you have the chance.'

'No,' Michael said raggedly, and staggered to his feet.

And Shane said, 'We're not going without Claire.'

'I assure you, boys, you will be going, one way or another,' Amelie said. 'Myrnin. Give the girl to me, and I will deal with this intrusion.'

'But—'

'Do you doubt that I will act in the best interests of Morganville?' she asked, holding his gaze. 'Have you *ever* doubted that, in all our years together?'

'But they have Ada,' he said, and his voice was small and lost and plaintive. 'You have to make them give her back. Please.'

'I will,' Amelie said. 'But first, let me have the girl.'

Myrnin nodded and shoved Claire at her.

Claire tried to twist aside, but Amelie, without seeming to move at all, was somehow in the way. She took hold of Claire's arm in an ice-cold iron grip, and looked at her with even colder eyes. 'Be still,' she said. 'I'll deal with you in a moment.' Claire felt her last hope die, because there was no hint of real recognition in Amelie's face.

Frank said, 'You'd better deal with me before you settle with some little schoolkid, or I'll get offended.'

'You'd better deal with all of us,' Shane said. 'I'm not going to let you hurt her.'

'You sound brave, Shane, for someone who doesn't remember being in my presence before,' Amelie said. 'But I won't hurt her. Or any of you.' She looked at Claire again, and this time there was warmth in her eyes. A kind of reassurance. 'I assure you, I am fully aware of what I am doing here.'

She remembered. Relief hit Claire, and she made a sighing sound as the tension left her body. Things were still dangerous, no question about that, but with Amelie on their side, surely it was going to be all right. She could convince Myrnin to do the right thing.

'They have Ada,' Myrnin said. 'You have to find her. Please.'

Amelie let Claire go, and moved her off to the side, out of his reach. 'There's no need,' she said, and the compassion in her voice was a kind of pain all its own. 'We both know where Ada is, Myrnin. I know you remember.'

He didn't move, and didn't speak, but there was a frantic, feverish glitter in his eyes.

'You've been ill. Ada was caring for you, but she fell ill as well. Weakness has always triggered bad things in you, and she grew weak. One day—'

'No,' Myrnin said. It wasn't so much a denial as a plea for her not to keep talking.

'One day I came here and found her dead. Drained of life.'

'No!'

'It was too late to save her, but you'd tried, once you came to your senses. Heaven knows you'd tried. You did your best to preserve what you could of her, don't you remember?'

'No no no!' Myrnin sank down to a crouch, hiding his face in his hands. 'No, it isn't true!'

'You know it is,' Amelie said, and walked forward to put a gentle hand on his shoulder. 'My friend, this isn't the first time we've had this conversation. You become ill, and you forget, and you wait for her to come back. But Ada isn't coming back, is she? She's gone.'

'No, she's not gone,' Myrnin whispered. 'I saved her. I *saved* her. She can't die now. She can't leave me. She's safe. I'll keep her safe. No one can hurt her.'

He still thought Ada was in the machine. That hurt worse than his grief, somehow; it was another tragedy in slow motion, because Claire knew she'd have to see him remember, see him lose what he loved all over again.

Just like everyone else.

But the difference was that Myrnin wanted to hang on, *had* to hang on. He was three years in the past, and sick, and crazy.

He'd do everything he could to stop them from taking Ada away from him. *That* was why he'd treated Claire like an intruder in the first place...because on some level, he was still trying to save Ada, and he knew that Claire intended to destroy her.

'You can't take her,' Myrnin whispered. 'You can't take her away from me. Please don't do that.'

Amelie's expression had slowly gone still and cold. 'There's nothing to take,' she said. 'Ada's gone. Three years ago, you wept in the corner and ripped your own skin. I had to stop you from killing indiscriminately to keep from drowning in your pain. I won't let you go back to that...beast. You deserve better than that.'

Myrnin shuddered and dropped his hands down limply to his sides. 'What are you going to do?'

'Turn it off,' she said. 'Stop this madness while we still can. You'll be better once it's done.'

Myrnin's eyes flared bright, shocking white, and he leapt for Amelie, fangs sliding down. She twisted out of the way, pulling Claire with her. Her guards jumped into the fight, but Myrnin was strong, and as full-on crazy as she'd ever seen him.

He tossed one the entire length of the lab, and staked the other with a broken chair leg, and screamed at her in defiance.

She didn't move.

'Let me go!' Oliver yelled at Amelie, and shook

his chains impatiently. 'You can see I had nothing to do with any of this, and you need my help! Let me loose!'

She hesitated, staring at him, and then bent to expertly unlock the chains, which dropped from his wrists and ankles to the stone floor. Oliver staggered a little, breathing in a gasp of relief, and Amelie reached out to take hold of his arm.

'Oliver,' she said, and held his gaze. 'I remember what happened. I remember, and I am sorry.'

He hesitated, then nodded in response. It was as if he was waiting for her to make some decision... something more than simply letting him loose.

Amelie said, 'I won't be your servant in Morganville. Nor should you be mine. Equals.' She offered her hand to him, and he looked down at it, clearly taken aback. But he took it. 'Now defend what is ours, my partner.'

He grinned – grinned! – and whirled to meet Myrnin in mid-leap as Myrnin attacked.

He had Myrnin down in seconds, but it was a rush of adrenalin that faded, and Claire realised that the pain of the silver chains was taking its toll on him. He slowed down. Myrnin didn't, and in another few, deadly seconds, Myrnin's clawed fingers slashed at Oliver's face. Oliver ducked, but lost his balance as Myrnin threw him backward in a rush.

Oliver crashed with deadly speed into a wall, and

Myrnin ran in a blur for the back of the room. 'He's going downstairs!' Claire yelled, and grabbed up Oliver's fallen silver chains as Myrnin yanked the rug away. She heard the beeps of the code being entered in the trapdoor lock. 'Stop him!' He'd had days here by himself, doing who-knew-what. Creating...things. Letting him go down there was dangerous, even more than facing him up here.

Somehow, she still wanted to reason with him. *It isn't Myrnin, not really.* She remembered the Myrnin she'd got to know, the kind, almost gentle man, the one who'd brought her soup and held her upright when she'd been too tired to stand on her own. The one who'd fought for her time and time again.

She had to fight for him, now. She had to defend him against himself.

Frank Collins almost made it to the trapdoor, but it slammed shut at the last second, and Claire heard the lock engage with a sharp, buzzing snap of power. 'Don't touch it!' she yelled, as Shane's dad reached for the keypad. 'It's electrified!'

'It's the only way in,' Oliver said, as he climbed painfully to his feet. 'Someone has to open it.'

'It's not the only way,' Claire replied, and looked at Amelie. 'There's a back way. Isn't there?'

Amelie hesitated, then nodded. She turned and headed for the portal on the wall. Rudolph's body was lying there – well, half of it – and she moved it aside and stood in front of the black doorway. Colours shifted, pulsed, and faded into darkness again.

Claire found she was holding on to someone's hand. It turned out to be Shane, who'd come up beside her. She could feel how tense his muscles were, and how fast his pulse was going. Hers was at least twice as fast.

'There,' Amelie said. Nothing seemed different about the darkness on the other side of the doorway, but Claire felt a kind of energy radiating out of it. 'I warn you, it's not a safe course. Go quickly. I have to hold it open, or he might remember to block it.'

Oliver gave her a doubtful look, but plunged past into the darkness; it swallowed him up like a pit full of ink. Frank and West followed, and then Claire and Shane. Before they stepped through, Shane hesitated and looked over his shoulder.

Michael was right there – pale, a little unsteady, leaning on Eve's shoulder. 'Right with you, bro,' he said. 'Go.'

'Are we totally sure this is a good plan?' Shane asked, quietly, to Claire. The fact that he asked *her* made her feel a little faint; it felt like...trust.

No, it *was* trust. Trust she hadn't earned, but something that felt unbearably precious to her.

Claire tried to sound confident. 'I think so,' she said. 'Just watch your back, OK?'

'Nah, Michael's got mine.' He looked straight into her eyes. 'I've got yours.'

Shane jumped into the darkness, and took Claire with him.

On the other side, it was just as black – a kind of darkness that made panic twist up in a hard, hot knot in Claire's stomach. She knew this darkness. She'd been in it before.

'Easy,' Frank Collins said, and she felt his hand grab her shoulder to keep her still. 'Don't move.'

'There are holes in the floor,' she said. 'Pits. Can you see them?' She hoped he could; all the vampires she'd ever known could. She and Shane and Eve were about as blind as it was possible to be.

'Yeah, I see it, hang on. I've got a light.' That was Frank Collins speaking from somewhere right behind her. Light blazed out in a pure white cone that lanced out over rocks and pale, angular juts of quartz, sharp as razors. They were in a big cavern, silent except for the echoes of their movements and voices. 'Nobody move.'

He was right, because the area where they'd come through was the only reliably safe spot in the room. The rock floor was pitted with inky black holes that led, for all Claire knew, down to the centre of the earth and out the other side. Not only that, but she knew from experience that where the rock *looked* solid, it probably wasn't. It was like a maze, and the last time Claire had been here, Myrnin had helped her through. He wouldn't be doing that now. He'd be trying to send her screaming to her death, along with everyone accompanying her. She swallowed hard; in the distance she saw a metal eyebolt driven deep into the rocks, and a length of silver chain. He'd been imprisoned here, once, when he'd been...more himself.

But he might not remember that, now. Or care that he'd tried to save her life.

'I know the way,' she said softly, and took the flashlight from Frank. She tested every step carefully; some of the solid-seeming rock was fragile, eaten away beneath by unseen underground rivers that were long gone. Her foot broke through twice, and only Shane's grip on her arm kept her from falling forward the second time.

It seemed agonisingly slow, making their way along the little path. Even the vampires seemed to take each step with great care. Claire supposed it might be an even worse nightmare for them, plummeting down an endless black tunnel; what if they couldn't get back out? How long could they survive down there without blood, or light? And if they did survive...that might almost be worse.

Claire was worried most about Michael. He'd taken a lot of abuse already, and now Shane was quietly taking his other arm, helping Eve, who was starting to stagger under Michael's weight. *He'll be OK*, she thought. She had to believe that, and focus.

A sound went through the cavern, like a sigh; she frowned, wondering what had caused it. It wasn't wind; there was no breath of a draft in here, just cool, damp air that weighed down heavily over her skin. She shivered and waited a second, but the sound didn't come again.

Then she felt a whisper of air against her face – an unmistakable stirring that ruffled her hair. Claire pointed the flashlight in the direction from which the wind had come, but she saw nothing there. Nothing but the treacherous rock floor, the glittering quartz crystals jutting from the walls, and the dark, silent chasms that spread out in sheets.

Claire made her way carefully towards another patch of apparently solid rock, and as she did so, she felt the breeze again, more strongly.

It wasn't coming from above, or even from the walls.

It blew up straight out of the darkness. Claire braced herself carefully and turned the light downward, into the pit, trying to see what might be going on. Nothing. The darkness swallowed the flashlight's glow without a trace.

Claire put out her hand. Definitely that was a cool

breeze blowing up, as if a fan had been turned on.

She felt a little funny, suddenly. A little faint. A little...woozy.

'Hey!' Shane said, and grabbed her shoulders to drag her back from the edge. 'What the hell are you doing?'

She took in a deep breath. Her head hurt a little. 'Looking,' she said, and coughed. It hurt. 'Sorry. This way.'

Moving away from the chasm seemed to make her feel better, though she now had a kind of odd, twisting nausea inside, and she wanted to breathe deeper and deeper, even though she wasn't tired. Claire focused on each step, every careful movement. She heard someone stumble behind her, and Frank Collins's quiet curse.

And then she heard West cough, an explosively loud sound. 'Sorry,' West said, but then she coughed again, and again, and when Claire looked back she saw that the tall vampire woman was hunched over, hands on her thighs.

She was retching up blood.

It was in that moment that Claire realised that something was very, very wrong. It seemed obvious now, but she wasn't sure why she hadn't understood before. Her brain didn't seem to be working quite right. Her vision swam in and out of focus, and now Oliver was coughing, too, deep, tearing sounds that left him gasping and wiping his mouth. Claire caught the red glimmer of blood.

Frank was now coughing, too.

Claire suddenly felt it hit her, too, the ripping pain in her lungs, the overwhelming convulsion. She gasped, instinctively pulled in a breath, and coughed. And kept coughing.

Gas. It was gas. For some reason, the vampires were more susceptible to it; maybe it was attacking them through the skin, or it just took less to make them sick. Michael was gagging now, and Eve and Shane were starting to choke, too.

Claire staggered from the force of her coughing, and almost fell. Oliver lunged and caught her, then lost his grip as he coughed again; she wavered, perilously close to the edge of a big, dark abyss that was – she now realised – spewing out some kind of toxin. She tried to hold her breath, but couldn't do it for long. It felt like she couldn't get enough air. She heard herself making gasping noises, like a fish out of water. Her head hurt, badly, and she just needed *air*...

Claire felt hot and sick and scared and *dying*, but it came to her with sudden, brutal clarity that she had to get them out of there. She was the only one who could do it, the only one who knew the path. They weren't far from the exit to the cavern; she couldn't see it, but she knew it was there. It was right behind that outcropping of quartz – a quick left turn would put them on solid rock, and then they'd be out.

She had to get them there.

She reached back and grabbed Oliver's hand. It was wet; she didn't know if that was blood, and she didn't look. 'Hold hands!' she shouted, and plunged ahead, not bothering to test the rock anymore. If it broke, it didn't really matter. Being careful was going to get them all killed.

She didn't know if everyone was linked together, but she couldn't wait. She only knew the feel of the stone beneath her feet, the hot, burning pressure in her lungs, the throb of pain in her head. The unreal glow of the flashlight reflecting back white from quartz and grey from stone and disappearing into the black...

She couldn't feel her feet now, but she couldn't stop. Claire lurched forward, dragging on Oliver's hand to pull him with her, and jumped across a two-foot-wide black chasm, landing badly and nearly sprawling. She felt the cool, blowing pressure of the gas rippling her clothes as she passed over the pit. Oliver's hand almost ripped free from hers, but she pulled, and he made it. As soon as he was across he turned and yanked Shane over, who pulled Michael, who pulled Eve, who pulled Frank.

West.

Where was West?

Claire spotted her, standing a dozen feet behind them, staggering. Blood was a black mask on her face, and as Claire watched, West dropped the bow she'd been carrying, and fell to her knees.

She pitched forward, into the darkness.

Frank lunged, trying to get to her, but Oliver held him back. With his other hand, Oliver shoved Claire in the opposite direction. She hated him right then, hated him badly enough to push him in, too, but she knew what he was doing.

He was saving their lives.

She plunged on. They were on the path now, and even though she was coughing helplessly, even though it felt like strength was bleeding out of her with every step, she knew where she was going. She felt a wave of coolness against her face, and suddenly her coughing lessened. She dragged in a choking breath, and then another one, and tasted beautiful, delicious, sweet air.

She'd passed the quartz outcropping, and was in the narrow tunnel that led to the black emptiness of another portal.

Claire made it there, staggering but still upright, and the others joined her. Oliver had dropped her hand as soon as he could, but Shane took it, and that was good. She squeezed tightly, and he gave her a thumbs-up as he coughed again and wiped blood from his mouth. His eyes were bloodshot, too. Everyone seemed to be OK, even Michael.

Claire kept breathing in deep, cleansing gasps, and focused on the portal. This part would be tricky if Myrnin remembered to lock it, but she didn't think he would have. This hadn't been used in so long, according to him, that he'd actually forgotten it existed – at least he had, until Ada had trapped them both in the cavern.

If he'd forgotten all that, he'd have forgotten this secret portal, too.

She hoped.

The frequencies tuned in her head, and she saw a wash of shimmer across the black, then a glow, then pinpoints of light. An eerie wash of colour, somewhere between grey and blue. It finally resolved into shadows, and overhead lights, and the weird, sprawling, organic shape of the computer that lay under Myrnin's lab.

'Quietly,' Oliver said, and squeezed her shoulder in warning. She nodded. 'Let us go first.'

She stood back, holding the portal open, as Oliver stepped through, and then Frank. Shane, Eve, and Michael all looked at her, and she nodded.

'You guys go on,' Shane said. 'I'll go with her.'

Michael took Eve's hand in his and stepped through the portal.

'You don't have to do this,' Shane said. 'You could just let us handle it.'

'Us? Who's us?'

He jerked his chin at the vampires and Eve. 'You know. The rest of us. This is going to be dangerous.'

'Not going to happen,' Claire said. 'I might be able to get him to stop.'

'Who, crazy dude? Maybe. Or he might pull your head off,' Shane said. 'I kind of worry.'

She couldn't help but smile. 'Yeah?'

'A little bit.'

'That's...nice.'

He studied her, and returned the smile. 'Yeah,' he said. 'Kind of is, actually. So. I'm going, then.'

'Me, too.'

Shane held out his hand, and she took it, and they went in together.

On the other side of the portal, there was no sign of Myrnin at all. The machine hummed and clanked and hissed, steam whispering from valves at all angles. *He's here*, Claire thought. *Somewhere*. Oliver and Frank were moving silently through the shadows, hunting for him. Eve, Michael, and Shane were sensibly staying put where they were.

The switch on the wall was the master control for the power. Claire pulled free of Shane's grip, and they had a mime-style argument, him shaking his head, her holding her finger to her lips, him mouthing words she was pretty sure would have got him expelled if he'd actually been fifteen. Or at least put in detention. She made a definite 'stay here' motion, and moved towards the power switch.

When she was still about two feet away, she felt the prickling warning around the metal. Myrnin had wired it, somehow, and there was live current running through it. If she – or any of them – touched it, they'd roast.

She studied the problem for a few seconds, then turned and went back to her friends. She grabbed Eve by the arm, bent close, and whispered, 'I need your boots.'

'*What?*' Eve tried to keep her voice soft, but it came out a little too startled. 'My *what?*'

'Boots,' Claire hissed. 'Now. Hurry.'

Eve gave her a wide-eyed, doubtful look, shook her head in a way that indicated she thought Claire had gone completely mental, and bent over to unlace her heavy, clunky, thick-soled boots. She slid one off, then the other, and stood there on the cold stone floor in red-and-black-striped socks. She held the boots out to Claire.

Claire stuck her hands inside the boots like they were giant, awkward gloves. They were warm and a little damp from Eve's feet. Under normal circumstances that would have been gross, but Claire was kind of over that now.

She went back to the switch, took a deep breath, and clapped the rubber soles of Eve's boots onto the red-painted lever. She closed her eyes when she did it, half expecting to get zapped into oblivion, but instead, nothing happened. She could still feel the power, but the boots were insulating her, as were her own rubber-soled shoes.

Claire yanked down on the switch, using all of her strength, and for a second it seemed it wouldn't give – but then it did, snapping to the off position with a sudden, shocking clank of metal.

And it didn't matter. *Nothing happened.*

The machine kept running.

Claire stripped the boots off her hands and tossed them to Eve, who quickly bent over to put them on her feet, unfastened.

'I knew someone like you would come,' Myrnin said, and Claire thought he was somewhere behind the machine, hard to see, harder to reach. 'Someone who wanted to destroy everything. Someone who wanted to bring down Morganville. I've been working for days to be sure you wouldn't succeed. Save yourselves. Leave now.'

'Myrnin, there's nothing here to save! It's just a *machine*, and it's broken! Ada's gone!'

He hissed, and there was fury in his voice when he said, 'Don't you say that. Don't you *ever* say that.'

There was a choked cry, and a sudden, violent flurry of motion in the dark where Myrnin was hiding.

Oliver staggered backward and fell into a pool of light. His face was twisted, and there was a silver stake buried deep in his chest. He went limp, and stayed that way.

Claire rushed forward, but before she could get to him, Myrnin stepped out of the dark and grabbed her. She hadn't seen him coming, and couldn't twist out of the way in time. He had her in a split second, dragging her away from Oliver and off into the shadows with his hand over her mouth.

'No!' Shane yelled, and ran forward to yank the stake out of Oliver's chest. Oliver convulsed and rolled over on his side, but Shane hardly even paused.

He came after Myrnin and Claire with the weapon.

Frank Collins grabbed his son from behind and slung him out of the way just as Shane hit a trip wire, almost invisible in the dim light.

All that Claire could see from her perspective was a brilliant flash of light, which was followed almost immediately by an incredible, numbing roar of sound. She felt stinging cuts open up on her body, even as Myrnin shoved her down to the floor and fell atop her, and a choking wave of dust washed over her. She twisted free of Myrnin, who was lying dazed, and tried to scramble to her feet.

In front of the machine, a huge metal column had tipped over and pinned Frank Collins across the middle in a pile of rubble. Shane was lying a few feet away, covered in pale dust but still alive and breathing; as Claire pulled herself up, she saw Michael get to him and check his pulse. He gave her a thumbs-up gesture, then moved to where Frank was pinned down. He tried to lift the metal, but it was too heavy even for vampire strength.

And Frank didn't look good. There was a steady, thick stream of blood running from his chest to pool on the floor around him.

'Help me!' Michael yelled, and Oliver managed to crawl over and put his shoulder to the pylon as well. 'Push!'

'No use,' Frank gasped. 'I'm done. Finish this. Claire, finish it.'

She turned towards the console of the machine. It was covered in dust, and the screen was cracked, but it was still alive and working. She reached for a handful of wiring, but stopped just an inch away as she felt the hair on her arms stirring and standing up.

'You can't,' Myrnin said, as he rolled over and stared at her. 'You can't stop it. It's all right. Once you let go, it feels better. You'll feel better. Just...let go.'

'I can't do that.' She was crying now, out of sheer

frustration and fright. 'Help me. *Help me!*'

'It can't be turned off now,' Myrnin said. 'I made sure. Ada won't ever be hurt again. Not by you, not by me. She's safe.'

'She's *killing us!*' Claire screamed. 'God! Stop!'

'No, she's *fixing* us,' Myrnin said. 'Don't you understand? I read the journals, the ones upstairs. Morganville hasn't been right for years. It's been changing, turning into something wrong. She's made us right again. All of us.'

'Bullshit,' Frank Collins said, and coughed blood. 'Shut it down, Myrnin. You have to do it.'

Myrnin looked at him over the pile of rubble. 'Don't you want to go back to when you were happy, when we were *all* happy? You, your wife, your daughter, your son? It can all come back. You can feel that way again. She can make you feel that way.'

Frank laughed. 'You're going to give me my family back,' he said. 'Is that what you're telling me?'

'Not me,' Myrnin said. 'Not really. But I can make it all as it was, for you as well as me. You, of all people, should want that.'

Frank's throat worked, as if he were swallowing something unpleasant. His eyes were bright and very, very cold. 'So you're God now,' he said. 'You can bring back the dead.'

'I can give you a new family. This girl can be your

new daughter. We can find you a wife. I can make you forget. You'll never know the difference, and she'll forget all about who she once was.'

'You really think that's tempting,' Frank Collins said, very softly. 'It's sick. My wife and daughter are dead, and you're not going to make me believe a lie. You're not going to pervert their memories. My son loves that girl, and I'm not letting you take her away from him, too.'

Myrnin looked up, as if he'd sensed something. 'It's too late,' he said. 'It's starting.'

Claire heard the pitch of the machine's hum changing, shifting to something higher, more urgent. She felt a pulse of power from it, and something went weird in her head. Something she needed.

Something that held her in place in the world, in time, in space.

It *hurt*. It felt like her brain was being shredded, ripped in half, and memories spilt out in a silvery stream, she couldn't hold onto them, it was all just... noise.

The pain stopped, but something worse took over. Panic. Horror. Fear. She was looking at a room full of strangers. Scary people, in a scary place. How had she got here? What was...what was happening? *Where was she?*

Why wasn't she at home?

No, that wasn't right. She knew them, she knew them all. That was Shane, getting to his feet... Then everything shifted and he was a boy she didn't know, dark-haired, dusty. A stranger. He started towards her, but then he wavered and stopped, and put his hands to his head as if it hurt. Hers still hurt, too. There was a sound, a weird sound that wasn't really there, wasn't really a sound at all, and she felt...

Lost. She felt so lost, and alone, and terrified.

It was like having mental double vision. She knew these people at some very basic level, but she'd also forgotten them. She didn't/did know the man with the scarred face, and the boy reaching out to her, and the girl with the dark hair and the pale face, and other golden-haired boy. She could see them in one way, with names and histories, but it kept fading out. Disappearing.

No. She didn't know anyone here, and she'd never felt so vulnerable and horrible in her life. She wanted to go home.

There was another stranger dressed in funky old Victorian clothes, like some steampunk wannabe, staring at her with big, dark eyes. He reached out for her, and she knew that wasn't right. Knew she had to stumble away from him, into the arms of the boy.

Another older, grey-haired man elbowed her out of the way and slammed the Victorian man into the wall, then dragged him out and down the tunnel. He was yelling at them all to follow. Claire didn't want to; she didn't trust them, any of them.

But the boy took her hand, and said, 'Trust me, Claire,' and she felt something inside that had been howling in fear...go quiet.

Another wall of pain slammed into her, and she almost went down. It was all going away, everything she was, everything...

She fell to her knees, and realised that she was kneeling next to a man with a scar on his face. He was trapped under a fallen metal pillar, and it looked bad, really bad. She tried to move it, but he reached out and caught her hand in his. 'Claire,' he said. 'Get out of here. Do it now.'

He let go and fumbled in a bag that had fallen next to him. He brought out something round and dark green, about the size of an apple.

Grenade. The word floated through her mind and dissolved into mist. There was some reason she should be afraid of that, but she couldn't really think what it was.

The dark-haired boy was yelling at her now, pulling her to her feet. He looked down and saw the thing, the *grenade*. 'Dad,' he whispered. 'Dad, what are you doing?'

'Get out of here,' the man said. 'I'm not going to

lose you, too, Shane. It's starting to all go away, and I can't let that happen. I have to stop it. This is the only way.'

The boy stood there, looking down at him, and then dropped to his knees and put his hand on the man's head. 'I'm sorry,' he said. 'Dad, I'm sorry.'

'Don't be,' the man said. 'I need a little help, and then you need to get your friends out of here. Understand?'

The boy was crying, and trembling, but he nodded.

He reached down and took hold of the metal ring in the grenade, and his dad yanked in the other direction. It sprang free.

'Go,' the man said. 'I love you, son.'

The boy didn't want to go. Claire practically dragged him across the room, in the direction all the others had already gone. They stopped at the mouth of the tunnel, and Claire saw the man roll the grenade slowly across the floor, until it clicked against the metal of a huge, Frankensteined tangle of cables and clockworks, pipes and keyboards.

She knew him. She was almost sure she did, as he turned his head and smiled at her.

His name was Frank. Frank Collins.

Frank said, 'Goodbye.'

Claire gasped and yanked Shane into the tunnel.

He tripped and went down, and she did, too, and it was a good thing.

In another second, the world exploded behind them.

She woke up to a ringing sound in her ears. Her whole body ached, and her head felt like it had been filled with battery acid, but she was alive.

And she felt...whole. Herself again.

When she moved, she found she was pinned under a heavy, warm weight. *Shane.* She wriggled out from underneath and turned him over, frantic with terror that he'd been hurt, but then she saw he was breathing, and his eyes fluttered open, looking momentarily blank and oddly surprised. They focused on her face. He said something, but she pointed to her ears and shook her head. She helped him sit up, and ran her hands anxiously over him. He had some cuts and bruises, but nothing bad.

Shane pointed to her and raised his eyebrows to make it a question. She made an okay sign. He gave her a thumbs-up on his own behalf.

A sudden burst of light overhead caught her by surprise, and she looked up to see a trapdoor fly open as light poured down. A lithe figure in a white suit dropped, landing lightly on her high-heeled feet, and looked around at the damage. If Amelie spoke, Claire couldn't hear it; she moved over to stand beside

Oliver, who was bending over Myrnin and holding him down.

Myrnin didn't seem as if he needed to be held down. He was shivering, pale, and hollow-eyed, and when he met Claire's eyes, he looked quickly away.

She saw tears.

Michael and Eve were standing together, wrapped in each other's arms, looking like they didn't intend to ever let go. Claire reached down and took Shane's hand, pulling him upright. She felt a cautious kind of joy, a dawning realisation that they might actually be OK, after all.

Until Shane turned his head and looked down the tunnel, and Claire remembered. Worse, she saw *him* remember. His lips parted, and she saw him yell, *Dad!*, and he ran down the tunnel towards the machine room.

Claire ran after him, heart pounding.

The machine was destroyed. Really, truly scrapped. It was hard to believe just how ripped apart it was, actually; she supposed that there'd been some kind of chain reaction inside of it, because it looked like it had just crushed in on itself at some points. There were pieces everywhere, bent and scattered. Nothing moved. There was a thick, choking haze of dust hanging in the air.

Shane headed straight for the wreckage. Claire tried to stop him, but he shook her off, face white and blank. *Dad?* She heard a dim echo of the shout this time, and heard the dread in Shane's voice.

She grabbed Shane's arm, and he looked down at her. She had no idea what to say, but she knew her expression would communicate how sorry she was.

Shane pulled free and ran over to the machine's wreckage – and stopped. Just...stopped, staring down.

Claire didn't know what to do. She felt awful and scared and sick, and she knew she should go to him, but something told her not to. Something told her to wait.

Amelie touched her shoulder, frowning, and Claire jumped in tense surprise. Amelie looked from her to Shane's motionless figure, and Claire saw knowledge dawn in Amelie's face. She went to Shane and put her arm around his shoulders, then turned him around, and Claire knew that he'd seen something behind that tangle of metal. Something awful. There was a burnt-out, dead look in his eyes again, and it felt like her heart turned to ash in sympathy for him.

Claire rushed over and into his arms, and after a few seconds, he hugged her. Then he put his head on her shoulder, and even if she couldn't hear him, she felt the way his body shook, and the dampness of his tears against her skin.

Claire combed her fingers through his hair and did the only thing she could do.

She held on.

CHAPTER SIXTEEN

The only thing that approached the sadness Claire felt for Shane was the sympathy she felt for Myrnin.

Maybe it was all wrong; after all, it was his fault. All of it. But in destroying the machine, Frank Collins had reset things back to the way they should be – including Myrnin's sanity.

Sane, he understood what he'd done, and Claire could hardly stand to look at him, to see that awful, stunned, horrified expression in his eyes. He hadn't said a word, not a word. When Amelie tried to speak to him, he averted his eyes and sat, motionless and quiet, head down.

Oliver, as usual, had no sympathy at all. 'West is dead,' he said flatly. 'Or worse, perhaps. Collins sacrificed himself to put it right. Let him brood, if he wants to brood.'

Myrnin raised his head then, slowly, and fixed his dark, tragic eyes on Oliver. He said nothing, but there was something very nasty in the way they looked at each other.

'Well?' Oliver demanded. Myrnin looked away. 'All because you couldn't lose your precious Ada without going mad. Promise me, Amelie, that you'll crucify me with silver before you allow me to fall in love.'

'I hardly think there's any chance of that,' Amelie said. 'I doubt you have the capacity.' She sounded remote and cold, but there was something almost painful in it, too. 'There is some positive news, I suppose. Most people seem to have recovered their memories. Whatever damage has been done seems to be temporary.'

'Positive news,' Oliver repeated. 'Except that our boundaries are down, and all our defences. You *know* that can't continue. The machine—'

'Isn't working,' Claire said, and got up from the chair where she sat next to Shane. 'It isn't working. It isn't *going* to be working, not for months, if it ever does again. Get over it, Oliver.' She was angry, she realised. Shaking. And she knew that it was because of Shane's dad. 'Could you maybe take a minute or something? Just *feel* something?'

Amelie and Oliver both looked at her with identically surprised expressions. 'Feel what?' Oliver asked.

'Grief? For Frank Collins? Are you sure your memory is entirely restored?'

Claire gritted her teeth and resisted the urge to flip him off. She shouldn't have. Eve silently did it for her, from where she stood near the portal, slapping dust and debris off of her Goth black. Her boots were still untied. 'Hey, Oliver?' she called. 'Didn't see *you* biting the bullet back there and taking one for the team. You were out of there faster than me.'

That put Oliver's mood dangerously towards the dark, but Eve clearly didn't care. She was distressed, too. And angry.

Myrnin finally spoke. 'I knew,' he said, very softly. 'I knew that I wasn't...myself. I let myself believe that what I was doing was safe, but it wasn't. Maybe even then my mind was...going.' He looked up, and there was a faraway, miserable look on his face. 'If I'd believed Claire in the first place, we could have stopped this. It didn't have to happen this way. But I wanted...I suppose that deep inside, I wanted things to be...' He took a deep breath. 'I wanted her back. I wanted the past. I wanted to feel...less constrained by the rules. And that's what the machine picked up from me. That's what it tried to do.'

'Well,' Oliver said. 'You got your wish.'

Amelie shook her head. 'This gets us nowhere,' she said. 'Frank Collins did us a great service, regardless of his history. I will honour that.'

Shane looked up. 'How?' His voice was hollow and empty. 'A plaque?'

'How would you prefer he be honoured?' Amelie asked. 'If it's within my power, I'll grant it to you.'

Shane didn't hesitate, not even for a second. It was, Claire thought, like he'd already figured out what he was going to say. 'Let Kyle out of the cage in Founder's Square,' he said. 'Put him on probation. But don't kill him.'

Silence fell, long and heavy, and for a few dreadful seconds Claire thought that Amelie was angry. But she was just...pensive. She finally said, 'All right.'

Oliver made a frustrated, furious noise in the back of his throat, picked up a glass beaker that had somehow survived all the destruction, and smashed it to smithereens against the far wall. 'Enough!' he barked. 'Will you continue to bend to every breather who—'

Amelie grabbed him by the arm, pulled him to face her, and said, 'Stop.' Her tone was chilly, and quiet, and deadly serious. 'We will *stop* tearing at each other, Oliver. It does neither of us good. It solves nothing. It breeds mistrust and paranoia and ill feelings, and we are not so numerous in this town that we can afford our ambitions. I told you we will rule as equals, but mark me: unless we change, unless we learn how to risk our safety and compromise, the humans *will* rise up. They *will* destroy us. I don't grant this because the boy is innocent. I grant it because mercy is more to our cause than justice.'

Oliver stared at her without speaking or moving. There was something odd about his expression, something...vulnerable? Claire wasn't sure. She'd never really seen anything like it. 'And what if I decide I want to rule alone after all?'

'I won't fight you for it,' she said. 'But your arrogance would destroy Morganville, and all of us.'

'I've ruled men before,' he said.

'Not to any lasting effect. You tried to change those you ruled. You couldn't.' Amelie let go of him, and put her hand on his chest, lightly. 'Your ideals didn't survive you. Mine must, or we will all perish together. I'm sure you don't want that.'

'No,' Oliver said, oddly quiet. 'No, that's not what I want.'

'Then what do you want?'

He hesitated, and then he inclined his head. 'I'll let you know,' he said. 'But for now...for now, a truce.'

Amelie let another second tick away, and then stepped away from him. 'I'll dispatch police to monitor the roads out of town. We'll have to hope that we can maintain order with more conventional means until—'

'Until what?' Myrnin asked bitterly. 'Until I create another miracle? Another brilliant feat that turns fatal because you won't allow me to build it as it *must* be built? No. No, I'll create nothing else, Amelie. This cannot be done properly unless you stop telling me how to do my job!'

'Ah,' Oliver said. 'I think I have thought of what it is I want. To never have to listen to him complain again.'

Amelie raised her pale eyebrows, staring at Myrnin, and then turned to Claire.

'It's no longer Myrnin's job,' she said. 'And I suppose you'd best begin thinking how you'll solve our problems, Claire.'

'What?'

'It was going to be your responsibility in a few years. This merely moves up our plans, I believe. Myrnin can assist you, but I will expect results within the week.'

Claire realised, with a sinking sensation, that she'd just become...the new Myrnin? How was that even *possible*?

Things could not possibly be worse than that – until she failed. She supposed then things would take a turn for the extra bad.

At least she had a week.

Myrnin shook his head. 'Amelie. Don't be ridiculous. The girl isn't—'

'Enough,' Amelie said, and the iron snap of command in her voice made him fall silent. 'You've done enough. People are dead, Myrnin.'

Claire couldn't even say she was wrong. Not about that.

Shane cleared his throat. 'Uh, about Kyle—'

Amelie turned to Oliver. 'Make the call,' she said. 'Unless you're planning to take my place.'

He let a few seconds go by, then pulled out his cell phone and ordered the prisoner in Founder's Square released.

Well, Claire thought. At least *somebody* would be happy.

She didn't see how it was going to be her.

Back home that evening, the four of them sat down to dinner. It was a quiet kind of thing, a little awkward, as if none of them knew where to start. They were all bruised, cut, and exhausted, for one thing; for another, nobody really wanted to say what they were all thinking. Or to bring up Shane's dad at all.

Eve, of course, decided to go at it from the opposite direction completely. 'I can't believe I went home to my *parents*,' she said, a little too brightly. 'Ugh. Revolting. My mom made my room into a hoarder's paradise, you know, full of boxes of crap. She ought to be in some freaky reality show. The weirdest part about it? I didn't really expect anything else, somehow. I just figured she'd pitched out my stuff and was pretending I'd never even been there. I pretended that often enough.' Eve played with her plate of spaghetti, but she wasn't really eating it. 'I kept asking her where my dad was. She kept saying he was on his way home.' Eve's father, Claire remembered, had been dead a year. No wonder she was playing with her food instead of eating. Eve swallowed a gulp of water. 'I wonder if maybe I should call her, see if she's OK.'

'We can go over there if you want,' Michael offered. 'I know you don't like going by yourself.'

Eve gave him a grateful little smile. 'You're awesome,' she said. 'Maybe tomorrow?'

'Sure.'

Shane wasn't talking at all. He was eating, though; he'd already cleaned one plate of spaghetti and was working on his second one. She wanted to talk to him, but she knew he wouldn't want her bringing it up, not in front of the others. Shane didn't like to be vulnerable, not even with his friends. He knew they'd understand, but that wasn't the point. He just needed to be...stronger than everybody else.

Eve said, 'At least you've got an appetite, Shane.'

That fell into an awkward silence, because Shane didn't come back at her at all. He just kept eating. Claire twirled some noodles on her fork and said, 'My mom called. Dad's getting surgery this weekend in Dallas.

They said he needed some kind of valve transplant, but it all looks like it's going to be OK, really OK. I'm going to ask for permission to go up on Friday.'

'You don't have to ask permission,' Shane said then. 'You can just go. The machine's dead. Just go.' His voice sounded flat, and wrong.

They all looked at one another, the rest of them. 'There'll be roadblocks,' Michael finally said. 'It's not that easy.'

'Yeah, it never is, is it?' Shane threw down his fork, pushed back from the table, and took his stuff into the kitchen. Claire went after him, but as soon as she came in the door, he dumped his food in the trash and his plate in the sink and turned to go.

'Shane—'

He held up both hands, pushing her off without touching her. 'Give me some room, OK? I need room.' He left. She stood there, looking at his plate sitting in the sink, and felt her heart breaking again. Why wouldn't he talk to her? What had she done? It hurt; it really did. She felt like...like she was losing him again.

She was tired of losing him.

Claire walked back out to the table. Shane had already disappeared upstairs, and his door shut with a slam. Michael and Eve were looking down at their plates.

'Awkward,' Eve finally said, but her heart wasn't in it.

Michael shook his head. 'He lost his dad. It hurts.'

'I *know*,' Eve said sharply. 'Remember? Not like I don't have the T-shirt for that one.'

'Sorry. I just meant—'

'I know.' Eve sighed, and took his hand. 'I know. Sorry. I'm just a little...weird. I guess we all are.'

'The truth is, he lost his dad a long time ago. Maybe when his sister died. Maybe when Frank...uh...' Claire didn't quite know how to say it.

Michael did. 'Got turned.'

'Yeah,' she said. 'I don't think he ever really faced it, though. Now it's right in his face. He can't really avoid it anymore. His dad's just...gone.'

'That's not it,' Shane said from the stairs. They all jumped, even Michael, whom Claire guessed hadn't heard him coming, either. Shane could be quiet when he wanted to. 'It isn't that he's gone. My problem is that I knew my dad. I was afraid of him, and then I wanted to please him, and then I hated him because I thought he was just a hundred per cent evil, especially after he turned vamp. But he wasn't. I was wrong about him. He came to help. And when he had to, he died so we could make it through this.'

They all looked at him silently. Shane sat down on the steps.

'The point is,' he said, 'it's too late for me to really love him now. That's what hurts.'

Claire got up, holding her plate, but Eve took it away from her. 'Go,' she said. 'I've got this. But you owe me laundry duty.'

Claire nodded and went up the steps. Shane raised his head, and their eyes met. She held out her hand.

After a long moment, he took it and stood up. 'You know, even when I didn't know you, I wanted to know you,' he said. 'So I guess you're stuck with me. Sorry.'

'I'm not,' Claire said, and led him upstairs.

Her cell phone rang at about four in the morning, vibrating around on the nightstand and sending her fumbling for it in a bleary haze. Claire pulled herself carefully out from under Shane's heavy arm and slipped out of bed, grabbed a robe, and walked out into the hall to answer the call.

The screen said, *Myrnin*. Claire closed her eyes tightly for a moment, then flipped the phone open and said, 'It's four in the morning. And it wasn't exactly an easy day.'

Myrnin said, 'I can put up the boundaries.'

The way he said it gave her pause, because it wasn't manic, it wasn't crazy, it was just...a simple statement of fact. 'You can? How? The whole thing was...destroyed.'

'Yes,' he said. 'It was. But as I once told you, the

machine was a support system. An amplifier. The important part of creating the boundaries and the memory control isn't the machine; it's the mind.'

'Myrnin—' Claire wanted to scream, throw the phone, do *something* crazy. But she didn't. She swallowed all that and forced herself to say, very carefully, 'Myrnin, I am not putting my brain into a jar to get you out of the doghouse with Amelie. That's never, ever going to happen.'

'I know that,' Myrnin said. 'You don't need to.'

Claire drew in a deep, calming breath. 'I don't.'

'No.'

'Why not?'

'Come to the lab,' he said. 'Come now.'

He hung up. Claire stared at the phone through narrowed, bleary eyes, then turned around and went back into her room.

Getting dressed in silence, in the dark, was a little challenging, but she managed, and sneaked carefully down the hallway, down the stairs, and hopped on one foot as she put her shoes on in the living room. She turned on a light and looked at herself in the mirror. She looked...well, pretty much like she'd been rousted out of bed without enough sleep. Bedhead. Creased skin. Wrinkled clothes.

'I'll kill him if this is for nothing,' she told her reflection, and grabbed her backpack, which was sitting in the corner. She threw it over her shoulder and walked over to the section of blank wall where the portal would appear. A few moments of concentration, and the black doorway appeared, stabilised, and she walked through, into Myrnin's lab.

It was still a whole lot worse for wear. Broken glass glittered on the floor. Tables were overturned. There was still a faint haze of dust in the air.

Then it occurred to her tired, lagging brain, with a real shock, that she shouldn't have been able to do that. Not coming through the portal. The machine had controlled the portal...and the machine was a crushed metal mess in the basement.

Why had it worked?

Myrnin was in the back of the lab, standing in front of...something she couldn't see too clearly. He didn't turn around. 'Claire,' he said. 'Thank you for coming.'

'Yeah. Does Amelie know you're doing this?'

'She instructed me to rest,' he said. 'So no, in fact she doesn't. But ultimately, I don't think she'll be angry.'

'You don't think so? Are you crazy?'

He didn't answer that directly. 'I've been working all night,' he said. 'Some of the parts were still usable, but I was only able to cobble together the very basic elements.'

'Elements of *what*?'

Myrnin finally moved, and Claire walked a few more steps towards him before stopping cold, her breath locked in her throat, her heart lurching, then hammering very, very fast.

Because that was a *brain*. In a *jar*. A jar of faintly green liquid that bubbled. There were tubes, copper tubes, circulating liquid, and there were wires, and there were clockworks ticking along, but there was a *brain*.

In a jar.

'What did you do?' Claire's voice didn't sound at all like her own. She didn't even realise that she'd said it out loud, until Myrnin looked directly at her.

'What I had to do,' he said. 'It won't work any other way. It's too dangerous. I can't risk anything like that happening again, and neither should you, Claire. Next time, we may not be so fortunate.'

'You killed somebody,' she said. Her throat was so tight that she thought she might choke on the words. 'Oh, my God, you killed somebody and...put their brain...in—'

'The point is that the barriers are up,' Myrnin said. 'And we are safe. I did what I knew had to be done. But you mustn't tell him.'

'Tell *who*?' Claire couldn't decide whether she was furious or terrified. Probably both.

Myrnin didn't answer.

The voice came out of her cell phone speaker, slightly muffled by her pocket – an eerie, disembodied voice that nevertheless was familiar.

The last thing she'd heard it say was, *Goodbye*.

'He means Shane,' said Frank Collins. The brain in the jar. 'Don't tell Shane, Claire. This is going to have to be our secret.'

Track List

Ghost Town had a more eclectic mix of music than ever. I hope you enjoy the song suggestions, and remember: feed the artists. Buy the music!

'Unconscious Thoughts'	Absolution Project
'What's in the Middle'	The Bird and the Bee
'Hero/Heroine'	Boys Like Girls
'Suzie Silver Wings'	Caution Cat
'The House Rules'	Christian Kane
'Late Nights and Street Fights'	Steve Smith
'Unbreakable'	Fireflight
'Lust for a Vampyr'	I Monster
'Blue and Evil'	Joe Bonamassa
'Can't Treat Me That Way'	Kate Earl
'Bad Romance'	Lady GaGa
'This is Halloween'	Marilyn Manson

'Enter Sandman'	Metallica
'The Big Sleep'	Oliver Future
'Black Heart'	Photoside Cafe
'Kill Your TV'	Photoside Cafe
'Death of Me'	Red
'Oogie Boogie's Song'	Rodrigo y Gabriela
'Maybe Tonight, Maybe Tomorrow'	Wideawake
'When She's Gone'	Slang
'Out in the Real World'	Stream of Passion
'Fire It Up'	Thousand Foot Krutch
'Blood on My Hands'	The Used

More playlists at *www.rachelcaine.com*

ACKNOWLEDGEMENTS

Steven Smith

Joe Bonamassa

Charles Armitage

Lucienne Diver

Barbara Tibbles

Anne Sowards (for above and beyond...)

*My friends and family at NAL, Allison & Busby,
and all of my other wonderful publishers worldwide.*

╔══════════════════════════════════╗

Morganville Vampires
EXCLUSIVE
Short story for UK readers only!

╚══════════════════════════════════╝

WORTH LIVING FOR

A Morganville Vampires short story

This story is set between Fade Out *and* Kiss of Death

When Shane came limping home, he was bleeding all over the place, and even though he was drunk off his ass, Shane knew that wasn't a good idea. Not with a vampire for a housemate.

The vampire housemate stared at him with a really blank expression, standing in the kitchen doorway, as Shane dropped down on the couch, grabbed a handful of tissues out of the box and started mopping at his mouth and nose.

'What?' he snapped. Michael shook his head. He was holding a beer in his hand. At least, Shane hoped it was a beer. It had a Budweiser label on it, anyway. 'I had a fight.'

'No kidding. Looks bad.'

'Nah.' Ow. Shane probed at a sore spot in his jaw and felt a sickening creak in one of his teeth. *Dammit.* The only thing worse than hitting a doctor's office in Morganville was suffering through dental work. Not exactly the best and the brightest, setting up shop around here. He was convinced that the jerks had never even heard of Novacaine.

Shane spat blood into the tissue, sniffed experimentally, and didn't feel any tell-tale drippage. Not so bad. Maybe the worst was over.

Michael walked over, but not close. Not close enough to worry about, anyway. 'What happened?'

Shane shrugged. 'You know, the usual. Couple of vampires got hold of some girl, started dragging her off. Some of us got into it. No big thing. Nobody got hurt bad.'

'Was she Protected?'

'College girl, out partying in the wrong side of town. You know the type.'

Michael nodded and held out the beer. Shane stared at it, then him.

'Don't be an asshole,' Michael said. 'It's not blood. And I didn't even take a drink yet.'

Shane took it and drank. The beer burnt in cuts, but it was a good kind of burn, and it washed the copper taste out of his mouth. He sat back with a sigh and closed his eyes. The room started making loops, so he opened them again. *Really shouldn't be drinking, on top of the drinking I already did.* Yeah, there were a lot of things he shouldn't be doing. Like living in the house with a vampire, for one thing. His dad would have—

His dad. There was a reason to drink. Shane toasted the absent ghost of Frank Collins, Major Douchebag, and gulped down another mouthful.

Michael sat on the couch, but at the other end. Safe distance, like he knew Shane was still feeling raw about the whole bloodsucking issue. He picked up his guitar and started playing, some Coldplay song Shane half-remembered. 'Which girl?'

'What?'

'You know, the girl the vamps were trying to drag off. Who was she?'

Shane considered that, rolling the beer between his hands. 'Didn't know her. Why?'

Michael shrugged. 'Doesn't matter, I guess. She probably never even knew they were vamps. But, dude, you really need to do something about your hero complex one of these days.'

'It wasn't just me. There were two other guys who jumped in.'

'But you started it.'

Oh man, Michael knew him way too well. 'Kinda.'

Shane tipped his head back and laughed, a little. It hurt. 'C'mon, man, you would've jumped in too. I know you. I'm not the only one riding around on a white horse.'

Michael studied Shane for a long moment, then said, 'You are way too drunk, you know that?'

Shane choked and nearly did a spit-take with the beer. 'Uh...yeah. Not really my fault, though. I was playing poker. Bunch of college guys, easy money. Only they kept buying rounds. The more they lost, the more they bought. Don't blame me. I made almost a thousand bucks tonight. *And* free beer.'

'And then you got into a fight with vampires, and walked home. Drunk and bleeding and carrying cash. In Morganville.' Michael's face was still, and way too sober. 'Man, you really do have a death wish. Why didn't you call? I'd have—'

'I don't need a bloodsucking babysitter,' Shane snapped, even though he knew Michael had a big frickin' point. The beer made him feel hot and sick, but he forced down another mouthful anyway. 'Weren't you supposed to be out with Eve? What are you doing here?'

Michael shrugged. 'She had to go in to work,' he said. 'I'm picking up her up later. Claire's at Myrnin's lab. She ought to pay rent there instead of here, the time she spends doing his crap.'

That gave Shane a bad, even sicker twist in his stomach. 'You don't think he's hitting on her, do you?'

'Myrnin?' Michael's fingers went still on the guitar, and Shane got a flash of startled blue eyes. 'Jesus. I think she'd have said something. Maybe not to you or me, but to Eve, for sure.'

'And Eve would tell you.'

Michael smiled. 'If she thought Claire was in trouble, she'd tell us both.'

That made Shane feel a little better. Just a little. Because when your potential competition was some ancient, occasionally suave dude who dressed in velvet and still looked twenty-something, nothing could make you feel a *lot* better.

Speaking of looking better, Michael was wearing better stuff than usual, probably because he'd been planning on impressing Eve. Blue shirt, blue jeans. Diamond stud earring in his left ear. 'Dude,' Shane said, distracted. 'Can vamps get pierced?'

'What?'

'Your earring.'

'Don't know.' Michael flicked his earlobe with one finger. 'I did this last year. When I was still the old me.'

'I never noticed.'

'And here I thought you cared.'

Shane laughed a little, and kept on thinking. 'What

about tats? Do they stay on a vampire?'

'I doubt it. We'd probably heal. Doesn't sound like something I want to try if it isn't going to stay on.'

'Sucks to be you, don't it? No pun intended.'

Michael looked up and grinned, and all the bullshit faded away. All the bitter anger (it always tasted like blood and tinfoil), all the weird complication of his best friend *drinking blood, for God's sake,* all that just up and left, and it could have been two years ago, or three, or more. They could have been twelve years old again, thinking of ways to stick frogs in Alyssa's shoes, worms in her underwear drawer, whatever.

Shane felt the hot sting of tears in his eyes and looked away. 'I missed you,' Shane blurted. It felt right to say it, and then it felt stupid because Michael was right there at the other end of the couch, and besides, guys didn't say that crap to other guys. 'Whatever.'

Michael got real interested in his guitar all of a sudden. 'Yeah,' he said quietly. 'I missed you, too. How'd we get like this?'

'Well, you vamped out, my dad made me promise to kill you—'

'Seriously.'

'That wasn't serious?'

'We used to hang. I miss you having my back.'

'I still have your back.'

'Do you?'

Shane looked at him in silence for a long few seconds without blinking and said, 'If you don't know that, you don't know shit about me, bro. Do I like it that you're sucking down O neg like it's Slimfast? Hell, no. Creeps me the hell out and it always will. But it doesn't matter. I'll always have your back.'

'Then let me have yours once in a while,' Michael said, and held out his fist. Shane bumped it, or tried; his coordination was way off. 'Next time, don't go wandering around out in the dark, bleeding and wearing a BITE ME sign.'

'Oh, blow me,' Shane groaned. 'I'm *fine.*'

'Please. You're so fine you're about thirty seconds from telling me all your deep, dark secrets and crying, or else puking your guts out.'

'Yeah, screw you too, buddy.' Shane closed his eyes and leant his head back on the sofa. The room was doing loop-de-loops, and it was kind of fun at first, and then not so much.

'I worry about you,' he heard Michael say, very quietly. 'I wasn't kidding about the death wish. Jesus, Shane, you keep doing this kind of thing, you'll end up dead in a ditch. Or worse.'

'Maybe it's what I deserve.' He couldn't believe he'd just said that out loud, but it was true. Maybe it *was* what he deserved. He hadn't been able to protect

Alyssa. He hadn't been able to save his mother. The pain – the pain helped, because it was like paying back a debt. Nobody understood that, though. They just thought he was nuts.

He felt a cold hand on his shoulder, and looked up to see Michael standing there, staring at him with so much – *everything* – in his eyes that it made him feel scared. Nobody should know him that well. Nobody.

But at least Michael didn't say it. He just said, 'Come on, man. Let's get you upstairs before you puke all over my guitar.'

'Don't tell Claire I came home drunk,' Shane said.

'Hell no.'

'Because I will *end* you.'

'If you survive the hangover,' Michael said, 'we'll see who wins *that* throw-down.'

Michael was right about the hangover. It sucked. Shane woke up with his guts heaving and his mouth tasting like he'd sucked on old sweat socks, and he rolled over in bed and moaned. He hadn't ralphed, but it had been close. He figured he still might. His head was pounding like Metallica's drummer, and he wanted to just make it all go away.

Not an option, though. He got up, slipped on a pair of cheap sunglasses and a ratty T-shirt and jeans that had seen better days, and shuffled downstairs to grab a tall glass of water. There was a pot of coffee on the burner, so he poured a cup of that too and took both to the kitchen table. He'd downed the water and was about to start on the coffee when the knocking came at the back door.

Well, not so much knocking as pounding. Which was really *not good* with his head already keeping the beat to a different, sadistic drummer.

Shane groaned, got up, and opened the door without checking to see who it was, mainly because death was preferable to the pain his head was giving him as long as that pounding was going on.

It was two someones, actually. Shane stared at them for a long, bloodshot second, then stepped back to let them in. 'Wow, a visit from the mayor,' he said. 'And it's not even election season. How you doing, Dick?'

Richard Morrell – who was *never* known as Dick, except to Shane – gave him a pained, long-suffering look. For all his faults – and God knew he had a lot, starting with being related to that psycho-bitch Monica – Dick never let the little things get to him. Which was why it was so much fun to try. He looked tanned and fit, and he was wearing an expensive suit, though why he bothered in Morganville was anybody's guess.

'Shane,' said the second person, a tall dark-skinned woman with a scar on her face, tightly cornrowed hair pulled back in a bun, and wearing a crisply ironed police uniform, all her brass gleaming. She wore the gun like she'd been born with it on her hip. 'Sorry for the early visit. I heard you had a late night.'

He shrugged, but he was glad he was wearing the sunglasses to hide his expression. And the bloodshot eyes. 'No problem, Chief Moses,' he said. 'Coffee?'

'I never say no to coffee,' Hannah Moses said, with a charming, professional kind of smile. Shane got a couple of mugs out of the cabinet and filled them, brain churning furiously against the numbing fog of the hangover. *Why are they here? What did I do?* Because the chance they could be here for anyone else seemed pretty long, and pretty small. He was *always* the one in trouble with the law.

He carried the mugs back to the kitchen table, which was piled with old, discarded copies of the *Morganville Daily* and flyers for things he never paid attention to; he shoved it all to the side. 'Sorry,' he said. 'Not my kitchen duty day.' As Hannah and Richard sat down and started sipping their drinks, he said, 'No offence, but we've got a coffee shop about six blocks away. Vampire owned. Any particular reason you're dropping in on me for your caffeine fix?' *Please say no.*

Richard and Hannah exchanged glances, and then Richard Morrell said, 'We need you to do something for us.'

Well, that was different. Really different. Shane cocked his head and tried to sort through it, because it wasn't making any sense. 'You. Need something. From me.'

'Don't make it a thing, Shane.'

'Kinda is a thing, though.' Neither of them cracked a smile. They both looked very, very serious. 'What is it?'

'Michael.'

Michael? Shane's eyebrows rose on their own, and he said, 'You have *got* to be kidding. *Our* Michael, the Boy Scout? No freaking way. What's he supposed to have done – littered? Jaywalked?'

'No,' Hannah said. She sounded regretful, and very sure of what she was saying. 'We think that he's hiding a fugitive from justice. A dangerous one, and one who could easily get him killed. We need to find out why, and where.'

Shane didn't mean to, but he sat down, hand cradling the hot ceramic of his coffee cup. *No way.* It wasn't like Michael, not at all. But Hannah wasn't one of those people who went off half-cocked, either. She knew her business, and if her business was Shane's best friend...well, that was bad. Real bad.

'Who's he supposed to be hiding?' Shane finally asked, through a throat that felt way too tight. 'Osama bin Laden?'

'He's hiding a vampire. I'd rather not tell you who we believe it is.'

'What, *Dracula*? Man, that guy gets around.' Neither of them smiled. 'Kidding. Jeez. Lighten up a little.'

Richard reached out and grabbed Shane's wrist as he started to raise the coffee cup. 'Lighten up,' he repeated. He looked way too pale, and way too angry now. Not the usual Dick Morrell at all. 'You stupid punk, you don't know what you're talking about. If you want to save Michael's life, you'd better get your head out of your ass and quit joking around.'

'If you want to save *your* life, you'd better take your hand off me, asshole!'

Richard did, sitting back and crossing his arms. Hannah's gaze darted from him to Shane, then back again. 'We're all going to just calm down,' she said. 'Because this doesn't help anyone, least of all Michael. Shane, he's not wrong. This is serious, and if we don't do something, it's going to go bad, especially for your friend, and maybe for the rest of you too. Please. We need your help.'

'To do what? Spy on my best friend? Screw that.' Shane felt his jaw muscles bunching up, and his aching hands – still bruised from last night's little scuffle – tightened into fists. 'Never gonna happen. Not unless you're straight with me. Who is it you're looking for, exactly? I'm guessing not Dracula, probably.'

The house seemed very quiet to Shane. He knew Claire could feel the house's moods, somehow, but he didn't really. It was just a house. Except it wasn't, and, somehow, he knew it was...listening.

'I can't tell you that,' Hannah said. 'And you don't need to know. It's better if you don't.'

'Yeah, for you. But for me, trust me, it's better if I believe you when you say I need to stab my best friend in the back.'

Another moment of silence, and then Richard made a frustrated sound, like a dog growling, and said, 'Fine, Shane. But when I tell you this, it means you are exactly the fifth person in Morganville to know it. You, me, Hannah, Amelie, and Oliver. And guess which one we'll be looking at if it gets out.'

Shane was starting to think it really *was* Dracula they were talking about. 'All right,' he said. 'I'll sign a paper or whatever you want. But I need to know who you're talking about.'

'Bishop,' Richard said. 'I'm talking about Bishop.'

Shane felt his entire body turn cold. The hangover headache disappeared, just like mist. He slid his sunglasses off and stared at Richard, then Hannah. 'You're kidding,' he said. 'You didn't kill him yet? Or at least keep him in prison?' He *had* to be in prison. Bishop was, hands down, the most terrifying guy that Shane had ever seen in person. He'd never met a serial killer, not a real one, but damn, Bishop was the next best thing. Shane was willing to bet that Bishop would have intimidated Dahmer, Gacy and Bundy put together.

And he *lived* to cause destruction. It was his thing. That, and undoing whatever good things his daughter Amelie had managed to accomplish.

Not somebody you wanted to have roaming around loose on the streets of Morganville.

Jesus, Shane thought. *I walked home last night, bleeding and drunk. Michael wasn't kidding about the death wish.*

'Bishop was in prison,' Richard confirmed. 'Amelie had him walled up in a cell. And now he's out. He killed four guards along the way.'

'You've got to be – wait, you think *Michael* is hiding him? Why the hell would he do that?'

'I'll be honest with you, we don't *know* that Michael is involved. But there are only a few people in Morganville that Bishop could potentially use, and Michael's one of them – he was under Bishop's influence before. If so, your friend is in deep, deep trouble,' said Hannah. 'If you can find out where Bishop is hiding, we can take care of this quickly and quietly. Michael never has to be involved. But if you can't, we'll still find Bishop, and we'll bring Michael in as an accessory. Amelie's already said that this

time, she won't be so merciful – not to Bishop, or to
any vampire who gives him help. This could save his
life, Shane. Help us.'

Shane stood up and walked away, arms folded. He
was aching inside now, angry at them for putting him
in this position, angry at Michael for – for whatever.
*If you weren't a bloodsucking leech this would never
have happened.* Not that Michael had asked for it, in
the beginning, anyway. He'd been a casualty of war,
even at the start.

Even if Michael forgave him for this, Eve never
would, Shane just knew that. Eve held a grudge like
nobody he'd ever seen when it came to Michael. And
how the hell was he going to explain any of this to
Claire? He couldn't tell her about Bishop. No way.

Save his life.

Shane put his sunglasses back on, turned around,
and said, 'What do you want me to do?'

Following a vampire around was not as easy as it
sounded. For one thing, Michael had wheels – a
Morganville-issued sedan, with blacked-out windows.
The transportation Shane could get were all too
obvious – Eve's big black boat of a car, with tail fins,
or the murdered-out black Charger he was making
payments on with Rad, down at the repair shop. But
there *was* a way to do it.

Rad had motorcycles. Lots of them. Most of them were way too flashy – chrome, bright paint, all that stuff. No good for staying anonymous.

'How about this one?' Shane asked, pointing to a dark blue Honda. 'That'd probably do.'

'Pretty drab,' Rad – Radovic – said. 'I could maybe put some paint on it if you want.' Rad didn't feel that any of his rides were worth much unless they were memorable, which was kind of funny; he didn't have to work to make people remember him. Rad was a big, tough guy, all muscles. He was one of the few Shane would back off from in a fight, because when Rad swung a punch, it broke things. 'How long you need it for?'

'I don't know,' Shane said. 'Hopefully just tonight.'

'Twenty-five dollars a day,' Rad said. 'Friends rate. I won't ask you if you have a motorcycle license. You don't, that's your problem.'

Shane didn't think Hannah was going to quibble about some paperwork, not right now. He nodded. 'I need a helmet. Something that covers my face.'

Rad nodded. 'No problem. You want maybe night vision?'

'What?'

'My own invention,' Rad said proudly. 'Night vision built into helmet. Very handy for Morganville. You want?'

'How much?'

'Oh, another twenty-five dollars a night for the helmet.'

'You're killing me.'

Rad shrugged. 'Cheap if you can see trouble coming out there. Right?'

Well, Shane really couldn't argue with that. He finally nodded and shelled out fifty from the cash he'd won off the college boys. It was a good value, in Morganville, no question about it.

'You want two?' Rad's lips split in a wide, blinding grin. He had big, square teeth that could have done work in a toothpaste commercial. 'One for the girlfriend, eh?'

'Just one,' Shane said. 'I'm on my own tonight.'

As a precaution, Shane parked the bike behind the garage, in the deepest shadows he could find. He'd got to know it on the way home and it was a sweet little ride, not as loud as a lot of motorcycles. That would help, probably. But the important thing wasn't to keep Michael from seeing the bike following him, just that he didn't know it was Shane.

At least, that was Shane's best idea.

When he came in the kitchen, Claire was already there, looking in the refrigerator. She was wearing the same clothes she'd had on yesterday, which meant she'd just got back from the lab, and when he started towards her she held up her hands, looking miserable. 'I smell,' she said. 'No, I'm wrong, I stink. I can't smell it, but I can feel it. I don't want you to smell me right now.'

'I love how you smell,' he said. 'Besides, I didn't take a shower this morning either. My bad.'

She considered that, catching that cute lower lip between her teeth in a way that made him tingle, and then nodded and stepped into his embrace. God, she felt good – small and fragile and warm, soft in all the right places. Her lips were hot and sweet under his, and for a few seconds, at least, he felt all the way better. Kissing Claire did that to him.

He kissed her a second time, lightly, and asked, 'Did you eat anything today?'

'I think I had a graham cracker yesterday,' she said, and yawned. 'I think I'm too tired to eat, though.' When she turned her head, he saw the shadow of bite marks on her neck – scars, not fresh. She was growing her hair longer to cover them up. 'Where's everybody else?'

'Michael's at the music store, he had a late lesson. Should be back soon. Eve—' Right on cue, the front door banged open. 'That'd be Eve.'

'Yo, losers, where's my dinner?' Eve yelled.

'Yo, Gothic Princess, your name is on the kitchen duty list today!'

'Is *not!*'

Shane rolled his eyes. Claire was smiling. 'I'll help,' she said, and started pulling stuff out.

'Not your turn,' Eve said, breezing into the kitchen. 'You don't have to, Claire.'

'I know, but I'm hungry. I think. Maybe.' Claire frowned doubtfully at some leftovers. 'Is this any good?'

'If you have to ask, the answer is usually no,' Eve said, and dumped the bowl into the trash. 'Ugh. I don't even know what that was, but it isn't anymore. How about spaghetti?'

It was always spaghetti with Eve, unless someone else stepped in. Today, though, Shane's heart wasn't in it. 'Sure,' he said, which made her turn and narrow her heavily made-up eyes at him. Mistake.

'Wow. Mister I-have-a-better-idea, stumped? That's crazy talk. Are you running a fever?'

'Spaghetti sounds good.' He shrugged and let it go, because he was starting to wonder how he was going to gracefully ease out of here and follow Michael, if Michael left again.

'Not to me,' Claire sighed. 'You know what? I was right the first time. I'm more tired than I am hungry.' She grabbed a can of Coke from the fridge and covered another yawn. She really did look exhausted – dark circles under her eyes, her skin paler than it should have been.

'You're working too hard,' Shane said. 'Promise me you're going to get some rest, OK?'

'OK,' Claire said, and gave him an absolutely beautiful smile. 'Promise me you'll wake me up tomorrow?'

He had a flash of what that would be like, sitting on the edge of her bed as the rising sun streamed in, bending over to kiss her awake, seeing her eyes open and that same, lazy, delicious smile on her lips. Just for him.

All of a sudden, his pants felt two sizes too small, and he had to clear his throat. 'I promise,' he said, and meant it. That was something to live for, if everything else failed on him. 'Go on. Get to bed.'

She kissed him, ran her fingers through his hair, and left, practically staggering. He stood there watching her, not really thinking about anything until Eve smacked him on the back of the head. 'You're a good boyfriend,' she said.

'Then why did you hit me?'

'No reason,' she said, and grinned. 'Spaghetti it is. You're in charge of sauce.'

'Sauce is most of the work.'

'Really? I had no idea.'

Shane actually liked being around Eve, mostly, although she could get on his nerves; tonight, when he was anxious and trying not to show it, or think about it, she was perfect company. Her way-too-much-caffeine-powered chatter kept him concentrating just to keep up with her. He made the spaghetti sauce, which mostly involved opening a jar and dumping in more garlic, because it bugged the hell out of Michael, and the time seemed to go incredibly fast.

Michael arrived before the sauce was boiling. 'Hey,' he said, around kissing Eve's upturned lips. That took a while, and Shane grunted back a greeting that somehow managed to convey both that he was at the point of gagging, and a welcome home. 'Shane, the garlic thing? Getting old, man.'

'I like garlic,' Shane shrugged. 'Blame Eve, she told me to make the sauce.'

Michael just shrugged. Eve went to the fridge and got out an opaque sports bottle, which she held up. 'I already ate,' Michael said. Which meant that he'd stopped by the blood bank, which was why his skin was flushed almost to a healthy normal colour. The hungrier he got, the paler he got. When you could mistake him for a marble statue, it was time to run for the stakes. 'I can't stay,' he continued. 'I promised I'd do a late lesson thing.'

Michael earned his living at the music store — mainly because he refused, so far, to live the way the rest of the vamps did, by taking on a human, or preferably humans, to Protect. What a joke. The only

Protecting the vamps did was protecting their own interests. The humans had a choice – pay twenty per cent of their earnings into the vampire's account, or make regular donations at the blood bank. Most people chose blood, weirdly enough. Money was tougher to come by in Morganville.

Technically, Shane supposed that his Protector – and Claire's, and Eve's – was the Founder. So far, Amelie hadn't asked him or Eve for anything – no money, no blood, no nothing. Maybe Claire's hard work at the lab for Crazy Mad Bloodsucking Scientist Dude was paying all their bills. That did not make Shane feel manly.

'Who are you teaching?' Shane asked, trying to make it sound offhand and casual. From the glance Michael shot him, he wasn't sure if he'd got it right.

'Raoul Garza,' Michael said. 'Why?'

'Just curious. Seems like you've got a lot of late-night clients. You starting up some kind of undead band or something?' Not that it was a bad idea, now that Shane thought of it. 'You got a bass player, drums, that kind of thing?'

'Not yet. I'm not sure there's a lot of interest in that among the vamps.'

'Doesn't have to be all vamps, though. I'm just sayin'.'

This was almost a normal conversation, Shane

thought. Michael didn't seem paranoid about it, which was good. 'Yeah, that's true,' Michael said. 'I'll think about it. Might be fun.'

'Just make sure I get my fifteen per cent. It's fifteen for agents, right?'

'Bite me.'

'Think you've got that backwards, man.'

Michael hugged Eve from behind as she stirred the spaghetti, and kissed the side of her neck. He might have lingered there just a little too long for Shane's comfort, but so far there weren't any scars on Eve's throat. So far. 'I'll be back as soon as I can,' he said. 'You guys have fun.'

And just like that, he was gone. Eve looked after him for a few seconds with a sad expression, then turned the heat off under the pasta and started hunting around for the strainer. She didn't talk about Michael's absence after that, just focused on the food.

Shane was hungry, and he wolfed down a bowl, barely stopping to provide mmm-hmm commentary to Eve's monologue, which was like a bright, manic soundtrack he barely understood. He was thinking about Michael. About what he'd promised to do. Five minutes after sitting down, he was rinsing out his bowl at the sink.

'Hey,' Eve called from the other room. 'I know it was good and all, but what's the rush?'

'Got someplace to be,' he called back, feeling a stab of guilt at her silence after that pronouncement. 'Sorry.' That sounded lame.

'I needed some me time, anyway,' Eve said. 'Where are you going?'

'I'm dating a supermodel on the side.'

'Ha ha, very funny, is that what you want me to tell Claire?'

Shane stuck his head back into the living room, where Eve still sat at the dining table in the corner, poking morosely at her half-full bowl. 'I can't tell you,' he said. 'But it's important, OK?'

She raised her head and looked at him, and for all the Goth white paint on her face and the thick black lines around her eyes, not to mention the screaming purple lipstick, for a second she looked just like his mother. Back when his mother was still...herself. 'You need to say where you're going,' Eve said. 'It's not safe if you just – take off. You know that. You grew up knowing that.'

'Yeah,' he said, and avoided her stare. 'Well, this time, I can't. I'll be back.'

He was out the back door before she could yell anything after him. He stuck the helmet on, grabbed the bike and rolled it silently down the drive to the street, where he kicked it into gear. Michael's car was long gone, of course, but that didn't really matter; he kicked the motorcycle into a dull growl, and then into a roar as he rounded the corner. He liked the way it responded to him when he leant one way, then the other, dodging around imaginary obstacles. It was fully dark now, and Morganville wasn't big on security lighting, but the night vision built into the helmet was freaking amazing – everything looked ghostly green, but perfectly visible. There were a few cars on the street, mostly the dark-tinted variety that Michael drove, but he ignored them. All the vamp-mobiles looked alike, especially at night, but Eve had given Michael a glow-in-the-dark bumper sticker and it easily distinguished him from the rest.

Shane caught sight of the green-glowing Death's head in less than three minutes, and eased back on his speed. The engine noise faded to a throb, and he hung back – as much as possible, in Morganville – trying to look inconspicuous. Not easy to do, but he was wearing a black jacket and black helmet, and the bike's paint blended in with the darkness.

Michael made some turns, leading him off into the broken-down industrial area on the south side of the town; they passed by the old tyre factory, for which Shane was grateful because he had bad, creepy memories of that place. They also passed the old hospital, shuttered and half-destroyed. There were a bunch of not-very-stable rusted barns that passed for workshops and storage warehouses. Again, no stopping.

Michael kept going, heading for the edge of town. Shane started to worry about that; as a vampire, Michael could conceivably have permission to go outside the boundaries, but he knew that if he tried it, somewhere, someone would notice. Plus, he didn't fancy getting any of the town's memory tinkering, especially now that he knew who – and what – was doing it. He'd heard way too much on that subject from Claire to feel comfortable. Shane unconsciously backed off on the speed and watched the sedan's glow-in-the-dark skull begin to get smaller. He hesitated for a second, then pressed the throttle again, harder. The engine growled a threat, and he headed for the wrong side of town.

But Michael didn't go past the town limits sign. Instead, he took a left turn into the darkness, down a street that looked as if it had been built dilapidated, not to mention deserted. Shane slowed right down, almost coasting. Michael was turning his car right into a dirt yard in front of one of those almost-falling-down tin buildings, streaked with rust like mould.

Shane parked, killed the engine, but kept the cool night-vision helmet on. He crouched down, well aware Michael could see in the dark if he tried, but his best friend's attention was all on the building ahead of him.

Michael looked hesitant, even from as far away as Shane was; he stood by his car for a long second, then walked forwards. Slowly. From what Shane could tell, it was like a man walking to his own execution.

Dammit. Shane realised that he couldn't just... wait here. He'd have to follow Michael inside, which was nine kinds of crazy, not to mention suicidal. If the mayor's info was correct – and he had no reason to think it wasn't – Michael was into something bad, maybe not by his own choice. It was no place for a human to be, especially without back-up.

But he couldn't let Michael go by himself.

Shane moved as quietly as he could – which, given a lifetime of living in Morganville, was pretty damn quiet – towards the dark, sinister-looking doorway through which Michael had vanished. It occurred to him that Eve was never going to forgive him if he got himself killed out here without telling her first.

He didn't want to even think about Claire. Not right now. It might make him turn around and leave.

Shane pulled in a deep, slow breath and stepped into the dark.

A hand closed around his throat and jerked him off balance and into the shadows. The chin strap on his helmet broke, and the whole thing was ripped off, but there wasn't any sound of it hitting the ground so his attacker had kept it, maybe the better to beat him with later. Shane flailed a little, feet scuffing the broken concrete floor, but he couldn't get any traction. The hand around his throat felt cold, and very strong.

And then Michael said, in a whisper like mist, 'Shane?' He let go, and Shane tried to slow his heartbeat down, and breathe without wheezing. 'You idiot, what the hell are you doing?'

'Following you,' Shane whispered back. 'What do you think, I came here for the scenery?'

'You are a fucking moron.' Michael was really pissed; he didn't drop the f-bomb very much anymore, not since Claire had moved in. It was probably unconscious. 'Seriously, what are you doing?'

'Following. You.' Shane said it very slowly, just to be sure. 'You're in trouble, man. I got a visit.'

'What kind of visit?'

'You want to discuss that here?' Shane waved a hand – which he couldn't see in the inky darkness – to stress the point. 'Now?'

'No, I want you to get back on your little rice-burner and leave me alone,' Michael said. 'Jesus, did you tell Eve, too? Is she lurking around here?'

'Give me some credit. You know Eve, she's not stealthy. You'd have heard her first, in those damn boots.'

Michael made a sound that was not quite a laugh,

but should have been. 'So you came by yourself. To what, rescue me?'

'Absolutely,' Shane whispered. 'Now, can we go?'

'No,' Michael said. 'I have to be sure he's still here.'

Shane had a sudden, urgent bad feeling. 'Please don't tell me it's who I think it is.'

'Mean old guy who nearly killed us all before?'

'Oh man.' Shane took in a deep breath. 'They think you're helping him.'

He didn't need to be able to see Michael's face to imagine his expression – shock, outrage, anger. 'What? Who thinks that?'

'Tricky Dick, for one. And Hannah Moses. That ain't good, Mikey.'

'No damn kidding.'

'How did you get yourself into this?'

Michael was quiet for a second or two, then said, 'There was this girl. I knew her back in junior high. She came to see me.'

'What, for a booty call?'

'No, asshat, to get me to bite her. Turn her. Bring her over. Give her eternal life. Pick your euphemism.'

'I think I liked the booty call explanation better. Wait, this relates to Bishop how, exactly?'

'I was worried about her. I thought she might get herself hurt, so I followed her. While I was following her, she got grabbed.' Michael's pause was painful. 'She got killed. I couldn't – I was too far away to stop it. I saw it happen. And I saw who did it.'

'Bishop.'

'I didn't know why he was out, but I knew it was important to find out what he was doing. So I tracked him. He came here, finally. He spends days here, sometimes nights.'

Shane swallowed hard. 'Is he here?'

'Not right now, I checked. I was planning to wait until I was sure he'd come in, then go get the cavalry.'

'Why didn't you turn him in already?'

'The first time I was going to, but he left again and I lost him. I figured he'd come back here, so I waited. He did. This is the second time I've been here. I just want to make sure before I get Amelie and Oliver on to it.'

'You know, I'm not usually the on-the-side-of-caution guy, but I think this is a prime time to call the heavy hitters and get the hell out of the way.'

'Probably,' Michael said. 'But I was afraid they'd think I was with him.'

'Guess what? Barn door, horse, et cetera. Come on, let's go drop a safe, long-distance dime on this old bastard.' It seemed, to Shane, like the best plan ever. Particularly the part where he didn't get killed, or turned vamp, which for him would be worse. No offence to Michael.

Michael seemed to be torn, but finally, he said, 'All right. I just want to make sure he's here when they get here. He's got away from them once. It can't happen again, Shane. It can't.'

Michael was taking this real damn personally, Shane realised. It wasn't just about Bishop, and general-principles anger at the evil old crow. It was about the girl, the one Michael had refused to turn, who'd got way more than she'd bargained for from the next vamp she bumped into.

Shane could understand that on a level so deep it was practically atomic. 'Right,' he said quietly. 'It won't. Let's go.'

And they would have, honestly, except that in that moment, as they headed for the front door, something made a sound at the distant, lightless back of the warehouse. It echoed weirdly around the metal structure, and Shane couldn't decide what it was. A struggle? Someone dragging something? Michael's hand tightened on his arm, pulling him to a sudden, silent stop.

And then Shane heard a child crying.

It was a lost, desperate sound, and it got inside him and pulled in painful places. He couldn't see Michael but he understood the rigid way his friend was locked in stillness. Michael could hear more, maybe see more.

And it wasn't good.

Shane was trying to decide whether or not to whisper a question when he heard, very distinctly, a little girl's voice say, eerily calmly, 'Please let me go, sir. I won't say a thing. I won't tell anybody.'

No wonder Michael was so still, so quiet.

It was happening all over again, like a nightmare.

Shane felt a shiver go through Michael, an impulse, and he knew what it was. 'No,' he whispered, just a thread of sound. 'Don't do it.'

'No choice,' Michael whispered back. Shane nodded, because he got it, he really did, and he took out his cell phone and texted Claire, mainly because he didn't have any bloodsuckers on speed dial. Claire did. He gave the address, or as close as he could guess it, and added a 911 on the end, just to make it clear this wasn't going to be pretty. If she'd turned her phone off, or left it somewhere...

But she hadn't, and seconds later, the screen lit up with a message from Claire. SENDING HELP GET OUT GET OUT NOW.

Which was a sensible kind of plan, really,

But that left Michael here, all alone, without help. Without anybody. And that ultimately wasn't something Shane could live with. He texted back WILL DO, even though he knew he wouldn't, and in the glow of the cell phone screen looked up at Michael. Michael could see what he was texting, but it was pretty obvious that Michael knew he was lying. Textually speaking.

It was really hard to fold up the phone and lose the light, but Shane knew he had to do it. The darkness fell like a thick, smothering blanket, and for a second he imagined he was drowning in it. Michael had let go of him, and the disorientation was total. Shane stayed where he was, trying not to think about all the things that could go wrong with this non-plan, and almost jumped when he felt Michael's fingers grip his shoulder in warning. He knew what that meant, without any words being said.

Bishop knew they were here.

In a weird kind of way, that was...better. The suspense was over. Now it was just about the fight, and the fight was where Shane lived, inside. It was like...home.

'Tell me you brought weapons,' Michael said. He wasn't trying to hide, either. Shane wondered if he felt the same way; probably not, he thought. Michael didn't run from a fight, but he never seemed to have quite the same thirst for it, either. It was more of a grim acceptance of the inevitable.

'Don't say I never give you anything,' Shane said, and reached into his jacket to retrieve two silver-tipped wooden stakes. Guaranteed to leave a mark, even on a vamp of Bishop's age and power. He handed one to Michael, then checked his other pockets. He found a bag of silver nitrate powder, which he kept. 'When I throw this, stay out of the way, or you're going to be sparkling, and not in that fashionable vamp kind of way.'

'How do you want to do this?'

'You keep Bishop occupied, I save the girl.'

'Really? Come on.'

'What? You think I've got a better shot at him?'

'No, I think you're better at keep-away,' Michael said, 'and Bishop likes going after humans first. He likes the easy kills.'

'No offence intended.'

'I didn't say you'd be one of them.'

Shane considered it. Bishop frankly scared the bejesus out of him, but Michael had one thing right – he could get to the girl faster, pick her up, and run her out of danger much better than Shane could. He could be back in seconds to jump in the fight, too.

Shane just had to keep Bishop at arm's length for maybe...a minute. Maybe less.

It didn't sound that hard, which was why Shane knew it would be ridiculous. 'Sure,' he said. 'Let's do this thing.'

'I'll get the lights,' Michael said. 'Five seconds.' And then he was gone, moving like a ghost through the dark, and Shane was left alone, gripping the stake in one hand, and his plastic bag of silver powder in the other. He counted down in his head, focusing on the numbers instead of all the things that could go wrong.

He was still on two when the lights blazed on in the warehouse, ranks of greenish, flickering things that cast a weirdly alien colour over everything – which wasn't much. Piles of debris. Old, sagging cardboard boxes. And over at the far end of the warehouse, some kind of broken-down forklift that was missing its wheels.

And there was Mr Bishop, holding the wrist of a little red-haired girl about twelve years old. Growing up in Morganville, you knew people by sight, even if you didn't want to have anything to do with them, and he knew that kid. Her name was Clea Blaisdell.

Not that it mattered whether or not he actually knew her. He wouldn't have left anybody, even Monica Morrell, to Bishop's non-existent mercy.

So he stepped out in full view, twirled the stake in his fingers like he actually felt that cocky, and yelled, 'Yo, Grandpa, you eating snack sizes now? Trying to lose a few pounds?' He kept walking, closing the distance between them. He couldn't see Michael, but that didn't matter; he knew he was there, working his way around to a good striking distance.

Shane was still twenty feet away, but that was close enough to see Bishop's lips part in a smile like the edges of a knife wound. Bishop was, frighteningly, even more horrible than he remembered – stringy white hair clinging to his scalp like it hadn't been washed, ever; grey, dirty clothes; a face so white and sharp it hardly looked human at all.

'If it isn't the Collins boy,' Bishop said. His voice sounded rusty. 'I would have thought your father's example had taught you to mind your manners. No matter. I won't waste my time on turning you into one of my own. I'll just settle for having you dead at my feet.'

'Nice fantasy,' Shane said, and kept walking. His heart was thumping so fast and hard it hurt. 'Never happen, sucker. Come on. Show me what you got, you lame old—'

He didn't have time to finish the insult, because Bishop dropped the girl's wrist and flew at him in a blur. Shane took a running step – not back, *towards* him – and threw himself flat on the concrete in a slide as Bishop's leap carried the vampire over him. Shane twisted and rolled to his feet as Bishop landed, ten feet too far, and twirled the stake again. He was breathless, and his whole body was screaming at him to run, dammit, but he covered it with a wolfish grin and a *come-on* gesture as he twirled the stake. When

Bishop let out a low, unsettling growl and lowered his fangs, Shane started backing away. Strategically. Keeping Bishop's back to the red-haired girl...

...who was caught up by another running blur, which didn't slow down as it whipped through the air towards a gap in the back wall. Bishop's private entrance, most likely. *Go, Mikey*, Shane thought, and then he didn't have time for thinking because he had the world's oldest, meanest vampire on his ass, and Bishop meant business.

Shane tried to keep away, and he dodged a swipe of Bishop's sharp fingernails that would have gutted him; his feet felt clumsy, even fuelled by adrenalin and terror. Bishop was fast, very fast, faster than Michael, maybe. Human agility wasn't enough.

As Bishop's hand closed on Shane's arm and yanked him forwards, Shane figured he was pretty much already dead. It was only a matter of how it would happen...drained and left some dry corpse, or ripped apart in a bloody spree. On the whole, Shane thought maybe the ripping thing was better, but then, he'd never actually had time to give it much thought. His arm would break first, and then...then...

Then, suddenly, a silver shower of dust exploded around Bishop like fireworks, glittering dully in the fluorescent lights, and Shane blinked and coughed as it hit him, too. About one second later, Bishop's grip on his arm loosened, and his red-rimmed eyes widened as his mouth split open in a scream.

His hair caught fire around his head in a weird flaming halo. Shane pulled his arm free and stumbled backwards, his brain just catching up with what he was seeing.

Bishop, on fire where the fine, silvery powder had hit him. As Bishop whirled to see who'd thrown it, Shane saw Michael standing ten feet behind him, arm still extended from the throw. There were burn marks on his palm.

Now, Shane thought, and as Bishop started to lurch towards his best friend, Shane brought up the stake and lunged, fast. He didn't let himself think about it, or try to direct what he was doing. Sometimes, his body just knew these things.

Sometimes, it was better if the mind stayed out of its way.

The stake hit Bishop in the back on the left side, punched in through the still-burning skin, and slammed straight into Bishop's heart.

Shane fell backward, slapping out the flames that had caught on the sleeves of his jacket, as Bishop screamed and danced madly in place, trying to reach the stake that had pierced his heart...and then slowly toppled to his knees, then forwards onto his face.

He was too old to die quickly. In fact, Shane wasn't

sure even silver would do it — but he hoped. Man, he really, really hoped.

Shane stayed where he was, lying propped on his elbows and watching the vampire, but nothing happened. Bishop didn't pop up, snarling; the silver burnt him, but not really very much. It was like a slow, reluctant sizzle around the stake.

Bishop blinked, very slowly.

Not dead. Not yet.

Michael came to his side and offered him a hand.

'We should cut his head off,' Shane said, not taking the hand. Michael didn't pull it back.

'Not ours to do,' he said. 'But promise me something.'

'What?'

Michael's face looked so pale, so strange in the greenish glare of the lights. 'Promise me you'll do it for me if I become like him.'

Shane hesitated, then reached up and took his hand, and let Michael pull him up to his feet. 'You won't,' he said, and didn't let go. 'You won't, bro. I won't let you.'

He let go. They tapped fists and nodded. It was a bargain.

There was a sound of engines outside, and squealing brakes, and in under five seconds the place was swarming with guys in stark black suits and ties and sunglasses, all with vamp-pale faces and weapons. They surrounded Shane and Michael, and the inert – but not dead – corpse of Bishop.

Nobody said anything.

The newcomers parted ranks and a woman dressed in white walked through like she owned the place, which technically she probably did. She was carrying the little red-haired girl, who had her chubby arms around the woman's long, elegant neck. The Ice Queen, which was Shane's private nickname for her.

Amelie. The Founder of Morganville.

She was pretty, but in a cold kind of way that made Shane shiver; there was something about her eyes that wasn't quite…right. Not even the other vamps had eyes like that.

'You did this?' she asked, and looked at the burning body. There wasn't much of an expression on her face, no hint of how she really felt about the whole thing. Shane traded a look with Michael.

'Yeah,' Michael confirmed. 'Sorry. We had to.'

'Oh, indeed,' she said. 'It's good you did. For his sake. Had I caught him in this situation, I might not have been quite so…merciful.' She paused, then shifted her gaze directly to Shane. 'Who staked him?'

Before Shane could answer, Michael jumped in. 'I did,' he said. 'Shane saved the kid.'

Amelie didn't blink. 'It's good it was you,' she said.

'Were it Mr Collins, I might have to convene a Council meeting and order punishment. Humans don't stake vampires in Morganville, Mr Collins. Not without consequences. But of course it wasn't Shane at all, was it, Michael?'

'No,' Michael said. 'It was me.'

Shane opened his mouth, got a cold glance from Amelie, and shut it, fast. He didn't nod. He decided that maybe it wasn't a lie, exactly, if he didn't move. Or breathe.

Amelie turned away, towards one of her guards, who leant towards her expectantly. 'Take care of this,' she said. 'No one finds out about this. See to it that my father goes back where he belongs. And don't be in any hurry to remove the stake.'

'Ma'am,' he said. He looked over at Michael and Shane. 'What about them?' Meaning, Shane realised with a sinking feeling, that they were security risks. Not that they'd hurt Michael. But he was just a breather. Nothing to lose sleep over, assuming Amelie actually slept.

She hesitated a moment, one pale, elegant hand smoothing down the girl's red hair, and then said, 'I think we can trust Shane and Michael to understand the importance of keeping this to themselves.'

'And the girl?'

Amelie looked down at the kid. 'Clea,' she said. 'Her

name is Clea. I'll take her home. I'm sure her parents will also understand how to keep quiet.' She looked at Shane. 'You have something to say?'

He shook his head. 'Just surprised. You know her name.'

Amelie's pale lips curled into a smile, and there was a shadow of warmth in her eyes. 'Of course,' she said. 'I know all the names.'

She didn't look back at Bishop. With a nod to Michael, she turned and carried Clea out of the building, into the night. Probably to a limousine, with a driver. Which beat the hell out of the little motorcycle Shane had ridden in on.

'We should go,' Michael said. 'Need a ride?'

'Are you kidding?' Shane asked. 'Do you know what Rad does to people who don't bring back his bikes?'

The sun was just coming up when Shane sat down on the edge of Claire's bed. He didn't wake her up, not right at first. She was curled on her side, the morning glow turning her skin gold, making her hair burn red at the ends. Shane curled a strand of it around his finger, and it felt like warm silk.

He let the hair fall away, and moved his finger gently over her cheek, then lightly over her lips. Claire's eyelids fluttered, and she made a soft, vague, pleased kind of sound deep in her throat.

And then she focused on him.

Her brown eyes went all gold in the sun, and he felt golden inside, too. She didn't say anything. Neither did he.

He bent over and kissed her, and her lips were warm and sweet, and he thought, *worth living for*.

When he finally sat up, she smiled at him, and it was so beautiful he forgot whatever he was going to say to her. Probably something lame, like *good morning*.

'What did you do last night?' she asked, and scooted over.

Shane slowly lowered himself down next to her, never looking away from her warm, sunlit eyes. And that smile. 'You know,' he said. 'The usual.'

If she had any suspicions about that, she kept them to herself. Besides, they had more to think about...and none of it involved vampires.

And all of it was...good.

The Morganville Vampires series so far...

Check out our website for free tasters and exclusive discounts, competitions and giveaways, and sign up to our monthly newsletter to keep up-to-date on our latest releases, news and upcoming events.

www.allisonandbusby.com